In B'tween: The 3 Claps of Thunder

Also by Nandita Banerjee

Novels

No.7: They're Calling

No.7: The Date

In B'tween: The Wisp

Poetry Anthologies

Thoughts Recollected in Tranquility

Alice Through Wonderland

"In Banerjee's supernatural thriller, family devotion collides with dark magic.... Banerjee's prose is vivid and fast-paced, rich with cultural details and suspense ... the story's ingenuity, heartfelt relationships, and narrative ambition combine to deliver a compelling and original paranormal thriller. A vivid paranormal mystery that will haunt readers long after the final page." – *Kirkus Reviews*

"Another moody and compelling plunge into a cursed family drama. Playing out in both the spirit and mortal realms, the plot toys with common conceptions surrounding the afterlife, while also artfully blurring the lines between magic, science, and religious tradition. This is a surprisingly multifaceted read in this genre, given the intricacy of the plot, the timely thematic undercurrents, and a collection of complex but relatable characters." – *Self-Publishing Review*

In B'tween: The 3 Claps of Thunder

Nandita Banerjee

ISBN: (Paperback) 9798991535038

DEDICATION

I dedicate this book to my grandmother, Shantih, whose enduring patience and affection have been my anchor through my most difficult years. Her love remains forever etched in my heart.

Chapter 1

The churning waves and raging sky clashed in a tempestuous dance, embodying the raw force of nature at its most intense. The storm had come on quickly in dune-backed Old Digha, engulfing the coastal resort town in a torrent of rain.

Thunder screamed across the skies. To the discordant drumroll, the gale added its heavy thrash-metal song and the gulls, their brazen-sharp squawks.

Deepak's voice rang out to me in the pandemonium. "Priya!"

His radiance cast a surreal light upon the thick, bruised clouds, as if the sun itself struggled to pierce their shadows.

My knight in shining armor even in death.

I soared only to plummet, and he blurred and faded into the ominous clouds.

His divine aura repels my sickly green glow. If only I could have retained the supernal hue. Perhaps it was not meant for me. Heaven wasn't. I got in by mistake, and they chucked me out . . .

Feet dragged along the sand miles beneath me. Hard soles clomped.

Not Uncle Dev, the evil sorcerer. The fiend smells different. But he could still be around, searching for me with his spirit traps.

Quaking like the churning sea, I plummeted down to Leda's two-story store apartment.

I worried about the young detective. A close friend of my children, Sunny and Sonya, Leda had tried to break the sorcerer's curse on my family only to become the object of it. Yet she had taken the help of Rao, a renowned theologian, to burn the bewitched book, the tool used by the fiend to cast the spell. Unnoticed and without warning, the ashes had coalesced into an ash bat above their heads, all except one flake that had descended upon Leda's wrist. There it had melted, leaving a burn mark in the shape of the bat.

Has she been able to get some sleep?

All seemed quiet at her apartment.

I might have relaxed for a second when a living mass swooped down beside me in a frenzied dive. I catapulted from the sill at the suddenness with a startled gasp.

It was a gull. It hopped over the sill, its yellow beak drooping downward to a point like a witch's nose.

This cannot be the fiend. He might be good at changing his appearance, but he cannot hide his natural scent.

The gull leaped closer, screeching, its glare pure evil.

My core rattled. I turned myself into a plain gray moth. Like my heightened senses, disguise was another of my ghostly perks.

The gull fixed its dark eyes on my glow.

I pulled my wings tight over my bosom.

It spread its wings and whipped away into the bruised skies to continue its mocking tones aloft.

The sky turned purple. The wind raged fiercely, bringing with it flurries of ash.

That poured gasoline onto the spark of fear in my core. I phased through the wall.

The ash darkened to soot; the flakes danced and crashed against the windowpanes, turning into hand-like assemblages of bone, muscles, joints, tendons, and skin.

The sorcerer's bat!

How heinously the fiend uses the spirit of my childhood friend, Hema, to get to his victims, now as that creature of ash, now as a living, breathing book.

Why is the bat back?

She peered in, watching the young detective emerge from her tiny bedroom and turn on the light in the tiny open-plan kitchen living room. Leda did not hear her; the bat's ultrasonic chirps were beyond the frequency limit of sounds humans could hear.

Leda filled the kettle and plugged it in. The scar pulsed like an ominous cage of trapped energy. She doubled over with a gasp.

Is it just the bat's presence that affects the scar, or is the fiend manipulating it?

There was no sign of him in the neighborhood. *Perhaps he is close enough to impact the scar but beyond my perception range of five miles.*

The bat crawled up the walls, clicking rapidly.

Is there no end to this nightmare?

Leda collapsed on the floor, writhing and groaning.

Sonya, my daughter, tossed and turned on the makeshift bed in the commercial space downstairs, the store, unaware of it all. Not like she could have helped to relieve Leda's pain. The sorcerer was too powerful. And he was both illusive and discreet.

He must be crushed. If only there's a way.

Leda's whimper intensified, then quickly faded as the bat flapped her wings and immersed herself in the stormy darkness. Deadly pale, Leda's gaze drifted to the window.

In obscure silhouette, the bat glided among the pitch-black clouds.

Chapter 2

Leda poured the golden oolong evenly into three cups, and Sonya walked in groggily.

"Oh, Leda, you shouldn't have bothered." Sonya glanced at the bat-shaped scar on her wrist. "I am so sorry for bringing all this on you."

Sonya cannot stop blaming herself for being the bearer of the sorcerer's tool—the cursed book.

Leda shook her head. "You did not. I am responsible for what happened to me."

Sonya sighed. "H-how is the scar?"

Leda dipped her head in an equivocal nod. "Have your tea." She passed Sonya a cup. "Tell me how it tastes with the ginger and cardamom. Thought you might like some special tea this morning."

Bless her!

Sonya sipped a mouthful. "Mmmm. Love it. Thank you so much, but you didn't have to." Sonya's gaze drifted to the third cup. "Who's that for?"

"Your brother. He's coming to double check on the scar," Leda seemed to have full confidence in my son, Sunny, a resident doctor at University College London. "He thinks it's just a burn like Meghna said."

Meghna, a nurse by profession, had taken care of Ma after her stroke following my death. She had however, left Ma's household and followed Sonya and her friend, Randy, to Digha where he had died in an accident. Meghna loved Randy and was pregnant with his baby.

Sonya squinted at Leda. "I swear I woke up to your groans. I would be happy if you told me I was imagining them."

"No, you weren't." Leda was calm as always. "The pain flares up now and then, but it's barely been twelve hours. Give it some more time." She offered Sonya a cookie.

"No, thanks." Sonya swallowed hard to steady her breath. "I'm so scared for you. Wonder why the fiend branded you. Rao burned the book. Nothing happened to him."

"Perhaps I was the more threatening—private detective Sergeant from the Roma Police Department. Dev didn't like the thought of a formidable outsider meddling in his affairs." Leda patted Sonya on the shoulder, then carried the two remaining cups and the cookie jar into the living area. "Anyway, Sunny should be here any moment. I'm counting on him to advise me on the next course of action."

Sonya followed Leda. "But Sunny knows nothing about black magic, which puts you completely at the fiend's mercy."

"Not if I can manage to get far away from Dev." Leda picked up her cup and sipped a mouthful.

"But the scar?"

Leda grinned. "My husband, Patrick, and I will find a skilled plastic surgeon to remove it."

Either her sense of calm was anchored in her well-earned self-confidence, or she was trying to stay strong for Sonya.

This is all part of her inherent sense of compassion. She always puts others before herself.

Even as the wings of the bat-shape on Leda's wrist moved like they were real and preparing to take off, the ash bat's ultrasonic chirps pierced my core.

I tugged my silken wings over my glow. Again, I did not catch any signs of the fiend's presence.

Leda fisted her hand with a groan. "I saw an ash bat earlier, exactly the shape of my scar."

Sonya glanced around. "She is here, flying out."

Leda, deadly pale, squinted at the weird creature.

"Rao couldn't really help," muttered Sonya.

With a furtive glance at her, Leda drained her cup and set it back on the tray.

The door creaked open, and Sunny walked in. "Hey, how are you, Leda? How's the scar?" He examined it quickly, and his eyes drifted to the steaming cup of fresh tea on the coffee table.

Leda offered him the cup. "Masala tea."

"Thank you. It's good to see that you are doing well, Leda."

"I want to go about the day as normally as I can, though I'm planning on keeping the store closed."

Leda had arrived in Kolkata as an undercover agent to gather information and evidence against Randy, a suspect in a murder investigation. He had befriended Sonya in London and accompanied her to India for my husband, Ravi, and my funeral. Initially, Leda conducted her investigations from the Kolkata store she helped her friend run. Later, she moved her base of operations to Digha.

Sunny breathed a sigh. "Of course. As long as you are well. At least Rao was of some help, tough and enormous as he is."

Sonya scowled. "No, he wasn't, despite his knowledge and experience."

Sunny glanced from her to Leda's wrist and back again. His brows knitted together.

Expressionless, Leda opened the cookie jar. "Cookies, anyone?"

Sonya leaned forward to pick one and spilled a little tea on her skirt. She tried to brush it off and made a bigger mess. All the while, her fingers trembled.

She's stressed and anxious. The curse had wrecked her confidence.

Sunny's cheeks pushed up.

Sonya's face contorted, and my core went out to her.

Sunny has changed so much toward her since she brought that book home.

Leda rose and passed Sonya a handful of kitchen towels.

"Thanks," said Sonya, cleaning herself.

"Cookie, Sunny?" Leda held out the jar to him.

Sunny helped himself to a cookie. "Any new developments since last night?"

"An ash bat, a bat made of ash, was here a little while ago," explained Sonya. "Leda was in a lot of pain."

"Really, Leda?" Sunny peered down at the scar. "It looks okay now."

Leda merely smiled.

"Leda, you should have this removed ASAP." Sunny's voice shook.

Leda managed a smile. "Patrick, my husband, has been talking to the best surgeons in Dallas. They might be able to remove the scar, but the magic? Dev is controlling it. He's a very powerful sorcerer."

"He must be crushed," muttered Sonya.

Exactly. If there was only a way.

"We're trying to arrest him." Leda sighed. "The police can't find him. I've got the forces involved in Kolkata, as well as in the rest of Bengal. I'm dead certain he's using magic to conceal himself."

Sunny scoffed. "Sonya, why don't you find him? He's your special friend. He gave you the book."

Sonya flinched.

"One of my aunts, Aunt Camelia, is into all sorts of mumbo-jumbo." Leda quickly shifted the conversation away from Sonya. "She once said that spirits can be engaged to find solutions to problems."

Sunny frowned at her.

"Ever heard of a thing called planchette, Sunny?"

"Um—"

"It is a respectful way of approaching a spirit. Spirits are known to see a lot more than us, and they can go places without being noticed. If you call someone, a well-wisher, they would be only too glad of the opportunity to relieve you of your problem."

"I can only think of Mom," said Sunny.

As much as I would love to help, I had warned myself against it. Spirits did not have the energy to interact with humans. If they did, they only drew on the life spirit of the person involved.

"She might be right beside you at this moment, trying to send you signs," said Leda.

Sunny glanced around. "All I see is a gray moth, though I must admit that sometimes I see this gleam—kind of orange, varying in brightness."

I used to be orange . . .

"I see those and others too," said Sonya. "They are shades of green, even filthy green. Don't know if they're Mom or Dad or both or some other known or unknown entity."

I have been every shade they mention in the few months I've been dead.

Leda fiddled with her phone. "You two decide if you want to speak to your mom or your dad, and we will communicate with them tonight. I'll go try to call Patrick. His phone is always switched off." She rose and left the room, her brows scrunched.

"I'd rather they hover as mute and evasive glows," Sonya said.

"Hmmm." Sunny sighed. "When I was carrying Mom and Dad's cremains to India for the funeral, a bright orange glow tried to get too close at the airport. Perhaps it was Mom, and she wanted to say something. I'd never experienced anything like that before and freaked out."

It was one of the few times I revealed myself to him. I shouldn't have, but he was travelling all by himself with the urns.

"My experiences have been much worse," Sonya muttered. "I've been ill."

Exactly. I must be unresponsive during the séance, even if it means disappointing them.

"You could have been ill for a thousand reasons," Sunny snapped. "You don't eat well, probably do drugs—"

"Well then, let's connect with Mom." Sonya's lips quivered. "You could talk to her about all your grievances."

Leda returned. "There are different ways of venturing into the occult, but we must follow the rules. Are you both happy to call your mom's spirit?"

Sunny swallowed. "It would be a great opportunity, but will she really talk?"

I haven't been offered the perk yet.

"Not exactly." Leda laughed. "We'll use a little plank, attached to a pencil. She will produce mystical drawings or writing, as she pleases."

If only Leda knew about the consequences.

"I can't wait to talk to Mom." Sunny leaned in. "Would there be any dangers involved?"

Leda met his gaze. "This board is a portal. If you don't know how to handle it, things can go very wrong. But I've used it in the past, and it has worked just fine for me. As I said, my Aunt Camelia is into all this, so I kind of know how to go about it. I'll be the spirit medium. All you and Sonya will have to do is listen to me talk to her."

"Where shall we see the drawings?" asked Sonya.

"There may not be drawings. The response might include ghostly voices in the corner of the room, clanging bells, knocking, or a 'spirit hand' appearing and vanishing upon occasion."

Just at that moment the curtain over the doorway twitched, and Sonya let out a little yell. "Who is that?"

A slender young woman in a cheap cotton saree and flip-flops emerged through the door. "It's only me, Jalebi." She pulled her curly hair back in a bun and adjusted the Mangalsutra at her throat. Her big, black eyes looked sad.

Jalebi! That's a popular sweetmeat in India, crisp and sweet. She is more a Cinderella.

"I am a caregiver," she said quietly. "My client, an old man, died a few weeks ago, and I'm out of work." She cast a furtive glance at Sunny. "Dr. Gupta asked me to come see you."

"Yes, yes, of course," said Sunny. "I see you found the place." He glanced at Leda. "I met Jalebi at the hospital yesterday. The nurses seem to know her."

"I am on the lookout for a nurse's job," Jalebi chimed in, "though I didn't quite finish my degree."

Sunny nodded. "As I was saying, yesterday, she came to Paul's cabin to find out if he needed a caregiver after he was discharged from the hospital."

Sonya stiffened, her face etched with guilt. Paul was her ex, though they still loved each other. She had made a deliberate decision to distance herself from him, yet she was hanging around in Digha, living within a few miles of Paul's hospital.

"Does he need one?" Leda asked.

Sunny shook his head. "He is going back to the US with his dad. James is arriving tonight. Hope you will have the decency to come and say a final goodbye, Sonya. Paul wouldn't have broken his leg if he hadn't tried to save you."

Sonya winced, looking away. She had gotten too close to Randy, Paul's cousin, and he had crashed his car a few days ago with Sonya in the passenger seat.

Sunny turned toward Leda. "Anyway, Leda, I know you are managing things on your own, but under the circumstances, I think you could do with some help with household chores. Jalebi does housework too."

Jalebi nodded. "I have some experience."

"That is very thoughtful of you, Sunny." Leda beamed. "I think we could do with your help here, though it may not be for long."

"That's okay. I take whatever comes my way." Jalebi smiled sadly. "What would you like me to do?"

She makes a good first impression.

Leda opened her purse and handed her some change. "Would you please get me some milk, bananas, eggs, and bread from the grocers? It's just down the road."

"Of course." Jalebi left without a backward glance.

Chapter 3

Jalebi was quick to return with the groceries, and the subject of 'planchette' was dropped.

Sunny left, and Jalebi cleaned Leda's store apartment until it sparkled. She emptied and wiped the wastebaskets, changed and washed the bedlinen. And when the chores were completed, she engaged Sonya and Leda with many a story from her childhood spent in the wild and mysterious Sundarbans, a mangrove area, in the delta of the Bay of Bengal.

It's amazing how quickly she shed her sadness for the very qualities her name suggests.

"Isn't the forest habitat home to the Royal Bengal Tiger?" asked Sonya.

"Yes—" The kettle whistled in the kitchen, and Jalebi rushed across the living area to grab it. "Tea?" she asked.

Leda and Sonya nodded.

Jalebi found herself the spices for a masala chai. "Spotting a tiger in the Sundarbans is extremely difficult compared to any other forest."

"That must make it scarier living there," remarked Leda.

Jalebi creamed the milk. "More so for poor fishermen, crab, and honey collectors who sneak into the forbidden, dense forest areas without permission or protection. They serve as easy prey for the tigers."

Sonya shivered. "Do you know anyone who was attacked?"

"My mother." Jalebi barely looked back. "She was a wood collector. We found her decapitated head in the river behind our house."

There was an awkward silence, but only until Jalebi brought the aromatic tea to Leda and Sonya perched on the edge of the settee.

"Thank you." They took the cups squinting at her.

"Thank you for letting me work for you." Jalebi instantly immersed her listeners in yet another story, happier by far.

The girl was a delight. Yet her eyes were alert with inquisitiveness that seemed to take in her surroundings and catalogue each aspect. She spoke very good English considering she was from one of the most underdeveloped suburbs of West Bengal.

Does Leda notice? It was hard to tell. Calm and composed, the detective worked alongside her new maid, her warm smile never leaving her face.

That evening Sunny was back at Leda's store apartment and Jalebi cooked coconut shrimp curry and basmati rice for dinner. She served the meal in green coconut shells that she found on the beach and left for what she called her little hut in the slums. She said she would not be back until the following day. Apparently, her friend had called to inform her that her absconding husband had returned home.

After dinner, Leda took Sunny and Sonya down to the store. Leda rummaged through the merchandise and retrieved a big wooden frame, some thick cardboard, a flat board, marked with the letters of the Latin alphabet, the numbers zero to nine, the words "yes," and "no," and various other symbols and graphics. "Here's everything we need." Leda glanced from Sonya to Sunny and back again. "So, who are we talking to, your mom or dad?"

"Mom," said Sunny.

They will be so disappointed with me.

"Great." Leda fetched a pair of scissors from the kitchen. "Now, the next step is to choose the shape for the planchette. I've seen hearts, teardrops, and even a simple rounded triangle."

"I would like a heart, please," said Sonya.

"Heart okay, Sunny?" Leda glanced at him.

Sunny nodded.

Leda cut the cardboard into the desired shape, ensuring that it was large enough for them to sit around and comfortably place their fingertips along the edges. She then snipped a hole in the middle to act as a "window" they could look through to see the answer. "As I mentioned before, there are cautionary tales that the board opens a door to evil spirits, making the game sound like a supernatural dare. That can be prevented by using a silver coin as the planchette, but unfortunately, I do not have one. Shall we still play?"

Neither Sunny nor Sonya objected.

"What exactly will you ask her?" Sunny seemed to be already in game mode.

"About Dev, where he is, how to find him, how to crush him. There is no escape from the curse until we do. Now, press down gently on the cardboard heart with the index finger of your right hand and repeat a prayer after me. "O great soul in the divine plane, please cooperate with us in this our attempt to know some answers through your prediction."

Even as they chanted the words several times, a gleaming, chauffeured Bentley stopped a few blocks away. An unfamiliar woman in a purple, embroidered hijab stepped out and walked toward the store-apartment.

Where have I seen this car before? In Ma's neighborhood?

Unaware of the stranger, Leda asked the first question. "Where is Dev?"

The scar shifted on her wrist, yet there was no sign of the bat.

"Where is Dev?" Leda repeated her question.

The heart jerked slightly and moved over some letters, in sequence—c-l-o-s-e.

Who is this?

A thick gaseous mass grazed past me. *Asha?* I recognized her scent and leaped toward her, but she warded me off to the corner of the store.

This cannot be Asha!

"Mom?" cried Sonya.

"Priya?" Leda frowned.

The cardboard heart pulled out of Leda's hand and moved across the board, making a triangular pattern over the letters, "A-S-H-A."

Leda grimaced. With a furtive glance at her scar, throbbing and reddening, she scanned the store.

Unaware of the reactions of her scar, Sunny whispered, "Mom's best friend."

Hesitantly, Leda asked the next question, "Is it possible to find Dev?" She pursed her mouth as if in pain. Her eyes darted.

There was still no sign of the bat.

At the window, the strange woman adjusted her hijab to reveal her face momentarily.

The fiend! How did he disguise his natural scent?

Leda's gaze drifted to him. She froze.

The heart zipped to the letter 'y' then shot to 'e' where it whizzed around in circles.

"Why doesn't it move?" Sonya asked.

The Ouija board sparked beneath the heart shape. The scar on Leda's arm glowed green as if with some luminescent chemical.

Leda groaned and the cardboard heart leaped off the burning board in flames.

Sunny and Sonya raced around in the uncanny surge of smoke, coughing and gasping, grabbing whatever they could find to stop the fire. They smothered the flames, only to find Leda, lying still as a corpse on the floor.

The glow on her wrist foamed along the edges, fizzing in a shocking spritz of effervescence.

Sunny checked her vital signs, while Sonya rushed to open the window, but the fumes, the smoke, and the foam vanished before she touched the crank handle like they had been magically sucked out.

Sonya craned her neck to scan the street.

Alas, the fiend had disappeared. I could not catch any sign of him even with my heightened senses. *The power of magic!*

Leda shot up. "Where am I?"

"In your apartment." Sonya frowned at her wrist. "Your scar was all weird."

"There was something pulsating beneath my skin, something alive. It felt like, um, what they call quickening," Leda spoke as if in a trance. "You know when you first feel a baby's movement in utero?" Her fingers skittered over her belly.

Someone must have described the feeling to her in detail.

"How does it feel now?" Sunny asked.

"Normal. Completely normal, but I . . . I—" She glanced at the window, and her brows scrunched.

Both Sunny and Sonya peered down at the scar. There was no swelling, no redness. Not even the green fizz had left its mark.

Sonya scowled. "How is this possible? Your wrist effervesced like a boiling cauldron, only minutes ago."

A passerby peered in through the window.

Leda pointed to him. "Dev—"

Sunny and Sonya swung around.

"He's a neighbor," said Sonya.

Leda turned beetroot red. Her teeth clattered, and she shivered like she'd been submerged under the Arctic ice.

Sunny and Sonya helped her to the makeshift bed and wrapped her up with every stitch of fabric they could find. Yet she shook uncontrollably, muttering incoherent phrases about some dreaded monster holding her in his clutches.

It must be the fiend.

Sunny gave Leda a diazepam injection. It calmed her down, and she slowly drifted off to sleep.

Hours passed

It was nearly ten when he left for his hotel, assuring Leda that he would be back at six the next morning.

He did not even look at Sonya.

Leda's phone chimed with a message from Patrick just after midnight.

On my way to Digha. Should be there in less than an hour.

Great! Leda replied.

Sonya sat up groggily on the floor. "Is everything okay?"

"Yes. Come and sleep on the bed. I'm going upstairs. Patrick's going to be here in less than an hour."

"Really!" Sonya heaved a sigh.

Leda texted Sunny. Don't worry about checking on me at six. I'm fine and Patrick's almost here.

Good, Sunny replied. Gran's not well, and I'm on the phone with Auntie Diya advising her what to do.

I left them for Ma's house, following the instructions of my first lesson in Phantom Travel to a T—inhaling to bursting point, thinking only about Ma, my target person, until the air pushed out of me, propelling me forward like a rocket, at triple the speed

Chapter 4

Ma was unusually restless when I landed on her four-poster bed. "My grandchildren get engaged but not married," she said in a rapid blur. "Sonya's not even allowed that. Someone help her, please. Those waves are tossing her around like a ball."

Diya stood by Ma, crushing her pills and mixing them into apple sauce. "Perhaps, Yash should not have called and introduced his fiancé to me."

"But you his mother," said Dolly, Ma's maid, and her daughter, Leena, added, "He have right to be happy. The greatest happiness in this world be when we love someone and that someone love us back." Her eyes glistened, and she cuddled Miss Rosy, the dog.

My core went out to Leena. The eighteen-year-old's husband, Ganesh, was in hospital for weeks now after a near-fatal accident he had suffered at the construction site where he worked. He was lucky that Deepak, then a top neurosurgeon, had arrived in the nick of time and taken charge of the situation.

Ma drew in rasping breaths. "Help, Sonya is drowning. And all because of me."

Sunny called and spoke to Ma.

She did not recognize his voice. Her eyes darted around the room and settled on my gray wings. "Priya comes, but never Ravi."

She loved Ravi like he was her own son.

"Ravi will not forgive me," she muttered, "and neither will Sonya. She drowned, didn't she?"

"Sonya's fine, Gran," said Sunny reassuringly. "Couldn't be better."

Diya spooned the concoction she prepared into Ma's mouth and then wiped her lips clean. A person of uncommon gifts, Diya, had the makings of a perfect nurse.

"Everything will be alright," she whispered in Ma's ear. "Just you wait and see."

Ma continued to ramble about her fears until she tired herself out and fell into a deep sleep.

Approaching Digha early the following morning, I noticed a youngish man with long, tousled hair, ambling up to Leda's store-apartment with a suitcase. He planted it on the ground and rang the bell.

Patrick? Did he only just arrive? Hope the girls are okay.

Sonya emerged from the store warily and opened the door. Her skin shone like polished stone in the morning light; her hair lay like a second skin over her cheeks.

Why is she sweating?

Everything looked fine inside the house. Leda slept in her room.

"I am Patrick." The man grinned.

Sonya gave him a ghost of a smile. Her fingers trembled.

Something doesn't feel right.

Patrick burst into a loud guffaw. "Now, Sonya —"

"You know my name?"

Patrick raked his hand though his unkempt hair. "I thought all pretty girls with a southern twang were so called."

Sonya did have the twang, having grown up in Houston.

He laughed again. "Only kidding. Leda can't seem to stop talking about you. Now, if you would please excuse me, I would be much obliged if you invited me in instead of just staring at me."

He seems like a genial sort.

"Of course. Come in." Sonya opened the door wide for him to enter.

Patrick stepped in and swept his gaze around the hallway. "So, where is my dear wife?"

"Um—" Sonya began and glanced up the stairs. "I'll see if she's up." She led Patrick to the bedroom where Leda slept like a rock.

"This is so unusual," said Patrick. "She's always up by this hour."

"I'll go get some tea. You must be exhausted from the flight, Patrick." Sonya sidled away.

Patrick bent down over Leda and touched her gently. "Leda? Babe?" He kissed her on the lips.

Leda's eyes flung open at once.

The Snow White reaction!

"Sorry, I dozed off." Leda stared at her husband. "Where were you? I waited for you, tried to call, texted, but you did not reply."

"I had a flat tire, and my phone died." Patrick heaved a sigh. "Where's the scar?"

Leda turned her hand around, and he scooped it up, squinting at the shape.

"You seemed to disappear off the face of the Earth since I told you about it."

Patrick stared at the scar. "Darling, I got on the plane as soon as I heard about your ordeal." He explained how lucky he had been to get the flight ticket at such short notice even as he examined the scar from different angles.

Sonya returned with two cups of tea and some snacks on a tray and planted it on the nightstand.

"Thanks, Sonya," said Leda.

"Thanks," said Patrick, barely looking up from the scar. "It's exactly as you texted—a bat."

"It's not always the same," muttered Sonya.

Leda silenced her with a glare.

"What do you mean?" Patrick scowled.

Sonya swallowed.

"What was Sonya talking about?" Patrick looked Leda dead in the eye.

"Oh, Patrick, you know that the anxious brain can play tricks on you."

Patrick's brow furrowed. "The book that was burned was demonic, right?"

Leda nodded, and Sonya crept away.

"What did Sonya mean when she said it's not always the same?" Patrick insisted. "You must be honest with me."

"Well, sometimes it might look like it changed color, or the edges shifted."

Looked like? Is she lying out of compassion for his nerves?

The clock struck eight.

"Take a shower, Patrick, and relax." Leda yawned, hugging her pillows.

"Why are you so groggy? You're not on sedatives, are you?"

"Sunny gave me diazepam injection."

"The doctor from the UK? Leda, I have a feeling you're not telling me everything. He wouldn't give you that injection for nothing."

Leda yawned again. "You'll be with me all day and night now. Find out for yourself."

Her words were drowned by the loud, excited voice of Jalebi entering the apartment. "Hello, Sonya. Good morning! Where is Leda? Look what I got you all for breakfast." She opened a four-tier stainless-steel lunch box and out popped alu bhondas, cabbage pakoras, and egg parathas.

Her intentions seem good.

"Wow!" exclaimed Sonya. "How is your husband?"

"Oh, he's always bad news."

Patrick peeked his head out of the bedroom.

Jalebi grinned at him. "I am Jalebi, the new maid."

"Go get changed, Patrick, and Jalebi will serve you a lovely, hot, Indian breakfast." Leda curled up beneath her blanket.

"As you wish, darling." Patrick plucked a clean set of clothes from his suitcase and vanished into the bathroom.

Leda fell asleep at once.

The noon sun was fierce when Leda awoke. Patrick chomped away on an egg paratha with Sunny, listening to Sonya's account of how Leda got branded and what happened since.

"You must take Leda out of here, ASAP," said Sunny. "Not that I understand or believe in black magic, but what I saw last night was real, and honestly, I am terrified."

"How did it all start?" Patrick demanded.

Even as Sonya explained, Patrick glanced at Sunny repeatedly. Sunny looked away, perhaps in silent fury at his own ignorance.

Sonya's lips trembled. "We lost our home, No.7, to the fiend's curse." Her voice choked.

"No.7! The house in Houston that burned down?" Patrick looked at Sunny incredulously.

Sunny nodded, blinking.

"Did you have a pet dog?" Patrick squinted at him.

"Dog?" Sunny and Sonya cried together. "No."

They wouldn't know.

"Well, around two months ago," continued Patrick, "I picked up a dainty little dog, an expensive, rare breed from the sidewalk along your property. I was driving to one of my business meetings. I was a bit too early and was taking the scenic route, when he leaped in front of my car."

I listened in amazement. A silky terrier belonging to the big bosses of Ravi's gang had turned up at No.7 not long before the fire, but he had run away.

"Must've been someone else's," said Sunny.

"I asked around. No one seemed to recognize him. Of course, he was filthy." Patrick's brows scrunched. "Someone said they had seen him run from your back yard before the fire with a little bag of cocaine."

True, though, the statement earned him a scowl from Sunny. Neither he nor Sonya knew that Ravi's gang were distributors of illegal drugs, including cocaine, in the United States. They stored some of the cocaine in my study drawers in little scented bag when I was indisposed.

Sonya swallowed. "Sorry, no idea about that. My parents were decent folks."

Until Hema's book arrived at our door. Ravi got so involved with his gang, the rogues came to dominate our home, turning our sweet haven into Hell.

"Of course." Patrick looked apologetic. "I just told you all this because I literally picked up the silky terrier from outside your property, a few days after we first met," he rambled on. "As I was passing by your property, it was pouring with rain, though not at No.7. I stopped to ensure that my mind was not playing tricks on me. Perhaps it had intrigued the terrier too, for he leaped in my path again. He looked so lonely and hungry, I took him home to Dallas."

"That was so sweet," said Sonya. Both she and Sunny smiled at the man approvingly.

"All I wanted was to give him a home," Patrick continued, "but I worried that he might have an owner somewhere, clueless about his whereabouts. So I brought him back to Houston the following week and took him around the neighborhood. We talked with so many people, and still no one seemed to recognize him. The shame, because with a thorough scrub at the groomers and regular brushing, the pup turned out to be quite a dish!"

That's his name, Dish.

"Dish rings a bell," said Sonya. "Dad's friend Auntie Sue and her husband, Uncle BLZ, had a silky terrier by that name. He was the cutest puppy possible, and Uncle BLZ the most prolific arsonist of the seventies in India."

"Your dad's friend?" Patrick stared at them, mouth agape.

Sunny levelled a glare at Sonya. "How could their dog come all the way to No.7 from Victoria?"

"Victoria, Texas?"

Sunny nodded, evading Patrick's eyes.

"The owners could have brought him over." Patrick squinted at him. "Did they deal in drugs?"

"No idea," muttered Sonya, "but I'm glad Dish is with you, Patrick. He would have found a good home—that beautiful dog!"

"So, we have a dog now? You didn't tell me, Patrick." Leda stepped in. "Where is he now that you are here?"

"With my friend, Marco and his wife, Gladys."

"Marco?" Leda frowned.

"Marco Bianchi and his wife, Gladys, are from my village in Naples. They moved to the US a year ago and invested all their money in a start-up. It failed. They ran up significant debts and were devastated."

"And you left the pup with them?" Leda looked surprised.

"He did them a world of good. Especially since they lost their cat recently. They are okay, they'll be fine. I employed them both in my company and took care of their health insurance."

God bless!

"You are an angel," said Sunny. "You too, Leda. Shame that you should have to suffer for Sonya's indiscretion."

Sonya shifted uneasily on the settee.

"I am a detective, Sunny," Leda said quietly. "It is not rare for a detective to pay for getting involved in dangerous cases."

Sunny drained his cup and shot up. "I must get back to the hotel. Nice meeting you, Patrick, but do take Leda back to the US ASAP."

Patrick nodded.

Sunny walked to the door and stopped. "Um, Sonya, sorry, I forgot. James would like to talk to you about the internship. I think you should call him tonight if not actually go and thank him in person for all his kindness."

Sonya swallowed hard.

She has avoided that internship for months, and James was so kind to offer it to her after she dropped out of Yale.

"Think about it, Sonya." The glare of contempt was evident in Sunny's icy stare. "You owe him that call." Sunny glided out of the door.

Sonya stared after him.

Would she go with him if he asked? This place is too tiny, and Patrick's here.

Sunny and Sonya have grown so distant, yet six months ago, they were the most loving siblings.

"I'll take an early night," said Sonya. She returned to her bed in the store. She did not make the phone call. Instead, she gazed at Paul's pictures on her phone for a while and then dozed off.

Chapter 5

A clap of thunder echoed around the sky and a howling wind picked up. The old windows of Leda's two-story store apartment rattled.

Leda yawned in the tiny living area as Patrick slept in the bedroom.

"Tea?" asked Jalebi.

Leda shook her head, rising from the settee. "I need something stronger to hit my reset button. Do you drink alcohol?"

"Pints to reset my button." Jalebi laughed.

She can be fun.

"You are so full of surprises, Jalebi." Leda fetched a bottle of vodka, two cartons of juice, cranberry and pineapple, and two chilled martini glasses.

"You store your glasses in the fridge?" Jalebi looked surprised.

"Uh-huh, and it is the key to a perfect cocktail." Leda poured a shot of the juices in the glasses, swished them around, then dumped them out in the sink. But as she was about to add the ingredients to the shaker full of ice, Jalebi stopped her.

"Can I have the drink without the vodka, please."

Huh?

Leda frowned.

Jalebi swallowed. "I have this sudden intolerance to alcohol."

Leda mixed the drinks separately and strained the concoctions into the glasses. "There, enjoy." She offered Jalebi her glass.

"Thank you." Jalebi mirrored her smile.

"I wish I could throw on some great music, but oh, well." Leda sipped a mouthful of the cocktail.

Jalebi swirled the beverage in her mouth. "These juices scream Hawaii."

"Hawaii?" Leda's eyebrows cinched together.

"A soft drink with a special, tropical flavor." Jalebi gulped it down. "I've known happier times."

The rain hammered down, lightning flashed, and thunder cracked.

Leda filled Jalebi's glass.

"Honestly, Leda, you are so nice." Jalebi glanced at the scar. "Who would hurt you so bad?"

"No one hurt me." Leda traced the shape with her finger. "The magic did. I was meddlesome."

"But the magic came from someone."

"A sorcerer."

"An evil sorcerer," Jalebi said with marked vehemence.

That's a strong reaction.

"Would you happen to know one?" asked Leda.

I would guess so.

Jalebi looked away. "I would stay as far as possible from anyone I suspected had anything to do with magic."

"So, you do not have the nosy streak like me." Leda laughed.

Jalebi shook her head.

The storm grew intense; the rain came down in sheets. Thunder exploded and hail pounded on the roof.

"This evening's been one of my happiest, but I've got to go." Jalebi drained her cup and carried it to the sink.

"In this weather? Have another glass, or is your husband waiting for you?"

"No, he isn't. He's gone again. He may not be back for months."

"You're welcome to stay for the night if you want to. There's a bed in the little enclosure at the top of the stairs."

Jalebi nodded with a sigh. "How long will you protect me against the storm? Aren't you going back home soon?"

There was something more in her voice than just sadness because Leda would be going—a firm, persistent, and unwavering quality as if demanding a definite "yes" or "no" answer; that coupled with the dark look in her eyes made me wonder. *Why this urgency to know?*

Leda smiled. "We could talk about your future before I do. Tell me about yourself, your life—how you came to live here, how you met your husband, how you fell in love?"

"I married for anything but love."

"Then leave him."

"It's not so easy. I provide him with his booze money. He will kill me."

"If he comes back! You could move on by then. Not like you depend on him. And you sound educated."

"I did not finish my nursing degree."

"Why?"

"I had no money."

"Who supported you before?"

"G-gran. She died last year." Jalebi blinked. "If a nice lady like you loaned me money, I would finish my studies, find a job, and pay her back. But you won't be staying, right? You're going back home with your husband, aren't you?"

Again, that insistence.

"Um—"

Lightning cracked the sky, the crash of thunder almost drowning the thud of the street door.

Sonya's bed was empty.

I couldn't find her, despite my heightened senses. She seemed to be nowhere within a five-mile radius of the house, my perception range. *How did she disappear so quickly?*

In the distance, a patch of flickering dots, like television static, winked out of existence.

What is that?

Even as Leda and Jalebi scooted down the stairs with the flashlight, I scanned the beach.

There was no trace of Sonya.

Does the fiend have a hand in her disappearance? Stress bubbled through my core, tearing it apart. *No, Leda's scar would react to his presence.*

I flew far and wide in search for her, unwittingly delving into the woods bordering the coastal resort town.

The wind rose, making queer sobbing sounds as it swept over the little town. I caught a whiff of sulfur and the agonizing cries of other spirits and veered away.

Why would Sonya even venture out here?

I rushed to Sunny's hotel. *Perhaps Sonya's here. Perhaps she realizes she should move out of Leda's apartment.*

At the Ritz, Sunny squinted at his cell phone screen. He had sent Nikita, his ex-fiancée, a text message asking if he could call her.

Her reply arrived. Sorry, not now. Only just arrived in Kolkata and am trying to find a nursing home for my grandparents. They are stuck at the Oberoi Grand.

Nikita's grandparents' health had suffered since Nikita's parents—Ruby, their daughter, and her husband, Vinay, had died in a car crash six months ago. Asha's mother, Auntie Bina, now looked after Ruby's parents. Auntie Bina and Ruby's mother were sisters.

Where's Auntie Bina?

I could help, Sunny texted.

He seemed unaware of Sonya's disappearance.

Why hasn't Leda informed him? Has Sonya returned?

Several streets away in Leda's store apartment, Sonya talked with Leda and Patrick outside the store.

Relief wobbled into my core, jellylike, thick soothing.

Leda watched Sonya with narrowed eyes. "You didn't tell us where you went."

"Nowhere really."

Leda swept her gaze over Sonya's clothes and hair. They were perfectly dry.

How strange!

"You must excuse me." Sonya sighed, then yawned. "I need to go back to bed. Goodnight."

"Goodnight." Leda left the store with a scowl.

I lingered, trying in vain to solve the mystery.

Chapter 6

Lightning flashed and thunder boomed. Rain sang upon the rooftops and drummed on every window.

I rested on the table lamp by Sonya in the store, my wings spread open.

Upstairs, Patrick slept through it all. Leda was constantly on the phone with Meghna, persuading her to move in with her. Finally, when the clock struck twelve, Leda tiptoed up to the little enclosure at the top of the stairs.

Jalebi was still awake, reading.

"Meghna's coming. Are you okay to share this cubbyhole with her?"

"Of course."

"Thanks, dear." Leda bolted down the stairs. Her footsteps echoed on the wood.

Sonya emerged from the store in her pajamas, pulling her hair back in a moss-green satin scrunchie at the base of her neck.

"Sorry, Sonya, did I wake you up? Meghna is almost here."

Sonya frowned. "Now?"

"Yes, thank God. Now I can talk some sense into the girl, coax her to keep Randy's baby."

Sonya sighed heavily. *It must be the memories.* Randy had been more than a friend, a brother born for adversity, or so she thought.

"Meghna says there's a stigma around unmarried motherhood in this country. I reminded her that this is 2009! The world is seeing significant shifts in people's mindset."

"Not in India though, especially about unmarried motherhood," said Sonya. "For one thing, Gran won't have her back, and she is not the only conservative person round here. Meghna should have thought about the consequences before throwing herself at Randy."

Leda swallowed.

"It will get harder, I'm afraid, with that telltale stomach walking ahead of her."

Leda sighed. "I could help her."

"You are going away."

"Even then."

Leda has only been here a few months. She does not have a clue about our culture.

A taxi pulled up outside, and Leda opened the door.

Meghna, dripping wet, rushed in, dragging a suitcase behind her. Her eyes were sunken with dark circles underneath.

It must be grief taking its toll, but why the green skin tone?

Leda and Sonya gasped.

"Stop looking at me like that." Meghna shook the rainwater from her clothes. "I used green tea face mask to cleanse my skin. Couldn't really wash it off in my rush to get here."

They looked away, their expressions still quite baffled.

The wind blew in the house with a powerful passion, banging the door as if it were its chaotic drumbeat. Sonya closed it with all her might while Leda led Meghna upstairs.

"I am so glad you came." Leda grabbed Meghna a towel. "Let me make you some tea."

"No, thanks. Tea and coffee make me feel sick." Meghna wiped herself dry. "Thankfully, I shall be rid of this nausea very soon. I've spoken to a doctor who is willing to perform an abortion right away."

Leda pressed her lips together.

Jalebi walked in, smiling at Meghna like she had not noticed her green face. "I'm Jalebi, the maid. Let me make you a mug of Horlicks. It's mango pudding flavored."

"Mango? I crave mango all the time."

They seem to have gelled instantly.

"Have you made Meghna's bed, Jalebi?" asked Leda.

Jalebi nodded. She prepared the drink and brought it to Meghna posthaste.

"Thank you." Meghan beamed.

Leda led Meghna to the settee, and Jalebi made herself scarce.

Meghna heaved a sigh. "I can't wait to unburden myself."

Leda swallowed. "Think again. Give yourself some more time, in case you should regret this later. Ask you parents—"

"Are you crazy? They would rather let me die." Meghna gulped down the drink. "I've booked in for termination. It's best done as early as possible. It is easier, safer, and costs less."

"You know what? You should see the baby in an ultrasound scan—"

Tears sprang in Meghna's eyes. "Why are you doing this to me, huh? You know I love Randy, and the baby is a part of him." She choked a sob. "Bringing a bastard into the world was not my plan."

Leda leaned in. "But if I stand by you, ensure he has a happy life?"

Meghna squinted at her. "W-why would you? And you won't stay here forever. You will be gone well before the baby comes."

"What if you come with me?"

Oh, Leda!

"Leda, I know you are kind, but this is taking things too far. You will regret this sooner or later, and then I won't know what to do in that strange land." Meghna sniffed. "I can start afresh here and do very well for myself without the baby. Randy's left me a lot of money."

"Okay, but my offer stays open." Leda smiled. "Let me know if you change your mind. You will have my full support."

"But why?"

"If I say I need you."

"You need me?" Meghna scoffed. The wind echoed her laugh.

The expression of hurt on Leda's face saddened me. *She sounds so genuine.*

"You don't know everything about me."

Meghna met her gaze. "What is there not to know about you? You have a great career, a good marriage, a house, a beautiful face, a lovely smile—everything!"

"Really?" Leda blinked.

For a long moment neither spoke. Thunder deafened the silence. The wind hammered at the door and the windows. The rain thudded on the roof. It raced in the gutters and poured from the leaders.

"Are you hungry? Let me get you some coconut laddus Jalebi made today." Leda rose.

"I am terminating the pregnancy anyway." Meghna spoke with finality.

"You are the mother." Leda found the sweetmeats and packed a handful in a stainless-steel container. "There. Come, Meghna, let's take these up to your room."

Meghna followed her to the little enclosure at the top of the stairs where Jalebi was waiting for her and slumped down on the bed. "Honestly, I couldn't stick around in the hotel. The cleaners guessed I was pregnant and with no vermillion powder in the parting of my hair or a Mangalsutra, I quickly became an object of contempt." She sighed. "Thank you, Leda."

"My pleasure. Now try and get some sleep." Leda started to walk away.

"Wait!" Meghna grabbed her arm. "Did you really mean it when you said you would support me as well as ensure my baby has a happy life?"

Leda's gaze swept over Meghna, lingering on her belly. "Yes. You would do well for yourself while watching him grow." She moved briskly to plump the pillow on the bed, and Meghna missed the tear that rolled down the detective's cheek.

It's not like Leda to get emotional over little disagreements.

Meghna scowled. "But, Leda, I'm so not comfortable raising a bastard."

"You could give him up for adoption."

"That easy? Can you guarantee that I will find someone? Do you have anyone in mind? Where do they live?"

"Please, Meghna, five minutes ago, you were determined to terminate the pregnancy."

"What you said set me thinking. My family's forever wallowing in poverty, no matter how hard I try to help them. I could dump Randy's money on them and run." She glanced from Leda to Jalebi and back again. "But how would you benefit from the arrangement?"

"I would have the satisfaction of watching the baby grow in front of your eyes." Leda attempted a smile. "Anyway, good night."

"You are an angel." Meghna reclined against the pillows. "You should settle down and start a family, Leda, not travel round the world investigating crime."

"Hello." Patrick knocked on the door, standing ajar.

Leda glanced back. "Hi. Come in. Meghna, meet my husband, Patrick. Patrick, this is Meghna, my friend. She is expecting."

Patrick breathed a heavy sigh. "Congratulations! Is it a girl or a boy?"

"Too early to tell though not to dream," Leda muttered.

They seem to be very much in love. Have they never tried to have a baby?

"Dream about a bastard, Leda?" Meghna sniffed. "I know it's not an issue in the US, but here, unwed motherhood is heavily stigmatized. I will be challenged, questioned, and criticized at every step. They will whisper about me behind my back, every day."

"We could take her to Dallas. Couldn't we?" Leda lifted her eyes to Patrick's.

He swallowed but held her gaze. "Of course."

"Am I to go there just to have the baby? And what will I do with myself after?"

"We'll find you a job," Leda said softly. "Patrick has his own company."

Patrick narrowed his eyes at Meghna. "What is it that you do?"

"I am a nurse."

Leda pursed her lips. "Meghna is quick to learn. She can make herself useful in any situation."

"Hmmm. Perhaps Meghna could throw some light on the whereabouts of the sorcerer who gave you that scar."

Leda's face fell.

"Leda, I have been meaning to tell you something," said Meghna. "You know the old, abandoned house opposite Aeshna Estates where Randy used to work? Things happen there. I have seen Aghoris meditating on corpses. Though I cannot claim that Dev is actively involved in the goings-on, I suspect there could be a connection. You could investigate."

"We leave for the US in less than seventy-two hours." Patrick's phone rang. He ignored the call.

Leda checked her phone. "There has already been a police raid there, but I could drop by real quick, catch them unawares."

"You must be super careful," said Meghna. "It is a real-life living hell of torture,"

She knows alright. Desperate for Randy's love, she landed up there in pursuit of him.

Patrick grimaced "Leda, you're not going to a nasty place like that."

Leda just smiled.

"Not alone. I forbid you."

Meghna met his gaze. "But that is exactly how you go to that place, alone, and enter unnoticed. If you must explore the place, you must do it in complete secrecy."

Patrick's eyebrow shot up.

"Don't worry, Pat." Leda murmured with a half-smile. "The police found nothing there except some poor sadhus."

"The police might have been bribed," said Meghna.

"Leda," said Patrick firmly, "you must promise to stay away from the place."

Meghna grinned. "Patrick, you love your wife too much. If you do not give her freedom, how will she do her work?"

"Oh, he is just nervous about all this black magic," said Leda. "He knows I've handled dangerous criminals, notorious killers."

"But not black magicians." Patrick squeaked. "How about I come with you, Leda?"

"I am not going anywhere now," said Leda. "We need to book Meghna's ticket. Remember, she is coming with us."

"I applied for visa months ago when I first met Randy." Meghna sighed.

"Don't worry about anything," said Leda.

"I too applied for visa ages ago," muttered Jalebi.

Leda smiled with a nod. She bade Jalebi and Meghna goodnight and left with her husband.

Jalebi stayed with Meghna. They chatted through the night about all things under the sky.

It looks like they've known each other for ever.

Chapter 7

The moon shone in the watery sky when Deepak's scent filled my core. He hovered over me, baring his glow—the brightest shade of orange.

"Hey!" I fluttered my bedraggled wings. Surprisingly, I did not repel him.

"You've brightened. Doing something right?" Deepak's voice echoed around me.

"Disengaging from humans."

"You must regain your radiance."

"The little that rubbed off on me in Heaven?" I scoffed. "That tinge of orange did not secure me a place in our eternal home anyway."

"You must try harder and get brighter. The Devil is out hunting for green spirits. He has cast his net wide. You will smell his stench—"

"I'm more concerned about the fiend. He has cast the spell and is using various tools to achieve his goals. He must be crushed."

"Priya, no, please! Harbor pure thoughts only, be kind, and stay out of the lives of humans."

"That's easier said than done. I am stuck here with my children all the time, and the curse plagues them. How can I not get involved?"

"Problems are inevitable in life. People find their way around them, eventually."

"But the curse?"

"Wait for the final outcome. Trust in divine timing. Getting involved will—"

"I know, Deepak."

"Well, try. You must move on, Priya. An increased status entails perks."

"Like?"

A quiver of flame darted through his core. "SMS from the Heaven-elders. I have been away from Heaven for far too long."

He was gone.

Down below Leda headed toward the highway in a taxi. She was on the phone with Rao, talking about the scar.

I will not follow her but hide in her apartment, harboring the purest of thoughts . . .

Alas, curiosity got the better of me. *Where's she going? Is it about the curse?* I dove into the taxi and crawled under Leda's collar. She touched me and smiled.

My safe haven.

"Yes, it moved like a live object or rather a bat," Leda spoke on the phone. "It's like someone is controlling it. Who else but Dev? Anyway, see you in a bit." She hung up and texted Patrick.

I am on my way to see Rao about the scar. Keep it quiet.

Patrick did not reply. I guessed he was fast asleep.

The sky changed from charcoal to dull gray when the taxi approached the narrow potholed lane leading to the old, abandoned house opposite Aeshna Estates. The woods that ran along the boundary of the estate were deep and foreboding.

My core trembled. *She can't be here just to talk about the scar.*

There was no sign of Rao.

Leda squinted at the time on her cell phone. 5:15.

I shuddered for her.

"So isolated. Is it this building?" The taxi driver pointed to Aeshna Estates.

"Y-yes." Leda paid him, and the taxi pulled away. She was all alone in the netherworld.

The daredevil!

The old derelict building peeked through a gap in the trees. There was not a light in the windows.

Leda ventured up the path overtaken by weeds and stepped in through the doorless entrance. Even as she faltered in the darkness, I felt the gruesome pull of snares located at all the pivotal points, the splintered window frames and the crumbling walls.

It's like someone's expecting me. Who?

There was no sign of the fiend.

I mingled with the creepy crawlies in the soil.

Leda lurked in the shadows of the tall, winding staircase leading up to a rugged, gaping hole in the wall.

Someone was cleaning. There was a calmness in the sound of furniture gliding over wooden floors and the soft swish of a broom as it swept.

Leda seemed distracted by voices chanting in unison, carried in by a gust of sweet-smelling wind.

Is it the sadhus?

She rushed out and bolted into the thicket behind the house. She ventured deep into it, until beneath a wide canopy of angel's trumpets, she stopped.

The sweet, heady smell of the pendulous blossoms mingled with the sacred aroma of Hindu religious rituals—sandalwood and Indian frankincense smoking on coconut husk, and of course, pure ghee flaring in the fire. The clarified butter and fire combined, generating an energy in the surroundings, powerful enough to chase away negative energies and attract positive vibrations.

The whole area throbbed with spiritual activity. In a vast clearing beyond, bunches of young sadhus with matted hair hummed, strumming their ektaras to create a haunting melody. They wore nothing but simple saffron loincloths. Older sannyasins meditated, each meditation session followed by offerings and chanting of the Gita. An elderly sadhu sat among sādhvīnes, speaking of how he had been healed through prayer.

Quite the religious site!

Someone has definitely informed the fiend that she's coming. Who?

A faint whiff of blood drew my attention to Rao, skulking in the darkness, a few blotches of blood on his sleeve. I must've gotten a little too carried away by the rituals to notice him.

"Hey, Leda." Rao tapped Leda on the shoulder.

She swung around.

"I was looking forward to exploring the indoors with you. Did I misunderstand what you wanted to do?"

So, they did come here to investigate.

"There's nothing inside, Rao. I have a feeling they got wind of our visit and cleaned up thoroughly."

"Not quite as thoroughly as you think."

He showed her some broken pieces of cheap, glittering glass bangles he had found along the side of the staircase. "There weren't many," he said. "I don't know whether they broke under my body weight as I fell on them, or they were already lying there that way."

"Let's go back, check the place out."

They rushed back when Leda's phone chimed with a text from Meghna.

Sonya has disappeared. Her phone is gone too, and she won't pick up when we call.

Meghna's worried about Sonya's disappearance?

Leda called Meghna at once.

"The front door banged at around three," she said. "I heard some sounds and footsteps and went downstairs. I saw no one. The store door stood ajar. Sonya was not in sight. Terrified that she had been abducted and the abductors would come back for me, I woke up Patrick. We searched everywhere for Sonya. We didn't find her."

Hmmm.

"Did you let Sunny know?"

"Of course." Meghna turned on the speakerphone and Patrick added, "We're on the beach, but Sonya is nowhere in sight." He sighed. "There's something she's not telling us."

"I'll get back ASAP," said Leda.

Chapter 8

The first light of dawn stretched across the horizon when I returned to Digha.

Sonya's scent flooded the barnacled rocks where she sat before the rising sun, lost in the rhythmic percussion of the waves on the sand. Her lips bore the semblance of a smile.

It's like she's found a solution to her problems.

A mile away, Patrick and Sunny trudged along the sand toward the rocks.

"The girl could have wandered off anywhere," said Sunny. "We are just wasting time."

I winced at the rage in his voice.

Patrick's gaze searched the beach meticulously. He said nothing.

They ran into Jalebi, squinting into the distance where Sonya sat on the barnacled rocks.

Why doesn't she tell the others?

Patrick craned his necks to scan the far end of the sea wall. "Isn't that Sonya on the rocks?"

"Yes." Sunny scowled.

Jalebi frowned.

Patrick squinted at Jalebi. "Why didn't you tell us, Jalebi?"

"My eyesight is bad. I couldn't even be sure there was anybody there."

Hmmm.

They all walked up to Sonya.

"Sonya, why did you go away without telling anyone?" Sunny demanded of her.

"I'm an adult, Sunny," said Sonya with cool composure.

"Of course," bellowed Sunny. "But why weren't you answering your phone?"

"Do you care?"

Sunny glowered at her. "We happen to come from the same family. Honestly, Sonya, you're so ungrateful. I wasted my time looking for you."

"She is your sister." Patrick gave a little laugh.

Six months ago, Sunny would have behaved very differently, but again, that was before the book arrived.

"Is Leda back?" he asked, and Patrick's phone chimed with a text from her.

"She says she's in the parking lot." Patrick grinned.

We found Sonya, he texted her. How was your meeting with Rao? Could he help with the scar?

Not really, came her reply.

Patrick dropped her a "crying face" emoji.

"Are you all set to return to the States?" asked Sunny.

"Yes."

Leda came running up.

"Here she comes." Patrick grinned.

Leda pecked her husband on the cheek and slumped down by Sonya.

"Hi, Leda," she said.

"Hi. Where were you?

"On the beach."

Really!

"Where were you, Leda?" asked Jalebi. "Why did you leave at that unearthly hour?"

"I had work. By the way, Sonya, have you ever been to the abandoned house opposite Aeshna Estates?"

Sonya shook her head. "I didn't know there was one. Was that where you were all this time?"

"I was checking out the property as part of the investigation."

I was surprised that she said it in front of Jalebi. *Or is it deliberate?*

"The place is rumored to be a gangland," Leda continued, "All I saw was this immaculately clean place, a haven of peace, with these monks and nuns seeming to persevere wholeheartedly in their spiritual pursuit." She paused and her brows scrunched. "Yet there were glass bangles on the staircase."

"Celibate ascetics in an abandoned house and glass bangles? What an interesting combination." Jalebi chuckled. "Did you know that the melodious jingle of bangles is all about titillation?"

"There's been some foul play." Leda scowled.

"Not necessarily. You forget that the house is old and abandoned. In India love is not free. It is strictly put in chains. People in illegal relationships use places like that to make love." Squawking seagulls wheeling over their heads drowned Jalebi's voice.

Jalebi picked up a stone. "Shoo, shoo." she cried.

"Oh, please let them stay," begged Leda.

"Yes, please," pleaded Sonya. "I can only stick around here because of their sharp squawks. They drown that voice of conscience that can never shut up."

The guilt is consuming her.

Jalebi giggled and tossed the stone at the birds.

"Stop!" Leda grabbed Jalebi's arm, but the rock had already left her hand. In moments the gulls were like dark shadows against the sky. "One of them could have got hurt."

"And dropped." Jalebi smirked.

Sonya and Leda stared at her aghast.

There is a streak of cruelty in the girl.

"What would you do with it?" asked Leda.

"Nothing. The meat I've heard tastes like trash. But you could have pulled off the feathers and bones and used them to create stuff for your store." Jalebi touched her natural brown feather earrings.

"I never used live animals. Anyway, would you like anything from the store, I can let you have it for free."

"I have no home." Jalebi sighed. "Are you selling the store?"

"No. It belongs to my friend. I was only managing it for her."

"But I heard you handcrafted the display cases, shelves, racks."

"Yes, Jalebi. We'll donate those." Leda smiled. "Anyway, I've got to go. I'll hire a car and give Patrick a tour of this place. There are so many scenic beaches—Sonya, you coming?"

"No, thank you. I'll stay out here for a bit longer and enjoy the scenery. Please don't worry about me. I promise I won't get lost."

Chapter 9

Leda and Patrick returned from their tour of the beaches mid-afternoon and began to sort through the merchandise of the store.

Can't believe she'll quit the investigation to follow her husband back to the States. She must have a plan in place.

It was hard to tell.

They worked in silence, careful not to disturb Jalebi and Meghna who they assumed were enjoying an afternoon siesta. Yet the friends were wide awake in the little enclosure at the top of the stairs, deep in conversation.

"I was in the middle of my period when I found my bathroom door wouldn't lock," said Jalebi. "I told him, and he promised to fix it. Only he didn't. He said he had ordered a special lock that never arrived."

Who's this man?

"Then?" Meghna was barely able to hold her curiosity, yet she did not ask who the man was. I guessed she knew.

"One day, as I was getting changed in the bathroom, he walked in," Jalebi continued.

"And he saw you naked?" Meghna giggled.

"I had tiny boobs, and my body was changing. I was embarrassed, but he was great." Her description of the foreplay was highly specific and descriptive.

It sounded like the man was a lot older and experienced. Revulsion stirred in the pit of my core.

"How old were you again?" asked Meghna.

"Fourteen."

So young!

"And you enjoyed it?"

"Well, the outercourse, yes. He trained me to enjoy the main event gradually. I was too young to understand abuse. I feared the punishments and loved the rewards he gave me like a special drink with tropical flavors."

Hawaii?

A mysterious smile dribbled out of the corners of Jalebi's mouth. "In time, the activities became his special rewards."

They roared with laughter.

The clock struck five, and Jalebi came racing down. "Leda, Patrick, you're already back? Why didn't you tell me?" She put the kettle on and grabbed the broom.

"We're going to miss you, Jalebi," said Patrick.

"Yet you choose to take my friend with you, not me."

Leda and Patrick exchanged glances.

"You knew—" began Leda.

"We'll pay you for the rest of this month as well as for the next," said Patrick. "Ten thousand rupees, okay?"

Two hundred dollars—that's quite a sum!

Patrick slipped out his check book from his bag, but Jalebi shook her head.

"I don't want the money. Take me to the US if you ever can, Patrick."

"I'll try, but no promises."

Later that evening, Patrick and Leda called on the landlord to inform him about their decision to move out.

"At last, nothing stands in the way of our homeward journey." Patrick looked the picture of happiness upon their return to the store apartment.

He stumbled on a broken stair tread. "This building needs repair," he said.

"I wish we could help." Leda sighed. "The landlord and his wife have been so supportive of me during my stay here."

"I will give the landlord some money. That should take care of it all." Patrick beamed.

It's what they call "helper's high."

They walked up the stairs holding hands like a couple on a date.

Jalebi had been waiting for them. "Look what I cooked. Crab masala and basmati rice. Come, have it while it's still hot."

Leda and Patrick thanked her profusely. They devoured the dish and applauded her culinary skills. Meghna avoided coming to the table for fear of throwing up at the sight of the humongous shellfish.

Sonya was on the phone with Nikita. She didn't want any dinner.

"When do you return to the UK?' asked Leda.

Sonya shrugged.

"I can continue to cook and clean for you," said Jalebi. "How long are you planning to stay?"

"Don't worry about me,' said Sonya. "I will go crash on Nikita's couch."

Everyone retired to their bedrooms early that night.

I stayed with Sonya in her room, where wrapped up in blankets, she watched *Revolutionary Road* on her laptop. She seemed lost in the story of love and family, ambitions and frustrations, dreamers and conformists, and fell asleep almost instantly after the movie ended.

I wondered at her calm facial expression. *What has brought her so much peace? Is it Nikita?* The girls had been best friends forever, but then they fell out over Nikita and Sunny's breakup. It was nice that they had managed to patch things up and become friends again.

"Paul," Sonya muttered in her sleep.

Is she dreaming about him? Hope it's a happy dream.

Yards from her, Leda glided down the stairs, harnessing her binoculars on her chest. With a furtive glance at the store, she stole out of the apartment, jumped into the hired Maruti Suzuki, and vanished into the darkness.

I knew beyond a shadow of doubt that she headed toward the abandoned house. *She was not satisfied with her investigation last night.*

I sneaked into her car.

The sky was at its darkest when Leda arrived at the house. She drove past and parked around a mile from it, by the thickets bordering the street.

Isn't Rao coming today?

Leda slipped out noiselessly, then glancing to either side, she sprinted down the road. Approaching the property, she slowed down, switched off her phone, and melted into the thicket.

There was no fragrance of molten ghee in the breeze or of any other pooja paraphernalia. Instead, the air reeked of burning wood, clothes, metal, and carboard.

The sadhus and sadhvines had vanished.

She drew a calming breath.

What if the fiend is back today?

I followed but stopped at the house. The spirit traps lingered on the door and window frames.

Leda entered through a broken window, and a car pulled up on the road.

I recoiled.

Familiar scents wafted into my core. I recognized the driver, Neel, the deadliest rogue of Ravi's gang. and his blue-eyed boy, Damien.

Why are they here? My core pounded. *If only I could give Leda a fright and make her leave.*

She remained unfazed. With a quick glance at her unreactive scar, she tiptoed out to hide among the tall weeds in the front yard.

The men slipped into the house.

Damien hummed a happy tune.

"Too happy, eh?" asked Neel. "Going straight for your honeymoon after the cremation?"

Who's dead?

The men seemed oblivious of Leda observing the goings-on through her binoculars. Neel yanked his cell phone out from his pocket and called someone.

Within the house, someone received the call. Almost at once a trapdoor opened under the staircase, revealing a secret passage.

A hefty man emerged, bearing a sack. In it was the body of a young girl, stone-dead. Her soul still fluttered frantically on the sack as if to get back into the body.

Is she finding it hard to accept death?

I descended on the spirit and hugged her with all the warmth in my core. "You're free." I whispered. "Enjoy your freedom."

She leaped out of my grasp. "Thanks, lime-green spirit."

Lime-green? Me?

I was indeed a bright, yellow-toned shade of green. *When did that happen?*

I realized that my disguise had fallen away. Something like a mirror ring on Neel's finger pointed at me. I could not move.

Neel's phone rang.

"Yes," he responded, "I got the two air tickets Rishabhdev asked for and sent them to him."

That's the fiend. Battling the constraining force, I could not help wondering where the fiend was going.

A giant tug from the ring severed my core from me and slapped it against Neel's palm. At once he squeezed his fingers over it into a fist.

I blacked out.

When I came around, Neel had not moved. I felt drained. I had lost my heightened senses.

"Dump the body in the car," said Neel. "Damien and I will leave with it immediately. Where is that firangi—that detective? Have they taken her back to her car?"

I quaked with fear. Leda had disappeared from behind the tall weeds. *What have they done with her?*

The hefty man nodded. "Yes. They had to knock her out. But she's with Jalebi, our expert."

She was the informer last night.

"Enough!" Neel snapped. "Now, hurry up. The house will be demolished today and the rubble burned. We want all the evidence destroyed ASAP."

A stranger called Neel to inform him to prepare for a police raid in less than two hours. He went berserk; his fist slackened.

My core tumbled away and came crashing back into me. I was whole again. For several minutes I lay immobilized, my strength and my heightened senses returning slowly.

Neel still held his hand in a fist.

He has not realized that my core has gotten away.

The rumblings of the hydraulic excavator sounded in the distance. The miles around the house sprang before me, yard by yard. The bulldozer rose to view, rolling toward Leda's car.

Cold dread coiled in my core.

Covered in black, Jalebi jumped out of the driver's seat and ran, leaving Leda unconscious and bleeding in the passenger seat.

Neither the bulldozer nor Jalebi was fast enough for the robust Rao. Appearing as if out of nowhere, he landed a resounding kick on Jalebi's shin and sent her catapulting into the path of the bulldozer.

Even as the dozer operator engaged the brakes, Rao leaped into the car and grabbed the wheel. He drove in reverse down the street, turned into a narrow dust road, and hurtled away.

Leda muttered incoherently. She was coming round.

Jalebi writhed on the road, unable to move her numb leg. Yet she texted Neel:

Leda's escaped.

Chapter 10

Neel rushed out in response to Jalebi's text.

Free of the trap, I transformed into a Common Mormon, the commonest butterfly in India, and slid onto the underside of Leda's car.

The car bounced over the rutted dirt road. Leda slouched on the passenger seat, blood dripping down her face.

"Where am I?" she began as the car emerged onto the main road, then gasped. "Rao, we must go back. There's a dead body at the house."

"Not much you can do about it. They're knocking down the house." Rao glanced back over his shoulder and his gaze drifted over Leda's face. "You need first aid." Grabbing the bottle of water in the driver's door pocket, he thrust it in her hand and accelerated the car.

Leda chugged the water. "W-where did you find me?"

"In this car. It was parked in the middle of the road. You were unconscious, possibly knocked unconscious by the hooded, masked rogue in the driver's seat who fled at the sight of me. Sorry, I had no time to investigate. The bulldozer was rolling toward us. Can you remember anything?"

"T-there was a dead woman. Two men had come for her. One spoke on the phone about air tickets—two—one for Dev, and another for a woman travelling with him."

I had missed that bit of the conversation. *What else did they say?*

"I got too engrossed trying to find out about this woman. I ventured too close." Leda sighed. "I can't remember what happened after—how did you get there? When?"

"Just after four and thank God I did." Rao swallowed. "I could not fall asleep last night. I did some research on the house and ventured out to explore it upon a sudden whim. I took the dust road through the once-green fields behind Aeshna Estates. The road joins the street about a quarter of a mile from where you were parked." He inhaled sharply. "Your assailant jumped out of the car and ran. I kicked the person in the path of the bulldozer, and it stopped. I took advantage of that and escaped with you." He sighed. "You didn't tell me you were coming here tonight. Why? And then you switched off your phone. Didn't you realize the risk you were putting yourself into?"

"I wanted to keep it very, very secret." Leda switched her phone back on, and Patrick called.

"Where have you been, Leda? I must have called a thousand times."

"Sorry. I had switched off my phone." She blurted out the truth.

Patrick erupted in rage. "Are you completely out of your mind? We fly back to the US in less than forty-eight hours. Did you take Jalebi and Sonya with you? They've been missing for hours now."

Is the fiend flying somewhere with Sonya? Leda said something about two air tickets.

I dashed to the airport.

There was no sign of the fiend or Sonya.

What if they have already boarded their plane and the plane has taken off? Where would they be heading?

Despite the perks I enjoyed as a spirit, I could not reach Sonya. The rules of Phantom Travel required me to know the exact location of my target person, and I did not have it.

I returned to Digha hoping that Sonya had turned up at Leda' store apartment.

She had not.

Leda searched for her on the beach with Patrick. A wide Band-Aid covered the wound on her forehead

"I wanted to catch Dev unawares," she explained. "His people were there, just not him."

"How do you know he wasn't hiding?" asked Patrick.

"The scar was still." Leda sighed. "Besides he's leaving. I heard people talking about air tickets—two—one for Dev, and another for a woman travelling with him."

"Hope the woman is not our Sonya," Patrick muttered. "There are rumors that Sonya was seen among the rocks talking to someone on the phone last night, and that later, a woman, tall, slim, and dressed in western clothes, picked her up at the gas station across the road in a Mercedes."

It could be Nikita. Sonya said she would crash on her couch.

"Could be Nikita. I've heard she's tall and slim. Let me call Sunny. He can find out." Leda dialed his number.

Sunny did not pick up.

Meghna walked up.

I lingered, wondering what she had to say about Sonya's disappearance.

"Any news of Jalebi?" She coughed.

"Nope. Leda and I walked as far as Jalebi's hut. The door was locked." Patrick squinted at Meghna's heavily made-up face.

The greenness beneath the make-up intrigued me. *Is it just the remains of a face mask?*

"Jalebi didn't even take the check yesterday," said Leda.

"Jalebi is too nice." Meghna coughed again. "I doubt she cares about the money. She might never come back."

Meghna should know where Jalebi is if they are as close as they appear to be.

"Did you hear any rumors about Sonya's whereabouts?" Leda told her what she had heard.

"Yes, everything you said and more. Apparently, she had been telling her caller that she was looking forward to a hearty brunch with them at the Oberoi Grand."

That must be Nikita. Her grandparents are stuck at the hotel.

I set off for Kolkata, certain that Sonya was with Nikita.

Chapter 11

I arrived at the Oberoi Grand, and Nikita rushed after a vacant taxi sailing past. Sonya's scent had not mingled with hers.

They couldn't have been together, especially for a hearty brunch. Besides, where's the Mercedes?

The taxi stopped and Nikita stepped in. "Manderville Gardens, please."

 The driver pulled away.

I chased after it. Auntie Bina lived in a condominium complex in Manderville Gardens, and she also matched the description of the woman rumored to have picked up Sonya at the gas station opposite Leda's store apartment the previous night. She was both tall and slim, and she owned a Mercedes.

Approaching the condo block, I detected Uncle Dev's scent among others, though not Sonya's.

Is he flying with Auntie Bina? I had seen him get close to the socialite over the months.

Auntie Bina had gone to great lengths to decorate the condo. The lights had been dimmed and scented candles dotted the large living room. A familiar song, "Can't Help Falling in Love," played on the stereo in Elvis's voice. Suddenly, it sounded more powerful than it ever had, even somewhat operatic.

I spotted the fiend in Auntie Bina's bed, between her bare legs, twirling his fingers in the sparse, coarse hair. With his mussed-up wig and his youthful features, he looked decades younger than his actual age.

"You are my fantasy and desire." He swept his fingers over her folds, teasing her entrance until she jerked upright with a moan.

"Every moment with you feels like a dream I never want to end." Auntie Bina tangled herself around him. Seemingly lost to a deep and carnal desire, she had no idea that Nikita had arrived at the condo.

For shame! I thought she had class.

The clock chimed one.

Nikita peeked into the kitchen, and the butler offered her some coffee. She carried it into the living room and sipped the beverage, waiting.

The butler wheeled in some savories and sweetmeats. "Mrs. Singh should be with you shortly."

"I must see her today about my grandparents. They are so ill and have been stuck at the Oberoi Grand for months. I have been out looking into senior centers, which is why I came here all the way from the US. I need Gran Bina's advice to decide on one I could move them into ASAP."

This confirms that Nikita did not carry off Sonya.

The butler swallowed. "Why don't you come to the kitchen and help me make some mutton biriyani while you wait?"

"Me help you! You are an expert." Nonetheless, she followed him with a frown like she knew Auntie Bina entertained her lover in her bedroom.

On Auntie Bina's humongous bed, the lovers rubbed their genitals against each other blissfully, and that did not drive them into a frenzy.

The fiend helped Auntie Bina adjust herself on his belly. "The best thing about tantric sex is, there's no rush."

If only they would talk about Sonya or the fiend's flight.

They spooned, kissed, licked, teased, nibbled. They did not mention Sonya.

What if Auntie Bina brought Sonya to the condo and then sent her off somewhere?

I focused on the butler's conversation with Nikita, hoping he would tell her something in strict confidence.

"Mutton is hard to digest." Nikita rested against the countertop, squinting at the ingredients: clarified butter, caramelized onions, saffron milk, cumin, coriander seeds, garam masala, whole and ground ginger, garlic, and chili paste. "Gran Bina would not usually have a spicy mutton preparation. Is she having guests over for lunch?"

"Y-yes," the butler said somewhat hesitantly, stirring the concoction in the pot. "Why didn't you inform her that you were coming? She would have waited, done her best to entertain you, like she usually does."

"I didn't really want that, not after I broke up with Dillon. Gran Bina spent a fortune on the dowry." Nikita sighed. "Did she ask not to be disturbed?"

The butler grimaced.

Nikita glanced out of the kitchen at the bedroom door.

Behind it, Auntie Bina locked eyes with the monster. She had abandoned her silk chemise "What about the full-body massage you promised?"

He ran his fingers along the contours of her body. "I am still admiring your perfect Jane Fonda body."

"I follow along with her classic step aerobics routine regularly." Auntie Bina's voice trailed as he pressed down against her. She released a rumbling growl full of need. "I'm going to miss this."

So he is going somewhere without her.

"When we're together again," said the fiend, "we will perfect the art—take it slow, enjoy the deeper levels of sensation."

"Is her guest already here?" Nikita asked the butler.

He let loose a sigh. "Mrs. Singh could have let him in. I was here in the kitchen."

Nikita cocked her head to the side.

A low, wondrous moan rippled through the apartment.

The fiend ran his fingers over the squirming Auntie Bina down from her head to her toes in long strokes. "There. Now, what are the most neglected parts of your body?" His voice was liquid velvet. "Let me give them love."

She rattled them off in a husky voice, "Behind my ears, elbow, butt hole—"

"Slower, dear." He stooped over and kissed, licked, and even nibbled the areas, teasing them with his gentle touch, with his lips, his tongue, his teeth.

"Feet, knees, belly button . . ."

Though the words were indistinct, there was no way Nikita was deaf to their voices.

Auntie Bina probably did not have a clue, or perhaps she chose to be oblivious to the world.

Nikita slipped out her phone and texted her a message.

I am here about my grandparents, but it seems you're busy. I'll come back later.

Auntie Bina's cell phone chimed. She leaned over to read the message, but the fiend shook his head.

"No, Bina. Sorry, but I have little time."

He is leaving soon. With whom? If it's with Sonya, where is she?

The fiend rubbed the massage oil in his hands, slowly warming it up. Then he dripped the warm oil from his cupped hands onto her back.

She stirred with a prolonged moan. He massaged in the oil gently, slowly increasing the pressure, kneading her muscles with his thumb and forefingers.

Got to take off, have a lot on my plate, Nikita texted.

Auntie Bina's phone chimed again.

Wiping his hand on his hand towel, the fiend typed on her behalf:

I'm with my massage therapist. Doctor's orders. Will call you later.

"I'm not an idiot," muttered Nikita.

Auntie Bina didn't seem to care about anyone's opinion. "Dev, tell me how you manage to make the massage oil smell just right?"

"I mix the oils very gently with cinnamon and a few other 'warming' spices and let stand overnight. They blend and balance out nicely."

"Did you hear the masseur? He's loud." Nikita started walking toward Auntie Bina's door.

The butler nodded as he drained the cooked rice in the sink. "The rice looks completely cooked. Will you please taste it for me?"

Nikita did with a scowl. "Great! Since when has Gran Bina been prescribed massages by her doctor?"

"Long time." The butler concentrated on layering the fragrant rice over the cooked mutton and masalas in a metal pot.

"How often is he here?"

"On and off." The butler drizzled a ladle of mutton gravy over the rice before topping it with handfuls of chopped mint and coriander leaves. "She um, was not expecting you."

"But I really need to talk to her about my grandparents. When is she leaving for the US?"

If Auntie Bina is going to the US, the fiend couldn't be going there too. She said she would miss his ways.

The butler stiffened as he covered the pot with foil and then with the lid. "If she told you that, she should've given you a date."

"Well, she said something like in a few weeks, but that was all."

Then the fiend could be going to the US, and with Sonya. My core quivered within the Common Mormon disguise. *I'll stay put and listen to them talk.*

The butler's phone chimed with a message from Auntie Bina.

Get a bottle of Bombay Sapphire and kebabs from the Shiraz Mahal, right now. He must leave in an hour.

So he is going today.

The butler swallowed. "Nikita, I have some errands to run. Come, I'll ask the chauffeur to drop you off."

Nikita's face contorted, but she left with him.

In Auntie Bina's bedroom, the lovers had relocated to the jacuzzi. "Wish I used your place, Bina," he said, "but it's so predictable."

How? Why on earth don't they speak more clearly?

Chapter 12

I paced the air outside Auntie Bina's condominium complex, still hoping to pick up some information about Sonya's whereabouts from the lovers' conversation.

Neither Auntie Bina nor the fiend divulged any.

Nikita's voice drifted through the air as Auntie Bina's chauffeur drove her away in her Mercedes-Benz. "Yes, Leda, just got Sunny's text. Thanks for calling. I've heard a lot about you from Sonya. Um, she sounded pretty chilled last night. We talked—"

The car sped away, and a green shape charged at me, oozing the stench of sulfur.

It must be the Devil.

I dove in and a little boy almost grabbed me. "Daddy, a Common Mormon. Love the patterns on her wings. Can I take her home?"

The yearning in his voice!

I darted for cover in Auntie Bina's condo, and the lovers emerged from the bedroom.

The butler had returned, and he served the food and alcohol as they settled at the table. He then made himself sparse. The happy couple ate, drank, laughed, and flirted without uttering a word about the fiend's plans for the evening.

Just as they finished, a Chevy Impala pulled up outside the condo. After a prolonged kiss, the fiend rode away in it, talking in hushed tones with the chauffeur.

"Good, I'm glad that she likes the Red Lake house." said the fiend.

Who? Sonya? Is that where she is? The car was headed that way.

I threw caution to the wind and zipped through the older part of the city with its narrow lanes and old buildings.

Somewhere in their midst, I caught a faint whiff of Sonya's scent. It came from a sprawling mansion, almost consumed by the surrounding wilderness.

I swooped down into the dark thickets, listening for any sound betraying her distress. I heard nothing, despite my heightened senses, though Sonya's scent intensified.

There were spirit traps everywhere. Paranoid, I zipped around the property, too afraid to settle anywhere.

Headlights flashed on the house, revealing layers of peeling plaster and exposed brick. The Chevy Impala had arrived with the fiend. He stepped out, his gleaming, beadlike eye scoring the overgrown garden. I darted to the boundary wall, not the straight perfection of the modern buildings I was used to, but one that was curved and flawed; each curve and flaw rendered it solid and impenetrable.

Lights sprang up around me—fireflies. I had never known their lanterns to glow so green or stink so foul. In the stench, I caught a whiff of BLZ's scent.

Is this the eternal home Baalzebub chose for himself? Poor Asha could not rid the world of the rogue even by murdering him.

The fireflies were identical. *Which one is him?*

A torchlight swung across the stretch of green, searching.

I meandered among the tall trees for cover, not risking contact with the bushes for fear of those sneaky spirit traps. What I did not expect was for a bunch of popsicle sticks to come flying at me. The straight rows of yarn looked irresistible.

I succumbed.

The trap stripped me of my disguise and dragged me up against a branch. The first crippling spasm hit, doubling me over. I struggled to suppress the whimper that escaped my core.

It was drowned instantaneously by the shrieks erupting from within the house.

What is going on here?

Fighting the threads in sheer panic, I noticed an entity writhing in one of the rooms, so intensely green, I could mistake him for a weed. But then his scent suffused my core.

Ravi! How did he get here?

Needle-sharp tweezers pulled him on either end, elongating him to twice his size. I had never heard a spirit squeal that loud or wriggle so hard.

He broke away. Acetylene torches chased him up what looked like a drainpipe.

"There's no getting away!" spooky voices hissed. "We will grind you to a pulp."

I glimpsed tangling wires and electronic boards in the background. Multi-jointed appendages moved among them. Their reverbs, pitch shift, and delayed echoes created sound effects of terror as if from some other dimension.

Intrigued by the drama that unfolded before me, I was oblivious of a giant beefy man scooping up my trap. It was only when he hurled me in through Ravi's window that I realized.

I landed only inches from him. The trap tightened around me. Each row of thread was like a hot knife cutting into my core. I pounded against them, twisting, twitching, and writhing. I could not break free.

Ravi zipped around the torture chamber, battering against the walls, groaning piteously. His cries echoed through the grounds. He crashed against the machinery and slammed into me.

Does he recognize me, or is he blind in his agony?

I thrashed against the binding threads screaming as loud as a spirit can.

"Am I to share this hellhole with you, whore?" He smacked me with his distended core.

He does recognize me.

"You ruined your life and everyone else's." He corebutted me mercilessly.

"I did not—" A thread snapped somewhere in my trap, then another.

"Shut the fuck up, you half-witted cow." He struck me again.

I groaned.

He continues to be the violent, vulgar monster he had turned into. Memories of the screaming, swearing, terrorizing, humiliating Ravi surged. I recalled his affairs, his lies, and his every act of abuse in revolting detail.

"You flirted with my two best friends—Jay and Vinay—

goodness knows what you did with them behind my back." Ravi winced like the pain was growing within him like a tumor. "Surely, I was always worth more." His green glow flashed livid purple.

"Ravi, I was madly in love with you, but you changed so suddenly. It was your gang. I turned to anyone who showed me some kindness."

"And they did, did they? Those losers." Ravi buffeted me from side to side.

"They were already dead when they did." I felt my trap slipping. *One more smack and I fly.*

"I just tried to cover up my pain." Ravi's voice cracked. "I adored you, Priya, and you knew it, yet you humiliated me time and again with your suicide attempts."

"They were not suicide attempts, but near-death experiences triggered by spirits. We fell under a spell. Remember the kids went to Kolkata just before Sonya dropped out of Yale. She brought home my childhood friend Hema's book, jinxed by her uncle, Dev, and that generated a series of unfortunate events. I am sorry I became such an inconvenience—"

"Oh, cut it out you, yellow belly!" He lurched at me, and the trap fell away.

I shot out the window, glowing neon yellow.

How did it brighten so significantly? Was it the apology?

Every bit of me hurt. It felt like I didn't really belong to me, and every movement was a negotiation rather than an order.

Yet my thoughts were with Ravi. *He is still in shackles. I should set him free.*

My return only incited him further. He lurched at me hissing and spitting, his exertions only worsening his agony. His groans were racking.

The sound of soft humming wafted into the room: notes of Taylor Swift's "Love Story."

That must be Sonya.

Donning my old disguise of the simple gray moth, I nestled within the folds of the brocade drapes in the master bedroom where she reclined on a carved teak diwan, beneath a brass-and-crystal chandelier, The latest *Vogue* magazine lay open on her lap, and she took little bites of caviar, served on a fine porcelain platter with creme fraiche, lemon wedges, hard-cooked eggs, yolks and whites chopped separately, mini potatoes, minced onions, and toast points lightly coated with butter.

The fiend's treating her like a queen. His queen? Heaven forbid!

A uniformed woman ran Sonya's marble clawfoot bath. The fragrance of Jo Malone bubble bath filled the air.

"The towels are in the bathroom, ma'am," she said.

Sonya nodded "Thanks, Linda."

"You're welcome." Linda unlocked a Burma teak wardrobe with brass elephant handles, slipped out a Burberry shirt dress in cotton twill, and laid it on the bed. "The dress you ordered. It arrived last night. Boss flew it in from London."

Wow! It looks like Sonya signed a pact with the fiend.

"Great! I love it," Sonya squeaked. "Did you get me a burner?"

Why a burner? Where's her own phone?

"Of course." The woman handed it to her. "You must discard it after use. Boss must not get wind of you using such things, not until he gives it to you."

"This is all I need right now. Thanks!"

Linda left the room.

Sonya sat up and glanced around, her gaze lingering on the overpriced accessories adorning it. I doubted she had the faintest clue that her dad's soul was trapped and writhing in agony a few doors down the corridor.

The exquisitely carved gold resin pendulum clock on the dresser chimed eight.

With a sigh, she texted a quick message to Sunny:

I have come away of my own accord on important business. Will be back when I am done.

What important business?

As if on second thought, she added another line:

This is my decision. Nothing you can do about it, unless you want me to march around the place I'm at—hup, two, three, four.

Is that to prove that the message is from her?

As a father, Ravi had been more indulgent toward Sonya than toward Sunny. Sunny had grudged it, and Sonya, sensitive to her brother's feelings even as a toddler, deliberately got herself into some act of mischief after Sunny's tellings-off so he could punish her. He had invariably made her march around the house in rhythm to the first beat of a four-by-four military cadence—hup, two, three, four. Nobody outside our immediate family knew about it.

Sonya messaged Paul too, kissed the words, then deleted them. She held on to the phone for a couple of minutes, a weird half-smile in her eyes, only to toss the device into the gilded wastepaper basket.

It looks like she's here by choice. Has the fiend worked some magic on her?

Sonya picked up the Burberry dress and held it over the one she wore before the mirror. Her eyes traced every curve and line. "Mmmm." She stood tall with her head held high. Then she laid the dress back on the bed and stepped into the bathroom.

Minutes passed. I waited for Sunny to answer her text.

Sunny did not respond. *Perhaps he hasn't read it yet.*

I whizzed around the house. Every room was as lavishly furnished as Sonya's bedroom. Linda prepared dinner in the kitchen with large quantities of ingredients from the best gourmet grocery stores in town.

Is Sonya hosting a party with the fiend tonight? What is the occasion?

Caught in the throes of irrepressible angst, I plummeted, and almost bounced off the fiend's head, and landed several yards behind him. *Phew!*

The fiend did not notice me. He seemed somewhat preoccupied as he walked to the Chevy Impala, disguised as a much younger man, and checked his suitcases in the trunk. With a smirk he settled in the back seat of the vehicle.

He's all ready to pick up his companion. It cannot be Sonya. Linda is preparing a rather large dinner. The fiend and Sonya can't both be gone.

I gave a little murmur of relief. *Good riddance*! But then I wondered what Sonya would be doing at the property while he was gone. *Did he give it to her?* With Kolkata's real estate market booming, it was no doubt a priceless gift. *What is she giving him in return?*

My unease surged back.

In the master suite, Sonya sat before the antique, gold mirror, pulling her hair back and wrapping a moss-green satin scrunchie around a low ponytail.

It looks like she's enjoying "the lady of the manor" feeling.

A disconcerting thought crossed my core. *What if the fiend dumps his suitcases somewhere and returns to enjoy Sonya's company?*

Auntie Bina said he had to leave in an hour; she did not mention the flight time. I assumed he was leaving in the evening.

I shot out.

The Chevy drove past Red Lake mall, nearly ten miles, northeast of the Red Lake house.

My senses have gotten sharper with the brightening of my glow.

Focusing on the car, I noticed that the fiend had left the car with his luggage. *When? Where?*

I searched the roads, flying low over the traffic. There was no sign of the fiend or his bags.

I flew over Auntie Bina's condo. She sat alone in her bedroom, drinking, as she listened to Elvis. *The perfect picture of a lonely lover.*

Has he returned to Sonya?

I rushed back to the Red Lake house, and an empty taxi emerged through the gate. The driver was surrounded by static like dots.

I did not think much of it, not at the time. It was only when I flew through the house searching frantically for Sonya, that I recalled the slight static I'd noticed on our street in Digha a few nights ago.

It's so strange that I see it only when Sonya goes missing.

I peeked into the kitchen. Dinner was ready. Linda had cooked enough for at least five people.

Yet she is alone in the house.

The whirring of the miniature gyratory crusher sounded in the torture chamber. The machines beeped and whirred in their usual chorus.

I did not see anything remotely resembling the color green in the equipment. Ravi was gone.

Have they grounded him to pulp? But where is the mush?

Chapter 13

I revisited Kolkata airport. The fiend and Sonya were nowhere in sight. I searched for that haze of static amid crowds boarding the aircrafts, at the security checkpoints, and the waiting areas in vain.

Despair swamped my core. Unanswered questions came in rapid fire all pointing to the same unsolved problem—the curse and its downward spiral.

It will just get worse, unless the fiend is crushed. Yet Deepak insists that I harbor pure thoughts only.

The sky lightened, and I remembered Sonya's text to Sunny.

He must've read it by now. Could he have spoken to Leda? But Leda and Patrick are leaving today. Is Sunny leaving too?

I returned to Digha to find Sunny bolting up the stairs to Leda's living room, his phone held firmly in his hand. He noticed Nikita on the sofa and stopped short.

Nikita stiffened.

"Nikita left her grandparents and rushed here to help us look for Sonya," said Leda.

My love for her surged. *She cares so much.*

"Sonya has her own plans." Sunny took a sharp inhale. "Leda, did Sonya take her phone?"

"I would think so, though she is not picking up." Leda scrolled through her texts. "There's nothing from her or from Patrick. He left last night to drop off the merchandise at the original store in Kolkata and isn't back yet."

"When is your flight?" asked Sunny with a furtive glance at Nikita.

"Eight in the evening." Leda squinted at his trembling fingers, "I'll go put the kettle on."

"Thanks." Sunny perched on the edge of the sofa.

Nikita raised her eyes through her dark, full lashes, and they locked full on to his.

Time seemed to have stopped for them. It was like a scene out of the movies when two lovers connected in the mutual knowledge that something magical was happening, and the rest of the world faded to gray.

It might have gone on everlastingly but just across from them, Leda collapsed on the floor. The impact was jarring—a sharp jolt that reverberated through the apartment.

"Leda!" Sunny leaped toward her, and she curled up into a ball and bounced on the floor, frothing at the mouth. "Stop, Leda!" he cried. "You're scaring me."

Nikita walked up behind him, her reflexes slower, as if recovering from the world that had just melted away. One look at the young detective knocked her back to reality. "Leda!" She tried to grab her, but Leda shot several feet away from them, spinning at a monstrous speed. "Looks like she's possessed."

My core rattled like a pebble in a tin.

Leda's wrist hit the floor incessantly like a mechanized toy, so rapidly as to become increasingly blurred. "Out, out, go, you are hurting me,' she muttered.

"What is?" Nikita frowned. "Who are you talking to, Leda?"

Leda tried to grab at something, still rotating. "How did Dev get in here?" Her words were garbled.

Sunny and Nikita exchanged glances. They had not seen him and neither had I.

But she could be right. *He might have been here. The fiend seems to be evolving as a sorcerer and getting more skilled.*

"Never seen anything like this in my life." Sunny scowled. He and Nikita dragged chairs in Leda's path. Bashing hard against them several times, she slowly spun to a stop.

Sunny stooped over her, trying to check out the scar, but her wrist twisted away from him.

Nikita seized Leda's arm with both hands. Leda screamed and fainted.

Sunny and Nikita carried her to the sofa, and she shot up.

"Has he left?"

"Who," said Sunny softly.

Leda squinted at him. "Dev. Where were you?"

Sunny frowned. "We did not budge from this room."

Leda swallowed. Her brows furrowed. She glanced down at her scar. It looked like a normal burn scar.

Sunny slumped down on the chair opposite her with a sigh. "If only Sonya had spoken to me about the book when the sorcerer gave it to her."

"What book?" asked Nikita.

"Last year when Sonya, you, and I went to India," explained Sunny, "Sonya befriended a sorcerer, Dev, Gran's then next-door neighbor. He gave her a book belonging to his niece, Mom's childhood friend, Hema."

Nikita frowned. "Was it in a newspaper package? I remember seeing her pack it carefully in her suitcase."

She noticed it alright though the subject of the parcel never came up with her. During the trip, Sonya had kept her distance, watching Nikita and Sunny's deepening bond and afraid of intruding.

Leda sighed. "I believe things started going wrong in your family after the book arrived."

Sunny nodded. "Yes, Sonya dropped out of Yale. Apparently, she had been having an affair with a married drug dealer. Dad got furious about it all. He was nasty to Mom, but she had her own problems." He cast a quick glance at Nikita who dropped her eyes. "Of course," he continued, "Sonya wasted every opportunity to get her life back on track. Paul coaxed her to apply to LSE out of the goodness of his heart, and she got accepted for the fall semester. I don't think she'll go back. Paul got his father to offer her an internship at his firm in the spring, and she did nothing about it."

"This book was no ordinary book." Leda sighed. "There were sketches in it, sketches of ghosts. When Sonya flipped through it with Priya, she recognized them as the spirits of Hema's friends and relatives who visited her during her last months. Apparently, they sucked her life-spirit out of her. Sonya found the sketches morbid and trashed the book."

Nikita frowned. "Sonya never said a thing."

"Probably because she thought she had gotten rid of it, but it removed itself from the garbage can." Leda inhaled sharply. "It was everywhere. We burned it at the advice of an expert theologian, Rao, but a flake of ash from the remains flew onto my wrist and burned it."

Nikita squinted at the scar

"How does it feel now?" asked Sunny.

"Like nothing ever happened. I strongly believe Dev is trying to scare me off the investigation. The West Bengal police have pulled plain-clothes cops in to stake out different neighborhoods where he could be lurking." Leda rose. "So sorry, I forgot about the tea."

"Don't worry. Let me make you some." Nikita put the kettle on.

"You need to rest, Leda," said Sunny.

"Not until I get to the bottom of this business."

She's about to leave the country.

"Leda, I'm so glad you're going back with Patrick," said Sunny.

"The fiend is leaving too."

"Where's he going?"

"No idea. I heard that he's gotten some air tickets. He might have left already."

"Well, he's not following you to the US. The man's old, around eighty." Sunny scoffed. "Anyway, we'll all be gone before he even dreams of landing there."

He doesn't spare a single thought for his sister.

"We can't go back without Sonya," said Nikita.

Sunny scowled. "I'm losing my patience with her. She is so self-centered."

Nikita looked surprised, hurt even. "Sorry, I don't agree with you. Sonya is my best friend. She used her contacts to find a perfect care home for my grandparents. I only texted her that I needed help just hours before she's supposed to have disappeared, and on my way here, the Administrator of the best care home in Kolkata called me to confirm that I could move my grandparents into the facility any time next week." She sighed. "I could have returned to the US with complete peace of mind, but now it worries me that my dear friend has completely disappeared."

Sunny met her gaze. "Sonya is not lost. She went off on her own accord last night."

Nikita's face contorted into a frown.

"Who told you that, Sunny?" asked Leda.

"Well, I wasn't quite finished speaking when your scar acted up, Leda. In fact, the very reason I came here was to show you the text message Sonya sent me." Sunny pulled it up on his phone. "Here."

Nikita and Leda read it.

"What is this 'hup two three four' punishment?" asked Nikita.

"Oh, you don't know about it either, Nikita?" Leda was back to being her calm and composed self again. "I thought I was the only one."

Sunny explained it to them.

"So, the text is from Sonya alright. Wonder what this important business could be." Nikita poured the golden oolong into three cups and carried them over to the living area.

"It can't be to destroy the book. We tried and it transformed into the ash bat. Is Sonya trying to capture the bat? Is it even possible?" Leda handed Sunny a cup and helped herself to one. "Thanks, Nikita." She sipped a large mouthful. "Sonya did talk about crushing Dev."

Sunny rolled his eyes.

"She wouldn't attempt that all by herself." Nikita mumbled.

Patrick returned, dabbing his forehead with a handkerchief. "Is there enough tea for me?"

"Of course." Nikita beamed.

"I was beginning to wonder what became of you," said Leda.

"Well, I bumped into the local headmaster on my way back, and he needed help to install your handcrafted fixtures and equipment at the school."

"If generosity had a name, it would be you, Patrick." Sunny grinned.

Patrick chuckled. "Well, I'm so relieved that at last, nothing stands in the way of our homeward journey."

No one mentioned a word about Leda's ordeal. Nikita brought Patrick some tea, and the conversation moved to the fiend.

"Why can't the police catch him?" asked Patrick.

Leda sighed. "Because he can hide himself."

Diya, my sister, called.

"Sunny, Ma is not doing too well. She's constantly vomiting, can't keep anything down. The doctor prescribed her some sedatives, but she won't sleep. She keeps asking for Sonya. Why don't you and Sonya come back here tonight? Ma hasn't got long." Diya's voice caught.

"Sonya has left Digha on some 'important' business." muttered Sunny.

"Oh, okay," she said. "It would be nice if you could come."

"Of course."

The call disconnected, and Sunny paced the room. "I'll go back to Kolkata today, spend some time with Gran while she lingers, and then fly out to London from there."

Patrick sighed heavily. "If only Sonya would contact us."

Sunny told him about the text. "I don't see any point in waiting for Sonya. If she does decide to come back at some point, Leda's landlord is always there to receive her."

"Of course." Patrick nodded.

"When is the next train to Kolkata, any idea?" asked Sunny.

Leda smiled. "Why would you take a train when Nikita has a car?"

Nikita checked her watch. "The driver went into town to see a friend. He should be back in an hour. I could drop you off at your gran's on my way back."

"But I have to get my stuff from the hotel and check out." said Sunny. "The hotel is a fifteen-minute walk from here. I'll go. Start packing."

"Let's walk back together. I'll ask the driver to pick us up at the hotel." Nikita texted her driver.

"Sure!" Sunny's eyes sparkled.

How easily he brushes off responsibility for his sister. My core ached with concern for her.

Chapter 14

Distraught over the turn of events, I flitted about restlessly in the briny air.

Deepak approached me in one of his bird disguises. "The Devil's on the prowl, corralling souls off to hell." He zipped across the sky with incredibly fast wing beats.

A tiny feather wafted down, rollicking in the gale, drifting in and out of reach. It appeared to have dropped from his wing.

I felt an irresistible tug toward it. Before I could grab it, a pitchfork stabbed into it, missing me by inches.

The stench of sulfur flooded my core.

Trying to swerve past the Devil's herd of green souls huddled together in his net, I collided with a flock of spirits fleeing in terror. That sent me catapulting into the waves crashing on the beach.

Nikita walked along the shore, leaving footprints in the damp sand next to the drifting seafoam. "It feels so wrong to go away without even knowing where Sonya is or if she's okay," she mumbled.

Is she trying to persuade Sunny to stay?

Sunny did not seem to hear her. He walked on, glancing at her repeatedly.

It's like he's constantly checking to see if she's really there with him.

"Thank goodness, the storm has passed," he said.

The sun struggled to penetrate the thick, shadowy clouds and cast an eerie, surreal light over the landscape.

"Not quite." Nikita noticed me floating on the sea foam and scooped me up. "Hello, beautiful!" She stroked me.

"That moth needs to dry off before flying." Sunny slowed down to a stop, squinting at me.

"Remember our picnic in Galveston?" She set me down on the sand.

"Oh, yes. You and Sonya drowned the poor butterflies."

"Because you made us sit and appreciate the true 'nature' of the beach. All we wanted to do was to dance barefoot on the warm sand. Mom had brought a radio."

"And all I wanted was to build a coastal diorama. I asked you to wait and watch."

"But your cove got more and more attractive, and we encouraged the butterflies to take a soak in the runny gel you used to create the ripples." Nikita met his gaze. "Sonya and I were little devils, and yet you were so wonderful with us, always patient, always sensible, trying to guide us in the right direction,"

Is she deliberately giving him reminders?

"Anybody knows it's wrong to drown butterflies," said Sunny.

"We were only five." Nikita searched his face.

He looked away.

Nikita's eyes glistened with tears. "I'm sorry, Sunny."

A couple of street urchins ran over with paper boats. "Why she crying?" they asked Sunny.

He quickly walked away.

Nikita followed. "I know you will never forget how I broke up with you and—" Her voice choked.

She did, but I've watched the girl grow up. She loves no one other than Sunny.

Sunny blinked furiously.

Nikita swallowed. "I never loved Dillon half as much as I loved you, Sunny. I was just so angry with life for snatching away my parents. I was angry with my parents too, for keeping me in the dark about their associations. The necklace I blamed Uncle Ravi of stealing—" She pursed her mouth and wiped a solitary tear that snaked down her cheek.

"Dad did acquire it somehow, though it belonged to the gang, and he made alterations to it before giving it to Mom for her fiftieth birthday. So, you were not entirely wrong. You had the right to be mad at us."

"But the necklace did not really belong to Mom. It belonged to the gang." Nikita turned her teary eyes upon him. "It feels so strange that my parents, your dad, Uncle Jay, Auntie Asha, Auntie Sue, and Uncle BLZ, all got involved in the drug trade, and let it mess up their lives. Auntie Asha committed suicide."

"Really?"

"She literally ended her life by stepping in front of a bus near your gran's house. I didn't know until Sonya told me."

"Sonya never said a word to me."

"You really need to have a heart-to-heart with her when she gets back."

Sunny's phone chimed. He glanced at the text and pursed his lips.

"Another message from Sonya?"

"No. It's Auntie Diya. Gran's sinking."

Chapter 15

The gray sky hung low, a flat ceiling pressing down on the world. A faint fall of rain whispered against the windows. Traffic clogged the narrow road.

Nikita's rented car crawled through the seaside resort with the lovers. I camouflaged against Sunny's door.

Oddly silent, he focused his unflinching gaze on the horizon.

It must be the memories. Ma and he have always been close.

Nikita laid her hand over his. All he could manage was a thin, wan smile.

The heavy downpour began suddenly, as if someone switched on a hose. Muddy waters gurgled and bubbled all around. The car splashed through giant puddles filling the ruts of drier weather.

Through the veil of moisture, Sunny watched Bengal's rural scenes—paddy fields, dirt roads, mud houses, cow-drawn carts—masterpieces of Impressionism art.

Nikita rubbed the condensed water droplets on the windows and pressed her nose against the glass.

The rain gradually petered out.

The sun broke through the dark storm clouds bringing a brighter palette to the view. The grass, lush and glossy, waved softly in the breeze. Children crowded around the puddles. Some jumped right in, splotching the passing car with gooey mud, then whooping and giggling at their own brilliant silliness.

Sunny laughed and Nikita sprang around.

"What I loved about my Indian vacations was playing in the rain." She grinned.

"And we never caught a cold." Sunny mirrored Nikita's smile.

Chatting merrily about the fun monsoons of their childhood in India, they approached Ma's house.

Nikita was keen to pay her last respects to Ma, and Sunny thought it was a great idea. However, as they walked in through the open gate and up the garden path, voices floated in the still air.

Ma's maid, Dolly, and her seventeen-year-old, mother-to-be daughter, Leena, were talking in Ma's bedroom, their backs turned to the window.

"Nikitadidi so selfish," Leena cried. "She not just leave Sunnydada, she plan to marry her new boyfriend on the same day she to wed Sunnydada."

"But she not marry," her mother said.

"She crazy or what?"

People will blame Nikita, and she her tragic loss, when actually the fiend's curse will not allow Sunny any happiness.

Nikita stopped in her tracks. Her eyes filled. "Sunny, you go. I must get back to my grandparents, pack their stuff."

Sunny glanced back. "I'm sorry about Leena."

"It's okay. Talk to you soon." Nikita rushed away.

Sunny didn't stop her.

Miss Rosie, the family dog, bounded up. Sunny picked her up and carried her to Ma's room.

Dolly and Leena had relocated to the kitchen.

Diya looked up from the book she was reading. Her face lit up. "Hi."

Ma turned her head toward the door. Her lips moved silently, forming the word "Sonya."

"It's Sunny, Ma," Diya corrected her.

Sunny walked up to her bed quietly.

"Everyone comes and goes," Ma muttered, "but never the girl. Never."

Sunny swallowed. "S-she will come."

Ma bent over, gagged, and vomited between her legs.

Diya cleaned her up. Sunny helped.

"I am sorry she has gotten like this," Diya blinked.

"You are doing your best, Auntie Diya. With Meghna gone, it must be so hard for you."

Ma retched, tried to clamp her mouth shut, then spewed blood.

While Diya started the cleaning process all over again, Ma lay back against her pillows. Her eyes were so weighed down with wrinkled folds that she looked sound asleep.

"Priya and Ravi's deaths took their toll, and now she's obsessed with Uncle Dev's curse on your family," Diya whispered. "She has lost her appetite and her will to live." Her voice choked.

Dolly wheeled in some puris and sabji.

Leena followed, with a tall glass of icy-cold Thums Up. "Sunnydada, drink this first. You thirsty after long journey."

Sunny grinned. "Thank you."

"Why Sonyadidi not come?" Leena asked. "She not like us?"

"Of course she likes you. In fact, she likes you very much." Sunny's reassurance was instantly rewarded by the lopsided grin of Leena's doting husband, Ganesh, who slowly walked into the room.

He's back! I hadn't noticed him with everything that was going on.

"Hey, how are you, Ganesh?" Sunny beamed at him.

"Okay." Leena spoke on his behalf. "He little slow, but he very observant, like he looking for someone—perhaps Dr. Deepak Kapoor." She sighed deeply.

There was silence.

Ma opened her eyes and glanced at the man. The corners of her lips quirked up a little. "The light," she muttered.

Sunny frowned. "What light?"

"Yesterday, there be light next door, in building coming up." Dolly said softly. "You remember, Priyadidi's friend live there?

"And Uncle Dev." Sunny's frown deepened into a scowl. "Nobody lives there anymore."

Diya shook her head. "The builders work all day, but they all leave before sundown. It gets very dark. But last night here was a light, and Ganesh noticed it first."

Was the fiend here? His scent did not linger in the air. *He's gotten adept at manipulating scents.*

Ganesh took a wobbly step forward. "I see light," he stammered, then stumbled.

Dolly guided him back to his bed.

"Ganesh see light first," said Leena. "Miss Rosie rush there, barking like maniac, and she bring scrunchie back." She produced a moss-green satin scrunchie from Ma's nightstand, a mirror image of Sonya's ponytailer.

It smelled of her.

She was definitely here last night.

Sunny didn't seem to recognize the scrunchie. "So, what happened after? Did the light turn off?"

"It was like a flashlight," said Diya. "Yes, it turned off. We assumed some curious neighbor had come and then left, but it could have been Dev. He might have been lurking in the neighborhood, for around midnight, a Mercedes pulled up at the curb. I have seen him around in expensive cars. Anyway, by the time I got out of bed, tucked the mosquito net back in, and ran to the window, the car pulled away."

"But you saw the logo?" Sunny polished off the puri and sabji.

"Yes, and the Mercedes was black. I know Asha's mom has a black Mercedes. You don't see a lot of those around here."

Did she visit them here?

"Gran Bina wouldn't know the likes of this Dev guy." Sunny swallowed.

If he only saw them together!

The sun started its downward journey. The orange gold stretched across the garden.

A little bird whistled upon a blossomed twig of the old Gulmohar. There it hopped over sprigs of leaves, chirping, as if the branch was its trampoline. It's chitter rippled through the fiery blossoms, bringing a small smile to Ma's face.

It's like an angel.

Ma pulled herself up as if with some renewed energy, and the bird took flight. Its beating wings seemed to capture her mind in the most calming of ways until it was a mere silhouette against the fiery sky.

She turned unusually restless. "I gave Yash's share of my zewar to Diya," she muttered. "Sonya shall have my bangles. Goodness knows when she will find a husband." She moved her wrist feebly, perhaps to hear the playful jingle jangle of the gold circles layered at her wrists one last time. "And my pair of Meenakari gold kangans,

I shall leave for Nikita." She looked up at Sunny, and he swallowed hard.

They are the most impressive and valuable of all Ma's jewelry. Ma had really set her heart on the marriage. *How can she be so sure of the union?*

"Tell her I left her my blessings . . ." Ma's words were incoherent and ended in a sigh.

"I'll get Maji a cup of warm milk." Leena hastened away.

Diya tried to lay Ma back against the pillows, but Ma rested her head on her shoulder and gazed upon Sunny's face. "Take care, my prince." She attempted to smile as she drew her last breath. Time froze in her eyes. When her hand dropped by her side, I knew she had passed on.

Sunny closed her vacant eyes. His own eyes flowed.

Tears coursed down Diya's cheeks unchecked.

Leena rushed in with the milk, Dolly in tow. "I already warm it and put in thermos flask." They saw Ma and stopped short. Their shrieks echoed through the house. "Maji no more."

A twirl of mist whooshed over Diya, hovered in circles over the wailing Dolly and Leena, and then slowly drifted out.

"Ma?" I followed.

In the gray skies, the wisp of mist condensed into an apparition—Ma. She looked younger and sturdier. Her hair was silver, in various stages of oxidization.

"It's been my last wish that we meet after death, and here we are." She wobbled and stumbled midair. "Why do I feel like a fledgling or is it normal?"

No idea. I had flown into Deepak's embrace straight after death. I grabbed her. "You are fine."

We rode through the sky as if we were on sleek and perfect tracks.

"Priya, I am full of remorse. I should've told you and Sonya about Dev."

"I already know a lot about him, perhaps more than you ever will."

"Except what I left unsaid." Ma clung to me, warmer in death than ever in life. "He was professor of Quantum Physics at the university. When I first came to the household as a bahu, he was a regular visitor and an honored one. He had one obsession and that was quantum entanglement, a quantum phenomenon that Albert

Einstein called 'spooky action at a distance.' He began to research the subject, more the spooky aspect of it than the phenomenon itself. That turned him more and more into a recluse."

She leaned back in dreamy awe through space and almost got tugged away by the gusty wind.

I pulled her back.

"Phew. I thought I lost you. I need your help to seek out your father."

I chuckled. "Of course, but only after you finish the story."

"Well," she continued, "Dev's parents suddenly became very ill. His sister, Hema's mother, and her family moved in to take care of them. She was pregnant with Hema, and I with you. We got close. She told me Dev had shifted his research to the dying brain and was doing some mischief she didn't quite understand. She seemed somewhat uneasy about it, but then her parents died, you and Hema were born, and we got busy. If I had taken her seriously, perhaps her husband and children could have been saved."

Dawn broke, and a billion pure eyes of light upgraded the world to some higher definition.

Ma trembled. "Now that I see how high above the ground we are, isn't there someplace we could rest, call home, like Heaven? Shouldn't you be there already? Is it the affair? That rogue of a surgeon!"

I did not tell her that Deepak was already in Heaven. "We'll get there eventually, Ma. Don't worry. Tell me more about the fiend."

Ma rambled on. "He invited Aghoris into the house. These sadhus transfer health to and pollution away from patients as a form of 'transformative healing.' Dev allowed the sadhus to use his healthy family members, and once they were way into terminal diseases and sinking, he would remove them to hospitals of his choice, put them on ventilators and pacemakers and monitor their brain activity."

Too engrossed in the tale, I must have loosened my hold on Ma. When I realized, she had started plummeting. I swooped down after her, but the wind blew her away.

I searched the skies.

Morning graduated into afternoon. When evening cast her dusky light, I glimpsed two souls disappearing over the brow of a cloud, engaged in merry conversation—Ma and Mashi, Hema's mother.

Ma has company. I heaved a sigh.

A new day dawned and set, then another. I nestled on a cloud, a simple gray moth, hoping to catch a glimpse of Sonya somewhere.

A mesmerizing light exploded in the skies, sweeping me in a whirlwind. I drowned in Deepak's scent and forgot my troubles.

"At last, Priya," His voice was velveteen. "I should be at Heaven's festival, but I spotted your neon yellow hue. Wow! What have you been up to?"

"Only been a little supportive of Ma, apologetic to Ravi."

"You are an angel. I missed you so much, my core was in pieces—the worst illness in Heaven. I've been recuperating under the care of fairies in their 'hospitium.'"

"And you're already flying?"

"The world over, with nothing but fairy dust holding me together. I am out for a test 'levithon.'"

"What's that?"

"You choose a purpose, your destination, inhale, exhale the gas, defy gravity, and lift off."

"I've done that, but doesn't that take you to one specific person in one specific place?"

"My perks take me to several, though I have one starting point. For this trip, it was Houston. and flying out over the Gulf, I swear I saw your Sonya on the Seawall in Galveston."

"Excuse me." I rushed away at once.

"She is completely at peace with herself, so don't interfere," Deepak called after me.

I had already landed on the island's historic pleasure pier. The merrymakers had retired for the night, and a stoic calmness had descended on the moon-bleached amusement park.

There was no sign of Sonya.

Chapter 16

Dark, brooding clouds, turbulent waves, and strong winds created a raw, untamed atmosphere.

I scoured the miles of sand for my daughter. *Deepak said Sonya's here in Galveston. He can't be wrong.*

I scanned the sea and the cliffs. I dove into the high-rise, multistory dwellings and hotels. Nowhere was there a trace of my girl or even that mysterious, odorless static.

I didn't stop to ask Deepak when he saw Sonya in Galveston. Sonya might not be staying in Galveston. Sonya might have been visiting from Houston and gone back.

I braved the storm. Thunder crackled like shots from a cannon. Jagged bolts of lightning split the sky. The silver blaze illuminated the land beneath.

I glimpsed Houston, then No. 7. Charcoal lay thick over the property like winter's first snow, though depressingly gray.

Fierce winds blasted the houses in the neighborhood. The rain whipped down like crystal nails all around. The water-motes did not touch the ash. The deafening blast of thunder did not rock the layers. No.7 slept, waiting as if for someone to uncover it.

A sharp pang of sorrow shot through me. *My home turned into a waste land.*

Deepak asked me specifically not to harbor evil thoughts, but honestly, is it possible to break the spell without crushing the fiend?

Lightning came in great networking forks. An old man's spectral face blazed bolder amid Heaven's light.

The spirit of the house? Saint Ignatius?

Transfixing me with his large, lustrous eyes, he uttered three words—Datta, Dayadhvam, Dāmyata—each sharp and loud as a thunderclap.

The three Sanskrit words from the Upanishad symbolized the three aspects of a virtuous life: giving, compassion, and self-control.

Lightning illuminated a brilliant pathway above. The silhouettes of Patrick and Leda, stood out in the molten silver. *They personify the qualities of Datta and Dayadhvam—giving and compassion.*

Up ahead on the white road, there was another human shape walking with them. Dāmyata? The Sanskrit word meant self-control. I could not tell whether the third entity was a man or a woman.

"Shantih. Shantih. Shantih." The words boomed through deeper drumrolls of thunder.

Shantih translates to peace, representing inner peace, rest, calmness, tranquility, and bliss. This must be a prophesy. Perhaps peace will be restored at No.7 with the three 'Da's.

The baffling question returned to plague me. *How can that be accomplished unless the fiend is squashed?*

Waves of ash rose from No.7 and rolled away like a wraith's veil of sorrow. The stench of sulfur filled the air.

The Devil is here.

The wind howled. It blew in a hellacious mood, spinning the ash into a whirlpool. The maelstrom sucked me in with a deadly force. A portal opened to another dimension, joyless and fiery. *Hell?*

I shuddered.

Thunder sounded a deep warning. The rage of the tempest bore down. Lightning tore through the churning ash, steering me away from the vortex.

The ash cascaded down and settled back on the property.

In the sudden calm that descended over No.7, the stink faded, and I was free.

Who saved me? Saint Ignatius?

All I saw were birds in the sky moving in choreographed melody.

The tune was interrupted by the strains of a violin. A Romni entered the scene, playing the instrument. Clad in a dark patchwork robe, she was shrouded in a peculiar violet light.

Sonya?

The woman was taller, and she wore casual tassel sandals with no heels.

The fiend?

The Romni's luscious fruity scent oozed out of her, vibrant and fresh, a far cry from his musky cologne.

The fiend can manipulate smells; he can make the Romni's scent feel integrally connected with his person.

She began a lively, solo dance, twisting and shaking. Her movements were curiously effortless. As her shoulders swung in sync with her hips, a million flakes of ash swarmed over her head. There they coalesced into the ash bat.

The Romni is the fiend in disguise. Who else can conjure an ash bat out of thin air?

The fiend held out his hand and the bat perched on his palm. At once they disappeared without a trace amid a haze of fluttering dots.

I no longer doubted that those dots had something to do with the disappearing act.

I glided over Houston, searching for Sonya. *If only I could see as far as Deepak.*

The sun rose. Daylight pulsed through the city. Perched on a cloud overlooking No.7 and its neighboring streets, I scanned the area.

The traffic was heavy for that time of day. Everyone seemed to be up and about. A great many people popped in and out of the Whole Foods Supermarket.

Among the shoppers, Paul hobbled on crutches.

He was barely recognizable with his facial stubble and unkempt hair. His tired eyes searched incessantly for someone.

"This way." Unrecognizable in a Wilma Flintstone wig, Sonya led yet another Romni into the alcohol aisle. Together they peered down at an Apothic Red Blend on the shelf. A single, cloying perfume followed them, a borrowed identity that obscured their own.

How powerful is the fiend's magic?

Has he disguised himself as a Romni again?

The Romni did not speak, and I had no way to find out.

"Let me find you a nice bottle of bourbon," Sonya said, and Paul dropped his phone in the next aisle, where he and James, his dad, were shopping for mixers and garnishes for cocktails.

"I swear I heard Sonya," cried Paul. He glanced around wildly, trying to push past the crowds.

"You seem to hear her everywhere," James mumbled.

"Yet not see her anywhere." Paul craned his neck to catch a glimpse of her.

Sonya adjusted her wig and bent right over as if to pick up something from the floor.

The Romni sidled away.

Sonya left too, but through the exit door at the other end of the store.

Why did she choose to shop at a store just round the corner from James's Law Firm?

She speed walked into the parking garage, while talking with a friend on the phone. "I'm on my way. Yes, it was Paul and his dad. His dad's firm is just round the corner, but I had no idea Paul was in Houston. No, I don't have a clue when he's returning to London. No, of course not." Sonya glanced over her shoulder and dashed into the driver's seat of a black Kia sedan.

The Romni sat in the passenger seat.

"I'll never set foot here again, Uncle Dev," she said to him.

It's the fiend alright. Is she loyal to him out of fear?

The car headed toward Westheimer. I was certain they were on their way to No. 7.

I rose on a warm updraft and flew the short distance to the neighborhood. To my delight I could navigate the stratosphere with ease. *Did this new perk come with the neon yellow hue?*

Sonya slowed down at the T-junction upon which the house stood and pulled to the curbside of a new construction home several blocks away. They stepped out and walked back to No7.

Sonya grinned. "All yours now, Uncle Dev, with no one to contest it."

Hateful!

The fiend gazed lovingly at the black ash blanketing the property. "The toughest time for me was when people recovered from the initial shock of the fire and the deaths, and their eyes turned toward the coveted property. I had only just sown the seeds of evil in the scared site and earned the Master's blessings." He sighed. "It would be difficult to accomplish what I did here without your help, Sonya. Any new family coming into possession of the property would come with their own luck. We must stop that."

Sonya nodded and flashed her sweetest smile.

Disgusting! She can't really be that happy.

"At least the HOA can't win." The fiend rubbed the tip of his boot against the crusty layer of ash. "Irremovable except by magic." He chanted a mantra, and the ash glided away. He crooned another and the layers drifted back

"Wow!" Sonya applauded.

"Impossible without extensive research and my dear niece's drudgery." He guffawed. "Hema, the ash-bat! What an invention. I lent her the magic touch. Every dew drop she touched turned into ash."

"And how did the flakes all stick together and not get blown away in the wind?" Sonya sounded genuinely interested.

"There's a sweat-like substance secreted from her salivary glands that glues the ash together."

"Ingenious. No.7 will always be neatly buried under this crust." Sonya grinned.

"Um—what I do hate is your mother stalking us." The fiend narrowed his eyes to the skies.

Too wrapped up in the conversation, I had started plummeting. At once, I soared up into the clouds above.

"How do you know?" Sonya scowled

"She's that flying object up there." He pointed at the skies. "Looks like a simple gray moth, but it is just a disguise to cover her glow."

"Where?" Sonya scanned the skies.

"My special lenses catch the glow, and only because Priya is still not an expert at ghostly ways. She keeps flicking in and out of her disguise."

Clumsy me!

"Whoa, Uncle Dev, you're so clever, and I think your latest discovery, the scent-free invisibility disguise, is ingenious. Mom would never recognize us in that."

"Until she sees the static."

"It's only slight. The disguise should make it easy for you to catch her. You were thinking of replacing Hema's spirit with her, were you not?"

I could not catch a trace of emotion in Sonya's voice. But safely out of their reach, I awaited the information. *Does he trust her enough to tell her?*

"I have made some other arrangement for that," he said.

Sonya leaned in.

"It's her glow I'm after," He glanced up at me and adjusted his special lenses. "It changes color, a rare phenomenon. My latest invention can sever it from her, but not permanently."

Does he speak of what Neel used at the abandoned house? I shuddered. *It was sheer luck that I escaped.*

"I will help you of course."

"Hang on." The fiend played a quick tune on his cell phone. The ash bat appeared and squeezed into his pocket. "C'mon, Sonya, we need to get back to the hotel."

Sonya did not question the urgency. Only too eager to oblige, she raced back to the black Kia with him.

I followed the car to Budget Stay, a cheap motel in Hillcroft.

I did not see them step out of the car. All I saw was a slight static around its doors when they opened and shut in the parking lot.

Almost at once a beaded fancy fringed ornament cover floated toward me from the external walkway of the second floor.

This cannot be a spirit trap.

I was swept in with sounds like cameras clicking, then ejected by a sudden, violent force.

What was that?

Chapter 17

Certain that the fiend and Sonya would revisit No.7, I decided to return to the property. My own neighborhood was the most convenient place to eavesdrop on their conversations and observe them. Besides, I hoped to see more of Saint Ignatius and learn about the third hooded silhouette, Dāmyata.

Approaching the neighborhood, I glimpsed a light in what used to be Asha's home.

The landscaped gardens evoked memories of happier times, the picnics, the fun activities in the pool, the poolside parties, not to mention the outdoor movie nights. Fighting the sudden rush of emotions, I plummeted into the backyard and landed somewhere between Auntie Bina and Sonya, engaged in deep conversation.

Auntie Bina is already here? Why did she say she would miss the fiend's lovemaking?

I gravitated toward Sonya perched on the edge of the pool in a pretty Hermès summer frock, sipping a raspberry spritz.

Auntie Bina spotted me. "Do we have a moth infestation?"

Before Sonya noticed me, I flew into the tall hedgerows lining the backyard. A warm breeze swept over the tops of the trees, moving the deepening foliage. The fiend was busy among the shadows, flipping lamb steaks on the old-time pit barrel cooker.

There was no sign of the bat.

Did they leave her at the motel?

"It was so lovely to fly with you." Sonya smiled at Auntie Bina, seemingly relaxed.

Hmmm.

On the pool deck, Auntie Bina lowered her whiskey tumbler from her lips. "I couldn't stay back with Dev coming away. I called my travel agent, and he put me on the same plane as you two. He didn't take a penny. He said it was his wedding gift to me."

She married the fiend! She cannot know everything about him.

Sonya's brows scrunched. Quick as a flash, she masked her shock with a wide grin. "Congratulations!"

"Thank you." Auntie Bina beamed, and they chatted about the good old times.

The fiend brought over some lamb steaks for them. "Hey, taste some of this lamb and tell me if you prefer it well done."

"Would you be so kind as to fill up my glass, dear?" said Auntie Bina.

"You are drinking too fast," the fiend mouthed. Nevertheless, he scooped up the tumbler.

Their eyes locked. He held her gaze until she looked away to cut a small portion of the steak. Out gushed the juices. She forked the piece into her mouth and closed her eyes. "Mmmm."

A satisfied grin spread across the fiend's face. He hastened away.

Auntie Bina watched the octogenarian disappear behind the trees. "You haven't told Dev about Asha, have you?" she whispered.

"No. It was all so sad." Sonya blinked.

"She had nothing to live for." Auntie Bina sighed. "Anyway. Keep it all to yourself, the manner of her death, my stepping in to do the last rites. Dev has this friend called Neel who got my son-in-law killed. Jay's death wrecked Asha's life. Apparently, the man has resurfaced in Dev's life after many years, and they are getting uncomfortably close. I don't want Neel to know what happened to my baby."

"I won't utter a word. Auntie Asha has a special place in my heart, and you have one too, Gran Bina."

A wan smile floated across Auntie Bina 's lips. "When you and Nikita were little, Sunny would chase after you in the pool, and you and Nikita would flee, splashing so much water that the deck would be flooded."

A wave of nostalgia swept over me. *It feels just like yesterday.*

Sonya grinned. "You chased us too. What wouldn't I give to bring back those summer days. When you visited Auntie Asha,

Nikita and I would come straight to you from school instead of staying back at after-school club." Sonya blinked. "You would join us in the pool, be the big shark."

"And you two would squeal in your glittering mermaid swimsuits." The grand lady giggled.

Auntie Bina had no grandchildren of her own and had never missed an opportunity to play with the kids.

"Gone are those days." Her eyes glistened. "I tried to be happy, but the Gods are jealous." She wiped her wet cheeks. "Nothing ever goes right for me. I hope this marriage works out."

Soon it'll be the last thing she wants.

Sonya's lips turned up promptly. "I am sure it will."

The fiend returned with Auntie Bina's refilled glass, and shrimp skewers.

She beamed. "I am so grateful that Sonya is helping to keep your whereabouts secret from that detective."

The fiend nodded. "Me too. She has also been taking me around town, teaching me the rules of driving here. Thank you, Sonya."

That can't be enough to satisfy the fiend.

"Thank you." Sonya smiled. 'I so enjoy your company."

Really!

They settled down to eat.

"I wish Nikita were here too," said Sonya.

"The runaway bride." Dev chuckled. "Bina spent a fortune on her dowry."

"It will stay locked in my condo until she finds the right man." Auntie Bina sipped the bourbon. "I love this Old Forester. It's so smooth. Dillon had some of the finest quality in his bar."

"He's extremely well-to do, has hotels and restaurants in the UK and US, but Nikita didn't care for him." The fiend paused, studying Sonya's reaction.

Sonya swallowed hard. "Nikita has always been infatuated with Sunny."

True.

Auntie Bina laughed. "As a child she would call herself Mrs. Sunny."

Oh, yes.

Sonya nodded with a sigh. "They had a little misunderstanding."

"You mean a big one," the fiend corrected her. "She dumped Sunny and decided to marry Dillon on the same day she was to wed Sunny."

Sonya looked up and met his gaze.

Will she mention the book?

She only smiled.

"Let me get you the tandoori salmon." The fiend darted away to the BBQ grill.

"Has Nikita said anything to you about getting back with Sunny?" Auntie Bina asked.

Sonya shook her head. "No, but I think she still has a lot of feelings for him."

"My sister and her husband are so worried about Nikita. At least they are sorted. I am so grateful to Dev for doing that for us. I couldn't have looked after them forever."

So the fiend did that, not Sonya. Does he have her phone?

Auntie Bina sighed. "Sonya, beti, what do you intend to do with yourself? Go back to uni, I guess?"

Sonya shrugged.

"No plans?"

Sonya inhaled sharply.

Auntie Bina rose from her deckchair and slumped down by Sonya at the edge of the pool. "Everything okay with you?"

For a split second, I thought I noticed a frozen "deer in the headlights" look on Sonya's face, but it faded, and her wide grin returned to grace her lips.

She's faking calm for whatever reason.

Auntie Bina pressed closer. "There's this book I have been meaning to ask you about."

"W-what book?"

"The magical book that teased Ravi to distraction on the night your house burned down," Auntie Bina whispered. "Now, I ask because Asha told the butler, who was her regular visitor during her last days, that the thing brought your family bad luck, and she was pursuing it."

Sonya frowned. "She asked me specifically not to run after it before she died."

"But how did your family get to have the book? Who sent it?"

Sonya lowered her eyes to gaze into the pool. "M-mom would have known."

"You know, Sonya, I was thinking that maybe one weekend we, you and I, could go to Uptown Park and check out the shops together."

"You and Uncle Dev are just married. You two should be hanging out together now, without me third wheeling."

"You third wheel us oldies? I can't believe you are being so polite to me. I am not a stranger." Her gaze swept over Sonya's face. "How was your day with Dev? Where did you take my old man?"

"No.7."

"Oh! You took him there? Is he after the property?"

Sonya shook her head. "There's nothing left of the house."

"Hmmm." Auntie Bina sighed. "And did you have a nice time?"

"Yes."

The affirmative sounds more emphasized than it should.

The elderly lady tilted her head with a frown. "I would understand if you didn't. You look pale even with your makeup."

If only she could get Sonya talking.

"Oh, really? I thought I was getting my color back. I wasn't eating well after Mom and Dad passed, but now I am."

Auntie Bina squinted at her. "Look, I know Dev. Sometimes, things are good, but he can be easily misunderstood for his silence when, really, he is lost in his thoughts or concentrating on the tasks at hand. He's a writer; he's writing about extraterrestrial life."

She knows so little about him.

The fiend was back with a fresh bottle of bourbon and smoking hot salmon steaks to fill the glasses and platters. "What says the grand dame, Sonya?" he asked.

Is he scared that they might be gossiping about him?

Sonya's lips turned up at once in response.

"My Bina loves to talk." He blew her a kiss, and Auntie Bina blushed.

"I'll leave you two lovebirds," muttered Sonya, rising.

"Not at all. You sit right down." Auntie Bina grabbed her hand. "Dev and I are here to look after you. You look too pale for my liking. You should go for a health check ASAP."

Good idea.

"Oh, please, Gran Bina," Sonya protested. "I am perfectly alright. Never felt better."

The fiend glanced at Sonya furtively. "All she needs to do is have her meals and take regular walks, preferably in the evening. She can walk down to No.7."

Sonya nodded.

His sly grin in response left me with a deep sense of unease. "And you, Bina, will ensure that, won't you?"

"Of course. Anything for Sonya."

"Thank you." He breathed a long, deep sigh.

Chapter 18

Sonya and the fiend seemed to vanish from Asha's house the next morning.

I hated her closeness to the fiend and hoped to observe her during her evening walks in our neighborhood.

I need to see her alone to figure out how happy she really is with her decision.

She did not turn up for her walk that evening.

Sunset blossomed red and gold. It cast a warm glow across the urban landscape. The hues did not seem to touch the dull, gray ash spread over No.7.

Will anything ever change here or in the lives of my children? If only the thunder would speak again.

A mist of incense swirled in the air instead. *How utterly divine.*

All at once, with a creak and a groan, a crack appeared in the ash. The fast-fading light ignited the murkiness within in a rose-petal blush. It looked like something soft-white and lustrous reflected the sunset. *Silver?*

There was a story associated with No.7. Apparently, hundreds of years ago an old monk, Saint Ignatius, buried some communion silver on the property. *So it's not a myth.*

An Audi Q7 pulled up to the curb. Leda stepped out, then Meghna.

I gasped at the sight of the young nurse. Her feet tapped the floor in the slow, doddering steps of a woman at least three times her age.

Her slight shoulders dragged in her long cotton dress, and she moved cautiously, pausing for balance before taking every step.

What's going on with her?

"I must show you something." Leda led Meghna toward the crack.

Alas, it had vanished.

"I never get to see the silver," Meghna whined. "Only you do."

Leda has seen it already?

"I don't understand why," she muttered.

Meghna retched.

Leda passed her a pack of chewing gum. "Let's go home. I shouldn't have dragged you here." They returned to the car, and she helped Meghna in.

Neither noticed Sonya sprinting up, her face a serene puzzle.

What is she thinking?

She would have merged into the deepening shadows of the evening when Leda looked up. "Hey, Sonya!" she said cheerily. "What a pleasant surprise. I didn't have a clue you were in Houston. How are you?"

Sonya came to a stiff, uncertain halt. "I thought you lived in Dallas."

"Yes, but I've rented an apartment here at Bell Heights."

"She's been looking for you." Meghna jutted her face out the open door.

"Well, it wasn't just for that," said Leda, "though it was partly the reason."

Sonya smirked. "You can go back home now that you've found me."

Meghna scowled. "Show some gratitude at least. It was so senseless of you to come away without telling anyone. Everyone has been searching for you frantically."

"Yet why?" Sonya met her lackluster stare. "I mentioned that I was on a mission very explicitly in my last text message to Sunny. Did he not tell you, Leda?"

The detective nodded. "Oh, yes, he did. Have you accomplished your mission?"

"Not quite, but I've made some progress."

Really!

"Enough to satisfy you?" Leda's piercing blue eyes seemed to x-ray her soul.

"My only satisfaction now is to visit this place. We lived here, a perfect family."

Meghna coughed. "You must let go, or the emotions will destroy you."

"I miss my home." Sonya blinked.

At last, I see some real emotion.

"Something interesting happened here the other day," said Leda. "I was alone, trying to clean the place with chemicals, when I felt a presence behind me. I turned back. I saw nobody, yet a crack had appeared in the ash, and I glimpsed some silver beneath."

"Silver? Where?" Sonya glanced around as if searching for it.

"Over there." Leda pointed to the sacred spot where I had glimpsed the treasure.

Sonya relaxed a little and told Leda and Meghna the history of No.7. "Funny none of us ever saw it"

"The house was built over it." A smile warmed Leda's eyes. "How would you?"

True.

"Sonya should see it now that the house is no more." Meghna cackled.

Sonya swallowed. "It's like the secret chamber is trying to hide from sinners like me."

"I believe it is not so much to hide, Sonya, as to protect the treasures," said Leda. "The silver is pricey. It stayed safe all this time from people like the fiend—Dev."

"You mean Uncle Dev?" Sonya pronounced his name with surprising respect.

Leda's brows furrowed. "Oh, so you've gone back to calling him that?"

If I had a mouth, that was precisely what I would have said.

"For my own sanity and well-being." Sonya sighed. "Anyway, I've got to go."

Meghna scoffed. "It's lucky the curse was deflected from you. Poor Leda."

Sonya cast a furtive glance at Leda's wrist covered by the long sleeve of her blouse. "How's the scar?"

"I tried to have it removed," said Leda. "It disappeared only to come back again. I think things should be fine as long as I have no encounters with the bat or Dev."

"It all began here." Sonya gazed into the horizon.

Leda frowned at her.

"Don't you understand?" Meghna muttered. "It all began here. Therefore, you should avoid this place."

"I can't do that," laughed Leda. "I'm investigating the fiend. Besides, Sunny asked me to keep an eye on the property. He arrives in a few days."

"Does he?" Sonya's brows furrowed.

"Yes. You two should get together and decide what you want to do with the property."

"Sure."

"You must do something about this unsightly ash ASAP," said Meghna.

"I believe the City Council tried but failed." Sonya sighed. "Anyway, I've got to go."

"May I have your number, Sonya?" asked Leda. "The old one doesn't seem to work."

Sonya slipped her hand into her pocket. "Oh! I left my cell phone behind. Sorry, it's a new one, and I can't remember the number off the top of my head."

Oh, Sonya!

"And your old phone?" Meghna coughed.

"I misplaced it."

The fiend must have it.

Meghna gagged and heaved.

"Sorry, Sonya. We'll have to head back home. Where are you staying? I could drop you off."

"With Mom's friend on Woodway Road, barely two miles from here. You go; I'll jog back."

I never had any friends on Woodway.

Leda scribbled her number and address on a Kleenex and handed it to her. "Here. Take this. Call when you have a minute, I'm going back to Dallas. Do come and visit me. Whenever."

"Thanks." Sonya tucked away the tissue in her trouser pocket and broke into a sprint.

"She's so weird, so terribly selfish." Meghna coughed and sneezed all at once. "Has she never been disciplined by anyone?"

The book turned her shaky and indecisive, but not selfish or rude. The fiend's negative traits are rubbing off on her.

"She's only being secretive. Everyone has a right to privacy." Leda watched Sonya disappear down the road.

Chapter 19

Leda and Meghna headed toward Dallas.

Sonya sprinted all the way to Woodway, stopped, glanced over her shoulder, then raced to Asha's house on Post Oak Boulevard.

Auntie Bina greeted her at the door. "Hey! You're back. Want to play a game of Scrabble?" She had already set up the board on the dining table.

"Sure." Sonya stepped in. "Where's Uncle Dev?"

"He has a severe headache and asked not to be disturbed,"

There was no sign of the fiend in the house. *Hope he's not stalking Leda.*

Leda had just exited the urban freeway and entered the interstate highway when I spotted her maneuvering her car in a sea of traffic.

The fiend was not in sight.

Neither Leda nor Meghna spoke. Their silence was punctuated by Meghna's gags, retches, and heaves.

Leda's phone chimed with a message from Patrick:

Jalebi's plane is delayed by four hours.

I'm sorry, she replied. We should be back in Dallas by then. I'll get dinner started.

Why is Jalebi coming to Dallas? Is it to complete what she failed to accomplish in India? I felt a deep sense of unease and slipped into Leda's car.

"I feel I need to throw up," Meghna cried.

Leda gave her a bag and Meghna vomited into it.

Leda passed her some water, and Meghna drained the bottle.

"You are past your first trimester, Meghna, and still feeling nauseous," said Leda. "You should talk with your doctor."

"I am a nurse. I know what to do."

"Then you shouldn't be looking so ill. You don't want me to come with you to the doctor, so I don't, but I can't stop worrying. Is the baby growing well? You seem to be losing weight, and you look so pale."

She's greener than she's pale.

Meghna swallowed.

"You should see a dietician and get some advice. If you do not gain enough weight during pregnancy, you will be at risk of miscarriage, or your baby may be born too early and face health problems at birth."

"Don't worry." Meghna yawned. "Everything will be fine once Jalebi is here. Thank you for letting her come."

Is she coming to take care of Meghna?

Leda narrowed her eyes over the horizon until they shone like two vivid points of light.

Back in her house, Leda showed Meghna up to the en suite guest bedroom. "How about you enjoy a nice soak while I get dinner started. Patrick and Jalebi should be home soon."

Meghna nodded, and Leda left her to thaw some fish for dinner.

Sunny called and she picked up promptly. "Hi, Sunny, I would have called, but it must be like five in the morning in the UK." She cast a glance at the clock.

"Precisely," chuckled Sunny. "I am wide awake, working on my thesis. How are things at No.7?"

"Same, but guess what? I bumped into Sonya at No.7."

"Hmmm. I knew your persistence would pay off. What did she say? Where is she staying?"

A high-pitched chirp pierced my core. Unease slid through me. *The bat?*

Leda continued to talk. "At your mom's friend's house on Woodway."

"Woodway?" Sunny bellowed. "Neither of Mom's two friends Auntie Ruby, Nikita's Mom, or Auntie Asha, lived on Woodway. Nikita's house is in River Oaks, and Auntie Asha's is on Post Oak Boulevard."

"Oh, really? I wish I could spend more time with Sonya, but Meghna wasn't feeling too good, and Jalebi is arriving today." She glanced back at the clock. "The plane must have landed."

"Wow!" said Sunny. "Did you pay for her airfare too? She disappeared on you."

The scar moved ever so slightly on her wrist. Leda didn't seem to have a clue.

I fought the irresistible urge to alert her.

"We didn't pay Jalebi for her services in India and there needs to be someone in the house to keep an eye on Meghna," said Leda. "She's unwell and won't have anyone other than Jalebi. I don't know how Jalebi can help though—never known anyone to turn so green during a pregnancy!"

"Hope she hasn't got anything to do with your sorcerer." Sunny chuckled.

"No, not her."

"Did you find out why Jalebi disappeared in Digha?"

"She had an accident." The bat squeaked, and Leda glanced around.

Shadows crawled up the wall. "Um, excuse me, Sunny, talk to you later." She hung up on him and rushed up the stairs, scowling at the dark shapes vanishing into the plasterwork of the high ceiling.

She did not see the bat glide over her head and crash into the wall, though the noise startled her.

Leda knocked on the guestroom door left ajar.

"Meghna, you, okay?"

"Y-yes." Meghna slipped on her trousers in the bathroom, thrust the piece of rubber tubing in her hand into a fabric bag, and dumped it on the bed.

Was she trying to abort the baby?

"Meghna, are you alright?" Leda peeked in.

"Yes." The nurse grabbed the fabric bag, then dropped it. Out flew the rubber tubing, landing on the ground right before Leda's eyes.

"What is that?" Leda gasped, stepping in.

"A piece of rubber tubing." Meghna met Leda's horrified gaze. "I just wanted to live again, you know, with Randy gone."

"Don't Patrick and I have a say?"

"Yes, you do." Meghna glowered at her phone. "I'm out of my mind with worry. I don't know what I'm doing. Randy gave me a lot of money before he killed himself, but I misplaced it while I was staying with you in Digha."

"Why didn't you tell me at the time?"

"I wanted to come abroad and work here. It felt better you thinking that you needed me and not me you. I'm sorry. I feel terrible, but you won't speak about the people who are interested in adopting the baby. It's like they don't exist."

"We've only just got you home, Meghna." Leda's scar pulsed and glowed. She seized the wrist with her other hand and looked around. She did not see the bat slip into Meghna's room. Her lips trembled for a long moment, before she spoke again. "Goodness knows what would have become of you if I'd been a minute too late."

"Vacuum aspiration is very safe and takes about five to ten minutes from start to finish," Meghna tucked the rubber tubing back in her bag. "All I would need to do after this was rest for an hour." She noticed the ash bat coasting over the ceiling and shrieked.

Leda's scar glowed like embers. Even as she collapsed on the floor with a deep, guttural groan, the bat flew out through an open window.

Meghna helped Leda to her bed.

"D-d-dev's stalking me, he's m-m-manipulating the b-bat," stuttered Leda. She looked deadly pale though the swelling and abnormal redness of her scar had already subsided significantly. "Meghna, have you heard from Rao?"

"No, I severed all relations with my family and their neighbors since I got pregnant." She paused, then said in a kinder tone. "You can call him."

"His phone is always switched off," Leda muttered. "Wonder if Patrick and Jalebi have left the airport yet. I've had no time to cook dinner."

She's thinking about cooking dinner even now!

"I'll help," said Meghna.

Together, they found some Chicken stroganoff in the freezer and slipped it into the oven.

"I thought I just might find you here." Patrick walked into the kitchen and pecked Leda on the cheek. "Why was the front door open?"

"Was it?" Leda poured wine into two glasses.

Meghna had already laid the table.

"It's so lovely to see you all again." Jalebi looked fabulous, though she dragged her left leg a little. "I'm sorry I could not see you off in Digha. I had a little accident."

Meghna retched. She excused herself and withdrew to her room, without so much as a glance at Jalebi.

How very strange.

Leda sighed. "I know, Jalebi. I'm so glad you could come. Our Meghna will have a friend."

"Of course. Meghna can have Marco's wife, Gladys, as a friend too. The poor woman is not too well. Thankfully she has Dish for company."

"We dropped by Marco's house on our way here," Patrick said. "Gladys really enjoyed Jalebi's company."

"Jalebi is lovely company," chirped Leda.

"You can talk all night." Patrick laughed.

"Tonight, Jalebi might be jet-lagged. We shall have a long chat tomorrow morning after you leave for work."

"I'm away the next few days," Jalebi began.

Is she meeting up with the fiend?

"Really?" Leda swallowed. "Meghna could do with a companion right now."

"Not to worry. I shall spend a few hours with my friend who will come and pick me up tomorrow and then be right back for Meghna."

"Thanks."

"It's okay." Jalebi sent a quick message to a friend, some Chumki, and slipped her phone into her pocket. "All sorted."

Leda gazed at Jalebi with those piercing blue eyes.

If only I could mind read Leda.

They had a quick dinner, and then Jalebi cleared the table and loaded the dishwasher. "Leda, Patrick, you must give me my list of chores ASAP."

"Sure," said Leda and Patrick nodded. They thanked her profusely and retired to their bedroom.

"I have a feeling the fiend is around," said Leda.

"What makes you think so?" asked Patrick.

"The bat was here."

"And you left the front door open."

"I got disoriented with so much happening. Meghna isn't well, and she tried to abort the baby, here in this house. She's past fifteen weeks."

"You should sit with her and talk. I know you're busy looking for Sonya—"

"We bumped into her at No.7."

"Really? Where's she staying?"

Leda told him. "I don't know why she is lying to me. I am her friend."

"There's a rebel lying deep in her soul." Patrick grinned.

Chapter 20

*Y*es, *Sonya can be a bit of a rebel, but she is not stupid. She knows she has nothing to gain from her loyalty to the fiend.*

A new fear squeezed my core. *What if she has no other option but to comply? What if she repents her decision and it's too late? What if . . . ?*

Unable to stop the spiral of anxious "what-if" thoughts, I levithoned to Asha's house to discover the truth about Sonya's situation.

The house was quiet except for the faint murmurs drifting in from the backyard, where invisible and odorless, the fiend and Sonya spoke in utmost secrecy.

"With Leda keeping a close watch on No.7, it's getting very difficult to visit the property," said Sonya.

"She's desperate to find me now she's branded." The fiend's eyes darted.

I camouflaged among the solar garden lights creating bright pathways through the lawn.

Sonya scoffed. "As if it will change anything if she does."

"Only if she can kill me, which is impossible."

Why? I hated the smile in his voice and struggled to find a word to describe the type. *Malicious? Smug? Predatory?*

Sonya did not ask why. She spoke of Jalebi instead. "The other person who worries me is Jalebi. She is so complex. Are you sure she won't give you away, Uncle Dev?"

"Fat chance." The fiend's voice took a serious tone. "Anyway, your job is to take care of Leda. Find out about that scar."

"I did. She said it disappeared when she went to the surgeon but came back later." Sonya's monotone did not betray her emotions.

"What does she plan to do about it now? Is she trying to get rid of it in any other way? Talk to her and report back to me the status of the scar, her emotional temperature—if it's getting warmer, hotter, going into potentially dangerous degrees."

"She's very calm, but she struggles when the scar plays up."

"Is she scared?"

"Well, not like she's said anything."

"Oh, she will, if you can get close enough. Spoil her with gifts— I'll pay."

Leda is different.

"Sure."

How I hated Sonya's mousy-meek compliance.

"And if you should need to finish her off, you have my full cooperation," Sonya added quickly. "They say good riddance to bad rubbish."

For shame, Sonya.

The fiend inhaled deeply. "Relax, Sonya. Leda's not going anywhere. The harder part is making sure no one suspects a thing."

He sounds like a mentor teaching a younger, inexperienced partner.

"I will do anything you want me to," Sonya's voice dropped to a conspiratorial hush, "be it Leda, or Mom or even Dad."

I winced.

"Dad!" He scoffed. "He escaped my torture chamber. Your parents are always bad news."

"I'll do whatever to get Dad back. And the spirit-camera at Budget Stay should provide you with pictures of Mom's changing core for your book. Squeeze her tighter if you want clearer pictures of that something unusual you noticed. It will hurt her, but you have what you need at the end of the day."

So that's what it was the other day—something unusual in my core that had to be photographed urgently. What?

I discovered nothing even with close examination and retired to the undisturbed, dark attic space at the house to sort through my thoughts. Honestly, I could barely recognize my daughter any longer.

Later that night Deepak's brilliant light flashed through the gloom. "Are you okay?"

I could barely speak; I felt so upset.

He dipped down, his fire flashing continually, and I made a leap for him, He grabbed me tight and shot though the skies.

"Sorry, Deepak, I disappeared on you so suddenly the other day. I was so worried about Sonya. Did you go to the festival?"

"Yes. It was to celebrate the return of the greatest souls to their eternal home. There was so much merrymaking, but it got a bit lonely. Everyone had friends and family."

"You had Rose."

Rose, his only child, born with cerebral palsy, had not survived her twenty-first birthday.

"Rose now belongs to the top rung of the celestial hierarchy. She only communicates through pheromones."

"Pheromones?"

"Perfumes, varying strengths of which constitute distinct meaningful elements of the very formal language of Heaven's elite. I belong to the lowest rungs because I had to purify myself in purgatory."

"At least you're in the know about everything."

"I would rather give up that knowledge to be with you."

We rode into the furthest regions of the atmosphere, enjoying the frisson of joy that only freedom could bring. "Whoa!" I exclaimed, wishing I was some exotic creature in keeping with the breathtaking views.

As if by magic, I turned into a vibrant blue morpho butterfly.

Mesmerized by my iridescent flash, I flew around with slow wing beats. "Deepak, do I get to stay this way?"

"It will attract too much attention," he spoke in a tender tone. "This is just Heaven giving you a taste of wish-fulfillment, your upcoming perk."

I reverted to a simple gray moth.

"You so earned the privilege," his thrilling cry numbed my disappointment. "You restrained yourself though Sonya was very provocative. You did not interfere in the life of humans. You were kind to Ravi despite all the grudges you bear him, you apologized to him for your mistakes, and you helped other spirits. I am so proud of you, and Heaven is all about rewards. The world you are in is not where you should be in. Remember Heaven is your home; you are only here temporarily. Think only of Heaven and dwell on pure thoughts. It will lighten you up. The lighter you feel, the closer you will feel to Heaven. The more you get involved in the lives around you—you know."

"Yes, but how do I stop feeling hurt at the way Sonya speaks about us—Ravi and myself—to the fiend."

We bumped into dark rain clouds, and Deepak navigated through the rain that poured. "Don't dwell on it." he said. "Let your inner rain meet sunny rays."

The raindrops met the sun's first hesitant rays piercing the receding clouds. Colors arced upon the sky reaching for the sun-kissed rain.

We flew to the peak of the arc and glimpsed the sunset glow of the Elysian fields. It was serene and peaceful, yet I could not stop talking about Sonya.

"The fiend's heartlessness is rubbing off on her. She said she would do whatever to get Ravi back—those were her exact words. You know, when I saw her luxuriating at the old crumbling house at Red Lake, I thought she was ignorant of her father suffering in the torture chamber, but now I think she was party to it." I sighed. "He has still not forgiven me."

We glided down the other side of the rainbow toward the horizon.

"Yesterday I saw Ravi with BLZ hovering over Red Lake," said Deepak.

"Ravi is free?"

"Apparently, BLZ rescued Ravi from Dev's torture chamber."

"Hmmm. Yet the arsonist is no benevolent spirit."

"Not at all. He is furious with Neel and Sue for selling Herenhuis, his home to Bina."

Really! It took me a few minutes to process the news. "Where is Sue staying?"

"At the Red Lake House. Sue's taking full responsibility for the property until the fiend is back. She and that cook, Linda, organize parties for the rogues—" Deepak stiffened. "Feel the erratic vibrations in the air?"

"Um—very faint."

"A meeting I signed up for is about to begin. I must go. Sorry. Remember what we talked about. You must come to Heaven ASAP and talk to the Heaven Elders about the curse. Who knows? They might be able to help you."

The vibrations were more regular, more harmonious. "We are approaching Dallas," he muttered and flew away in a steep trajectory toward the stars.

I beelined to Leda's downspout. *I will try and follow Deepak's advice. Who knows? It could solve my problem.*

Chapter 21

In the dim light of dawn, Leda and Patrick paced out the dimensions of their home.

Meghna had gone missing.

Just as I decide to follow Deepak's advice.

Leda called Meghna's number in vain. "She ran away because of me. I interfered with her life, guilt-tripped her, and as if that was not enough, I brought her here to live with me, under my nose, to micromanage her life. If anything should happen to her, I am to blame."

"That inner critic is a bit loud today, huh? We all mess up. Literally, everyone makes mistakes." Patrick craned his neck out of the window, hoping to catch a glimpse of Meghna.

She was nowhere in sight.

Jalebi walked down the stairs groggily. "You two are already awake? Sorry, I did not come down earlier. I fell asleep." She glanced around, covering her mouth to stifle a yawn. "Where's Meghna?"

"She has disappeared," Patrick said.

"What? Since when?"

Could she have had a hand in Meghna's disappearance?

Patrick sighed. "Leda went up to check up on Meghna a few hours ago and found her missing."

"Why didn't you wake me up, Leda?" asked Jalebi.

"I didn't have the heart to. You were fast asleep."

"Last night Meghna was a little nauseous, but otherwise she seemed fine. Are you sure she hasn't gone out for a walk?"

Leda shook her head. "My interference in her life became so unbearable, she had to leave. Now I don't know where to start looking for her."

"Meghna is new to this country and hasn't really been out and about by herself very much," said Patrick. "She couldn't have gone far."

Leda nodded. "I think so too. Meghna has gone where she has gone with a purpose. She has taken the equipment required for manual vacuum aspiration and the towels from her bathroom. All she needs is a bit of privacy to do the job, and that doesn't need to be far."

"I thought she was seeing a doctor," said Jalebi.

Leda nodded. "Yes, Dr. Perez. She does not open until nine."

Jalebi's phone buzzed. She glanced at the message. "It's my friend. He will be here in five minutes to pick me up. Sorry, I can't come looking for Meghna with you."

"It's alright, Jalebi, you go." Leda sighed. "Patrick and I will check the neighborhood one last time and then inform the police. Meghna thinks she can abort the baby by herself, but she's in the fifteenth week. There might be complications."

Jalebi's phone buzzed again. "My friend is here."

All I saw was a blue Honda Civic sedan with a driver I had never seen before.

"What does your friend do?" asked Leda.

"He's a taxi driver." Jalebi saw herself out.

Leda and Patrick were out in the neighborhood searching for Meghna when she called.

"Where are you?" Leda panted.

"I got rid of the baby. You don't have to let me stay in your house if you don't want to."

"Of course I want you to stay with me. I brought you here. I am responsible for your well-being." Leda glanced at Patrick who met her gaze with a scowl. "It's Meghna."

"Where is she?" he asked. "Is she alright? Is the baby okay?"

Leda shook her head, blinking furiously. "We must go pick her up." She dug her fingers into her phone. "Where are you, Meghna?"

"You don't have to, honestly."

"Where are you?" Leda insisted.

"Um, with a, a, a friend from Houston. Um, she um, helped with the abortion. I . . . I met her at the OB's."

The pauses . . . the fillers . . . the repetitions . . . A sense of unease slid through my core.

"So you didn't go to a hospital?" Leda looked shocked.

"I will be all right. I feel fine."

"Good." Leda's voice broke, and a tear slid down her face.

"Let me talk." Patrick eased away the phone from her. "Where are you, Meghna? I'll come and pick you up."

There was a long pause.

"Meghna?" Patrick's voice was firm.

"I will wait by Alamo Drafthouse Cinema opposite Vickey Meadows at one."

"See you then," said Patrick and hung up.

He and Leda returned to their house in silence.

Back home, Leda dragged herself up the stairs and unlocked the nursery, two doors down the corridor from Meghna's room. Tearfully she walked in and gripped the bars of a crib, aqua blue like the cabinets and the rug.

Her gaze swept over the Toy Story wall murals, the matching window valance, the curtains, and the plaid blankets, and a sob tore from her chest.

Did Leda decorate the room? Was it for her baby?

I had gotten too close, and Leda's hand landed on my wings. It lingered. I didn't budge, not until she moved her hand to wipe the tears coursing down her face.

Patrick returned with Meghna just after two.

She had reverted to the attractive unpregnant nurse.

That was quick!

"Where's Leda?" asked Meghna.

Patrick pointed to the baby room with his chin and the two walked up the stairs and down the corridor to the nursery.

Meghna recoiled, her brows furrowed.

"We lost our baby," Patrick whispered in Meghna's ear. "Hi, Leda." He stepped in and kissed her. "Meghna is back."

Meghna stared at Leda speechless. I guessed that for her as for me, some of Leda's baffling words had finally begun to make sense.

Leda's teary gaze drifted across the room and rested on Meghna's face. "Come in," she said, wiping her cheek with her thumb. "I don't often let people into my past."

"I could never have imagined," stuttered Meghna.

"I didn't tell you. I don't tell anyone. It's been five months—" Tears flowed down her face.

My core shattered to watch the good woman cry.

"I am so sorry." Meghna's voice trailed. Her eyes brimmed.

Leda rubbed her face with a heavy sigh and slumped down on the window seat. "Meghna, you should rest. You must be exhausted."

"No, I'm fine."

"I'll get us some coffee." Patrick sidled away.

There was an uneasy silence, and then Leda spoke in a near-whisper. "I have a uterine anomaly, you know what they call the septate uterus, when the uterus has two small cavities instead of one."

Meghna nodded. "It's still possible to have a healthy pregnancy and delivery."

Leda trembled. "I had multiple miscarriages."

Meghna nodded. "The condition can increase your risk of miscarriage."

"I had surgery, conceived, and carried the baby full term, thought it would be all alright. They said the baby had been dead at birth. Stillborn. They said my boy had perished inside me. But how? I felt him move, kick, and grow vital under my heart." Her eyes streaming, Leda bit into her lip.

"Did you get pregnant within six months of the surgery?"

"No." Leda dabbed her eyes with her sleeve.

"I thought you were the luckiest person on Earth when I met you in India. You kept smiling. Who could have imagined what you've suffered?"

"I pray despite everything." Leda managed a faint smile. "That trip to India unfolded a lot differently than I imagined."

"You made friends; you met me. I bet you thought God had answered your prayers, and then I crashed your hopes."

Leda touched Meghna's shoulder, opened her mouth as if to say something, then closed it again.

"I have no right to be here," Meghna sniveled.

"Of course you do." Leda took a shuddering breath. "Things don't always work the way we want them to. We thought you could help us, but obviously God has other plans. Perhaps he wants us to help you, and trust me, we have the resources to."

So much compassion cannot go unrewarded.

"You are so kind, Leda." Meghna sucked in her breath quickly and then let it escape in a relieved sigh. She did not notice Patrick bring in the coffees and chose the moment to confide a secret in Leda. "I too have something to say, something I haven't told you yet. Things have not been quite right since the beginning of my pregnancy."

Patrick planted the tray on the rocker and would have tiptoed out without being noticed when he stumbled.

Leda and Meghna both looked up.

"Sorry," said Patrick. "I didn't mean to pry."

"It's okay," said Meghna. "I think you should also know why I aborted this baby, the memory of my late partner, Randy, whom I love so much."

"It's okay, Meghna." Leda watched her, her face etched with concern. "You have already explained."

"There's more" Meghna cried. "And I need to get this off my chest. I harbored the Devil's child in my womb."

How?

Leda and Patrick stared at her in stunned silence.

"Did it not occur to you seeing me?" Meghna's eyes streamed. "I could not recognize myself. At first, I thought it was due to hormonal changes, but then one night I woke up to find . . ." Meghna braced herself shivering.

"It's okay." Leda handed her a mug from the tray. "Have this, and perhaps we'll talk about it some other day."

Meghna sniffed, rolling the cup between her hands. "Please listen, so I do not have to bear the guilt of wronging two such beautiful people. It happened the night you and Sonya went into the forest in Digha with Rao to burn the book and you came back branded. I suddenly found Hema's book on my bed."

"But the book was burned and reduced to ashes." Patrick scowled.

All three pairs of eyes focused on the scar on Leda's wrist. It looked like nothing more than an old burn wound.

"Exactly." Meghna drew a sharp breath. "At first, I thought I was hallucinating. But it started coming every night and settled around me as I slept. In the mornings, there were something like teeth marks on my belly like some creature had been pecking at it."

Was it the bat?

"I saw what Sonya claimed she did," she continued. "Those sketches in the book darkened before my eyes as the pages fluttered in the quiet of the night."

"Did Jalebi see all this too?" asked Leda.

"No, though she probably saw the book. We slept on the same bed."

"Why didn't you tell me about the book?" asked Leda.

"I was hellbent on coming abroad, and you didn't seem too curious about my green complexion."

"Because you said you used green tea face mask to brighten your complexion."

"But was my complexion glowing?"

Leda shook her head. "No, but if only you had explained. The things you say, I cannot imagine in my worst nightmares."

"Yet you are a victim of black magic." Meghna sighed. "I wanted to get the Devil's baby out of my system. It completely freaked me out."

"I would have helped you if you let me."

"You can't help yourself." Meghna looked away. "If I lost the baby, would you bring me here?"

"But once here, you didn't even let me accompany you to the doctor. And you never went after that first day. I called her and asked."

Meghna shifted uncomfortably.

"You guys heard from Jalebi?" Patrick asked.

Leda shook her head.

Meghna lowered her eyes.

Why does she clench her fist?

Leda checked her phone. "No messages. Has she sent you any, Meghna?"

Megha scrolled through her messages, her hands trembling. "No."

"Do you know this friend she's with?" asked Leda.

"Um—"

Almost at once the doorbell rang. "Leda, Patrick! Open the door."

Jalebi was back.

Chapter 22

Jalebi peeked into Patrick's study. "Hey, Patrick," she called. Patrick was in the middle of a complex project, surrounded by schematics and code on his multiple monitor screens. His focus was so intense he didn't hear her, and she rushed away to the kitchen where Leda and Meghna chatted over a cup of tea.

"Hi, Leda," she said, then noticed Meghna. "Hey, you look so much better, brighter. Where did you go?" She glanced at Leda. "Perhaps, we should not have worried so much."

Meghna's cup wobbled in her hand.

Jalebi squinted at her. "Baby, okay?"

"I aborted it," Meghna said in a monotone.

"Oh!" Jalebi cried. "Does that mean I'm fired?"

Leda shook her head. "No, you're not. Our Meghna needs plenty of care to get her back to health."

"You don't need to worry about a thing." Patrick stepped into the kitchen, and his phone rang. "Excuse me." He returned to his study.

Meghna yawned. "I'll go upstairs and take a nap, Leda, if that's okay?"

"Sure."

Meghna left without so much as a backward glance.

Did Meghna and Jalebi fall out over something?

"Let's have a heart-to-heart while Meghna rests." Leda poured Jalebi some tea from the pot and served it with an assortment of cookies.

Jalebi sipped from her mug, watching Leda over the rim. "Can't believe Meghna aborted her baby. So selfish of her. That was the whole point of her coming here."

Why does Jalebi keep tapping her feet?

Leda frowned. "She said she was carrying the Devil's child and apparently there were all the symptoms."

"Oh my God! I know she was losing weight and had this unhealthy look—wasn't she seeing an obstetrician?"

"She had stopped. She thought she could take care of herself." Leda looked Jalebi straight in her eyes. "You didn't see anything strange while you spent the few nights with Meghna back in Digha, did you?"

"No." Jalebi practically covered her whole face with the mug to take another sip, an incredibly long one.

Leda eyed her warily.

It's like she can hear Jalebi's palpitations.

"Well, Meghna slept fitfully at night, waking up from nightmares several times."

"What was she scared of?" Leda asked.

"Of a book of sketches."

"Did you see the book?"

"How could I? It was a book in her nightmares. In fact, I'm not surprised she dreamed about a book of sketches with all of you so worked up about some book Sonya brought home from a sorcerer."

There was an awkward silence punctuated by the drip of the faucet.

"Excuse me. I'll go tighten the faucet handle." Leda pushed back her chair and rose calmly.

Jalebi shot up. "No more questions?"

The sudden change in her attitude was shocking.

"Sorry, if I offended you, Jalebi." Leda met her gaze.

Jalebi rolled her eyes. "You think you have a right over me because your husband paid for my flight here. I can pay you back the money." She slipped out a stack of bills wrapped with a paper band from her purse and slammed it on the table. "There, two thousand dollars!"

Wow! Who gave her all that money? The fiend?

Leda's chin trembled. "I don't want the money back, and I'm sure Patrick doesn't either. You can keep the cash with you. This is a new country for you, and it's expensive. Consider us your friends."

"Friends?" she spat. "When neither you nor Patrick have the decency to ask where I've been all this time or what I've been doing. Well, let me tell you. I have skills that have earned me a job with one of the richest families here."

"Who if I may ask?" Leda squinted at her.

"None of your business. Besides, I am done with your interrogation. You might be a detective, but I am no criminal. I expect to be treated with respect." She stamped out of the kitchen.

Did she return to sever all relations with the couple?

The front door slammed with a bang, loud enough for Patrick to come running into the kitchen.

"What was that?" he asked.

"Jalebi left."

"Left?" Patrick's gaze darted out of the window. The Honda Civic that had picked her up in the morning, pulled away from the curb.

"She came to return your money." Leda pointed with her chin to the stack of cash beside Jalebi's half empty cup.

"But who asked for it?"

"No one. She now seems to have a lot of money at her disposal."

Patrick's face contorted into an almighty scowl. "How? She told me she had no money and no friends in this country other than the taxi driver."

"That is what she told you." Leda's gaze swept over his face. "Tea?"

"Coffee, please."

Leda made him a cup.

"Her behavior surprises me." He sipped his coffee. "I know I got her here for us, and the baby, but she agreed."

"Perhaps this is yet another sign that we should embrace our greatest fear, childlessness, and move on." Leda's phone rang.

It was Sonya.

Now what does she want? I recalled her conversation with the fiend and stiffened.

Leda picked up at once. "Hello, Sonya."

"Hey, Leda, how are you doing?"

"Okay."

"Look, I am sorry about the other night. It was the sight of the ashes."

"It's alright. Let me know when you're planning on visiting the property again, and I'll come along. I would like to show you the church silver if I can."

"Of course, but right now, I am trying to take my mind off all that. I have started looking after myself, eating sensibly, and exercising regularly. I've even joined a yoga class."

"Yoga is beneficial for both the mind and the body. That's wonderful news."

"I miss you, Leda."

Really! Yet, there was nothing in her voice suggesting that she was feigning her affection.

Leda smiled. "How about we meet up sometime? We have a lot of catching up to do."

Just the thing Sonya wants.

"Sure. Are you free the weekend after next—um, the Saturday? I have a free pass for a friend at the yoga studio. We could find a nice restaurant afterward for lunch."

"Of course. Let me save the date." Leda did not see Patrick walk up behind her as she circled it on the kitchen calendar. "What time is the yoga class?" she asked Sonya.

"The class starts at eleven, but we should arrive fifteen minutes early. I'll get us matching outfits. There are some really cute sets available online."

"Cute yoga suits can be expensive."

"I'm the one with the expensive taste. Let me get them, please."

Following the fiend's instructions to a T.

"You don't have to."

Sonya hung up abruptly.

Leda glanced at the black screen and sighed.

"Done talking with Sonya?" Patrick's gaze fixed on Leda. "One moment she vanishes on you, the next she invites you to a yoga class and is adamant to buy you the gear. Is she bipolar?"

"Keep your friends close, and bi-polars closer." Leda grinned.

"Heard that about enemies."

"Too early to tell if she's one."

Chapter 23

Why did Sonya invite Leda to the yoga studio? I do not doubt that the fiend is involved in this.

I raged in wretched restlessness. The fiend is turning Sonya into his accomplice, something neither she nor Deepak realizes.

Struggling to confine myself in the downspout on Leda's roof with the purest of thoughts, I took a free ride to Asha's house in Leda's car the following day.

Sonya was in a bedroom upstairs, deeply engrossed in *From Dead to Worse*, a southern vampire mystery, about a telepathic waitress who became involved with vampires and other supernatural beings.

Does she ever think of going back to school or accepting James's internship offer?

I returned to the undisturbed, dark, attic space.

Morning graduated into afternoon, the midday light bringing a brighter palette to view if not a bonnier mood.

Auntie Bina lay on the plush velvet bed, reclining against mixed pillows in rich colors, her eyes closed.

The fiend entered, conspicuously green.

He can't be carrying the Devil's child.

He darted across the room to his side of the bed. just as Auntie Bina's bloodshot eyes sprang open. He turned his face away from her.

He won't let her see the monster that he is.

"How do you feel with your new workout routine?" he asked.

"A little overwhelmed. All my joints and muscles are achy. My fingers are a little swollen too." She wiped a tear starting in her eyes.

The fiend's face cracked into a smug grin. "Expect muscle soreness when starting a new type of exercise. I shall talk to the maid. I heard she used to be a masseuse—um, what's her name? Gulabi?" He played with the table lamp pull-chain.

"Color of the English rose!" Auntie Bina scoffed. "You are so bad with names! Her name is Jalebi. Jalebi is an Indian street food."

What is his strategy for remembering names?

"Yes. That's it. Age! The name is the first to go!"

His humility is so attractive.

Auntie Bina sat up, and her gaze drifted to his green face. "Is this some face mask you are using?"

"Mask?" He shook his head. "No. It's just a green tea moisturizing oil. My skin was so dry, I used it, and now I can't get rid of the stain. Would you know of any remedies?"

"No. But you could ask Jalebi. She might know."

"Of course." The fiend nodded. "We should make the most of her. After all we are paying her five hundred dollars a month in addition to providing a roof over her head and four square meals a day,"

Four square meals a day! It had been a long time since I heard that expression. There was a time in India when only the wealthy could enjoy the "four square meals a day" routine, typically including breakfast, lunch, a mid-afternoon "chai time" snack, and dinner.

He still has that mentality!

Auntie Bina heaved a sigh, resting her head in the crook of his neck.

The fiend patted her cheek, gazing at the wall. "I wish I could take you out for a drive, but I hate taxis. They don't have the privacy of one's own car—you know if we should want to steal a kiss."

He's after the family's cars! Greed is a bottomless pit.

"I sent the Jeep for servicing. It's only just come back as good as new." Auntie Bina blinked. "It belonged to Jay, my son-in-law. Asha used the Mercedes—" She swallowed down a sob, but her eyes streamed. "After Jay died, my baby became a wreck."

The fiend used his thumb to wipe away her tears, still staring at the wall.

Auntie Bina continued to lean against him.

"I love you to the moon and back," he whispered. "Once in a while, when everything goes wrong, love gives us a fairy tale."

"I'm sorry for being so unappreciative of your love." She choked, breaking into heart-rending sobs.

This is the socialite who would never be caught in an unguarded moment. It's her grief spilling over.

"How often do you find a person who loves your sad face and admires your waterworks?" the fiend chuckled.

"Oh, Dev, you are such a beast!" Auntie Bina smiled through her tears. She did not see the fiend press his lips together and rub his brow. "Jay's car is all yours. He will never come to claim it back."

The fiend rubbed his nose. "You give me so much. For what? What can an old man like me give you?" His words were saccharine sweet even as his eyes wandered to the clock.

He's the embodiment of pure evil.

"You are my soulmate." Gathering his hands in hers, she brought them to her lips. "You have no idea how deeply I love you." She sniffed. "Perhaps I don't show it all that well—I lost my only daughter." She turned her gaze to his face. "Remember, I chose to be with you when Kolkata police fanned out across the town to find you."

"I would get away, scot-free, with or without you," he chuckled. "I am one hell of a lucky devil! You have no idea what you've got yourself in for."

"I've always had a thing for bad guys, Dev, for living on the edge with them, walking on the wild side. You swept me off my feet with your evil streak." She got closer, and their faces touched. "We have felt the real thing in our brief time together. I wouldn't have it any other way."

Honestly, how blind is love?

"What if I have secrets that would shock you beyond your worst nightmares?" There was a steely glint in his eye.

"I had only read about women marrying their worst nightmares sneakily disguised as perfect love objects when we first met. You stunned me. It was like my soul stopped the search for its mate that had been going on forever." Her breath heaved with emotion.

"Really?" He stared at her face. "What became of the 'cold, calculating, unpredictable, impossible to please' you?"

"I lost my only daughter." She sniveled.

His lips curled.

He's only after her money.

With not an iota of suspicion, Auntie Bina slid her hand under her pillow and drew out Jay's Jeep key fob. "Here, take this. Enjoy!"

Chapter 24

The sun began to sink, and the fiend steered the Jeep to the east. He did not come back that night and called early the next morning.

"Sorry, Bina, I ran into Neel and followed him here to Louisiana to take a tour of his pharmaceutical company."

"I have been worried out of my mind," she cried.

"Bina," his voice was a mere whisper, "try and understand. Neel might make me his business partner. Think of the money, the position."

"We have everything, Dev. I just want you."

"And I want to give you the impossible."

Huh!

"When are you back?"

"In a few days. All the while I shall work tirelessly, prove myself to Neel, and all for you." Even as he spoke, the ash bat flew into Sonya's bedroom noiselessly.

Sonya zipped down to the kitchen to steal some bananas and grapes for her and stopped in her tracks.

Jalebi had arrived with her belongings. She was in the process of moving into the room over the garage, the servant's quarter.

Their paths did not cross.

Sonya went upstairs to her room, and the bat ate the fruit out of her hand. Sonya stroked her wings, and she was calm as a sleeping kitten.

Downstairs, Auntie Bina gave Jalebi specific instructions regarding the household chores: washing dishes, doing laundry, dusting, and cooking. Even as she carried them out, Auntie Bina watched, expressing in no uncertain terms her strong preference for cleanliness, order, and attention to detail.

Jalebi must have satisfied her to a T, for Auntie Bina ordered her to make some masala chai and invited Sonya to join her.

"Sonya, this is Jalebi, my new maid."

"Hello, Jalebi," said Sonya, her face expressionless.

"Hi," said Jalebi. "You must excuse me. I need to call a friend." She stepped out of the kitchen, only to return within minutes.

Auntie Bina produced a pack of cards. She and Sonya played German Whist, munching on a variety of snacks Jalebi dished up from leftovers in the fridge. Auntie Bina laughed and Sonya visibly relaxed. Happily, they competed to win good cards from the stock to add to their hand.

Just what my girl needs.

Twilight faded to a comforting black.

Sonya did not come upstairs. The ash bat plunged into the air and alighted on a new yard sign at No.7:

Toxic

I doubt this fazes the fiend.

The bat seemed indecisive for a few moments, then hopped onto the ash. She walked on all fours, her long tongue slithering over the blackness, glistening with oozing saliva.

An insufferable burnt orange stench flooded the air.

Drowning in it, I remained oblivious of Sunny and Paul approaching the neighborhood. It was only when Paul pulled up to the curb, and the friends stepped out that I noticed them.

The bat stopped her activity and stole away, taking the stink with her.

Sunny squinted at the yard sign. "What's that?"

"It's from the HOA." Paul sighed. "They've been here no less than three times, resorting to extreme cleaning measures. The last I heard, they're getting an expert to look into it."

His phone chimed with a message from his mother:
Dinner is ready. Where are you and Sunny?

"Mom wants us back home for dinner," said Paul. "C'mon, Sunny."

They drove away.

This is as good as it gets. All I need to do now is to secure a place in Heaven and beg the Heaven Elders to help break the curse

I soared up into the clouds and nestled among them, determined not to budge except in an emergency like a call from Heaven or an attack from the Devil.

The sky was a living canvas where fluffy clouds painted the daytime scene and the stars and constellations, the nocturnal stage. The galaxies tumbled and darted beyond, their distant lights inspiring dreams of other worlds.

Days past. I missed Deepak and consoled myself with the thought that he was in Heaven.

Heaven's light blossomed on noctilucent clouds higher up There the angels hovered, too white to be daylight. They spoke in voices more soothing than a thousand kisses. Their radiance was blinding.

I ventured out in search of Heaven's gate.

Spirits as bright as Deepak sailed past, whispering about the Devil's "drag net."

"If only we could save those trapped souls," said one. "But I can barely tell one from the other with the mesh cutting into their cores."

The stink of sulfur overwhelmed me. Humongous nets rocked in the skies like ships on a tumultuous sea. Cries for help echoed through the air.

"The Devil has cast his net really wide," whispered another bright soul. "There is no safe way for earthbound spirits to fly the skies tonight."

Is he speaking about me? I hid behind the radiant spirits.

The nets swerved past their dazzle and disappeared into the distance. The malodor faded too.

The privilege of embodying that radiance.

The air took on a welcoming soothing quality. The blue sky stretched above, clear and serene. Each burst of birdsong was a joy, every fragrance was fresh.

I felt calm and refreshed, and the nets returned with menacing speed.

"Help!" the captives' piercing screams rent the air. "Help, pump us some cool air," they seemed to beg of me. "You can."

I?

The nets swayed as if in a drunken swagger. The trapped souls lurched, thrashing against the mesh, only to fall back with groans of agony.

What if I levithon somewhere high up, far away from the Devil, like the thermosphere?

I inhaled to bursting point. The air pushed out of me, propelling me all the way to the auroras amid eerie expressions of gratitude.

Plumes of bold light, like incandescent liquid rock, shot across the stunning display of vibrant fluorescence.

"Your color!" Deepak's scent wrapped around me.

My core leaped. "No match for yours."

"There isn't much of a difference now. What you see on me is an incandescent cladding, an assemblage of a million high performance mirror balls that reflect the rays of the sun. It shields me from the Devil by blinding him. You will grow it once you're in Heaven."

That's what protected the bright souls and me hiding behind them. "Deepak, what new perks am I entitled to, now that I'm so much brighter? Can I go to Heaven and approach the Heaven Elders about the curse?"

"Um, no, but you can expect a certain level of wish fulfillment."

"Like protection from the Devil?"

"Perhaps from the fiend, but not from the Devil, not yet. So you must be very careful like right now."

I sniffed. "His stench is gone."

"But danger lurks. The drag net is dangerous. It floats in the air, thanks to the hell-made gossamer in the mesh of fibers. Once you're trapped, you essentially experience a loss of purpose and die a slow spiritual death." He sighed. "You must go straight back to No.7. Though the net extends well into your neighborhood, you will be safe in the treasure chamber beneath the ash. Stay there, and focus your mind on whatever is right, whatever is pure—"

"Is your time up?" I asked. "Are you preparing to leave?"

"Not yet. I'll wait for you to dive down to No.7 and hide yourself among the silver."

"But there are photographers down there—HOA working tirelessly to restore the cleanliness and aesthetics of the neighborhood."

"You can see all that? That's at least a hundred miles. Congratulations!"

My senses had increased tenfold, and I knew why. My confidence soared. I plummeted without another thought.

There was a raw energy in the air. Spirits stirred everywhere. In the mayhem, I glimpsed a distressed spirit, orange like me, ensnared by the Devil's pitchfork.

"Please, help," cried the spirit. "It could've been you."

There was a faint whiff of sulfur in the air, but I heard Deepak whisper, "The key to the gate of Heaven is empathy."

I leaped to his rescue when a mass of green vibrant energy collided into me. Asha's scent flooded my core fleetingly as I reeled and spun, bouncing over woods and dales.

"That was the dissimulating Devil, Priya!" Her voice sounded from afar. "How can you be so naïve?"

"Thanks Asha!"

The good soul. If Heaven would only see past her greenness.

The air resonated with unrest. The Devil's nets tumbled across the clouds with their booty of lost souls, snagging on their brilliant white tufts, tearing them apart.

Did he take Asha?

I raced helter-skelter for a glimpse of her, now plummeting, now soaring.

"About time you hid yourself at No.7." Deepak's stern reminder jolted through my core. "You saw for yourself what can happen otherwise. I can't always be quick enough—"

"Asha was," I said.

"She saved you in the nick of time. She's a brave and courageous friend, but you were supposed to go straight back to No.7, remember?" He offered to carry me to the property.

"Is Asha safe?" I protested.

"She's headed that way." He carried me away in a blaze of blinding light.

Approaching No.7, I glimpsed a knot of green spirits by Asha's house wrestling a ferocious entity, none other than my friend.

"I alone am enough," she claimed.

I started plummeting to shield her from her attackers.

It was a rash decision. I only distracted Asha, and she was swept right away by the spirits and melded into the green tangle.

"Coming?" Deepak panicked that the Devil would be upon me.

"I will wait for Asha right here. I know my friend; she'll find a way to come back." I crept away into the spaces beneath the roof tiles.

Deepak's flaring glow vanished like the wind snuffed it out.

Chapter 25

Days passed. Asha did not return home. Every other green spirit in the neighborhood flitted around carefree.

There was no sign of the Devil.

Sunny spoke with various fire debris cleanup services. They could not remove a flake of ash from the property. He returned to the UK.

Sonya confined herself to her room, reading yet another southern vampire mystery, *Dead and Gone*, a book about weres and shifters revealing their existence to the ordinary world.

At least she engages in something other than the company of the fiend.

Beneath the roof tiles above her room, I tried to stay detached from it all.

Jay's Jeep pulled into the driveway, and the fiend, still quite green, stepped out.

Jalebi left the dirty dishes in the sink and headed out to the kitchen garden. There she picked up the watering can and started watering the potted vegetables.

What prompted her to do that?

The fiend followed her out. "Hey, don't forget the flats of annuals in the greenhouse." His form-fitting T-shirt looked like it was an extension of his body. "It's time to plant them outside." He invaded her personal space by leaning in too close.

Jalebi focused on her work. "You have a gardener."

"Even then. Do everything you can to keep Bina happy, and I promise you; it'll reap rewards." His fingers wound around her waist.

"You are expecting a lot more from me than we initially agreed to." Jalebi eased away from his embrace.

"Playing hard to get, eh?" With a quick glance over his shoulder, he grabbed her and kissed her mouth. "This is for every time you're stubborn."

"Then I must keep being so." She gaped at his face. "Why are you so green?"

"It's the fetus—Meghna's. I sucked out his soul before I touched his body, making sure it did not contaminate the blood, but I guess the blood had already become tainted."

So, he aborted the baby.

"The blood was impeccably red." Jalebi squinted at his face.

She was in it too. I recalled how Meghna acted a bit strange with Jalebi since the abortion.

"Wonder how it stayed that way." He let out a long sigh of despair.

"He's the Master's child."

Why did he choose Meghna?

"I returned the soul to him safely, but you're right, Jalebi. I should have guessed the fetus would be different from other fetuses."

Jalebi's eyes oozed sympathy. "Oh, the color can be fixed. You need a full body bleach. There's a skin clinic at the intersection of West Road and Antoine. But it's not a cosmetic treatment and will be irreversible. You will be at risk of sunburn and skin cancer for the rest of your life."

The fiend scoffed. "I will never have any fatal disease."

Is he immortal? Then the curse can never be broken.

Jalebi pursed her lips; she asked no questions.

The fiend rushed to his Jeep and drove away, silent and preoccupied.

Auntie Bina stepped out of the hydro massage whirlpool bathtub, weeping copious tears.

"Jalebi?" she called.

There was no answer from the girl. The shirtless gardener had entered the kitchen from the sweltering heat of the afternoon sun to fetch himself a glass of water, and Jalebi had pounced on him.

"Here, have some chilled beer." She handed him a can.

He chugged it down. "Thanks." The froth of the beer glistened on his lips.

"Napkin?" Jalebi passed him one and tossed the empty can into the wastebasket.

The gardener wiped his mouth and held onto the napkin. "You so kind."

She flirts; he plays along.

Jalebi's gaze swept over his glistening, strapping body and stopped at the silver locket hanging around his neck. "Teach me some gardening tips."

The gardener ogled her pretty face. "Why?"

"I love gardening." She locked eyes with him. "I could free you up to meet with your girlfriend."

"I single with cat." He chuckled.

She eyeballed the locket.

He unclasped it. "I on one side, and my cat on other."

"Aww. How sweet." With a disarming smile, Jalebi blew a kiss in the direction of his chest. "Muah."

Was that kiss directed at the locket or at his heart?

The gardener watched her entranced. "How old you are?"

"Eighteen." Jalebi licked her lips. "It's my birthday today."

Is it? I doubted it very much, though she could pass off as an eighteen-year-old.

"Really?" he asked. "How you celebrate?"

Jalebi shrugged. "I am a maid. Who cares for me?"

"I do. I take you out in evening."

She hugged him. "You will?"

Auntie Bina rushed in and froze mid-stride. "Out, out, you obscene, indecent profligate," she yelled.

The gardener shot out the door.

"Don't bother coming back." Auntie Bina slammed the door shut and scowled at Jalebi. "Finish doing the dishes and leave."

The girl fell at her feet. "I was washing up when he came in and threw himself at me."

"Hey! Hey! I saw what you did. You're married. You wear a Mangalsutra."

"My husband ran away," cried Jalebi. "I have a right to be in a relationship."

"But not to throw yourself at anyone and everyone, you whore!"

I recalled Jalebi's chat with Meghna in Digha. *She's been transformed into one early on in life.*

Auntie Bina turned to go, and Jalebi grabbed her arm. "Stop." Auntie Bina unclasped her fingers and pushed her away. "Do not touch me."

"Please don't fire me."

"I will do exactly what needs to be done. Now go, finish your chores."

The fiend returned to the servant's quarter above the garage that evening, a white version of himself with distinct patches of green.

"The green's back." Jalebi's face contorted. "The Devil's color is fast."

"But it disappeared." The fiend leaped in front of the mirror. "No!"

His phone rang. He was too distraught to notice, so Jalebi picked up.

"Hello?" boomed Auntie Bina's voice on the other end of the line.

Jalebi hung up at once.

The fiend scowled. "Who was that?"

"Bina." She teared up instantly. "Hope she didn't realize I picked up."

His brows furrowed.

"The gardener tried to take advantage of me in the kitchen today, and she thought—"

"What?" He eyed her with an air of impatience.

Jalebi shrugged. "Why does it matter? You have her."

"You are carrying my baby."

Really? She avoided alcohol in Digha, but she doesn't look pregnant.

"You didn't even pay for my airfare. You made me beg Patrick."

"You stole the money from me to throw back at Leda. If you used a bit of tact, you could've stayed at their luxury ranch estate and spied on Leda."

"Spy on that sleuth? She has eyes in the back of her head. Her interrogations!" Jalebi huffed. "The last thing I want is to rot in prison. Isn't it enough that I've been your whore since I was thirteen?"

A pedophile too? He's the man Jalebi spoke about to Meghna.

His phone rang again, and this time he picked up.

"Dev?" Auntie Bina's voice was teary. "Where are you? I am missing you so much."

"Me too. Just got back and realized I left my wallet behind at the store I stopped at. I must go find it." The fiend hung up on her.

The fiend was in full makeup when he stepped into his bedroom that night.

"Hey." He greeted Auntie Bina cheerily. "How are you doing?"

"Dev!" She took a long drag on her cigarette and then crushed the butt beneath her heel. "I am disgusted by Jalebi's inappropriate bantering with her man."

"Her man?" The fiend nearly jumped out of his skin.

"The gardener. I fired him."

"Excellent," he said. "I cannot commend you enough on your wise decision. All you must do now is take that young woman—she's barely budded—and mold her into a maid befitting your household."

Auntie Bina limped across to the bar and poured herself a drink. "Want one?" She glanced over her shoulder at him.

He nodded, dropping down on the ivory-white, velvet-upholstered chaise and hugging the throw pillow.

It's like he's embracing all that lovely wealth.

"How long have you known the girl?" Auntie Bina lumbered back with two overfull tumblers.

"Found her on Care.com. I could fire her and get another."

"No, as long as you give her a telling off, and ask her to be more respectful. Otherwise, she is okay." She handed him a glass.

"Cheers." The fiend raised his cup.

They clinked their glasses, and she perched on his lap. "Calumet Farm Single Rack Black—the best bourbon available in Houston."

He touched the glass to his lips. "Mmmm."

Auntie Bina visibly relaxed. "You bring back the thrill of romance that has been absent from my life. How much luckier could an old woman get at this stage of her life?"

Chapter 26

Ⅰ must have confined myself to the space beneath the roof tiles at Asha's house for an eternity when I glimpsed Leda, Patrick, and Meghna approaching the house in Leda's Audi.

Leda hung up on Sunny and shoved her phone into her handbag. "Sunny is upset because Nikita is reluctant to return to London to pursue her studies. She is trying to go back to Harvard. Sunny does not like the idea, and they've been arguing."

It's always one thing or the other. The curse will allow them no peace.

"Hmmm." Patrick stared at the road ahead. "Has he patched up his differences with his sister?"

"Um—"

I drifted out of my hidey-hole unwittingly, and Leda glanced out the window.

"This used to be Priya's friend's house." Leda pointed in my direction. "Sunny gave me the address. I have a feeling Sonya lives here."

The car drove past the gates.

"You have your yoga-date with her this Saturday," said Patrick. "You can ask her then."

Leda nodded half-heartedly.

Is she having second thoughts about attending the session?

"Yoga and lunch—I doubt Leda will remember to ask." Meghna sulked. "I'm getting so tired of my life."

Leda and Patrick exchanged glances.

"You can go to another yoga class later with Leda," said Patrick.

"I need a job more than anything." Meghna blinked.

"Of course." Leda smiled warmly.

"You can work as a nurse, but you might have to do a course," said Patrick.

"That will cost a lot of money," Meghna cried. "Why would you pay for me? I can't give you the baby you wanted, and I would not like to get pregnant again."

"Very well, come and work in my factory," Patrick said. "With a nurse's meticulous attention to detail, you would be well-suited for a role in quality control, where you would inspect products for defects and verify they meet all company and industry standards."

A tear snaked down Meghna's cheek. "What have I done to deserve this—the pair of you?"

"I am not taking you on the girls' day out." Leda's eyes were pensive.

If only I could mind-read like Deepak.

The day of the invitation to the yoga studio finally dawned.

Sonya and I arrived early. She went in, I lingered in the car.

It's so much easier to watch the girls from here without having to bother about my disguise or getting involved.

Leda appeared at the parking lot exactly fifteen minutes before eleven and parked behind Sonya's Corolla.

Sonya stepped out and greeted her with a hug. "Thanks for coming."

"Thanks for inviting me." Leda glanced around. "It's very quiet here."

"It gets busier in the afternoon. I take solo yoga lessons for increased focus and a deeper connection with my body." Sonya beamed. "Let's go up to the studio and wait. Mr. Zayn, my instructor, is running late."

What if Zayn is the fiend? The sorcerer is incredibly versatile.

Sonya handed Leda a two-piece slimming yoga suit in a sealed bag.

Leda broke the seal with a firm pull and checked out the suit. "Wow! Half zipper long sleeves with thumb holes top and high-waisted pants. Thank you!"

"Thanks for coming," said Sonya. "Let's change so we don't waste a moment. It's an hour-long session. Once we're done, we'll whizz off to a restaurant of your choice."

"Lunch is on me," said Leda.

"Sure."

They changed and waited for Zayn in the studio.

It had an irregular quadrilateral shape. One corner was terribly acute, and another hideously obtuse. There was no furniture in the room, except for a small, simple wooden chest of drawers, under the one and only window, seemingly lost in the ginormous space.

Leda gravitated toward the Kamishikimi Kumano-imasu shrine mural opposite the window. "Wow!" She scrutinized the intricate details and vibrant colors that created a unique focal point.

Sonya produced some candles and planted them in pivotal positions within the room. As she lit them, a frantic, drab, greenish blob passed through them.

Asha's scent flooded my core. *Is Asha here?*

Before I knew it, I was sucked out of Sonya's car and hurled to the floor of the studio. The blob moved over me in a coordinated pattern more like a disco light than a spirit. Too late I discovered that the wall mural emitted shades of green lights, intermittently, creating an impression of a roving spirit.

But the scent? Is that a trick too?

The dancing flames hissed and towered over me, tall and strong. Curls of smoke twirled into my path, drowning me in their midst. I flailed and floundered, rising with the hot air.

My disguise fell away. The wisps of smoke sank into my glow, each one cutting deep into my core as if to claim pieces of it. I felt something like being quartered, the grisly penalty awarded in medieval England for the crime of treason. The only difference was that in the yoga studio, I was tugged at from more than four directions, mid-air.

Sonya's face was expressionless, like she knew what she was doing but was remorseless.

My despair was overwhelming when a gusty wind caught me and tossed me against the window, open just a crack. In moments, I was outside, bolting to the clouds.

The window banged shut.

Who opened the window? Not like Sonya would do it sneakily. She doesn't seem to have feelings for me anymore.

Mr. Zayn arrived well past eleven in a taxi, in the same suit that Sonya and Leda wore. Only his was gray, which became his svelte physique. Strangely drawn to his outdoorsy scent, I clung to the clouds with all my might.

The man looked by no means familiar, and his cheerful accent was quaint. Yet when he wished the girls, "Good morning," the basic sound produced by the vocal fold confirmed my suspicions.

He is the fiend. How horrible of Sonya to bring Leda to him!

Leda visibly relaxed. Her scar did not seem to react.

Does the yoga suit block the fiend's aura from the scar just like it hides the wound from me? Sonya knows how the scar's reaction alerts Leda to the fiend's presence. Is that why she gave Leda the suit?

Sonya had become truly and completely the fiend's ally. *For shame!*

"So who have we today?" the fiend grinned.

"My friend, Leda," Sonya's voice betrayed no emotion.

"Namaste." His voice was deep and mellow.

"Namaste," echoed Leda.

The fiend grinned. "Any idea what it means?"

"I bow to you, you bow to me," said Sonya.

"Good," applauded the fiend. "It basically means that the teacher in me honors the teacher in you."

Leda nodded.

"Now, get comfortable, girls. You can lie down if you like."

"I'll lie down," said Sonya.

"I'll sit," said Leda. "It is very kind of you to let me join Sonya this morning, Mr. Zayn. I would like to let you know that I am a complete beginner, curious about yoga practice and all its wonderful benefits."

"Well then, I have a great sequence for you." He watched Leda warily. "Right now, I would like you to close your eyes. Concentrate on outside sounds. Hear that cuckoo? Listen to it."

Sonya lay perfectly still.

How can she possibly be at peace with herself?

A smile plastered on the fiend's face. "Bring your attention onto yourself, your head, your shoulders, your arms, the trunk of your body, your legs, and your feet."

Sonya tweaked a strand of hair into place.

That betrays a pang of conscience.

"Sonya, relax. You're stiffening. Adjust your position if necessary."

She said nothing.

The fiend glanced at Leda. "Now what is your favorite activity?"

Leda picked up her cell phone and peered down at the screen. "Checking my phone."

"That is an addiction not an activity. Could you please turn it off?"

Leda did with a quick word of apology.

"Your next favorite activity?"

"Cycling."

"Mine too," said Sonya.

"Imagine you're cycling, gazing into the distant skyline. Ride toward it, and let your deep, rhythmic pedaling lull you into a state of profound calm."

Sonya and Leda closed their eyes.

"Choose your preferred place of retreat. Your sanctuary should be somewhere, real or imagined, where you can feel calm and relaxed. It may be a beach, a bower in a garden, a mountain path—idyllic, restful." The fiend's voice was clear and warm. "Enter your sanctuary, the place of perfect tranquility. The air is sweet, the sun is shining in the brilliant blue sky, the birds are singing. Find a nook." He circled Leda with his arms folded and his eyes narrowed at the left elasticized cuff of her top.

Leda's eyes sprang open.

He smiled. "You have become tranquility." His voice was controlled though his nostrils flared. "You are now at the center of your being. You are one with everything around you. You are part of nature and in harmony with yourself and your environment. You are totally free." His gaze dropped on Leda, and she squeezed her eyes shut.

He returned to his mat. "Sit up, girls, and look at me." He sat down and crossed his legs. "Now, I will show you the Sukhasana—the pose of ease. Repeat after me slowly and steadily." He touched his toes with his fingertips.

The girls mirrored his posture.

He inhaled looping forward, and exhaled grounding down and back. "Slide your hands over your thighs and knees, gently, breathing in and breathing out."

The girls replicated the sequence of poses. Leda eyed his joints fleetingly, and then his face.

Is she trying to gauge his age?

"Now, move one ear over one shoulder, then repeat with the other ear. Go forward into the chest and up. You will find that you are saying 'yes' and 'no' with your body. Repeat with your arms reaching up, repeat with arms to the side, then arms to your hips."

The girls obeyed.

"Deepen your breath, nice and deep. Inhale in and exhale out." The sound of his breathing, amplified by my heightened senses, tormented me for what felt like hours up in the clouds.

The girls focused.

"Now, draw your palms together at the sternum, and lift your hearts up to your chest. This posture is called the 'Anjali mudra.' Anjali means 'divine offering.'" His liquid latex mask glowed. He looked like a saint before some God as he joined his palms in reverence.

I marveled at his health, his vibrancy, and energy. *The octogenarian! In India he fed off embryo blood from abducted women every day. Here he just had Meghna's fetus.*

Leda narrowed her eyes at his face.

Is she putting her detective cap on?

"So," the fiend's voice cut through my thoughts, "let's practice this mudra." He pulled in his stomach to meet his spine. "I bow to the divinity within you from the divinity within me."

The girls repeated it.

"Wonderful!" He interlaced his fingers. "As you inhale, pull the palms forward, up, and back. On your next inhale, release those fingertips, and drop them. Inhale again, forward, up, and back." He whistled mischievously instead of breathing, eliciting a grin from the girls.

Even as Leda and Sonya performed the movements with elegance and ease, he glanced furtively at Leda's left wrist.

It's like he can see the scar.

Unaware, Leda followed his instructions to a T.

His lips held a faint smile. "Good. Good." He glanced at the clock and turned on some calming instrumental music. "It's nearly time. Practice with this. I'll be right back to decide when I can squeeze you two in for another session."

His phone chirped. "That must be from home. Sorry, got to go. Happy moving!" he sang along to the music and disappeared out the door.

The girls practiced the moves diligently until the clock struck noon.

"I think we should stop now and grab some lunch," said Sonya.

"Sure." Leda beamed.

They rushed to the changing rooms, but at the threshold Sonya's phone buzzed. "Leda," she said, "you change. Zayn wants me downstairs."

She rushed away, and Leda struggled to peel off the yoga suit in the changing room. She burst out of her cubicle, shouting, "Sonya, help, the cuff of the left sleeve is stuck."

Alas, the elevator had already begun its descent.

Terrified for her, I started plummeting from my cloud, only to realize I could not stop. I landed at the entrance of the building.

The fiend's gasp resounded through my core. In the nick of time, I dodged a grabber stick he thrust in my path, but not the pungent spray it squirted. The spatter thickened, fiery-hot as lava.

I struggled to break free from a strong force tugging me upward.

Down below, the elevator opened in the lobby.

Sonya ran out screaming in a state of panic, "L-Leda is on the phone—"

The fiend seized the device and smacked her butt. "Get to the car."

They blurred in the black smoke, billowing around me in growing plumes.

In the scorching heat and overwhelming stench, I sank into an all-engulfing numbness.

Chapter 27

The sun had set when I came around, snug within the body of a large black witch moth.

When did I transform into this creature?

Tall trees surrounded me. A soft breeze carried the sweet fragrance of Dogwood flowers to my core still weak from my ordeal.

How on earth did I get here?

I remembered being lifted up by some force. *Did the fiend's spray fail to achieve its purpose?*

The more I thought about the incident, the more the depth of Sonya's betrayal disoriented me. Those core beliefs: "she loves me," "she has my back," "I can trust her completely," crumbled to dust. *When will she come to her senses?*

Dusk fell. My sad thoughts added to the gloom. *How did Sonya get so evil?*

A gleam sliced through the murkiness. It intensified into a dazzle, igniting the hedgerows. Their boughs arced into the light spreading like dawn in the black heavens.

Another day already! I struggled to shut out those billion eyes of light.

"It's only me."

"Deepak!"

The most brilliant of mosaics, reflected from each leaf.

"How do you like your new disguise?"

"So it was your doing." I searched for him in the gold tessellations. "I thought you had forgotten about me."

"Forgotten about you? I've been trying to revive you since I brought you down here five days ago. I'm sorry, Priya. I was assigned some duties in Heaven that kept me very busy of late." He apologized profusely. "How did you manage to get yourself in that barbaric contraption in the yoga studio?"

"The fiend numbed me with a spray. I remember going up, but not where or how I came to rest. Perhaps it took me all the way to the studio. It all started up there. Sonya invited Leda over to a yoga session with the fiend after everything he did to her. I don't know what has become of her. Perhaps the fiend is controlling her mind. She is pure evil."

"But she was not in the picture when I arrived. You were stretched in so many different directions that your glow was blurry. Your core was almost severed from you."

"The fiend is after it." I shuddered.

"It must be your radiance that's tempting him. He tried to pinch me when I rushed out of the studio with you and got singed by my cladding. He ran for his dear life—hang on. What's this?" He touched my core gently. "You have the first mirror ball of the cladding. It's rudimentary and evolving."

All I saw was a tiny bubble, I had not noticed before, rippling away reflections of his glow. *Is this what the fiend photographed at Budget Stay?*

I told Deepak about the incident.

"It must've been more insignificant when he spotted it. But he did notice it."

"How many must I develop before I go to Heaven?"

"No idea. My first bubble popped up in Heaven. You must be very careful with that mirror ball. Dev might try to steal it."

"Won't this thingy repel him? Your cladding wards off the Devil."

"Not until you have millions clustered together in a complete cladding, but I've seen spirits use solitary ones in other ways. Say, if you want to follow someone somewhere or find out what is happening at that place, you can detach the mirror ball from your core and send it there. It's called 'transveho.' It will instantly feel like you're travelling with the ball." Even as he spoke two new mirror balls sprouted.

"The bubbles look like they're fused with my glow."

"They are actually very loosely attached to the outside of your core. Use one at a time. State the location or the person you wish to send it to in two clear words, then spin your core repeatedly until the bubble falls off."

"But will it come back to me afterward?"

"No. It has its limitations. If I were you, I would wait to use it only after I had sprouted many, many more."

"I want to find out the reason for Sonya's loyalty to the fiend."

"Priya, please. Sonya knows what she is doing. I see a new determination in her, a quiet confidence, even joy, like she's on a mission and on the way to accomplishing it."

"She did mention a mission in her text to Sunny from the Red Lake house. But what mission? Not like the fiend will revoke the curse."

"Perhaps the Dev guy has given her some kind of reassurance."

"Reassurance? Sonya is not stupid. She knows the man for who he is."

"What if she's made a deal with him, something like she brings Leda to him, and he lifts the spell he cast on your family? After all Leda is prying into his life and trying to get him arrested."

"That is possible. If it is, how selfish and ungrateful of Sonya. Sonya has changed so much since she went to live with the fiend. She knew the scar reacted in his presence, so she gave Leda an outfit that blocked his aura from it. Poor Leda had no idea that the yoga instructor was him. She went into the changing room at the end of the session and struggled to remove the jacket. The cuff stuck to her wrist like a second skin. Goodness knows what became of her."

"Where was Sonya?"

"In the elevator. I plummeted all the way down, goodness knows how, and the fiend trapped me with the spray."

"And that transported you up into the yoga studio, exactly in the middle of the candles."

"But they had been extinguished."

"Someone reignited them. The sorcerer of course. It would just take him a mantra to do it."

"For a moment I thought it was Sonya. She's become such a slave."

"No! Don't blame her for everything. Sometimes, the only way to free oneself of a curse is to get really close to the man that cast it."

"But he will never—"

"Not directly, but she might be snooping around to find information about him, his activities, spells, antithesis of curses. And she can do that only if he has complete trust in her."

"I don't think you understand his diabolical nature, Deepak. He's demonic, and he has complete control over her. If only I could eavesdrop on them, find out what's going on."

"Don't, please. It could lead you into doing something drastic."

"Deepak, you know how difficult it is to remain passive—"

The sunlight sauntered in in honeyed tones, beautiful and soothing.

"Do you feel strong enough to fly?" he asked me.

"Y-yes."

We skipped, we flitted, we dove, we soared, and as we glided over Leda's house, he blended in the sunshine.

Chapter 28

The delicious aroma of wheat flour frying in hot ghee and egg curry wafted around Leda's luxury ranch estate. Meghna was cooking in the kitchen.

Leda sat on the back porch in her pajamas, sipping coffee out of a chunky pottery mug while watching birds flock to her bird feeder.

I crept into the downspout.

Leda's phone rang. She glanced at the caller id. It said "Anonymous."

She still responded to the call. "Hello."

"Hi." It was Sonya.

What has the girl got to say for herself?

"Sonya?" Leda's voice lacked its usual warmth.

"Yes. How are you?" Sonya chirped. "I'm sorry for disappearing on you after the yoga session. Mr. Zayn's wife had been admitted to the hospital, and he asked me to drive him there ASAP."

The lies!

Leda scowled. "Where did you buy the yoga outfits?"

"Online. Why?"

"Who is this Mr. Zayn really?" asked Leda.

"I don't really understand what you are trying to say."

"Sonya," Leda inhaled deeply. "I have reason to believe that Mr. Zayn is Dev."

Sonya swallowed.

"You and the fiend planned it well, especially that outfit."

"What was wrong with it? We all wore the exact same suit."

It's hard to tell if she is faking it.

"Did you or Mr. Zayn have problems removing the jacket?"

"I didn't. I don't know about him." Sonya sounded surprised. "Did you?

"Yes, I struggled. I was frantic. The left sleeve clung to the scar. Perhaps it stopped the scar from reacting to his presence during the session." Leda drew a sharp breath. "Did you get that outfit so that I didn't find out that Mr. Zayn was the fiend in disguise?

"No."

"Did you tell Dev that the scar alerted me to his presence?"

"I did not." Sonya's voice choked.

She may not be lying now, but she did bring Leda to the fiend with many a lie.

"Then why did you leave me just as it was time to change? You seemed to vanish."

"How was I to know you would have problems with the sleeve? As I said, I had to take Mr. Zayn to the hospital to see his wife. She was critically ill." Sonya sighed.

She's lying through her teeth. She must've known about the sleeve.

"You did not reply to my calls or my texts."

She had an excuse for that. The fiend took away the new phone she had been communicating with Leda on. *What happened to her old phone?*

"I'm sorry, but I was racing down the street like a maniac," Sonya said convincingly. "So how did you take that thing off?"

"I couldn't. I ran downstairs screaming for help. There was not a soul in the lobby or even another car in the parking lot."

Sonya swallowed. "Then?"

"Even as I struggled, it peeled off, sleeve and all, like there hadn't been a problem with it at all."

"Oh, so it was purely nerves."

Is it possible that she's completely ignorant about the nature of the suit?

"Sonya, I know what I experienced. I am certain the sleeve cuff messed with the scar and blocked the fiend's aura."

"All the suits came in sealed bags. You saw that for yourself. You don't always have an explanation for everything. Strange things have happened to me; it's the curse."

"You blame everything on the curse." Leda's mug shook in her trembling hand. She dumped it on the coffee table.

"Well, you could too." Sonya gave a little laugh. "Hey, why don't we talk about this over a cup of coffee? I could pick you up today. I'm here for a few hours. There are some nice coffee places in your neighborhood."

I did not see or smell her.

"Sorry, Sonya." The birds squawked and screamed crowding around, drowning out Leda's voice.

A blackness like carbon dust crept among the birds, melding into the ash bat.

Leda flinched, dropping her phone. The scar shifted on her wrist. It looked like something throbbed within.

"Leda? Leda?" Sonya cried.

Leda writhed.

"Leda, I need to see you," Sonya's voice trailed.

Don't Leda's groans concern Sonya?

The scar glowed like hot coal.

Leda whimpered.

I could not but rush out of the downspout.

The ash bat charged at me. She bared my core. "Wow, Priya! How orange you glow!" The coldness in Hema's voice stung.

"What have you got planned for Leda?" I dared.

The bat's lips pulled back revealing her enormous fangs. "A scare she will remember."

The scar on Leda's wrist swayed menacingly, cutting deeper and deeper into her skin. Blood oozed out of it. She rolled off the sofa, unconscious.

The bat perched on her arm, flashing her vampire teeth. "Too interfering, too analytical. We don't like her type."

Thankfully, the patio door opened just then, and Meghna emerged with a solid wood rolling pin in her hand. "Leda, Patrick isn't back from Trader Joe's. Should I start frying the parathas—?" Her gaze drifted to Leda on the floor with the ash bat on her arm. She tried to strike the bat with the utensil.

The bat screamed, dashing around in a vicious frenzy.

Meghna hurled the kitchen tool in her direction.

The bat disintegrated into a pile of ashes that dispersed in the bright sunshine. Miles away, they coalesced into a dense black cloud reminiscent of a giant mouse and drifted in a southeasterly direction.

I will track her. "Follow bat," I cried to one of my mirror balls.

As I spun my core, the ball burst. I tried detaching another. It fell away with little effort. At once, it felt like I chased after the bat.

Before long, the jetties of Galveston came into sight. Upon the seawall, the cloud tightened into a bat shape, complete with ears, fangs, and limbs. Her vocal membranes vibrated at extremely high frequencies, and Hema's voice emerged in chirps and squeaks. She folded her wings and withdrew into her own cocoon of velvety dark.

The beach stretched before me with its towering waves, creamy foam, and barnacled rocks. Hiding among them were a few stones decorated with chalk wildflowers—a far cry from the host of red-orange Indian paintbrush, fluttering and dancing in the breeze. The stones smelled strongly of the ocean and faintly of Sonya.

This looks like Sonya's artwork.

The pictures blurred and faded, and the sound of Patrick's heavy footsteps thundered through my core.

Did the ball perish?

"Come quick, Patrick." Meghna's voice trembled in the foyer of Leda's house. She struggled to explain what she had witnessed. "Leda has fainted. She might have been bitten by the bat."

"The sorcerer's bat?" came Patrick's high-pitched reply. "Where is the brat?"

"She scattered," she stuttered, dripping with sweat. "The ash scattered."

Patrick rushed out onto the patio. He crouched over Leda, and she stirred. Her face was like a marble slate.

He carried her indoors. "What happened? How's the scar?".

It looked like an ordinary burn wound just like it had before the bat's assault.

"It hurt like it does when Dev or the bat is close." Leda took a shuddering breath.

"Did the bat bite you?" asked Patrick.

She shook her head.

Patrick glanced around. "Was Dev here?"

"I just saw the bat."

"Meghna, can you put the kettle on, please?" said Patrick. "Make us some delicious masala chai while I run and fetch the red velvet cake from the car. What Leda needs is a sugar-fix.

Chapter 29

The intense day ended on a lighter note. Patrick encouraged Leda and Meghna to make a trip to Highland Park Village for a girls' night out.

"It will take your mind off the sorcerer's nuisance," he said.

The women took his advice and left.

Patrick remained at home.

I stayed back too in the downspout, debating what I should do with my third and last mirror ball. It hung precariously off my core, threatening to drop off at any moment. With careful thought, I transvehoed it to Asha's house with the instructions "Auntie Bina."

That is where the action is.

Auntie Bina lay on her bed, her face as passive as if she were asleep.

The door creaked open, and the fiend entered, strikingly attractive in a Mark Zuckerberg T-shirt. He held a glass of frothy milk in his hand.

"Bina," he called. "Bina, my darling. Have your milk."

To what does she owe this act of kindness?

"Dev?" She sat up with a jerk. "Where were you? I waited for you all night."

"In your sleep?" He laughed out loud. "I was here all the time."

"Oh, Dev. You make it sound like I sleep all the time." She loosened a deep sigh. "Sonya hasn't come home in five days."

She must be in Galveston. The artwork on the stones was hers.

"And you have waited for her too in your sleep?" He chuckled.

"I don't really sleep all that much, Dev. I have been awake all day today. You could ask Sunny and Paul. I bumped into them at Whole Foods. Even they don't know where Sonya is."

"I trust you Bina. I don't need to ask anyone." I hated the evil glint in his eye. "Perhaps the milk is helping. That is why you must drink plenty of milk." He handed her the glass. "Drink up."

"Thanks, Dev." She sighed, rubbing the back of her neck. "You haven't seen Sonya the last five days, have you?"

"Can't remember. Might have."

Perhaps he's hiding her in Galveston, scent-free, in the invisibility guise.

Alas, I had no mirror balls left to check that out. And I could not risk a visit. Knowing the person Sonya had turned into, I feared she might surprise me with some novel, torturous spirit trap where I least expected.

"You must promise to find her for me." Auntie Bina pouted.

"Of course, dear." He was the epitome of tenderness. "Now drink up your milk."

She did not see through his smile and drained the glass. "I am so worried about Sonya. She always texts when she goes somewhere. It's been days. If she doesn't call or text in the next few hours, we should do something about it." She yawned.

He laid her back against the pillows with a kiss. "Sonya has friends here. She grew up in Houston, and she is an adult."

"Even then." Auntie Bina closed her eyes and fell asleep almost at once holding his finger.

The fiend eased it away, shoved the bottle of Valium that stood by the milk-stained spoon on the kitchen counter into his pocket, picked up a gift bag he had hidden deep inside a kitchen cabinet, and rushed up to the servant's quarter above the garage.

"Happy Birthday!" he sang.

Jalebi sashayed up to him, in a short, revealing, red sequin "devil" style dress. Her messy hair was pulled back into a loose bun with a few strands hanging loose.

The fiend gulped, almost forgetting to give her his present.

But Jalebi's gaze wandered over the giftbag, and she let out a little squeal. "Nordstrom!"

The fiend pulled out a Loro Piana Hedge cashmere and silk stole from the bag. "Like navy?" He held it up.

"Love it."

He turned her around and draped it over her shoulders. "Beautiful mother of my unborn baby." His hands strayed to squeeze her breasts over the sequin dress.

Wouldn't a father-to-be take this opportunity to caress the belly?

Jalebi giggled. "Does your missus know?"

She's too charmed by him to even suspect.

"She sleeps." He shook his head.

Jalebi shot him a reproachful pout.

He grinned. "All in good time. Right now, I am in the process of making a complete inventory of all our marital property and assets as the first step towards getting the most out of the divorce settlement. When filing a divorce through the County Court, I will have to submit a Family Law Financial Affidavit, detailing our incomes, expenses, and everything we have earned, purchased, or otherwise acquired over the course of the marriage. I must ensure I get my share, I mean yours and mine, of everything: earnings, savings, real property, vehicles, household furnishings, collectibles, and personal belongings." His lewd gaze swept over her. "You're so worth it."

The scoundrel!

Jalebi laced her hands with his, a hundred words of love smiled behind her diamond eyes. Their foreheads met, then their noses and lips. What happened next was the most earth-shattering passionate kiss possible.

"Jalebi!" Auntie Bina yelled.

I thought I smelled Ruby, and Nikita dashed down the main staircase.

When did she get here? It's not like she's expected.

Her phone chimed with a text from Sunny:

Hi Nikita.

We need to start looking for Sonya seriously, Nikita replied, flying out the door. I've searched everywhere after Paul told me, and I'm scared. She seems to be nowhere. I don't understand how you can be so indifferent.

So she is here to look for Sonya. Nikita really cares about her. Sunny used to . . .

Auntie Bina dragged herself to the living area. "Jalebi," she called so loud that its echo lasted several seconds.

The fiend almost jumped. "The hag's up. I must be going before she barges in here."

"No." Jalebi held onto him.

"Let go." He gave her a gentle push. "And shush about everything that passed between us. Everything."

He raced down the backstairs and Auntie Bina grabbed him at the entrance to the kitchen. "You are here? Then who is in the lounge upstairs? Jalebi?"

"In the lounge?" The fiend bellowed and rushed up the main stairs.

Auntie Bina followed.

They switched on the light, illuminating the gleaming furniture. The room was quiet as a graveyard.

Auntie Bina whizzed around. "Everything seems intact."

The fiend inhaled deeply. "Jasmine, lavender—a rich floral scent."

There was a slight whiff of Estée Lauder's Beyond Paradise in the air

Auntie Bina sniffed, then sniffed again, taking in every nuance and detail of the fragrance. "I don't know if I am hallucinating, but I think I can smell Ruby's signature perfume." Her eyes glistened.

The fiend's forehead wrinkled. "Ruby?"

"You know Ruby—Nikita's mom."

"Does Nikita have the keys to this house?" The fiend scowled.

"Of course. She was like a daughter to Asha and Jay. But she is not even in the city,"

"Oh, yes, she is. I was in her neighborhood and saw her drive in and out of that property!"

"Why would Nikita steal into this house?"

"God knows what she has up her sleeve," he muttered.

"What?" asked Auntie Bina.

"She doesn't show you her face because she's too embarrassed. You spent a fortune on her dahej. I would call it reckless spending."

She sighed. "Dev, we're both guilty of it."

The fiend's brows scrunched. "I have to go out."

"Keep your expenses at a minimum," cried Auntie Bina. "I was going through our joint account. Did you spend four grand at the mall in the last couple of days?"

The fiend closed his eyes and shook his head. "Now don't force me to give away your birthday gift. I'm sorry I still have to use your credit card. One of my houses in India sold for forty lakhs, and I'm expecting the sale proceeds to be deposited into my bank account in Kolkata within the next few days. Would you prefer to have the money converted to dollars and transferred to our joint account here?"

Auntie Bina side-eyed him with a sigh. "Yours or mine, we have to spend our money wisely."

His phone chimed with a text from Jalebi.

Where's the hag?

He hastily switched off his phone, kicking the mirror ball unwittingly.

It struck the wall. The room blurred for a second and then became clear again.

"Who messaged you?" Auntie Bina snatched the device from his hand. "This thing no doubt is the Devil's handiwork. First you get addicted to it, lose your mind, and then wallow in financial indiscipline. My birthday is in July. I don't understand why you're on this shopping binge already. Money is running out of our account like water. The work the Devil makes for idle hands!"

"The temper he puts into old wives!" he muttered.

Jalebi giggled.

When did she get here?

"Get out, whore!" Auntie Bina shrieked, then lashed out at the fiend. "The Devil take you! I shall stop all your allowances and then you can fetch your money from India."

A punch to the gut!

"I can leave you alone if it would make you feel better, or I can stay, and we could leave the Devil alone." Before Auntie Bina could reply, he grabbed her face and planted a quick kiss on her mouth.

Auntie Bina melted. "Jalebi's staring," she whispered.

"Hey, you! Off you go!" The fiend seized Jalebi by the shoulder and pushed her out.

She stumbled to the door.

"Go," he spat and kicked her.

How vile!

The familiar smile Auntie Bina reserved for him was back on her features, though her teary eyes and trembling body did not match the brightness of her grin. "The girl's got to go."

He eased away his phone from her grip. "Sounds like a good idea."

Auntie Bina sniveled. "I really hate the person I'm turning into. We're in a fresh relationship. It's that blissful period where everything should be about love, but instead—" She clapped her hand over her mouth, as if she was trying to contain her feelings within her throat.

He pulled her flush against him, trailing kisses down her neck. "You are too wonderful to be true."

He's the greatest dissembler that ever existed!

She broke into a low, heart-rending wail. "If you only knew about my insecurities, my fears! I don't make a good wife."

"That's so not true." He held her as she wept. "If perfection was a person, it would be you."

The mirror ball popped, and Asha's house disappeared.

Chapter 30

Patrick paced the patio, absorbed in his own thoughts. Twilight faded to black, and he relocated indoors to search the internet for any information on black magic. When Leda and Meghna returned from their shopping spree, he was immersed in an article about sorcery.

"You can't get it out of your head, can you?" Leda asked him. "I have spoken to my aunt. She promised to send some antidotes. Now come help me in the kitchen. We're making pasta. It's so therapeutic."

Patrick obliged, albeit reluctantly. He made the dough, kneaded it, and refrigerated it.

Leda mixed the ricotta, parmesan, mozzarella and provolone cheeses, an egg, and dried parsley together and set the filling aside.

Neither spoke.

Patrick made the sauce, then whisked in the parmesan, his face twisted in a frown.

Leda rolled out the dough into sheets, prepared the individual ravioli. "We had a nice day out. Thanks for suggesting it."

Patrick merely nodded.

Leda boiled the ravioli, drained well, and mixed in the thick, creamy sauce. Just as she arranged the pasta envelopes on the baking tray and sprinkled them with parmesan, Paul called.

"Hi," he said. "I am in town and thought I'd drop by if it's no problem for you."

"We would be delighted."

"Thanks."

Leda hung up. "Paul is in town," she said to Patrick. She set another place at the table.

Patrick's expression relaxed. "I'll sauté some brussels sprouts and bacon, the perfect sides for our ravioli."

Leda torched her crème brûlées and Paul arrived. He looked miserable.

"How's your leg?" asked Patrick.

"Never mind my leg. Sonya has gone missing." Paul pursed his lips, blinking furiously.

Oh, Paul!

"I saw Sonya at the yoga studio five days ago," said Leda. "She invited me to a yoga class. And she called me from an anonymous phone this morning offering me another day out with her."

"Really!" Paul's gaze shot to Leda. "From where?"

"She said she was passing through Dallas."

Paul sighed. "She was last seen five days ago. I believe she was staying with Bina in Asha's house. Sunny and I bumped into Bina at Whole Foods earlier today. Apparently, Sonya left for some work five days ago and hasn't been back since. She has not texted or called."

Funny Auntie Bina doesn't suspect her husband.

"Sonya will turn up." Meghna sniggered. "Not like she hasn't gone missing before."

She is still full of anger and bitterness about Randy's partiality toward Sonya.

Leda elbowed her firmly, but Meghna wasn't one to shut up easily.

"The times Sonya disappeared in Digha, bet she actually met up with Dev," Meghna rambled on, "and now she's living with him. The yoga instructor, Mr. Zayn, was him. Sonya lied to Leda."

Paul looked away, his face so sad.

"I feel scared for the girl," said Patrick. "The sorcerer is a dangerous man."

Paul met his gaze. "Why would Sonya go to the fiend? She knows he's a rogue."

"It surprises me too," said Leda, "since now she is free from the spell. Rao deflected the spell from her and Sunny, and it hit me."

Paul inhaled sharply. "I'm so sorry, Leda, about the scar, but—"

"That creature, Dev's ash bat, was here earlier today and attacked Leda," said Meghna.

"Really?" Paul frowned. "Could Sonya have gone on a mission to rid you of the curse, Leda? She isn't scared to risk her life for those she loves."

If only Paul knew how much Sonya has changed.

Leda lowered her eyes.

Patrick opened his mouth to say something then shut it almost at once.

"You've got it all so wrong, Paul," Meghna blurted out. "Sonya took Leda to Uncle Dev. She gave her a yoga suit that blocked his aura from her scar, so she could not tell it was him. No one knows better than Sonya that the scar's reaction to the fiend alerts Leda to his presence."

Paul stiffened.

"Let's start dinner." Patrick glanced at the clock.

Meghna carried the ravioli with all the sides to the table and arranged them neatly on serving dishes.

Everyone helped themselves to the meal in silence.

"Do you think Sonya might have struck a deal with this Dev guy?" said Paul suddenly.

Meghna smirked. "And the fiend has sealed the deal for her soul."

"Meghna, could you please check if the brûlées are ready?" Leda asked.

She disappeared only to reappear almost at once. "They are."

"Thanks," whispered Leda.

Patrick devoured the ravioli on his plate and helped himself to some more. "I have a feeling that Sonya still feels the impact of the curse."

Paul nodded. "Me too."

"There was a lot at stake," continued Patrick. "Her happiness, Sunny's happiness. While we were in Digha, she spoke to me about the situation and how she felt guilty that Sunny had to suffer because of her indiscretion."

"But Sunny is back with Nikita." Leda smiled.

Paul shook his head. "Not really."

Leda's brows scrunched.

I could imagine her surprise. She had seen Sunny and Nikita together not so long ago.

"If Sonya has struck a deal with Dev, she will never get what she bargained for," Leda said softly. "The man is crafty and dangerous and has tricked her before."

Paul shifted uneasily in his chair. "That is precisely what I've been thinking. Why is she taking such a huge risk? He has isolated her from everyone; he can do anything to her."

"She knows some way to sweeten the deal," Meghna chirped in.

Leda glared at Meghna, and the nurse rephrased her sentence. "I mean she could be giving him something that he desperately needs."

"Like?" Paul glowered at her.

"He needs help with the ways of the western world, and someone who can bring Leda to him. Sonya would serve both purposes."

"Listening to you, Meghna, it feels kind of silly that I can't catch him." Leda sighed. "He is not a vulnerable octogenarian."

A grim silence fell over the table.

Leda slipped into the kitchen and returned with the crème brûlées. "I really should not have refused Sonya's offer of another day out with her."

Thank goodness she did!

"Good for you." Patrick heaved a sigh. "No doubt, Dev would get involved. Promise me, you'll stay away from him, Leda."

There was an awkward pause in the conversation. Leda took a breath and looked her husband directly in the eye, "I must do my job, Patrick."

Chapter 31

Paul had just taken leave of Leda and Patrick when his phone chimed with a message from Auntie Bina:

Friends in Galveston think there's someone in my condo. They've seen a light. I think it is Sonya. I texted Sunny too. He did not respond.

Paul typed Galveston in the car's navigation system. The driving distance was nearly three hundred miles from Dallas, and it was nearly midnight.

Paul rushed away into the dark night without a second thought.

Sonya is lucky in love!

I dove into his car. There could be no better opportunity to seek out my daughter if she were indeed in Galveston.

The night turned blustery as we approached the island city. Yet a hooded middle-aged man sat among the rocks chugging beer from a bottle.

Is this Sonya?

There was nothing about the man that suggested that he could be a young woman in disguise. His facial features were too masculine. His scent was strong and rugged. He had no feminine curves.

Paul parked on the Galveston Seawall beneath an overcast sky. His gaze swept over the hooded man. He did not stop to talk to him. Instead, he turned and headed toward Auntie Bina's dark condo just across the street.

The hooded man slipped out a pocket notepad and pen from his pocket and scribbled a message.

I love you, P. So stay away. S

Her sigh, the handwriting, and the content of the message gave Sonya away.

What a convincing transformation! It's not just careful attention to details; there's magic involved.

The first few drops of rain spit down on the rocks.

Sonya tore the page from the notepad and weighed it down on the rocks with a stone. Then she followed Paul to the entrance lobby of the condo complex and hid behind a pillar.

With a deep frown, Paul walked up to the receptionist and described Sonya to him. He had not seen anyone matching her description.

Paul zipped up to Auntie Bina's condo in the elevator and knocked. There was no answer. He asked around. Nobody had seen Sonya. He scooted back to the lobby, bolted out the double doors, and raced down to the rocks.

He will leave no stone unturned.

Sonya ran up the stairs to the condo, and flung herself on the bed, sobbing.

She hasn't changed toward Paul. Perhaps we are all misunderstanding her. I thought about the open window in the yoga studio and Sonya's succinct words to Leda at No.7, "It all began here." *She was trying to help, wasn't she, or am I reading too much into it?*

The rooms of the condo were immaculate. The fridge was stacked, the closets neatly arranged with young adult clothing—all top brands—that I had never seen before. And they were all her size.

Sonya is using Auntie Bina's property without her knowledge, which is outrageous. Yet, she is not happy. The fiend must be forcing her to stay here.

There was no sign of him.

The rain poured down. It drummed wildly on the roof of Paul's car. It splattered hard against the windows.

I flitted around restlessly inside the car. *Has Paul stumbled on the note? Perhaps I should guide him to it with my light . . .*

The temptation was irresistible. I ventured out and Deepak grabbed me.

"Paul found the note. It's slightly blotched in the rain, but he could still read the words." He did not sound happy. "Priya, you are not supposed to be here. You're lucky Dev is not out prowling the streets with spirit traps tonight. But he's close, launching a sales promotion for rainbow fentanyl with Neel."

"Deepak," I tried to explain, "Sonya is in Auntie Bina's condo, possibly living with the fiend. This is as bad as the curse can get. I want some prophesy about my children's future." I told him about the three 'Da's. "Datta and Dayadhvam represent Patrick and Leda and Dāmyata, some stranger. What will happen to Sunny and Sonya?"

"You could visit the future-telling mountains. However, you cannot ask questions. They will reveal what they will reveal."

"Okay."

Thunder growled.

We raced through a tunnel in the cumulus clouds. It rolled from side to side.

"It's like it is about to crumble down on us."

"It won't," Deepak said. "The rising air that helps it form, keeps it afloat."

Cracks appeared in the roof, fissures of brilliant light that rippled like puddles of rainwater.

"Hallowed portals to Heaven," announced Deepak.

They widened. Lacy white-edged cirrus clouds rolled in, forming a perfect line in the radiance.

"Shuttles to Heaven," he said.

We boarded one and glided swiftly to Heaven's outer limits.

Mountains rose before us, dressed in palmettos right up to their crowns—a celebration of golds, from flaxen through sweet corn, bumblebee, canary, mustard, and fire.

Mesmerizing.

The ridges parted, conjuring the prettiest of mosaics.

Upon the dappled shades of the palmettos, floated a watery light in a human shape—me—more youthful than my last human reflection.

"Recognize yourself?" Deepak chuckled. "Heaven has an admittee list; I suppose this is how it's announced."

"Amazing!"

The wispy silhouette boldened, effusing honeyed tones. As if permission to enter had been granted, she drifted in slow and graceful swirls and anchored herself in heaven's ether.

"Congratulations on your admission to Heaven, Priya!"

"Does it mean I get to stay?" I asked eagerly.

"You will know when you do." Deepak was almost inaudible against the steady hum of bees in the background.

"Deepak?" I cast around the dreamscape.

He was in the sunset ahead, melting into the watery "me," like we weren't really two separate entities at all.

A shiver crept down my spine as I experienced an acute sense of déjà vu.

The mountain ridges closed. The bright palmettos faded.

I felt myself plummeting.

Someday, I'll have a place beside Deepak in Heaven.

"Of course." Deepak's blaze pulsed through the graphite sky, illuminating a pathway below through the black that nurtured the evening street on which Leda's house stood.

"Stay put," he called. "This is your safe haven for now."

Slipping back into the downspout of Leda's roof, I planned ways to deal with my isolation. I would chat up the ash-bat and elicit information about the fiend's immortality and his plans for Sonya.

Sunny's fury pierced my core though he was only in a phone conversation with Leda. "Some people have no sense of responsibility, time, or duty. They are just drifters. But Sonya is worse. She's a narcissist with no regard for anyone but herself."

Patrick sighed. "I think she's desperate to accomplish what she calls her 'mission.'"

Meghna scoffed. "A mission impossible."

"A tough one no doubt," said Leda. "What worries me is that she's being pressured into making wrong choices."

Alone in the darkness, my anxiety peaked for my girl. Tossing restlessly in my self-imposed prison, I felt heavier than usual. My core shone brighter than ever.

I had grown a thin layer of cladding. *If only it will help me to reach my destination sooner and seek the help of the Heaven Elders.*

Chapter 32

Patrick stayed awake all night, reading articles on black magic online. When the dawn chorus broke the silence of the night, he left his chair, heaving a sigh.

It looks like he has found a solution to the problem.

"You are up early." Leda walked past like everything was perfectly normal and started filling the kettle.

Patrick followed her into the kitchen. "Leda, you must not budge from the house the next few days."

Leda switched on the kettle. "W-why?"

"I um, need your help with Gladys."

"Why? What's up with her?" Leda plucked two mugs from the mug tree and set them on the countertop.

"She's still grieving."

"I tried to visit her, but she never seems to be home."

"Perhaps we should try again. She told me she felt tired and nauseous when I called a few days ago." He sighed. "She's gone all quiet since."

"Why don't you call her and ask her to come and spend some time with us here."

"Sure. I think she would love that." He dialed her number. She did not respond.

"She could be resting."

The kettle whistled and Leda prepared two cups of coffee. "Here," she passed one to Patrick and sipped a mouthful from the other.

Patrick stared at her.

"What?" Leda smiled at him over her cup.

"Could you please work from home while she's here?" Patrick's eyes were beseeching.

"Investigate from within these walls? You can't be serious. I need to go out, collect evidence."

"Why not let someone else do it, someone who knows about black magic?"

"So, it's not Gladys." Leda narrowed her eyes at him.

"But I am scared for my wife." Patrick's eyes glistened. "Completely freaked out."

"Not everything is about us, Patrick. There are a lot of people out there who have been victimized by the fiend. Besides, think about Sonya. What will happen to her?"

Her compassion! It's so innate in her.

"After what she did to you!"

"It's my job to investigate Dev's activities and bring him to justice. Please, don't get in the way."

Patrick phone chimed with a text from Glady's manager:

Gladys has not been coming into work the last few days, and she isn't responding to my calls and texts.

Patrick's brows scrunched.

Leda glanced at the text. "You go check up on Gladys, Patrick, and I will start making breakfast."

"Okay." Patrick drained his coffee and rushed away.

Seemingly deep in thought, Leda chopped up some red onions, bell peppers, and tomatoes, grated some carrots and sautéed them with oregano, red chili flakes, and salt. She folded some freshly grated cheese into the concoction and mixed well.

The doorbell rang and a parcel arrived from her Aunt Camelia.

She finished preparing the stuffing and opened it. There were all kinds of creams, lotions, and sprays.

Are they enough to combat the fiend's powerful black magic?

Leda checked them out, put them away, then began to fluff the eggs.

Patrick pulled up on the driveway and came in with a grimace. "Gladys is not in her house. "I knocked; I called her. She didn't pick up her phone. I went in with her spare key. Everything was intact, only she and Dish were missing."

"She might have gone somewhere for a few days with Dish." Leda lit the stove and poured the beaten egg into the saucepan. "Her friends would know. Doesn't she have friends in the neighborhood?"

"Yes, a couple—I met them at Marco's funeral. I called them both. They haven't got a clue where she is."

Leda spooned the stuffing onto one half of the egg and folded the other half over it. "What if she's on the plane back to Naples, where she's from, with Dish?"

"That's a possibility, but she is always so worried about her debts. The woman hasn't been home since Marco passed."

Leda slid the omelet from the pan onto a dish and placed it before Patrick.

"Where's yours?"

"I'll wait for Meghna. She's still in the shower."

Patrick dug into his omelet. "I had a chat with Gladys's kids. Tino, her son, said she did not allow him or his sister to come over for the funeral because money was tight. I thought it was best to inform the police, and I did. Though I answered most of their questions, there were certain things about which I was completely ignorant, like her last activities."

Patrick's phone rang. "Tino," he cried. "That's okay. I'll pay for the airfare. You can stay with us. Yes, yes, I will pick you up. Yes, I understand about your sister. Senior year can be tough."

The man's generosity is overwhelming.

Tino, a photography student, arrived the following day. He was so tearful that the police had to be extra gentle with their interrogation of him. He was mostly encouraged to talk about his mother. He said how caring she had been, and how much he had missed his parents since they had come out to the west. He did mention that his mother was upset over his father's sudden death, but that her friends, especially one who was a doctor, helped her a lot.

"No one has spoken of the doctor friend so far," said Patrick. "Must be her health provider here in the US. When I offered Marco and Gladys jobs, I provided them with medical insurance and recommended my doctor to them."

He called the clinic; they seemed to have no records of her visits in their visitor management system.

The police intensified their search for Gladys.

It was no secret within a day or two that Meghna was attracted to the young and handsome Tino. She would charge into his room after work.

She seems to have recovered from her last relationship.

Tino, however, was cold and unresponsive. He locked himself in the bathroom and emerged at dinnertime with bloodshot eyes.

Leda played board games with him whenever the opportunity presented itself. She baked and cooked for him—the all-time popular Italian pasta, pizzas, lasagna, and risotto. Despite the delicious meals and Leda's warmth and compassion, Tino missed his mama.

Patrick encouraged Meghna to take him out. "He needs to be with people his age."

Meghna took him to the mall's international food court. As they rummaged through the mouth-watering menus, Meghna received a resounding smack on her backside.

"Hey!"

It was none other than Jalebi, practically unrecognizable in her traditional Lebanese long, flowing dress with elaborate silk embroidery, curtain bangs, fake lashes, and coin jewelry.

"Meghna, introduce me to your friend," she said.

Meghna swallowed. "This is Tino, um, Partick's friend's son from Naples, and Tino, this is J—"

"Rumki. I am popularly known by that name and would prefer to be called by it." Jalebi shared the fried chicken and potato wedges she had ordered for herself. "It's a big portion. I can't finish it." She broke a chunky piece in half and thrust it into Tino's mouth.

"Mmmm, love the lime-garlic flavor." Tino smacked his lips. "It's Levantine. Love it."

They talked about the east-facing lands along the Mediterranean coast. Jalebi showed off her knowledge about the people, the food, and the culture.

"Are you from Lebanon?" Tino stared at her in wide-eyed wonder.

"No." Jalebi giggled. "I just love all things Levantine."

Really!

"You have my exact interests."

Jalebi chuckled.

Laughter was easier for Tino minute by minute. It tipped out at Jalebi's words, burbling and chortling like siphons of soda.

Tino clicked random pictures of her. He excelled at candid photography.

Meghna sat alone, watching them. She was strangely morose and silent.

Perhaps she's thinking of Randy and her baby.

Jalebi didn't stay for too long. She claimed she had started studying to finish nursing school and left, but only after inviting them to Levant Grill, the restaurant where she worked, the following weekend.

"I am a server. You will be my guests."

"How long have you known her?" Tino asked Meghna on their way home.

"A few months." Meghna seemed oddly reticent about Jalebi. She didn't even mention the chance meeting to Leda or Patrick when she returned home.

This is odd. Why wouldn't she tell them she saw Jalebi? Meghna appears to bear her a grudge, yet Jalebi seems alright with her.

Chapter 33

Patrick approved of what he called "Meghna and Tino's friendship," but he was a strict boss. The thing he really tried to instill in Meghna was work ethic and commitment.

Meghna left home early on Monday morning with Patrick and returned late. She grabbed a quick dinner and retired to bed straight after to be adequately rested for the following day. Every day of the week was the same. Meghna ploughed on.

Impressive!

"I will help you build up a career here," Patrick promised her. He not only created opportunities for her professional development and growth, but he was generous with his compliments. The simplest accomplishment earned her a "well done."

And Patrick wasn't the only person who showed genuine concern about Meghna's well-being. Every night after Meghna returned from work, Leda provided her with hot meals.

The good woman looked after her like an older sister despite her busy schedule, but she was especially dedicated to Tino. She talked to him about relationships, while eliciting from him intimate details about his mother, her habits, hobbies, taste in clothes, food preferences, not to mention her friends back home. Tino seemed to enjoy his conversations with her, little realizing that she was tapping his secrets and most sensitive thoughts.

Together, they browsed through his online albums. "We were a happy family," said Tino, "until my sister and I went to uni. Suddenly empty nesters, Mama and Papa made a random decision to move here. They never should've. Papa invested all his money in a start-up, a flash in the pan. He became broke. Thankfully, Patrick gave him a job, but Papa's losses had already taken a toll on his health."

"Was your mama okay, health wise?" asked Leda.

"She had women's issues—menopausal complications. She was like forty-five, but she insisted she was in good hands."

"Do you know who her doctor was?"

Tino shrugged.

I'm sure Leda will get to the bottom of this investigation soon enough. Not all perpetrators are sorcerers.

In the late afternoons Leda and Tino parted ways.

Though Tino claimed to be taking pictures, he spent most of his time at Levant Grill. He did however tell Leda that he shared his parents' partiality toward Levantine cuisines. If only Leda knew that it was more the lure of Jalebi than the food that dragged him to the Lebanese eatery!

Leda diligently checked out every Levantine restaurant in and around Dallas for any evidence that could solve the mystery of Gladys's disappearance. She left no stone unturned. She snooped around Gladys's neighborhood too, stopping at random cafes, shops, malls, and parks.

One morning as she drove past Gladys's Street, Dish leaped in the path of her car. He appeared famished and injured.

At once she stopped the car and stepped out, but Dish charged into the hedges hugging Gladys's house. There he lay refusing to budge.

I almost ran over a terrier very much like the dog, Dish, you described, Leda texted Patrick. Come ASAP and bring some treats. He looks very scared.

Sure, Patrick's replied.

He arrived at the scene and recognized Dish. "It is him. Poor boy! He does have a way of running in front of people's cars."

Patrick tried to distract Dish out of the hedge with his favorite treats, but Dish barely budged.

"He loves chicken nuggets," he said and fetched Dish some.

The terrier crawled out, and Leda pointed at a vial sticking out from the soil where Dish had been lying. "Hey, what's that?"

Patrick dug out the Midazolam injection vial.

"Midazolam is used to produce sleepiness," said Patrick. "Wonder what they did to Gladys."

Leda went into the police station with the vial while Patrick took Dish to the vet who prescribed injections and medicines, not to mention rest.

By the end of his first week in Houston, Tino had become not only a regular visitor at Levant Grill, but every server's heartthrob.

Meghna was far from happy when she witnessed his closeness to the vivacious beauties, especially as she had been dragged there much against her will.

"Let's go," said Meghna. "I don't like the noise."

"I do. Where's Rumki?" He looked around and craned his neck, possibly to catch a glimpse of her.

Jalebi appeared, stunning in her uniform, but only after the food and drinks had both been served.

The light of lust flared in Tino's gaze.

Exactly how far along is she in her pregnancy? She still doesn't show.

Leaning into Tino, she ruffled his hair and straightened his shirt collar. She licked the pink gloss on her lips, and her phone chimed:

Duty calls.

Her face contorted.

Who's the message from? Her boss?

The only person of authority I noticed within the eatery was the manager, and he chatted cheerily on his phone.

Jalebi excused herself and disappeared into the employees' restroom.

The minutes ticked.

Tino's gaze lingered on the employees' restroom, the glow of lust in his eyes.

"Are you done?" Meghna tugged at Tino's arm. "I need to go."

"What now?" Tino stared into the shadowy darkness beyond the archway leading to the restroom. "Rumki will be back in a tick."

"Her name is not Rumki."

"She's popularly known by that name."

"Look, Tino, there are things you don't know about her." Meghna pushed back her chair and rose. "Anyway, I just got a text from Patrick."

Tino glanced at her. "What does he say?"

"They want us back home ASAP," she said with some urgency and left the table.

Tino followed.

As they navigated toward the door, Jalebi reappeared. "You're leaving, Tino? Why?"

"They need us at home." Lust screamed in Tino's eyes.

"It's Leda and Patrick," Meghna said in a flat voice. "They're waiting for us."

Swallowing hard, Jalebi stepped back to let them pass.

I saw a mix of disappointment and fear in her eyes. *I can understand the disappointment, but why the fear?*

Meghna called a taxi post haste, and it whizzed her and Tino away.

Still don't get y u had 2 go? Jalebi texted Tino.

I will b back alone bb, replied Tino. Wait 4 me.

Sure.

"I wonder why Patrick texted you and not me," Tino glowered at Meghna's phone.

"Tino," Meghna said in a monotone, "it's not them. Sorry, I had to drag you away from Jalebi."

"Oh, Meghna!" He scowled.

"Well, Leda and Patrick would too, if they were here."

"Do they even know her?"

"Oh, yes. Didn't you see Jalebi step back at the sound of their names? Several weeks ago, Patrick picked her up from the airport. He paid for her flight here, but upon arriving at their house, she acquired some money somehow and threw it back at them. She has a sugar daddy."

Tino's eyes were livid. "You think I'm too precious to waste myself on the likes of her?"

"Look. I'm not an angel myself, and I'm not trying to blame Jalebi for being in a relationship. Three months ago, what didn't I do to bag an American and have a child by him?" She blinked.

Tino's gaze swept over her. "You are pregnant?"

"Was. Anyway, this sugar daddy, Dev, is a dangerous man—a sorcerer. I don't know if you will believe me, but he branded Leda."

"What? That lovely lady?" Tino's frown deepened into a scowl. "However did that happen?"

Meghna took a deep breath and told him the whole story.

Tino gaped at her shell-shocked. "Poor Leda. She's so kind."

"Thanks to Sonya. You will see her. She ruined her own family, and now she's all out to wreck Leda's life."

Sonya did not ruin her own family deliberately, but with Leda, it looks like a different story.

"Is he here, this sorcerer?"

"Uh-huh." Meghna took a deep breath. "I told you I got pregnant. Well, there was something not right about the baby. I was losing weight, turning green. Jalebi, who was my caregiver at the time, said I was carrying the Devil's child. Not like we didn't have reason to. Sonya's grandma's house, where I conceived the baby, was haunted by spirits."

But not by the Devil. Why was she chosen to be the birthing vessel for the Devil's child?

"Did Leda and Patrick know?"

"Now they do, but I did not tell them a thing until I got rid of the baby." Tears welled up in her eyes and spilled down her cheeks. "What I did not know was that they had lost a few babies and were hoping to adopt my baby. At the time I was consumed with my own worries and preferred Jalebi's advice over everyone else's for her non-judgmental attitude. She promised me that if she could come to the US, she would take me to an OB she knew."

"Did she?"

"No, she had me taken to the sorcerer instead. It was only after she landed in Dallas the night before that she told me she would not come with me, and that a taxi driver would take me to an exorcist." She inhaled sharply. "I tried to abort the baby myself; I couldn't. The following morning, the taxi driver picked me up. He knocked me out on the way. After the fetus was sucked out and I regained consciousness I overheard Jalebi arguing with the sorcerer about how uncomfortable she felt about bringing pregnant women to him to provide him with his night cap. Apparently, he drank fetal blood every night to reverse the aging process."

How many crimes must a man commit before he is brought to justice?

"Really! What did Dev tell her?"

"He was furious. He reminded her that her father had sold her to him, that she was duty bound to do as he demanded. He condemned her for being ungrateful for all his kindness and generosity in bringing her up."

Tino gasped. "Oh my God."

"Now do you see why I am asking you to stay away from Jalebi? She might not be so bad, but she is controlled by the sorcerer."

Tino seemed far away, his mouth pursued, his body rocking. "I hope Mama wasn't expecting. The last time I spoke to Papa, he said Mama had women's issues. My sister told me she assumed that Mama was perhaps having menopausal complications. She was that age, around forty-five."

"But how would she know Jalebi?"

"When we asked Mama about her health, she said we had nothing to worry about. She was in the capable hands of this wonderful young woman who had just arrived from India with excellent medical knowledge. We thought she was the OB."

Meghna scowled. "We must ask Patrick and Leda if Gladys had any interaction with Jalebi."

Chapter 34

Meghna and Tino's taxi crawled in traffic when Leda's Audi approached her neighborhood.

Leda had left for Houston early that morning and asked specifically not to be disturbed, something she had never done before.

Has she found a lead?

She chatted cheerily with her Aunt Camelia as she drove. "Thank you," she said, "for bringing me the charmed surveillance camera. It caught images of static moving around No.7, briefly, though very clearly, something an ordinary camera would never do."

Relief swept through me. *Finally, someone at par with the fiend.*

"I am so glad you found it useful," answered Aunt Camelia. "It's lucky that Dev's invisibility spray is poor quality with all that static."

"I think there was more than one person because the mass of flickering dots split in half, and the two parts moved around the property like distinct entities."

I could only think of Sonya and the fiend.

Leda sighed. "If only I had the yoga gear with the hexed cuff."

"It's just a mantra away. Wait till I lay my hands on it. In trying to scare you, Dev showed you a way to get close to him without hurting, and you should use it to your advantage." Aunt Camelia paused for a second. "The plane's about to take off and I must switch off my phone. Take care."

"Thanks for everything, Aunt Camelia." Leda hung up and pulled up on the driveway.

Patrick opened the door at once. "Where have you been? I was worried out of my mind."

Leda whizzed in. "Lots happening," she announced in a sing-song voice. "Let me explain everything over a cup of coffee."

"Sure. There's some in the pot." Patrick followed her in. "Let me get it for you." He poured her a mugful, and Leda slumped in a chair at the kitchen table and sipped it slowly.

"Aunt Camelia got me just the thing I needed." She told Patrick about the surveillance camera and the images. "We are this close to capturing Dev," she said, holding her thumb and forefinger nearly touching.

It may be quite impossible to capture the fiend alive unless Aunt Camelia is more powerful than him, and it will be impossible to capture him dead if he is indeed immortal.

Meghna and Tino stepped in like high school kids in big trouble.

"You're back early?" Patrick looked from Meghna to Tino and back again.

"We need to talk." Meghna walked up, a sense of urgency about her.

Leda frowned.

Patrick scowled. "About?"

"We met Jalebi."

"Where?" asked Leda.

Meghna swallowed. "Actually, we bumped into her last weekend at the mall."

"Oh," Leda looked surprised. "You never said a word."

"I didn't have a clue you and Patrick knew her," muttered Tino.

His phone chimed with a message from Jalebi:

How long am I 2 wait 4 u?

20 mins max bb, Tino replied, his eyes narrowed and hardened.

The eye is the window to the heart.

All the while, Meghna tried to explain what happened. "I haven't been entirely honest about the abortion. I should have, considering everything you are doing for me." She took a shuddering breath.

Leda and Patrick exchanged glances.

"The baby was the Devil's child and—" Meghna's eyes glistened.

"I know, Meghna, you told me." Leda smiled kindly. "It was pretty apparent in your looks that something was very wrong."

"Jalebi arranged for me to be taken to Dev for the abortion. I didn't know I was going to him. Jalebi had promised to take me to an OB before she arrived here. We communicated regularly."

"Jalebi didn't go with you." Leda peered into her eyes.

"But she left soon after, didn't she?"

Leda nodded.

"She didn't want you to know she had a hand in this. That morning, I met up with a taxi driver as arranged by her. He knocked me out on the way to Dev's. After the abortion, I came around, and Jalebi asked the same man to drop me at Highland Village, but he chucked me out of the car near Alamo Drafthouse Cinema where Patrick picked me up. Only I don't recall how he did that. At some point during the ride, I must've fallen into a deep sleep."

The fiend is a meticulous planner and an effective executor.

Patrick clenched his jaw.

Meghna went on to tell them how she had eavesdropped on the fiend and Jalebi. She related Jalebi's life story in detail.

"Unbelievable." Patrick sighed. "Perhaps it's because of her past that she's grown so adept at taking advantage of other's goodwill."

"Exactly," said Tino. "I took her for a sweet, devil-may-care girl. Things were going so well between us, I fell in love with her. She was my get away and happy place this past week. We did so much together, walking, eating, watching telly, shopping. She made those common pleasures so much more fun. I'd never been in such a fulfilling relationship my entire life." He spoke quickly, a scowl darkening his face.

"So, you and he were not a thing?" Patrick mouthed to Meghna.

"No." Meghna shook her head. "Tino was always busy flirting with Jalebi, and she with him."

The look of disappointment in her eyes did not escape me.

"Oh, Meghna had to literally drag me out of the restaurant," said Tino. "I would not believe a word she said until I heard the whole story. And that made me wonder. Mama was having some women's issues."

Leda's brows furrowed. "You told me she had menopausal complications."

"Well, that is what my sister assumed, considering her age." He blinked furiously. "What if she was pregnant? What if she knew Jalebi?"

Leda swallowed. "Gladys knew Jalebi."

"Jalebi and I dropped by at hers on our way back from the airport," said Patrick. "They talked. In fact, I encouraged it, knowing how lonely Gladys had become since Marco passed and hoped they would gel. I have no idea if Jalebi went back."

"Jalebi commented on Gladys's health after the visit," said Leda. "She would have recognized the symptoms of pregnancy even without being told and could have taken her to Dev." She rose with a sigh. "Where is Jalebi now?"

"At the restaurant." Tino glanced at his phone, his teeth gritting. There were no new messages from her. He looked up. "She works eleven to eleven. If I go now, I'll be able to catch her." He walked toward the door, his teeth gritting, his fists clenched.

"No, stop," Leda cried. "We must plan our next course of action very carefully. Meghna, you dragged Tino away from the café?"

"Yes, she said that you and Patrick wanted us back home urgently with a glare," said Tino.

"How hard was the glare?" Leda squinted at Tino.

"Don't worry, I'm sure my sweet texts have balmed any fears that the glare could have aroused in Jalebi." Tino checked through his messages one last time. "I'll go catch her."

"Let me come with you, Tino," said Leda.

"No. I must handle it alone. You will scare her away."

He's smarter than I thought.

"You are putting yourself at risk," Leda pleaded.

"Anything for Mom." He opened the door. "Do not follow me." He rushed out, and the door slammed shut behind him.

Chapter 35

I was full of admiration for Tino's love for his mother, but deep down I was scared. Confronting Jalebi at Levant Grill had its own risks. It would no doubt involve the fiend.

The restaurant, a fifteen-minute drive from Leda's home, seemed to have closed early. And it stank of fresh blood, despite the use of heavy chemicals on the floor.

Someone got hurt.

The front doors were locked. The restaurant was dark inside. The chairs were stacked on the tables and in the vacant kitchen, the stainless-steel surfaces reflected the streetlights in a cold, metallic glare.

A low, drawn-out moan chilled me to the core. *Sounds like a ghost in trouble.* I could not ignore her wails and rushed to help.

The soul was rigidly stuck to her body, buried beneath several loose wood plank tiles in the flooring.

"Dev's doing," she sniveled. "He wants me within easy reach so he can use me for his experiments."

I recalled how Ravi had freed me from my trap and threw myself against her.

She remained stuck to her body, though my disguise ripped and the fine cladding that had developed around my core splintered in the process. *If I must linger here on Earth, I might as well make myself useful.* I used a sliver to cut between the spirit and her body. It worked like magic.

She was free. "Thank you," she sniveled. "Thank you so much. Neel, the owner, was whipping Jalebi, my coworker—he'd just discovered her relationship with the Roman boy, Tino. Jalebi bled. I tried to stop him, and he hit me so hard I had a fatal brain injury. The sorcerer, Dev, sucked me out as I was dying and slapped me against my body with a mantra. Then they buried me."

Tino arrived on the scene, and the spirit zipped away.

Tino frowned at the darkness shrouding the place and slipped out his cellphone.

Hi, where r u, he texted Jalebi.

Minutes passed. His taxi pulled away, and another pulled up.

"Hey!" Jalebi leaped out.

 Tino swung around. "Hey. Why is the restaurant closed?"

"A few of the employees, including the manager, are sick with a foodborne illness, so the restaurant has been closed indefinitely." Jalebi could barely move her bandaged arms, hanging limply at her side.

"What happened to your arm?" Tino squinted at her heavy makeup, barely covering up the cuts and bruises on her face and neck.

Jalebi is in worse trouble than my Sonya.

"I fell over." She turned away her face. "There was chaos. Anyway, I missed you so—?"

"Did you know my mom, Gladys?" Tino cut her short.

Jalebi started walking toward the isolated park down the road. "What makes you think I did?" She glanced back with a flirtatious smile.

"Can you take this seriously? My mom's gone missing."

Sonya's whimpers, soft but continuous, echoed through the air.

Without a moment's thought, I took off after the cries. *My child is in distress.*

Her cries faded.

Whipping through the skies, I glimpsed drops of blood on the road. They smelled of Sonya, though I did not see her.

The ash bat raced past me.

"Hema, stop," I said. "We need to talk." She smelled of Sonya's flesh and blood too. "Did you kill my daughter?"

"Me? Never. Sonya's my only hope." She flapped her wings and plunged into the darkness.

I speeded up and seized her. "But you must've hurt her. You reek of her blood."

"I only pecked at her arm. I didn't mean it to be so hard."

Anger surged through me. "A hard peck that results in bleeding is a serious wound that requires immediate medical attention."

"Not when a powerful sorcerer lives with her."

"That's the reason I need to find her, and you must help me. You used to be my best friend."

"Best friend! Can you come take my place? Relieve me?" She tried to grab me with her fangs.

"I was supposed to, but the fiend lost interest in me."

"The composition of your core will not buckle under the pressure of Uncle Dev's tools or his torture chamber. The black magic world has yet to invent a machine that will permanently sever your core from the rest of you. It's different. Look how it glows! Brighter by the second." She poked at the scant remains of my cladding. "How did you get so lucky when my fate is to wait for Meghna's baby to be found and trained?"

"Trained?"

"Evilness is not innate. That spirit needs training to do what I do, and hours of torture if he rebels."

A chaotic wind hurled us into gigantic columns of violently twisting air.

The bat exploded at once, her fangs, tongue, and tail scooted in opposite directions amid a cascade of ashes.

Shockwaves rolled over me, trying to pull my core asunder.

The stench of sulfur was overpowering.

It's the Devil!

The remains of my meager cladding were no match for him. Just his roar blew them to fiery smithereens. I was swept up with the pieces in a screaming whirlwind. Spinning in the chaos, I lost every sense of pattern and direction.

When I returned to the park. Tino and Jalebi were nowhere in sight.

Tino did not return that night.

Leda tried contacting him for hours but in vain.

Apparently, Patrick, Leda, and Meghna had made a trip to Levant Grill during my absence and found no trace of either Tino or Jalebi within miles of the restaurant.

Nobody slept that night.

Meghna tapped her fingers on the alarm clock ticking beside her.

Patrick watched the stars in the patio with Dish by his side. The terrier's health had improved since he had been found, thanks to the attentive care of the wonderful couple.

Leda sat at the study table, talking to Nikita.

"Have you heard from Sonya?" Leda asked her.

"No." Nikita sighed. "I don't understand why she won't contact me. I am her best friend."

There was an awkward silence.

"Leda, Paul told me what happened at the yoga studio. Now that is not my Sonya. I have known her since I was one."

"Yet Sunny thinks—"

"Sunny's attitude is unbelievable." Nikita's sneer resonated through my core.

If only her love and concern for Sonya would change Sunny's attitude.

There was another pause, and then Leda asked, "Are you in touch with Bina?"

"I tried to call her no less than five times. Four out of the five times, there was no answer, the call went straight to her voice mail. The fifth time, she responded, but she sounded woozy like she had been drinking." Nikita sighed. "And she only just got married."

"Have you met her husband?"

"No. I doubt he even lives with her."

Leda leaned forward in her chair. "Why don't you take her out sometime to some place nice, like Galveston?"

Galveston? Did Paul mention the note to her?

"Funny that you should suggest this, Leda. Paul hinted at the same idea a few days back. Gran Bina has a condo overlooking the beach, but she has been a little distant since she got married . . . "

Up above the luxury ranch estate, the bat prowled, darker and enormously magnified, recognizable only by her grooved lower lip and her rough, scaly, flickering tongue.

I curled up in the downspout. *There is no point trying to reason with her. Her circumstances have changed her into someone I don't quite know anymore.*

Her hiss echoed through the house. It was drowned by Dish's bark.

Patrick hushed him. "Dish, sit."

Dish backed down, growling.

Ash flakes landed on the study table where Leda sat talking to Nikita. Leda glanced behind her. There was no one. "Sorry, Nikita, something has come up. I'll get back to you later."

Leda rose, then collapsed with a groan. On her wrist, her scar throbbed. It lost color like it was flash burned with acid from the inside. Blisters sprouted, dark, shiny, and moist.

Dish's growl escalated into a snarl. He bared his teeth at the bat's shadows circling over the house.

"What is it, Dish?" cried Patrick. "You will wake up the neighbors."

The terrier continued to be restless, and Patrick picked him up and carried him indoors.

The agitated terrier jumped out of his arms, bolted into the study, and crashed into the desk. The collision brought a pile of books tumbling down. An envelope shot out.

Dish leaped onto Leda, sprawled on the floor, and covered her in slobber.

Patrick raced to her side. "Leda, you okay?"

"The bat was here." She sat up groggily.

"No wonder Dish was so restless." Patrick rushed to the window and craned his neck to scan the front yard.

"She's gone." Leda's gaze drifted to the envelope on the floor. It was addressed to her. She leaned forward and picked it up it. "Patrick, why didn't you give it to me?" She flipped the envelope, possibly for the sender's name. There was none.

"Sorry! I must have overlooked it."

Leda slit the envelope open carefully and slid out a piece of notepaper. "It's from Rao." She read the contents of the letter aloud:

> Leda
> I am sending you some clues about your assaulter I found at the ruins of the abandoned house. I shouldn't have gone. Someone

followed me back, invisible, but flickering like static. He cast a spell on my fingers. They're rotting.

    Rao

The last words were practically indecipherable. Leda and Patrick helped each other to get through them.

"Bet it was Dev." Patrick scowled. "See what could have happened to you."

Exactly what I'm thinking.

A tear rolled down Leda cheek. "Rao must be dead. He has not answered a single text since I came away from Digha."

"Do you have no common friends?"

"Megha. He was friends with her family. But Meghna hasn't been in touch with them or him since she got pregnant."

"Didn't Sonya's family know him too?"

"Barely. He lived miles away and probably visited them just once on his flashy scooter."

Leda peeped into the envelope and drew out a Ziploc pouch with a natural brown feather earring. "Looks like Jalebi's. I gave her the pair." Leda narrowed her eyes. "Rao said he kicked her on the shin and sent her catapulting into the path of the bulldozer."

Patrick frowned. "Didn't Jalebi go missing that night?"

"Yes, and she limped when she arrived here in Dallas."

"Tell me about it. She limped all the way through the airport."

Chapter 36

Nobody thought of breakfast the following morning, though the kettle boiled every hour, and cups kept piling up in the kitchen sink.

Patrick paced the kitchen, scrolling through his text messages. "Not one text from Tino."

"You forget he is with Jalebi now." Meghna's eyes brimmed with hostility.

Her jealousy!

Leda joined them at the table. "Didn't you ask Jalebi about the OB, like where she lived, how Jalebi got to know her?"

"Jalebi showed me pictures of this lovely woman, while we were in Digha. Apparently, she was an OB as well as her uncle's girlfriend." Meghna met Leda's eyes. "Sorry, we planned it all behind your back."

"But you tried to abort the baby in the bathroom the evening she arrived," said Leda.

"After Jalebi landed in Dallas, she texted me that since I was carrying the Devil's baby in my womb, I would have to go to a person with supernatural powers instead, like an 'ojha' or an exorcist. I was so scared, I tried to abort the baby myself." She took a sharp inhale. "I would have tried again after everyone fell asleep that night, but Jalebi kept watch on me until it was time for me to leave. My baby was her present to the fiend, and she ensured he was alive for him."

"Did you interact with Dev at all?" asked Patrick.

"No. It wasn't possible. When I came round after the abortion, I found myself lying on blood-stained sheets, on a table, in a windowless room. I was not in pain but felt kind of weak. There was no one around, so I slipped off the table and walked down a corridor. I heard Jalebi's voice. Peering in through a door standing slightly ajar, I saw her talking with a man she addressed as Dev. He was drinking blood from a glass tumbler."

How sickeningly disgusting.

"The room stank of blood. Besides, there was this kidney shaped basin with the bleeding fetus in it." Meghna's voice choked and her lips trembled.

"It's okay, Meghna." Leda touched her arm. "You don't have to tell us all this."

"I wouldn't, I didn't before, but now I feel it is important that you should know. Especially, if Tino's mom got herself into the same predicament."

Patrick swallowed. "You are lucky they didn't see you prying."

Meghna sighed. "I sneaked back to the table and lay very still until I fell asleep. Jalebi woke me up and walked me to the bathroom, where I changed into my clothes." Meghna sniveled. "Then suddenly, she blindfolded me and pushed me into the arms of the taxi driver who had picked me up from here."

Patrick sighed. "If only you had asked us for help, explaining your reasons."

"I made a mistake and learned my lesson."

If only Sonya would realize her mistake before it is too late.

"And the next you met Jalebi was at the mall?" asked Leda.

"Yes, last weekend. We bumped into her. She invited us to Levant Grill. I would have refused, but Tino was so excited, I couldn't."

"And he saw more of her over the course of the week when you were busy with work." Patrick narrowed his eyes at Meghna.

"Precisely. He fell madly in love. She can be so endearing and persuasive."

"He never told me a word. I was spending a lot of time with him." Leda heaved a weary sigh. "Perhaps, he didn't feel close enough."

"He has the highest regard for you but cannot pour out his heart to you," muttered Meghna.

"Why?"

"Because you are so perfect." Meghna's eyes welled up with tears of gratitude.

"Oh, Meghna!"

The day wore on.

Tino's scent continued to elude me, despite my heightened senses. A feeling of unease came over me.

Meghna left for Patrick's factory, and Leda for her daily round of investigations. Patrick stayed home, trying to distract himself with work. Dish watched him from under the bed.

Tino's sister called, distraught with worry. "Any news of Mama?" she asked.

"No, but they say no news is good news," said Patrick.

"Is it?" sniveled Tino's sister. "If only Tino would respond to my calls and texts."

"Guess his phone is switched off. As soon as I can contact him, I'll get him to call you."

"So he's not with you?" The girl's voice rose several octaves.

"No. He's out to see a friend. We'll keep you updated about Tino." Patrick hung up on the girl, his eyebrows tangled in a frown, and Leda walked in through the door.

"We should inform the police about Tino and have them put out a missing person's report," said Patrick. "It might be too soon but considering the risk level of the situation—wonder how I will explain to them that Dev could be involved in the disappearance of Gladys."

Leda peered into his eyes. "I've found a lead."

Really?

"What?" asked Patrick.

"Gladys has this wonderful collection of photos of herself in different hair styles."

"Must be old pictures. You know she's having a tough time paying off her debts."

Leda nodded. "I looked at the pictures differently—as a passionate interest in hairdressing. I went into the local salon to ask them if Gladys had ever shown any interest in their work." She breathed deeply. "It was quiet in there, and the manager and I got talking. Apparently, Gladys had been working there a few hours at the weekends and had left suddenly."

"Hmmm."

"Some new information came to light. The manager said that she had ventured out on a midnight tryst with her lover the night Gladys disappeared and noticed a silver Mercedes SUV at Gladys's curb."

Asha's Mercedes SUV is silver, but Auntie Bina uses it. The fiend uses Jay's Jeep.

"Something the manager noticed about the license plate stuck in her mind." Leda sighed. "The number was '431,' the digits added up to eight, and they were followed by the letter 'H,' the eighth letter of the alphabet."

That is Asha's car.

"Hmmm." Patrick scowled. "Who would be visiting Gladys that late?"

I hope Sonya had nothing to do with this. I do hate her loyalty to the fiend.

"Jalebi?" Leda inhaled sharply. "She can drive. She moved my car to the middle of the road for the bulldozer to crash into it."

"She might have pushed it. Maruti Suzuki cars are known for their lightweight design. But I think she had an accomplice. She couldn't have carried you to the car." Patrick sighed. "Gladys's late-night visitor could still have been Jalebi, but Jalebi with a driver."

"But where would she get a Mercedes?"

"Same place as she got the money to throw in your face."

Clever thinking. The fiend has access to both the Mercedes and Auntie Bina's money.

"The manager of the salon said she would have forgotten about the incident had she not bumped into the car a few days ago at Highland Park Village."

"Was there someone inside?"

"No." Leda shook her head. "It was empty. She waited around for several hours, and the driver did not return. Then she met a friend and got distracted for a few seconds, and the Mercedes was gone."

"Dev in his invisibility guise. You are on the right track. The two cases are connected."

Exactly!

The police asked Patrick very specific questions about Tino. Some he answered, some he could not. The officer asked for his address and verified his phone number so they could call him if there was an emergency or if new information came to light.

Patrick hung up and slumped down on the sofa.

Leda turned on the television and the newscaster announced:

I'm Diana Lucas with a breaking news report. A woman's slashed torso has been found in the Old River, west of FM 1409. The police continue their search for other body parts in the river and the surrounding forests and wetlands.

Patrick and Leda squinted at the tattoo on the collarbone in the shape of the letter "A."

What was Gladys's dead cat called? People tattoo letters to honor their loved ones.

My heightened senses did not allow me to see as far as the old River. Curiosity dragged me to the riverbanks.

The other body parts had still not been traced.

I thought about the mammals and reptiles inhabiting the surrounding forests and wetlands. *One of them might have attacked her.*

"Orange spirit," a ghost-soft whisper penetrated the gloom. "I'm Gladys. You are so orange, you must know if they've already killed my Tino? My body parts were sold as soon as they were severed from my body. I heard that they would sell Tino's too. I want to snatch his soul before Dev turns it to the Devil."

Oh my God, no! "Let me find out," I rushed away in a murderous rage. *The fiend must be crushed or there is no peace in this world. There must be a way.*

Chapter 37

Wings, distinctive with white and red markings and eyespots, fluttered on either side of me, jolting me out of my murderous thoughts.

"That's a Cecropia, before you ask." Deepak's voice lacked its usual warmth. "A little protection might be necessary for my browning love,"

"Browning?"

"Why can't you wait for the final outcome, trust in divine timing?"

"How much longer?" I yelled at him.

He was gone.

Restraining my murderous impulses, I levithoned back to Leda's house and a knock resounded through Leda's house.

Patrick rushed to the door and unlocked it.

Tino burst right through, disheveled and crying. "Sorry, I misplaced the key."

How did Tino survive?

"To Hell with the key." Patrick grunted. "Where have you been? We were worried."

Tino fell into his arms. His convulsive sobs echoed through the large house. "Mama is gone."

Leda and Patrick helped him to the sofa where he wept copious tears.

Meghna came running down the stairs. Wordlessly, she rushed to the kitchen to make Tino some hot tea.

"Mama is on the news—she, her torso with the tattoo," Tino blubbered. Sobs wracked his body. "When Amore, Mama's cat, died last year, she had his initial tattooed on her collarbone."

Just as I thought.

Leda and Patrick exchanged glances.

"Where did you watch the news?" asked Leda.

"I didn't watch the news; the taxi driver told me as he drove me home." Tino took a shuddering breath. "My phone had completely drained its battery and wouldn't turn on, so I borrowed his phone and called 911. Apparently, they had tried to notify me as I am next of kin. They asked me to come down and identify the body. I mean what's left of her." Tino sniffed. "But there was no way I could do that by myself."

"We'll come with you," said Patrick, "but first I must call the police and let them know you are back. We reported you missing."

"Hope you didn't say anything about Jalebi." Tino dabbed his eyes on his shirtsleeves.

Patrick squinted at him. "Um, no. Did you get a chance to speak with her?"

Tino inhaled sharply. "The restaurant was closed. She arrived there almost at the same time as I did, covered in cuts and bruises. As we spoke, I felt a pinprick, and I have no recollection of what happened after that."

Jalebi is an expert criminal.

Meghna brought in some tea and Tino gulped it down.

"When did you come around?" Leda rubbed her chin.

"Just after sunset outside a school. There was this note in my pocket."

Three pairs of eyes poured over the note.

Sorry, this is all I could do to save your life. Jalebi.

Tino blinked. "I don't know where Jalebi took me or what happened after, but I can assure you, she is not in this alone."

Patrick stepped into his office to inform the police of Tino's return while Leda and Tino continued talking.

"Why is Levant Grill closed?" asked Leda.

"I believe there was some infection in the kitchen," Tino replied.

"What was the issue??"

"Foodborne illness outbreak. I believe the manager was affected along with some of his employees."

"Hmmm."

Patrick returned sooner than I expected. "Tino, the police would like to conduct a 'Safe and Well Check' to understand what led to your disappearance."

Tino swallowed hard. "I shall not mention anything that might remotely get Jalebi in trouble. I seriously think she needs help."

He confirms my belief.

Meghna swallowed. For once she did not seem to have an opinion.

"You don't have to say anything if you don't want to," said Leda. "Anyway, the police are coming essentially to ensure that you're not a victim of crime or at risk of further harm."

Tino nodded. "When are they coming?"

"In a few hours," said Patrick. "In the meantime, please, let your sister know you are well." He handed Tino his phone. "Here, use this."

Tino sent a quick text to his sister and planted the device on the coffee table. "Leda, um, will you please come with me to identify—?" His voice trailed.

"Of course."

She accompanied him to the morgue.

Tino puked at the sight of his mother's remains. "What did Mama do to deserve such a horrifying death?" he cried.

No one deserves to die this way.

Leda consoled the trembling boy as best she could.

Leda and Tino returned from the police station, and a police cruiser pulled up on the driveway.

Patrick rose to greet the officer at the door.

"May I please speak with Mr. Valentino Bianchi?" he asked.

"Sure."

Everyone left the room, while the officer interrogated Tino about his whereabouts since his arrival in the country.

Tino maintained that he went looking for his mother, cleverly evading any mention of Jalebi and the fiend.

Leda spoke to the officer in private after Tino's interrogation.

"At this point we are certain that the torso belongs to Gladys Bianchi," he said. "The internal organs have been removed. Search and recovery efforts are underway for the missing remains."

The officer divulged other gruesome details about the murder. They had found signs of brutal torture on the body. He explained that forensics believed that Gladys had died three days ago, though her body was only discovered in the river that morning. He assured Leda that there was a whole bunch of officers working on this case and they would resolve it soon.

Leda's eyes narrowed, her lips pressed in a thin line.

No one knows better than her how difficult that is.

Tino was inconsolable when the officer left. "The questions made me feel like I was a suspect. Am I a suspect?"

"Only until you are proven innocent which you are," whispered Patrick.

Meghna merely nodded.

"It's because you're a relative," muttered Leda.

The next few days, Leda engaged herself in investigating the true reason behind the closure of Levant Grill.

The police found no witness testimony, physical evidence, or DNA evidence against Tino. He was ruled out as a suspect.

Chapter 38

Tino left for Naples at his sister's insistence.

Leda's investigations at Levant Grill yielded some satisfying results. The server's body was uncovered along with Neel's old passport and other important documents. Apparently, he operated under several fake names. Leda worked tirelessly to track down Neel and his missing crew.

"Now you can focus on finding the criminal, something you are good at." Patrick heaved a sigh. "And since Neel and Dev seem to be connected, you will eventually stumble on the sorcerer."

Leda's nodded, a faraway look in her eyes.

Patrick departed for work with Meghna, humming a tune.

Leda left for Houston in pursuit of new evidence with all her magical paraphernalia.

I slipped into her car. I had no mirror ball or cladding left, and I was desperate to find out if Sonya was involved in Gladys's murder.

The car sped down the long highways beneath a cloudless sky.

Leda called Sunny about Gladys's murder and confided her worst fears to him. "I hope Sonya has nothing to do with it."

Sunny hung up without any questions or opinions. He said he was busy.

He's only too eager to wash his hands off her. I withdrew to a corner of the Audi, very sad.

We entered the city limits of Houston.

A breeze of wind blew past carrying a whiff of the Devil's scent. An intense-green cloud of dust hovered over the horizon.

We were not far from Asha's street when a wall of dust rolled over. It shrouded the house, everywhere except around the kitchen.

I charged in and landed on crumbs of lamb kebabs. The meaty aroma battled for prominence with the foul stench of sulfur.

The Devil doesn't like meat?

I noticed the upturned canister of salt on the floor.

Salt wards off the Devil. The saltshaker was still three-quarters full, but I would not mess with the Devil.

Sweet highs of joy dominated the house. In the dimly lit lounge that sat atop the house, Jalebi, stark naked, stooped over the fiend, slurping off chocolate hazelnut spread smeared over his groin.

His purr!

He seemed to have no regard for Auntie Bina, asleep in her bedroom, oblivious of his dalliances with Jalebi. *Did he give her another sleeping pill?*

I fled to the distant corners of the house, but every sound was shockingly audible, every movement disgustingly visible, thanks to my heightened senses!

I need to get out of here.

Alas, the gardens were bathed in a ghastly green light, and the Devil's stench hung over the property.

I was stuck with the pervert. *If only he would spill some information about Sonya.*

Sprawled on the sofa, the fiend only spread his thighs wider. "You're darn good at this. Your mouth is magic."

"And you will give me all your worldly possessions for this?" Jalebi squeaked.

He raised his hand in consent.

"You are not serious, are you?" Jalebi spoke quickly with a kind of restless energy. "You don't take me seriously. You won't even talk to the OB despite all the problems I've been having."

Is this the OB she promised Meghna?

"I chanted mantras and the bleeding stopped. Oh, Jalebi. Now get on with it." He touched his groin. "You know the angles. You know my spots."

"Not until you do something about my abdominal cramping." Jalebi sprang up, and he shoved her head back against his crotch.

She picked herself up. "How can you give me all your property when you haven't even told Bina you want a divorce?"

The fiend rose hastily and slapped her. "Patience, girl. I am still trying to get a better understanding of my joint assets with Bina. Your crankiness is not making things any easier."

A sob tore from Jalebi's chest. "How do you not care that I'm well into my second trimester and still barely showing?"

"Oh, you will," he grunted. "You might have miscalculated."

"I have miscalculated!" Her dark eyes were pits of fire.

"With all the flirting you do, you would."

Jalebi flirts shamelessly with any man she sees.

"I flirt because I cannot envision a future with you. I flirt to find out if I'm still lovable. You said you would marry me and then married the hag. The baby means so much to me. I want to give him a family. It's about time you left the hag and started thinking about him, about us, planning for his future, for us!"

"Oh, Jalebi. You will ruin everything. Why don't you understand. Bina is so rich with all her own and her daughter's assets. If we rush her too much, she might call her lawyer and leave everything to Nikita." He rubbed his chin. "On the contrary if we wait, we can have all of Nikita's lovely wealth too."

He's got it all planned. The monster!

Jalebi's scowl permeated her entire physical presence. "Do you mean to seduce her too?"

The fiend shook his head. "She is not my type, but once married to Sunny, she will fall into his family spell. You may not see much of her, but should you chance to, remember to treat her with respect."

The sinister look in her eyes in response made me feel uneasy. "No one shall be more respected than your Rajrani, your name for me when you bought me from my father. That is how it was and that is how it shall be." Jalebi slithered into the fiend's lap, smashing her large breasts into his face.

"Rajrani! No polish! No poise! No elegance!" His mouth drooping as if in disgust, he pushed her away.

Jalebi staggered and struck the corner table. The crystal lamp on it rattled. She seized it before it crashed to the floor and wielded it over his head.

He dodged it adeptly, then seizing it by its ornate column, smacked her temple with the glass bottom.

The thud echoed around the lounge, as blood burst from her forehead, and she collapsed on the ground in a heap.

"The temper!" he muttered, pulling up his pants. "If only there were other sources of the precious blood—" His gaze shot to her. "She has guessed, has she not? The three other extractions aroused no suspicion."

Has he been extracting blood from his own fetus too?

Dabbing his sweating forehead on his shirtsleeve, he picked up the unconscious Jalebi and threw her on the sofa. For the briefest moment, he touched a minuscule dot near her pubic hairline.

It looked like an injection puncture wound.

He drew a little kit from his pocket. "If only I could use a higher dose of magic to numb her womb. But then it won't respond to the signals from the brain and to all those hormones. The fetus will die sooner than I need it to—my only source of blood."

Disgust tore through me.

He chloroformed the sleeping Jalebi and drew a slightly yellow liquid with traces of blood and mucus from yet another spot near the pubic hairline and chugged it.

He's helping himself to the amniotic fluid that protects the growing fetus? Poor Jalebi. Pity swamped my core. *No wonder her baby is not growing in her womb.*

With a weirdly placid look on his face, he texted Sonya:

Get some pomegranates and make a reservation for three tonight at Brenner's on the Bayou. Need to talk.

He put away his phone with a grunt of satisfaction. "As good as done. What would I do without Sonya?"

Sonya has earned his absolute trust. How utterly revolting!

Deep breathing punctuated the silence that ensued. I glimpsed sparks behind the perforated door in the corner of the lounge. It used to be the children's playroom where Sonya and Nikita had spent many an evening when we adults had been having too much fun to bother about them.

I neither saw nor smelled anyone among the empty bags and suitcases, then a few beads of sweat floated in the air, oozing Sonya's scent.

She's here prying? He will destroy her if he finds out. Frantic with worry, I whizzed around the walls, struggling to settle.

Seemingly preoccupied with his thoughts, the fiend picked up Jalebi's frock from the ground and checked its pockets. Out fell a little pouch. He unbuttoned it and inhaled the white, odorless, bitter, crystalline powder. "Strychnine! Stolen from my supplies!" Scowling, he thrust the pouch down his trouser pocket. "Jalebi is trying to kill me! Huh!" He shook his head at her senseless body. "I am immortal until I choose to die. There's no way you will ever lay hands on the 'Mrityushakti' mantra?"

Does such a Mantra really exist? I had heard about the Maha Mrityunjaya mantra, an ancient, powerful Sanskrit hymn that was chanted for protection, healing, and to overcome the fear of death, and the potent Mritasanjeevani mantra, an incantation that infused life into the dead, but never of the Mrityushakti mantra. I broke up the word into its component parts. "Mrityu" meant death and "shakti," power. *Does the mantra enable humans to bring death to themselves?*

Over-analysis led to action paralysis. I began to plummet. My glow jutted precariously out of the middle section of my disguise. Its thorax had ripped.

I froze mid-air.

A cockroach skittered across the floor.

If only I could slip into its body.

No sooner did I wish for the transformation than I snapped out completely of my disguise. The overlapping plates of the arthropod piled over me. Its three pairs of legs and wings—fell into position on either side of my core.

Is this the wish-fulfillment Deepak spoke of?

"Drown the stench of the cockroach," spoke a silvery voice within me.

Does it come with instructions?

"Drown it." The voice trembled. "Raise your temperature."

How on earth do I do that?

I was already struggling to come to terms with my skittish new form. Though I had never really considered the insect to be the freakiest creature in the animal kingdom like some, I could not bear the idea of being trapped within one. I tried to run from myself but only grew in every direction I attempted to flee. In no time, I assumed a strange and unimaginable size.

The fiend gasped at my antennae, swiveling back and forth. "What manner of cockroach is this? Is the world out to kill me?"

My papery wings fluttered maniacally. Before I could stop myself, I was zapping around the lounge, now perching on the antique wall mirror, now diving into the fiend's shirt.

"Awaken your pheromones," the silvery voice was back.

Pheromones? But they are chemical signals used for communication by the elite spirits in Heaven.

"You have a few within you, very powerful. Awaken them."

How?

"Raise your temperature."

Why does the voice repeat that command instead of explaining how to do it?

My anxiety led to increased cravings for the crumbs of kebabs that clung to the fiend's shirt. I devoured them post haste.

The fiend spun hysterically, cursing me in his wild efforts to brush me away. His shrieks and awkward jerks terrified me. I held on to him for dear life with the humongous teeth in my gizzard; they had grown in proportion to the rest of me.

"Ow! My nipples!" he screeched. "What species of cockroaches bite?"

Unwittingly I had nibbled on his nipples.

A hive-like rash spread over his chest. He gagged and retched. "I shall rip you to shreds."

Terrified, I sweltered within the cockroach.

"Perfect," sang the silvery voice. "This is key—hot. Your pheromones are roused. The cockroach's hemolymph is full of it. You have drowned its smell. Now slip out."

Shaking, I grabbed the fiend's finger instead with my overlong legs in a vice-like grip.

The fiend clenched the digit, sniffing. "Priya! The monstress!" He bumped into the furniture, trying to push me off his bleeding hand, stumbled, and fell on a loose floorboard. It caved.

"No!" Quaking, he pulled it out and straightened it with magic mantras. Then he thrust his hand in to feel a cloth bundle, crooning: "On frayed paper/ etched with scraper/ six words/ from the nerds/ of the cult/ for instant result."

Behind the perforated door, Sonya forgot to breathe.

I crawled over his hand, and he shrieked a vicious curse.

My antennae swiveled around faster and faster until they detached from my body. My forewings and hind wings stretched thin and ripped. My legs split at the joints, and the three body segments exploded, hurling me with an uncanny force beneath the sofa upon which Jalebi lay. I clung to the underside of the three-seater.

Chanting incoherently, the fiend crystallized the insect's hemolymph on his hand. The lucid drops swirled over his skin, dragging together the pieces of the cockroach into a regular-sized arthropod.

It did not move yet continued to smell eerily like me.

He slipped the cockroach into his pocket too, cackling. "Ha, Priya! Got you!"

There are gaps in his knowledge.

I transformed myself into a black-bodied peppered moth and watched him replace the floorboard over the secret compartment from my dark shadowy nook.

There's no rush as long as he is content with his acquisition.

Chapter 39

Jalebi slowly came around, her eyes fluttering open. "Pomegranate, sweet and juicy—where am I?" She pulled herself up on the sofa, and her hand shot up to the wound on her forehead, clotted with blood. "What happened?"

"You tried to hit me with the table lamp. I got even with you."

Jalebi's mouth twisted in a humorless smile. Even as she spread her curtain bangs over the clotted blood on the wound, she doubled over with pain. "Oh, my belly."

"Relax!" The fiend caressed her thighs. "It's a sign that our baby is growing."

The scoundrel!

"Oh, shut it, Dev" Jalebi dressed herself with a frown. "Like I don't know what is happening."

Does she have the slightest idea that he's stealing their baby's amniotic fluid?

He narrowed his eyes. "What's happening?"

Her frown deepened into a scowl. "Dev, I must see the OB ASAP about his development."

"Sure. I'll book you an appointment. I've already asked Sonya to get you some pomegranates."

Jalebi did not respond.

"I'll get her to deliver them all to your door, but tonight she will meet us at Brenner's on the Bayou. It's barely five miles from here and mirrors the picturesque scenery of Mr. Brenner's native Germany. It is so worth it, dining in the rustic elegance, you and I."

"Then why is Sonya coming? Why don't you try making babies with her? She seems quite enamored by you." Jalebi scoffed. "Sorry, Dev, it is getting increasingly difficult for me to bring you pregnant women without a car."

"You must manage. I'm using Sonya for a greater purpose."

"What greater purpose?" Jalebi echoed my thoughts.

"Never mind. Right now, we must think seriously about returning to India. Unfortunately, that cannot happen until the investigation into the firangi's allegations in the country is dropped, or in other words, we make her withdraw it."

Leda would never. I shuddered.

Jalebi laughed hysterically. "Leda will never. You could try killing her instead."

"Come, let's get out of here before the crone wakes up." The fiend led her out of the lounge.

The self-locking door shut with a soft thud.

They slipped into the garage in silence and drove away in Jay's Jeep.

The perforated door opened, and footsteps resounded on the wooden floor. Sonya moved like a ghost, scintillating stars in her wake. She stopped by the secret compartment where the fiend stored his belongings.

The flickering specks faded, and the floorboard moved. The fiend's bundle shifted within the hole and lifted out of it. The static returned, practically imperceptible, and then was gone.

What if the fiend should suddenly return?

The knot unfastened. The fabric unfolded, and the contents of the package, mostly pooja paraphernalia and exercise books, collided against each other. Out fell Sonya's old phone.

Sonya gasped audibly but did not touch it.

The pages of a thick almanac, among the contents, flipped swiftly.

Sonya's grunt of disappointment resounded through the air. The search resumed through the exercise books, way quicker.

With yet another gasp from Sonya, a piece of paper, old, with frayed edges moved out from between the pages of one. There were six Sanskrit words etched on it, possibly with a scraper.

Is this the Mrityushakti mantra? It matches the description in his song.

Sonya's old phone rose a foot or two above the ground, only to dance over the writing. Even as the camera clicked, Jay's Jeep pulled into the driveway. The fiend was back, and he was alone.

Oh, Sonya hurry.

Promptly, the things piled up, including the phone, exactly in the same order as they had been arranged before Sonya touched the bundle. The cloth folded neatly over them.

Her phone stays? But the image?

The fiend's footsteps approached speedily. Sonya's heart beat erratically.

I winced. *Will she make it back to the hideaway in time?*

The string returned around the parcel, one end moved to create a series of loops and passes, then locked together with the standing end.

The parcel returned to its place, and the floorboard closed over the hole.

The sparks reappeared only to vanish, and footsteps rushed back to the old playroom.

The key turned in the lock.

The fiend stepped in, and his nostrils flared. His eyes darted around the room.

Sonya's breaths were too quiet for human ears.

The fiend removed the floorboard and retrieved the bundle without delay. He removed the dust cloth, fingered through the contents, then pulled out the exercise book with the old and frayed piece of paper tucked between its pages.

He's after the mantra. It must be Mrityushakti mantra.

"Who has been having kebabs in my kitchen?" Auntie Bina yelled in the kitchen. "Dev? Are you home? Dev?"

The fiend packed away the other items, slipped out a labelless bottle from the hidey hole and squirted a purple liquid over himself and the book. The pearly drops mingled in millions and billions of bright white dots.

They vanished with his scent.

This is how Sonya makes herself invisible and scent free.

The floorboard returned over the secret chamber, and he sneaked out noiselessly.

Chapter 40

That evening Sonya posted herself by the elevated garden terrace at Brenner's on the Bayou. She was unrecognizable in a bob wig with razor-cut layers, lash-skimming bangs, and oversized Dior sunglasses.

She did not smell like herself, but the beads of sweat on her forehead, a normal physiological response to the June heat, gave her away.

I curled up in the dark, dank downspout in the corner of Asha's house, waiting for the drama to unfold. *It's so much more convenient to watch from my nook without constantly having to worry about my glow and the Devil.*

A taxi dropped off the fiend and Jalebi at the curbside.

It's clever of the fiend not to drive up in Jay's Jeep. People might have recognized it.

Sonya ran up, gesticulating frantically. "Hi, Uncle Dev. Hello, Jalebi."

The fiend wrapped an arm around her. "Lovely to see you, Sonya."

"You too," Sonya beamed.

"You look well." Jalebi gazed down at Sonya's dress with what appeared like a well-rehearsed smile. "The floral embroidery is beautiful."

"Thanks." Sonya grinned. "I love your cashmere and silk stole. Loro Piana Hedge! Present from Uncle Dev?"

Jalebi nodded, her lips mashed together in a hard line.

She hates him but can't leave him.

The fiend wedged himself between the two young women. "Sonya, how's your brother? Where is he? Getting any closer to—what's her name? N-Nikita."

Sonya swallowed. "They're both here in Houston, living separately."

"Really!" The fiend grinned.

"How do you know?" snapped Jalebi. "Did you meet up with them?"

Sonya shook her head. "No. I saw Paul drop off Sunny and pick him up from Double Tree during my walks. The hotel's a stone's throw from No.7."

Sunny must've just gotten here.

"And Nikita?" asked Jalebi. "Who does she hang out with?"

"Nikita, um, she's become a bit of a loner; she keeps to herself."

The fiend grinned. "Those two should be joined in holy matrimony."

Sonya's brows scrunched, but the frown faded quickly, giving way to an astonishingly wide smile. "Of course. Let's go in." She led them up the steps to the garden terrace. "Hope you will like the menu selections. I've heard that executive chefs from very famous restaurants worked alongside Mrs. Brenner to re-create some of the restaurant's favorite dishes."

"I'm sure we will," smirked Jalebi.

The fiend nodded, adjusting his black silk tie.

The double doors flung open, and the manager led them to a booth.

They sank into the richly cushioned seats and gazed out, spellbound, at the beautifully manicured lawns and gardens surrounding them with stunning water features and fountains of bright-blooming plants: tower of jewels, petunias, red bird of paradise, bougainvillea, and violas.

"The perfect escape from the bustling city life." The fiend chuckled.

Sonya crossed her legs and swung her foot, and I glimpsed a maze of interwoven threads.

Spirit catchers? My core welled up with grief, but it waned with the abrupt realization that she could be warning me to stay away. *She stole the mantra, and anyway, I am out of reach.*

"We should get Sunny and Nikita here," the fiend remarked, "to this lover's paradise."

Sonya smiled. "They are in a fight."

"I could patch it up with a potion like in the famous play." He laughed. "This place is full of violas. Dripping a little sap from the wild pansy on—who's causing the problem?"

"Nikita," muttered Jalebi. "Always the one playing hard to get."

That's not true. Guess Jalebi's still mad at Nikita because the fiend asked her to show respect toward her.

"Then we shall drizzle some on her eyelids as she sleeps and get Sunny in. You have her keys?" The fiend squinted at Sonya. "When does Nikita wake up in the morning?"

"She sets an alarm for half six. I can slip into the house in my invisibility disguise and leave the door open, but how will I get Sunny to come? Nikita won't invite him over."

"I'll do that." The fiend winked. "I can imitate Nikita's voice."

The server brought them freshly baked bread and butter. "Hey, how're we doing today? I'm Ella, and I'll be your server tonight." She passed them the menu cards. "Can I start you off with some drinks?"

"A glass of Cabernet Sauvignon, please." The fiend flashed his sweetest smile.

"I would like that too, please," Sonya said softly.

"Coke." Jalebi screwed her mouth into a grimace.

Ella wrote down the orders. "Would you like any appetizers?"

The trio agreed on batter-fried jumbo shrimp and lump crabmeat in Bearnaise sauce.

The server departed, and Sonya squinted at the fiend. "So, Uncle Dev, what are we talking about tonight? How can I make myself useful?"

I hated her bootlicking smile.

He peered into her eyes. "You couldn't get Leda to meet up after the yoga session."

"I'm sorry, but she's still furious about the yoga suit. What was wrong with the sleeve?"

So, she was not party to it.

"Design defect. Mine had it too."

The starters and drinks arrived.

The trio ordered the entrées before they dug in. Sonya chose cedar plank redfish with basil pesto and balsamic reduction served with grilled asparagus, and Jalebi ordered piri-piri chicken. The fiend picked filet mignon seasoned with the restaurant's signature steak seasoning, char-broiled and topped with their signature steak butter.

Jalebi retched. She excused herself and rushed to the ladies' room.

Sonya met the fiend's gaze. "Please, Uncle Dev, give me a second chance."

Again, the subservience!

The fiend forked a few shrimps into his mouth, chewed them, then washed them down with the wine. "Leda's harassing me. Make her stop. The last time the bat and I were at No.7, she nearly caught me." He drained his glass.

Wouldn't the scar react to his presence?

Sonya looked surprised, but she said nothing about it. "Um-weren't you in disguise?" she asked instead.

"Yes, but the static? It's unavoidable. The dots flicker as you disappear and afterward with every jerky move." He rubbed his hands together furiously. "What was worse was that Leda had planted her aunt at the property while she was probably watching from some hidden camera. The aunt was in an invisibility disguise too, and it was indiscernible."

"How did you know?"

"A trap for the bat with her favorite food suddenly appeared on the ash. Thankfully, I noticed it in the nick of time and grabbed the bat."

Sonya asked no more questions but listened with rapt attention as if to hear every word and absorb every detail.

That deep level of engagement can be so flattering. Is it a wonder that he trusts her?

The fiend's eyes swept over her face, lingering over each feature. "The aunt aimed a visibility spray in my direction, enough to counteract my spray. I had to cast a fog spell."

"Good, you outwitted her."

I quaked at his unnervingly sinister gaze.

"She was unprepared, but I'm sure she'll be back with wind spells and goodness knows what else. I eavesdropped on her phone conversations with Leda at Bell Heights, where she stays when she visits her niece. She's turning the sleuth into a sorcerer—a dangerous combination." His eyes glinted wildly. "I have only one option, and that is to finish both off ASAP."

The corners of Sonya's mouth turned up. She leaned in. "I can do it all, the whole nine yards, preparation, planning, leading them to some trap, if you will only tell me how."

She's only pretending. She photographed the mantra. But that smile!

"Sunny is here possibly about your property. Do everything in your power to stop him talking to prospective buyers without revealing yourself. And regain Leda's trust. You must bring her to me; there's stuff I need her to sign before we see the last of her." He rubbed his hands. "That done, we shall flee, you and I."

Where would they go? I felt deeply disconcerted.

"I will do exactly as you instruct me." Sonya's smile faded only to reappear almost instantly.

The server approached the table with the entrées.

Sonya smiled uncomfortably wide, with a dead gaze.

Silly girl! How long can she keep up this forced cheerfulness?

The server cleared the soiled dishes and planted the main courses on the placemats. "Enjoy," she said and vanished.

Sonya took rather small bites.

The fiend ate voraciously; his portion was large.

When Jalebi returned from the ladies' room, he had finished eating. Without looking up, he typed up a message on his phone:

Hey Bina. What are you up to? Missing you so much.

Auntie Bina's phone chimed with the text downstairs in her bedroom. She was sound asleep.

"You two get on with your dinner while I get the bells pealing." The fiend shot up and rushed out the door.

A gang of youngsters entered. They were Sonya's high school peers.

She paid for the meal and quickly departed with Jalebi.

Chapter 41

Auntie Bina was still sound asleep when the fiend arrived home and did not stir until the sun hovered mid-sky the following morning.

The fiend stepped into the room and planted a tray with two glasses of freshly squeezed orange juice, two mugs of coffee, and a plate stacked with pancakes topped with syrup on her nightstand. "Good morning, Bina!" He threw back the curtains, and sunlight poured in.

Auntie Bina scrunched her eyes, sitting up. "When did you get back?"

"Nine, but you weren't awake for me."

"I'm so sorry. It's these sedatives you got me. They're so calming."

Hmmm.

Her gaze drifted to the tray, and a smile flickered at the corners of her mouth. "Wow! Thanks."

He flashed a wide grin.

Auntie Bina helped herself to a pancake. "Lovely! So fluffy and buttery. It must've kept you very busy."

"Except when Sonya called."

Auntie Bina munched on the pancake, chasing it down with the orange juice. "Is she still at her friend's? She sent me one text, and then she is as good as gone again." Auntie Bina sighed.

It's all staring her in the face, yet she does not suspect her husband of being involved in Sonya's disappearance.

"Did she ask about me, Dev, when she called?"

"Oh, yes, though she mainly talked about Sunny and Nikita. They are both here, Sunny at Double Tree and Nikita in her lonely house, yet they don't talk."

"Hmmm. I would blame Nikita for this. She is being stubborn." Auntie Bina stared into the fiend's eyes and her lips quirked in a slightly mischievous smile. "You know a lot of magic. Don't you know any love spells?"

"Of course I do, and for intense, passionate love." The fiend guffawed. "If only I could have your permission to carry it out."

"Go ahead. Who's stopping you?"

"But once the spell is cast, they must get married. It will take them every ounce of will power not to make a spectacle of themselves."

The irony is that without his curse Sunny and Nikita would have been much the same.

The fiend laughed out loud. "Start the preparations." His phone vibrated with a message from Sonya:

Hema's vicious this morning. She's bitten hard and I am bleeding profusely.

You signed up for this, he replied to Sonya.

Shock waves rippled through my core, though I had had a hunch all along that Sonya had been forced into an unfair and harmful arrangement.

Will he spill some information about her whereabouts?

He did not. Neither did he rush to help her.

He lingered in his bedroom, his eyes darting and his head cocked to one side, as if he were listening for a sound. *What has he got up his sleeve? Isn't it enough that Sonya has become food for the bat?*

I ventured out of my hideaway. *Sonya is hurt; I must find her.*

I hovered over the urban sprawl, the suburbs, the woodlands, the parklands and the trails. There was no trace of Sonya. It was difficult when I did not have a location and Sonya disguised her scent.

Yet wouldn't the smell of her blood give her away? The odor of her sweat did. Or is she too far away for me to catch even a whiff?

Down below, Sunny stepped into his car in Trader Joe's parking lot, texting Nikita:

I miss us.

This "us" could work is if you were kinder to your sister, came Nikita's reply.

"What brings you here?" came Deepak's voice, and all at once the skies lit up.

"You are stalking me."

"How else do I save you when you're in trouble."

"My Sonya is hurt."

"Our Sonya is hopelessly in love." He chuckled. "Paul is in Galveston every few days—the criminal defense lawyer compromises work to take a leisurely stroll down the seaside boulevard every few days and Sonya watches him secretly."

"It's sweet, but scary. What if the fiend sees them?"

"Don't worry. Sonya is very careful. She never shows herself to Paul. I marvel at his persistence."

"Hmmm. I don't know if the fiend is aware of this." I told him about Sonya's text to him. "I'm shocked he didn't do anything about it."

"Cause it was fake news." Deepak paused as if checking to ensure he was right. "Even as we speak, Sonya is stepping into the elevator of the condo she lives at in Galveston."

"But why would Sonya send him fake news? She is like his little slave."

"She would if he asked her to."

"But why?"

"Your color changes are fascinating—" He gasped. "Guess what? Your cladding is growing back."

To my sheer amazement, I noticed a soft luster hugging my glow. *He is always in the know.* "Is it because I hid myself in the dark, dank downspout since I harbored murderous thoughts?" I asked.

"Y-yes, and it is also the reason why Sonya sent that text. The Devil is no doubt after your glow. He has insatiable scientific ambition; he needs to analyze your glow but can't come near you when you hide in the downspout, attic space, or under the roof. Of the few things that repel the Devil, iron is one. The downspout boot as well as the attic vent pipe that runs through the attic and the roof are both made of iron. So, he needs to get you out of there. And who can help him but Dev?"

"He is after my glow too. Last night I noticed a spirit trap under Sonya's shoes. He has even invented equipment to sever my core from my spirit." I shook violently. "I hate living in fear, Deepak, though the future-telling mountains predicted that I would eventually find a place in Heaven. How much longer do I have to wait?"

"Until it's time—come let me take you for a ride." He scooped me up, his cladding flapping at an incredible speed.

We lifted.

"Where are we going?"

"Outer space."

"And if the Devil should catch us there?"

"He'll be blinded by my cladding and yours."

We moved from the Earth into true open space.

The red planet came into view. Fleeting, chestnut humanoid forms orbited the planet. A couple flitted across our path.

We decelerated and dodged them in a graceful sweep, but they seemed keen to talk.

"Visiting from Heaven?" the female asked.

"He is." I snuggled against Deepak.

"Why not you?" asked the male.

"Not sure." I wondered at their warm reddish-brown hue. *Why are these spirits hanging around here?*

The male seemed to read my thoughts. "Originally from Mars, we're angels now, and we protect the planet."

"So there was life on Mars?"

"Mars was habitable in the past," explained the female, "but we Martians led an indulgent life. Our excessive consumption and negligence of responsibilities for personal pleasure ultimately drove the planet's climate toward the cold, inhospitable state it is today."

"But you are angels," I uttered in surprise. "Surely you had more sense."

"Yes, but only too late in life when we adopted a code of conduct, focusing on compassion and service to others," said the male.

His words reminded me of the code of conduct at No. 7. Perhaps Ravi and I would be angels after death if we abided by it.

"So much has happened on Mars," said Deepak. "Earthlings have no idea."

The female sighed. "Some, well a lot of you, do eventually. Come, let us show you around."

The humanoid forms draped around us as a protective shield in our slow and difficult descent through Mar's thin atmosphere and cushioned the impact of the landing. Together we dove into the solar system's largest volcano, Olympus Mons, and the largest canyon, Valles Marineris, played in the craters and dry lakebeds, and rollicked on symmetrical wave ripples on sandy shores.

"The best evidence of ancient water and waves on Mars," I said.

"Did you use surfboards?" chuckled Deepak.

"Yes, we did a billion years ago." The male led the way to the larger of the planet's polar ice caps. "This is made of frozen carbon dioxide. It grows and shrinks seasonally,"

"What is that?" I glimpsed a green mist-like entity writhing in the frozen hell.

"An evil spirit through and through, Ravi, surprised the angels by saving a young soul trapped in the net during the Devil's recent hunting spree," the female said.

I winced. "Please release him."

"Shush," Deepak nudged me. "I was in a similar situation, remember? This is his purgatory."

"He must go through the process of cleansing," the male's voice was firm, "though I must say that it's rare to find an evil spirit so thoughtful."

"He was the best father ever," I mumbled.

There was a little rumble.

"Rocks from outer space are striking the planet," muttered the male. "They generate seismic waves that travel through Mars' crust."

The planet swayed violently. Walls of dust rolled through, among them wisps of smoke, green and yellow.

"The evil spirits of Mars have stirred," said Deepak. "We must run!"

A stream of space debris tore through the atmosphere, creating bright trails of light.

He seized me and we boarded a shooting star.

We tore through space.

The meteor burned up in Earth's atmosphere. We plummeted through the atmosphere into the Atlantic.

I lost Deepak momentarily, and the Devil's net caught up with me

Deepak pinched me just as it was about to snag me with its grappling hook.

The miles of mesh receded promptly.

"Why didn't my cladding ward it away?" I asked.

"It can't just by itself." Deepak carried me to the coastal promenade amidst screeching gulls. They looped around in inverted arcs, noisy, tenacious.

"They're intrigued by our cladding. Our disguises have worn out with all our interplanetary movement." Deepak transformed into a gull while helping me turn into a sparrow. "There, that should help while I find you some place safe."

I jiggled and joggled, struggling to fit into my new disguise.

Deepak tightened his clasp.

An overwhelming pull tugged at me from all around. My feathers threatened to fall away. In my desperate efforts to pull it back, I began to slip.

"Deepak! Help!" I cried.

Gulls swooped through the air all around. They were mirror images of each other. They all smelled like Deepak. Their brazen cries sounded the same.

Which one is him?

A gull scooped me up. The next I knew, I was hurled into Auntie Bina's condo.

"Welcome," chirped the ash bat. She roosted within her folded wings in a corner of the ceiling.

The fiend and Sonya both seemed oblivious of my arrival.

"Sonya," the fiend addressed her as if in an urgent meeting, "you and I must flee this country ASAP, so that's as soon as the Sunny-Nikita episode is over."

"What about Jalebi? Isn't she coming?"

"She got involved in Gladys's murder. We can't take her with us."

So Sonya didn't have anything to do with it. Phew!

The relief was short-lived, for almost at once the fiend clicked his fingers. "Hema, to action!"

Action? Too late I realized my glow peeped through my ill-fitted guise in full view of the fiend. I froze.

The fiend ogled my new cladding.

The bat stirred, sprouting spigots at the end of her tail. Even as they spewed out black clouds of thread, her claws gripped the silk and constructed a web around me like a power loom.

I shuddered to think what trouble awaited me.

"She's stuck," said Sonya in a monotone.

Thank you, Sonya, but the fiend has eyes.

"Unless she turns into a spider." The fiend grinned.

That's an idea. No sooner did I envision myself as an arachnid, picking my way with ease through the tangled mass of threads, than I grew its body parts. Specialized and sensitive setae developed on my legs. The small bristles helped me tiptoe around the web.

Sonya gasped.

The fiend's eyes glinted. "See, why we need to capture her? She's magical. She changes shape and form at the drop of a hat!"

I should have been more cautious.

The bat lurched at me. She pecked at my thorax. "Juicy!" she squeaked.

"Patience." The fiend jabbed his knuckles into her face.

Outraged, the bat bit into my abdomen.

"You will wreck the core." The fiend grabbed the bat and hurled her into the night air. She maneuvered those wings of ash and glided into the moonlight.

I moved along the smooth "spokes" of the orb, avoiding the sticky strands that made up the spirals. There was no escape. The icy chill of panic hit me.

"Those that need to escape make a fantasy of it." The fiend turned excited eyes to Sonya. "Hema used to be like her at first."

Sonya responded with her disgustingly wide grin.

"The funny thing was, I had my eyes set on both of them." He suppressed a laugh. "A long time ago, when Hema was still alive and Priya's best friend, I started writing a book about extraterrestrial life. But I had neither the wealth nor the resources to pursue the subject. I had to stop for a while and used the time to read up extensively on esotericism, its doctrines and practices. I contemplated ways of researching life in other planets with the help of souls. I needed a soul. One of the girls had to die. I had only to inflict a fatal curse. I tried it on Hema first, and it worked. She became terminally ill, and I trapped her soul on the night of her death. I trained her as best I could and sent her into outer space as my personal satellite." He took a sharp inhale. "I lost her."

"Oh, no!" Sonya's disappointment sounded genuine.

I quickened my pace in a desperate attempt to flee. The web swayed with my frantic movements, tangling the radial and spiral threads.

"All my associates helped," the fiend explained. "Apparently, Hema had been carried away by the Devil and was in his safekeeping. The case was rare and interesting, and several renowned tantriks were very supportive. But I earned her back by myself."

"Wow!" Sonya gazed at him, wide-eyed.

He paused to soak up her admiration. "Well, it was through a simple pact with the Master. I would have to ensure that wherever I saw peace, faith, light, or joy, I would promptly sow hate, doubt, despair and everlasting sorrow. To that end, I trained Hema tirelessly in my torture chamber. Hema turned into a brute. Thanks to her, the Master has an equal footing at No.7 with the saint."

The scoundrel!

Sonya nodded appreciatively.

Is she on his side or not. I could not be sure anymore.

The fiend beamed. "It's wonderful that the Master is training Meghna's fetus. He is so lucky to spend the crucial months of his development in hell with his dad."

Sonya shot a glance at him. "I'm so glad you've got better candidates than Mom."

"Priya will be my new slave, prompt my new book, *Afterlife: What you did not know*."

Sonya squinted at me. "She changes the whole concept of afterlife, and that itself will provide enough content to fill fat volumes."

He heaved a sigh. "I will be so famous!"

Horrified, I tried every trick in my repertoire to flee—new disguises, resizing, willing myself to disappear—but in vain. The attempts only sapped my energy, leaving me limp and tired. At every turn, the web multiplied, and some overwhelming energy pulled me back.

The first flicker of doubt set in. *How accurate is the prediction of the future-telling mountains?*

"I'll whizz out and get a thorn bush to plant on the site where we shall bury her. Hopefully she'll grow numb by the time I'm back." The fiend eyed a glass bottle on the table.

Fear spiraled though me.

Sonya smiled, drops of sweat crawling down her back.

There, some emotion at last. If only she would ask more questions.

The fiend squinted at me. "Once we've got her in the bottle, we'll seal it with red wax. We must be super careful, though. Priya always finds a way to escape."

There's no hope this time. There is no sign of Deepak, and Sonya is all out to please the fiend.

Chapter 42

The fiend left, and I attempted new ways of escape, in vain. Sonya didn't seem to care. She rummaged through the grimoires in the drawers, her gaze lingering on spells, rituals, divinations, magical practices, personal notes, and even 'cookbook' style instructions.

"Tsk," her tongue clicked. "Not one clue on how to use it."

Does she mean the Mrityushakti mantra?

The lights flickered and went out in the entire condo complex.

The fiend rushed back in the pitch blackness. He did not notice Sonya step away from his drawers. "Power outage!" he bellowed. "Gah! Let me call the utility company." He tried to dial their number and grunted. "Seriously? No signal?" He restarted his phone, but it did not help. "Guess it's the waiting game now."

A light pierced the darkness, and the fiend opened the window blinds.

Arcing fireworks lit the sky.

He scowled. "Too early for the fourth of July!"

There was a whiff of Deepak's scent among them, so faint as to be insignificant.

Perhaps he's just passing.

Sparks cascaded down. In their lingering light, the fiend plucked me from the web. "Bottle, Sonya. I think your mom's up to something."

He overestimates my powers.

Sonya opened the bottle and held it for him patiently as he thrust me in.

How disgustingly compliant. I struggled to break free.

He pushed the cork down into me.

"There!" He planted the bottle on the countertop. His giant frozen smile loomed down at me.

I tried to slip out through the glass, but it was impassable. My constant thrashings against it exhausted me. I was dragged down and bound to the bottom by what felt like a thousand invisible shackles.

"Light the stove for the waxing, Sonya," he grinned.

Sonya obeyed like she had a gun to her head. And she stirred the gooey mass in the pan as instructed.

Terror rattled my core. I anticipated the torment coming.

The wax in the pan started bubbling when the entire room lit as if by a strobe light. Deepak's scent flooded the room. The light flashed a few times, and then the room was plunged into darkness once again.

"What was that?" Sonya, craning her neck to check out the dark corners.

Why isn't Deepak doing something? Is he powerless?

"Only lightning." The fiend sniffed.

"The sky didn't light up at all," cried Sonya.

"It could be an electrical issue with the stove hood. It's old."

"The light was a distinct white, LED-like light."

"Focus on the wax," the fiend bellowed.

"It's turned off."

"Who turned it off?" The fiend waved his hand over the wax and grunted. "It's getting cold."

How hot does he want it? It's still smoking.

The room blazed again, the whiteness lingering as if for an eternity.

Sonya recoiled, shielding her eyes.

"Positive energy—not a friend. Who?" The fiend glared at me, his eyes smoldering. "Priya has friends. I won't wait any longer."

The fiend picked up the bottle, held it upside down, and dipped the neck into the molten wax.

The bottom of the bottle tugged at me with incredible force. A million invisible pincers gripped my core. "Help!" I cried as loud as a ghost can.

Sonya did not hear me, but the fiend smirked in response.

My disguise peeled off.

"Got my prize at last!" the fiend dribbled.

So the future-telling mountains were wrong.

The fiend removed the excess wax, turned the bottle right side up, and dipped it into room-temperature water to solidify the wax. "There," he said with smug complacency. "All ready to be buried and retrieved as and when necessary."

He had barely uttered those words when a tongue of fire erupted midair, then slowly plummeted, wrapping around the bottle in tight coils.

"Priya has an accomplice." The fiend dropped the bottle, and it shattered with a sharp, high-pitched tinkle.

Even as I realized I was free, jagged shards flew at the fiend. "Help, Sonya!" He shrieked, collapsing to the floor upon the shattered debris.

Sonya rushed to him. She tried to dislodge the glass from his body with one hand, and texted Jalebi with the other:

We need your help. Come quick.

At the window, Deepak spun a bright red plumage around himself.

I flew to his bosom. "Where did you go?" I asked.

"The Devil snatched you from me. I was no match for him, so I waited."

"And outwitted him."

"He's gone, confident that the fiend has you." Deepak flapped his wings in preparation for a long flight. "Now hold on tight."

I snuggled into him, leaving Sonya with a semblance of a smile on her lips, just enough to show that she was enjoying her thoughts, whatever they might be.

Chapter 43

Deepak and I flew through the dark night and early dawn, his glow igniting a brilliance in the world around unknown at that time of day.

"Did you have a hand in the power outage?" I asked.

"Yes, I had to resort to all sorts of things just to save you." He sighed. "I'm sorry that despite your hue and cladding you must be stuck here."

"It could be the curse interfering. Have you heard anything about how the fiend is to meet his end?"

"Evil does not win in this world despite its apparent successes and the suffering it causes—"

"Philosophizing is the last thing I need. The fiend's power must be crushed for the spell to break. And that must happen ASAP."

The powerful notes of Mozart's Requiem, pouring through the speakers in Auntie Bina's bedroom, drew my attention to the house.

"Excuse me." I pulled away from Deepak and landed on the roof.

The music stopped abruptly.

"Don't you have anything livelier to listen to?" The fiend limped away from the CD player. A litany of adjectives crossed my core at the sight of him, including, but not limited to, pissed, irate, enraged, livid, seething, and certainly devastated.

On the bed, Auntie Bina's eyes sprang open. She gasped, rising. "Were you in a fight?"

Though he had managed to clean his hands and face with some form of magic, he had overlooked his shirt sleeves. "No! What makes you think so?"

"I don't know what to think anymore, but I have a right to know. I'm your wife." Tears streamed down her face. "A friend saw you and Jalebi at Brenner's on the Bayou."

"Really!"

Auntie Bina sniveled. "I got you out of India, away from that investigating detective. I saved your damned life."

His eyes hardened. "I don't owe you shit, and I warn you—"

"Warn me?" She dashed the tears from her face. "I-I will file for divorce."

No sooner did the "d" word leave her tongue than he came to his senses.

"I dropped Jalebi off at the restaurant. One of Neel's friends wanted a woman. How could you think I cheated on you?" His mouth descended on hers in an electrifying kiss. There it lingered, robbing her of the power of speech.

Auntie Bina clung to him.

She's scared to break up with him.

He knotted his hands in her hair. "You're beautiful, my bride and my best friend. I adore you. I can't imagine my life without you."

"I don't know." She sniffed. "Sometimes I think we are too different from each other."

"What's wrong with that? Haven't you heard that opposites attract?" He walked up to the DVD stand and grabbed the romantic comedy, *What Happens in Vegas.* "Let's check out what happens to these contrasting personalities."

Auntie Bina nodded, smiling through her tears.

The fiend slipped the DVD into the player.

The movie began.

The couple leaned against each other on the bed, their eyes glued to the screen. Halfway through the movie, he remembered that he had a breakfast meeting scheduled with a Neel in less than two hours.

"Where is this?" asked Auntie Bina.

"Victoria. I can't believe I'm so late. Sorry, I forgot to mention it."

"You are trying to run away from me," Auntie Bina cried.

Exactly! It's about time she does something about it.

"You must trust me. Try and understand. I'm doing this for us."

"How Dev? You keep disappearing every so often."

"It's work, dearest. I'm appreciative of how generous you are, but I hate having to keep taking from you. The sooner I have a steady income in this country, the easier our relationship will become."

Days passed. Dev did not return from Victoria.

Early one morning, Auntie Bina called him. "We've barely been married three months, and you've already forgotten me?"

She's trying in vain to save the marriage.

"I have said it before, and I repeat. I need financial independence." He sighed long and deep. "I'm sorry I must stay at Herenhuis, but I'm trying to prove myself useful to Neel. Now if you will please excuse me, there's a call coming. I won't be long, I promise."

"No, no, you can stay at Herenhuis. And you can continue to use Jay's car. The house and car are as much yours as mine." Auntie Bina hung up yet stared at the phone for several long minutes.

He did not call back.

The morning wore on,

Auntie Bina stood at bedroom window, a "far away" look in her eyes.

It's like her mind is with the fiend.

The clock struck nine, and she ordered a takeaway mutton biryani from Mughal-E-Azam, the Indian restaurant down the street.

She showered, dolled up in a pink chiffon salwar suit and diamonds, and drenched herself in Prada's Infusion de Fleur d'Oranger. The mixed rice dish arrived, and she set off for Herenhuis.

The door stood ajar, and Auntie Bina walked into the Dutch Colonial.

Memories flooded my core. Six months ago, the home reflected Sue's individuality, tastes, and lifestyle. Now the bespoke décor tailored spaces reflected Auntie Bina's personality.

Jalebi, fully dressed, arranged irises in a vase.

"You?" The bowl of biriyani shook in Auntie Bina's hands. "Are you the new cleaner?"

"No, I work at a restaurant." Jalebi smiled. "Dev and I are living together. Today he is away."

"Have you no dignity? The way he treats you!"

"Only in front of you," Jalebi corrected her, "so you don't get jealous. He's so cute when he begs for forgiveness. Look where's he's brought me. He says this is to be my new home—"

"This is my house!"

"He said he rented this place for me. Well, for us." Jalebi rubbed her belly gently as if connecting with her developing child.

Auntie Bina scowled. "You are with child?"

"Uh-huh."

The master bedroom door creaked open, and the fiend emerged from the shadows. "Bina! What a pleasant surprise!"

Auntie Bina almost dropped the bowl of biriyani. "You're still here!"

"I am about to leave." He rushed to her, tenderness oozing from his eyes. One hand wrapping around her waist, he eased the rice dish away from her and set it on the table. His gaze swept over her, and he sniffed. "Mmmm. Looks and kindness. Aren't I the luckiest man on Earth?"

Auntie Bina found her voice. "Jalebi says you told her that you rented this property for her and her baby. Who's the father?"

"How should I know? The woman's a slut. She's trying to split us up. You have no idea how much I've missed you." His lips descended on her mouth as I expected; what I could not have anticipated was the apathy with which Auntie Bina received the kiss. Her lips did not part.

His fingertips lifted to her cheek in an undemanding, but undeniably possessive caress.

She stiffened.

He swept his hand down her body.

She closed her eyes, digging her nails sharply into the flesh of her palms.

His fingers ventured to intimate areas, and she pushed him.

He stumbled back. "Bina?" His shocked surprise echoed through the old Dutch Colonial, only to be drowned by the honking of a taxi on the driveway.

"She cares two straws for you," Jalebi dared.

"Clear out from here, woman." He shoved her out the door. "Now Bina, where's that biriyani?" He scooped up the bowl and kissed it. "This is coming with me."

"Where are you going?" Auntie Bina asked.

"To Neel's factory. They are formally making me partner today. It's the money, nothing else. I did not tell you about it, Bina, because I knew you wouldn't like to come."

She swallowed hard.

Chapter 44

The rain pounded on the roof, a relentless rhythm against the quiet of dawn.

It's repetitive, and inescapable as this existence of mine.

Feeling her way through the house, Auntie Bina stumbled on every item of furniture.

"Oh, it feels claustrophobic in here." She sweated profusely, nursing her fifth or sixth straight bourbons. "My life is a mess. Asha's gone, Dev's drifting away," she cried, her body bucking from waves of agony. "Oh, for a butler to fetch me water. How will I possibly survive without house help?"

She should never have left India.

She staggered down the long hallway and stopped by the console table to stare at her marriage photograph. "I am not worthy of love, and she is?" Her glass dropped from her hand and smashed to smithereens.

Sniveling, she dragged herself up the stairs to the room above the garage.

The door stood ajar. She wobbled in and bumped into rows and rows of fabric storage baskets, each full to the brim with makeup products.

"The thief! The wastrel!" she slurred.

Her gaze drifted off to the framed wedding picture of a bride, Jalebi's look alike, on the open, empty wardrobe.

Is this Jalebi's mom?

Auntie Bina squinted through her fingers and braced herself against one wall to counter the effect the alcohol had on her equilibrium.

She did not notice the other half of the photo, the image of the groom, lying face down in the wastebasket. It was none other than Neel.

Is he Jalebi's dad?

The clouds had cleared when Auntie Bina swerved across the lanes and exited the freeway at Post Oak Boulevard. Shaking like an aspen leaf at the wheel, she braked at the green lights.

Cars honked.

Leda, a few cars behind her, slowed down, squinting at her license plate.

No doubt she recognizes the number.

Auntie Bina floored the accelerator and whizzed through the intersection only to skid into the curb.

The Mercedes came to a grinding halt. The driver's door flung open. Auntie Bina rolled out and lay in a heap on the road.

"Jeez!" Leda pulled over, leaped out, and raced down to the SUV.

Other drivers noticed the situation too and quickly came to their aid. Working together, they helped Auntie Bina into Leda's car and arranged for her car to be towed to the local auto garage.

The front tire rim was damaged.

"I have no one, nothing, no reason to live," Auntie Bina sobbed as Leda drove her home.

Leda gave a hilarious account of her own little accidents, cheering up the old lady.

Just the right person to take care of her.

When they finally arrived at the house, Auntie Bina was in a significantly better mood. "God bless you for coming to my rescue today. Please come in and have a cup of coffee with me."

"Sure." Leda followed Auntie Bina, her eagle-sharp gaze raking the grounds and the open, empty two-car garage. "Do you live here alone?" she asked.

"No. Well, maybe yes now."

"Why is that?"

She blinked. "My husband's away."

"What's he called?"

"Rishabh."

She's avoiding the name the fiend is popularly known by. She can't have guessed who Leda is. She's just protecting the fiend despite his indiscretions. The typical Hindu woman!

"Rishabh?" Leda squinted at her as if expecting her to give her his full name.

Auntie Bina nodded, steered clear of the main entrance and the foyer full of framed pictures, and led Leda into the house through the kitchen door. "Come in, please."

Leda stepped in after her, watching her every move. "Nice property you have."

Auntie Bina let loose a long sigh. "This used to be my daughter's home." Her voice choked.

Leda glanced around, and a smile warmed her eyes. "Wow! You have the best cappuccino machine. Shall I make some? I am quite an expert."

"Sure." Auntie Bina slumped down on an upholstered chair at the breakfast table.

Even as Leda prepared the coffee, Auntie Bina told her about her royal blood. "We are the Singhs of Punjab. I was married to Pran, my first husband, when I was only eighteen and blessed with the loveliest daughter." She grabbed a bunch of Kleenex tissues from the embroidered holder and stifled a sob. "They were all snatched from me."

"Grandchildren?" Leda asked without looking up.

"Nope."

Leda glanced back. "Sugar?"

"One stevia, please." Auntie Bina sat back in her chair. "My Asha was childless."

"Oh." Leda reached for the stevia pouches by the sugar canister and knocked it over. "Sorry." She tore a kitchen towel from the roll and cleaned up the spilled sugar granules. "I'm so sorry." She picked up the mugs and planted them on the table.

Auntie Bina sipped a mouthful of the coffee. "Mmmm. Thanks. Are you married?"

"Yes."

"Children?"

Leda shook her head, lifting her mug to her mouth with both hands. "Last January I had a baby." Leda's restless fingers swirled the coffee. "Stillborn. My boy perished inside me. But I felt him move, felt him kick, until the night before the delivery." She blinked furiously.

Her grief poured through her words. *If I had eyes I would be moved to tears.*

Auntie Bina listened in stunned silence.

Leda glanced at the clock. "I am sorry for taking your time. When is your husband back?"

"When he's done with his dalliances." Auntie Bina choked back a sob. "And it's like he's still not quite done when he's back. He must help himself to the maid, the voluptuous slut!" She huffed. "Ever tasted our Indian jalebis?"

Auntie Bina opens to her like she's her best friend.

"Crisp, fresh, and sweet?" laughed Leda. "Of course, I have. I'm only just back from Kolkata."

"She's a Jalebi."

Leda glanced around the room, craning her neck to look beyond the doorways. "Does she live here, this Jalebi?"

Auntie Bina shook her head. "No, I had to throw her out. She lives close, in Hillcroft."

Leda drained her mug. "The place where you have all the Indian eateries?"

"And saree shops. In fact, there's one right next to where she lives. Saree Palace—no, that's a lie. Silk Boutique."

"Hmmm. Interesting. I really must be going. Remember, I am just a call away if you need me." Leda gave Auntie Bina her business card. "Again, thank you for the coffee and your company."

Auntie Bina stared at the card.

Leda hastened back to her car, deep in thought.

Chapter 45

The fiend emerged out of his invisibility disguise in his suite at Budget Stay, hideously skeletal and wrinkled.

The ugly demon.

Jalebi's phone rang on the bed. He picked it up, and the anonymous call disconnected. He flicked through the images of young, half-clad men and their messages.

"Huh!" He deleted them all.

The bathroom door slid open, and Jalebi stepped out in a towel.

"When did you get here?" Jalebi sniveled.

"A few minutes ago." His gaze swept over her. "Got you a few things." He grabbed a goody bag from his side and planted it before her. "Here, embrace motherhood's radiant beginnings, beautiful mama! This luxurious cocktail of antioxidants will work wonders on your skin and help you sleep. You so deserve it."

The Devil incarnate!

Jalebi's phone chimed on the bed, and she snatched it away.

The fiend glanced at the screen. "So many young men in your life, my charming slave-girl, and you've been here for so little time."

Jalebi's lips trembled.

"Lust can be fun," he chuckled. "I'm not saying it can't, but where does it lead? You can't really trust any of these men, and without trust there can be no love or sense of security. You'll still be lonely inside." He took her hands in both of his. "I can give you everything. Why do you stray from me?"

Jalebi pulled away. "You spat at me in front of the hag. You threw me out of Herenhuis and dumped me here at this cheap motel. The bat lived here."

"You will have a bigger house than Herenhuis, I promise." He pulled off her towel and tugged her onto the bed. "Wait till I seize all of Bina's worldly possessions."

She sat up unabashed. "How long?"

"After I get out of this mess. I need Bina's help, her contacts, to get back to India safe and sound."

Jalebi rose abruptly, leaving splotches of blood on the bedsheet. "I am bleeding again. I thought it had stopped." She rushed into the bathroom in tears.

The fiend stroked his chin.

In minutes, Jalebi emerged with bloodshot eyes, dressed. "We need to go to the OB now."

"Don't worry. Your OB said it's normal to have some spotting or bleeding in the first trimester." The corners of his mouth curved up.

He really does have the perfect fake smile.

"I'm well into the second trimester. You don't even remember." Jalebi sniffed. "It's my karma catching up with me. I'm the reason so many women lost their babies. Now I'm about to lose mine." Her eyes streamed. "Please take me to the OB."

"When is your next appointment?" he asked.

"In two weeks. I cannot wait that long."

"Well, you do not have health insurance here. We're lucky that the OB is providing routine checkups for free. You cannot take advantage of her."

"But I need to talk to her. I'm so scared."

"Okay. Let me call Neel. She is Neel's friend."

Jalebi rolled her eyes.

Is Neel really Jalebi's dad?

The fiend called Neel. They spoke.

"I cannot request the OB to do more than what she is already doing," said Neel. "Perhaps a spontaneous abortion is the best thing that could happen under the circumstances."

A strangled sob escaped Jalebi's lungs. "I just want to be a mom."

"Mom!" Neel roared. "And the police are knocking on the door."

Jalebi wailed piteously.

The fiend's eyes glinted. "Rest and it will be fine."

The next morning, Jalebi waited at Auntie Bina's doorstep when she returned from a shopping spree.

Auntie Bina removed her Prada sunglasses and squinted at her bloodshot eyes. "What are you doing here?"

Jalebi fell at her feet. "Please forgive me. I have nowhere to go. Dev is so cruel."

"You lured my husband with your youth and helped yourself to him. And now you expect me to forgive you, you whore?"

"He never loved me, and he doesn't have half the respect for me that he has for you. You can have him back."

"Have him back!" Auntie Bina scoffed. "You had too much of him, eh?" She unlocked the door and stepped in. "You will miss him again if you starve yourself."

Jalebi grabbed her ankles. "Never. If you only hear what he has done to me." She looked pleadingly into the older woman's eyes. "May I come in, please? I will be good and do everything you ask me to."

Auntie Bina hesitated.

She struggles to survive without domestic help.

"You haven't got another maid, have you?" asked Jalebi.

"No, but I thought you worked at a restaurant."

"I did, but it closed. The owner killed a server because he fell out with her and buried her on the property. The police found out—any dirty dishes in the sink?"

Auntie Bina heaved a sigh. "The sink is full, and the laundry basket is overflowing."

"Anything to make enough money to go back to India. I would go back tonight if I could. Dev killed my baby." Jalebi squeezed her way in past a stunned, speechless Auntie Bina.

Auntie Bina tossed and turned on her lounge chair by the pool beneath the star-spangled sky.

Jalebi appeared with two mugs on a tray. "Can't rest? I brought you some more chamomile." She handed her a cup.

Auntie Bina brushed away a tear that had slipped down her cheek and took the cup. "Thanks, but I can't seem to fall asleep without the anesthesia of false hope. I liked to think there was some good in the man."

She really fell for the fiend.

Jalebi slumped down by the pool with her tea.

For a while they listened to the music of the crickets and the moan of the wind, then Jalebi broke the silence. "I was fooled too. The signs were all staring at me in the face, yet I liked to imagine he would spare my baby."

Auntie Bina sipped a mouthful of the chamomile, her brows deeply furrowed.

Jalebi's eyes streamed. "Every other night for like the past ten days, Dev drew amniotic fluid from my uterus."

Auntie Bina scowled. "Why would you let him?"

"He knocked me out." Jalebi took a shuddering breath.

Was he always as violent as he was in the lounge?

Auntie Bina's eyes, wide and fixed, held a blank expression of utter shock.

"Do you not know that he drinks fetus blood to prevent himself from ageing?"

"I knew there was something. He always looks so young."

"Right now, the supply is low, so he used our baby."

"Our baby?" Auntie Bina asked in an audible whisper.

Jalebi pursed her lips.

There was an awkward pause.

Auntie Bina inhaled sharply. "He was feeding off the amniotic fluid of his own baby?"

"It had traces of fetal blood." Jalebi dashed the tears from her eyes with her sleeve.

"You should have been more careful—did he use physical violence?"

"That always preceded the 'honeymoon phase' when he tried to draw me back in. He gave me these regular foot massages before my nightcap—Flower Sour, a mocktail made with fresh lemon juice mixed with the essence of chamomile and passionflower. I felt so drowsy after the initial sips that I never managed to finish my cup. I began spotting, but I did not suspect a thing."

Did she not suspect anything, or did she not want to suspect anything?

Jalebi drew a sharp breath. "Last night I accidentally spilled the drink."

Auntie Bina leaned forward, breathing heavily.

"Dev offered to make me another one. He rushed away so quickly, something made me want to follow him. I could swear I saw him shove a foil-backed blister pack of tablets behind the canisters on the countertop.

"I did not think much of it, or the little something he dumped in the trash at the time. He handed me the drink, and I returned to bed sipping it dreamily." Jalebi sighed. "I fell asleep before I could finish the cup and early this morning, I had a miscarriage. The fetus was deadly pale."

What did he do to suffer the fate? The Heavens allow humans too much free will.

"What did Dev say?"

"He pretended to be sorry. He took me to the hospital, and when we got back, he gave me a sedative. I took it and tried to sleep. I could not. I felt nauseous and vomited everything in my stomach including the Valium. Dev was not in the suite. I went to the kitchen area for some water and remembered the blister pack I saw him thrust behind the canister. It had disappeared. I had a banana, and opened the trashcan to toss off the peel, and I noticed a broken blister pack pocket. I searched the hotel suite thoroughly and found a blister pack of Rohypnol, with five missing, hidden away in the closet. The clear plastic pocket I found in the trash matched the pack exactly. It explained the five nights I had fallen asleep without finishing the nightcap."

"But how did you know he was extracting amniotic fluid from your womb?"

"I had been having cramps, but after these episodes, they were more severe and lasted longer. Besides, this morning I discovered a few punctures. I checked the disposable syringes. They were ten short. I have no idea when he's been using those, and that is strange because I oversaw the paraphernalia used to supply Dev with his drink. I found the women, brought them home to him."

"Even here?"

Jalebi nodded. "I got him Gladys—you recall the torso? Dev beheaded her because she squealed too much."

Auntie Bina trembled. "Oh, my God, Jalebi.

"She was the last. I stopped. I don't drive. I have acute myopia, my vision falls below the minimum required visual acuity, even with corrective lenses."

That is why Jalebi stared in Sonya's direction on Digha beach and did not quite see her. She didn't deliberately keep the information from the others. And she did not drive the Maruti Suzuki in the path of the bulldozer in Kolkata.

Auntie Bina scoffed. "Oh, so that is why he turned to his own fetus."

"He still had to ration his intake. He's lost his looks."

"He always wears a latex mask." Auntie Bina inhaled sharply.

"That's because he's all green—he lapped up every drop of blood in Meghna's fetus, the Devil's child."

Why would Meghna conceive the Devil's child?

"Devil's child?" Auntie Bina looked at her disbelievingly.

"The Devil sprouts souls periodically to preserve evil in this world. Only a selected few have access to the souls, and Dev happens to be one of them."

Auntie Bina winced. "Who is Meghna? Is she close to Dev?"

"No. Meghna was Sonya's grandmother's nurse. Mrs. Roy suffered a stroke when Ravi and Priya passed away so suddenly. You must know that the family was ruined because Dev cast a spell on the family, and he did it with something as trivial as a book."

Jalebi seems to know everything.

"I heard about this book." Auntie Bina looked deadly pale. "Sonya won't speak of it."

"Sonya is completely besotted with the octogenarian."

It does appear that way.

There was a glint in Auntie Bina's eye. She did not comment. "But how did Meghna conceive the Devil's child?" she asked instead.

"Sonya came to Kolkata for her parents' funeral with her friend, Randy," Jalebi continued. "They were together a lot of the time and were very close. Convinced that Sonya and Randy were lovers, the fiend sneaked one of the precious souls into Mrs. Roy's house, hoping to ensoul Sonya and Randy's baby in case 'they did it' and conceived. He wanted to keep all the "lovely evil" within the family. Alas, Randy and Sonya were not lovers, and the soul chose Meghna and Randy as his parents during one of their intimate moments at the house. Meghna was not intended to be his mother, so the Devil turned her green. She had no option but to abort the baby, and Dev did it."

"Oh, my God! Oh, my God!"

A twig snapped nearby.

Jalebi and Auntie Bina shot up, casting around.

There was nobody there, no body scent, no drops of sweat, or even any telltale static.

Perhaps it's just a squirrel or a rabbit.

Yet Auntie Bina hastened indoors. "I'll call Leda. I have her card somewhere."

Jalebi followed her in. "You have nothing to worry about. You're not pregnant, but of course, you don't know what the monster is capable of."

Chapter 46

Once within the house, Auntie Bina bolted all the doors. "Search the rooms, please, Jalebi."

Even as Jalebi carried out her request, Auntie Bina rummaged through her drawers and found Leda's card. "I'll call Leda, tell her there's a murderer on the loose."

"It won't change a thing," said Jalebi. "He's stalking her, waylaying her with jinxes, but she cannot catch him."

Has Aunt Camelia found the mantra that will prevent the scar from reacting to the fiend's presence?

"We must still talk to her," said Auntie Bina.

"Please don't. She will question you so hard that you will spill out my details."

"I told her you lived by Silk Boutique. She didn't come by, did she?"

"Might've. I never lived there. I lied."

"Oh. But what if you explain your situation?"

"Leda maintains strict ethical standards."

"But Dev abused you."

"I was addicted to the relationship. I worshipped him, committed all those atrocities for him. I cannot stop blaming myself."

"Neither can I. Every night, every day, every minute, every breath I take, it consumes me."

The fiend plays the lover well

They settled on the living room settee with some strong whiskey.

Auntie Bina sighed. "I had been warned. Just weeks before Dev swept me off my feet, an astrologer friend read my horoscope. He said that I was stepping into a difficult phase, he called 'Mahadasha,' and was about to meet a man of evil intentions. He said there was the possibility that I could surrender completely to his wiles."

Jalebi nodded. "When Rahu, the shadow planet that causes eclipses, is placed negatively in the horoscope, it impairs your sense of judgement. But there are astrological remedies to improve Rahu in your horoscope."

"The astrologer suggested I wear a gemstone, Gomed, a kind of garnet, but soon I fell insanely in love with Dev and forgot all about it."

He must've ensured she did.

"You could always wear one now." Jalebi took an extra-long sip.

"Yes, but my friend is dead. I must consult some other astrologer, someone trustworthy. Gemstones, I've heard, undergo many treatments from mine to shop, leading to the exhaustion of their vibrations."

"A Vedic pooja could help them to work with their full fervor. It's called purification. I can help you with that. I've been with Dev long enough; I am familiar with the rituals. Once that is completed and you wear the stone on your finger, you will regain control over your senses and your judgement."

"Thanks." Auntie Bina filled Jalebi's half-empty tumbler with the spicy bourbon. "You should get a stone too, Jalebi."

"Nothing can change my fate as long as Dev lives, and he has been granted immortality by the evil deity he worships."

She knows too.

"Really? That is a curse, don't you think? What if he should ever want to die?"

"He can whenever. He has a mantra—the Mrityushakti mantra. He was given it. I swear I did not imagine that incident."

"What incident, Jalebi?"

Jalebi had a faraway look in her eyes. "That night, Dev brought me a basketful of those pendulous flowers to chew—Angel's trumpets. He never really let me have them before. I had just learned from the other occupants of the house that the flowers contained large amounts of a substance nicknamed Devil's Breath due to its use by robbers in Columbia to knock out their victims. I was surprised, more so as he encouraged me to gorge myself on them and then quickly left. True, I had been curious about the taste and had begged him to bring me some, but a basketful?"

Auntie Bina stared at Jalebi, her brows scrunched. "Where was this? When?"

"Around twelve years ago in the outskirts of Kolkata. There's a house that looks abandoned."

"So Dev did not find you on Care.com."

"No. I've been with him since I was thirteen."

"Hmmm." Auntie Bina slumped back in the settee.

Jalebi continued with her story. "Suspecting something fishy going on, I followed him. It was unusually quiet, with none of that usual overlapping chatter and boisterous laughter of the sadhus who still retained their zest for life in that hell.

"I searched Dev out by his scent—the attar he wore. But creeping along untrodden paths through a jungle of angel's trumpets, I lost him. It was the flowers that hung straight down, as far as I could see, each trumpet twelve or more inches in length.

"Then, suddenly there was this sound—short, jagged scrapes of steel striking the ground. I froze on the spot. Two bare-bodied men were digging a pit by a thatched gazebo, where red-silk-clad sadhus sat in a semicircle before another pit, rectangular and brimming with blood. They rocked rhythmically as in a trance, chanting long monotonous mantras.

"Right across from them, several headless young boys, resplendent in red tulle and smeared with sindoor and sandalwood paste, lay on the grass. Blood gleamed on their severed heads." Jalebi drained her glass.

I quaked. *Does Sonya even realize what she's got herself into?*

Auntie Bina chugged the remaining whisky in her glass, her hand trembling. "Narabali. The government made it illegal with the Anti-Superstition and Black Magic Act in 1830."

"I was not too sure what was happening until the sadhus suddenly jerked their heads and with savage hand gestures, hissed an invocation to some dark goddess. Out of the blood bath, Dev emerged. The sadhus embraced him, their chanting rising to a crescendo. They showered him with red flowers, draped his gory body with black silk, and adorned his face with sandalwood paste.

"The decapitated bodies were set alight. Even as the fire crackled and spat and the fiery flames illuminated the famished bodies of the boys, the two bare-bodied men peeled the flesh from the heads. The aura of unmitigated gloom exuded a raw energy, so overwhelming, I fainted on the spot." Jalebi shuddered like she relived the experience all over again.

"Oh my God. What happened then?" asked Auntie Bina.

"I was lucky Dev did not return to my room that night or discover me amid the shrubs. When I came around, he was just yards from me, clean as freshly washed sheets and fragrant. With him was a dreaded sadhu I knew, presumably another devotee of the daemon Dev worshipped. Oblivious of my presence, they spoke in an audible whisper about the Mrityushakti mantra, how it was granted only to immortals, and how Dev was never to touch it, or read it, or even set eyes on it, except in the worst-case scenario. Apparently, it's composed of six words in Sanskrit that when read in the right order, would result in instantaneous death."

If only Sonya was here.

Auntie Bina grimaced. "Interesting. Did you see the piece of paper? Where does Dev keep it? Does he carry it around with him?"

"No, and I've seen him naked and even without his wig. Besides, I haven't got a clue about what medium—paper, canvas, stone—the sadhu used to pass on the mantra. I did not see him give it to Dev. The sadhu repeatedly visited the place after the incident. Every time he came, yajnas were performed. Animals were sacrificed, sometimes even humans. I was made to watch."

"How old were you again?"

"Almost fourteen then. At first, the angel's trumpets helped. Later the killings hardened me."

Auntie Bina stared at her in horror. "What if Dev is in the house right now, listening to us?"

I winced. *He could very well be.*

"I've checked every room," said Jalebi.

She did not mention the invisibility guise. *How does she not know about it?*

Auntie Bina shifted uneasily. "I wish we had a sensor."

Can a sensor pick up the clues? Even I can't with my heightened senses.

Chapter 47

As the night wore on, Auntie Bina and Jalebi restricted themselves to the kitchen.

"Warm me up some food please, Jalebi," said Auntie Bina. "There is chicken curry left over from last night."

Jalebi eased it out from the refrigerator and slipped it into the microwave. "I could make you some fresh chapatis."

"You don't have to. There's leftover rice in the fridge. You've had a long day." Auntie Bina spoke to Jalebi like she was her own daughter.

Sweet are the uses of adversity.

"Please, it's therapeutic. We could just have two each." Jalebi poured out some wheat flour from its canister, mixed in some yoghurt, and started kneading it.

Auntie Bina sighed. "Jalebi, you did not tell me about your parents. I do not mean to be nosy, but I can't help wondering why you went to live with that monster at the tender age of thirteen."

"Amma died when I was twelve. She was the best mom ever." Jalebi blinked furiously. "My father disappeared after the villagers found the half-eaten body of Amma." She took a shuddering breath. "She was out fetching firewood from the forest when a tiger attacked her."

Auntie Bina shifted uneasily on the settee. "I'm sorry."

"It's not uncommon in the Sundarbans where we lived." Jalebi's eyes streamed. "And no one feels sorry for me. Not even my own father. He sold me to Dev within a month of her passing."

She never mentions his name.

Auntie Bina's eyes glistened. Perhaps she felt sorry for judging her. I did. "Jalebi, I'm sorry, I've been so harsh," she sniveled.

Jalebi sighed.

Auntie Bina stared at her, as though fumbling for words. "That house you call abandoned, has Dev had it for years?"

"Yes. He renovated parts of it over the course of the years." Jalebi divided the soft dough into four portions. With a little oil she rolled them into small balls. "In those days it had a name— 'Bilash.' It translates to 'luxury' in English."

"More like indulgence, extravagance, a life of pleasure and comfort." Auntie Bina attempted a smile. "I know quite a bit of Bengali. I've lived in Kolkata for years."

Jalebi nodded.

Neither spoke for several minutes, then Jalebi broke the silence.

"I was lucky Dev was kind to me. You should listen to the stories of the women at his Tollygunge house, not like there are any still alive to tell them."

That was Hema's house. Things happened there.

"Dev asked me to call him by his name at home, but 'uncle' in public," continued Jalebi. "He sent me to a good school and to tutors to up my grades. I was doing well, though I was not allowed to visit my friends or bring them home. I didn't care because I had a good life, good food, nice clothes. I respected him until I hit puberty."

Auntie Bina shot her a side glance.

"He started making euphemistic references like 'private time together.' He said it was part of the arrangement and during the sessions, he discussed what he was seeking." Jalebi flattened each little ball of dough into thin circles using a rolling pin.

"When did you first realize you were being manipulated?"

"Did it matter?" Jalebi lit the stove and placed a small cast-iron skillet on it. "I was his prize, and he would enjoy me. There was no escape from it."

"Why didn't you run away?"

"Where would I go? I had no home. I was like a fishing boat, its line broken, washed away by the tide. I let Dev take charge." Jalebi placed a chapati on the skillet, browned and puffed it, then reached for the next one.

"You could have gotten pregnant."

"We had protected sex right from the start, except this one time I got pregnant." Jalebi cooked the third chapati to perfection and then the fourth. "I guess Dev ensured he had a backup fetus to supply him with blood when he came abroad. Of course, he told me that we didn't have to worry about an unwed pregnancy because he would marry me ASAP. Then he married you."

No wonder she was so angry with Auntie Bina.

Auntie Bina swallowed. "You have no connection with your husband?"

"My husband, Ved, is gay. He never touched me. He really belonged to Dev. My marriage was a ploy to introduce Ved into the close community at the abandoned house, a reason for him to live within its walls." Jalebi arranged the chapatis in the stainless-steel casserole and closed the lid. "There was another reason why Dev valued Ved. He was brought up here in the US and taught me spoken English. I told you about all those pregnant women I fetched to provide Dev with fetal blood. Well, we had an excess, and we sold them. I was the face of the business. I had more clients than you could imagine."

How utterly unthinkable!

Auntie Bina scowled. "So, everyone associated with Dev serves a purpose."

"Which changes with time. Women of child-bearing age always become his suppliers of fetal blood."

My anxiety spiraled into panic. *If I tell Deepak about this, will he still ask me to refrain from interfering in Sonya's life?*

Auntie Bina gritted her teeth. "Has he ever said why he married me?"

"You know why. He needed your help, influence, and money to get out of the country, and he will need it all again to get back in."

"Did he tell you?"

Jalebi nodded.

"But I gave myself to him, and to no other. I had suitors in Kolkata, rich and handsome. Did he never mention how much I loved him?"

"A man who drinks fetal blood to stay young?"

"My Botox bills are sky high. I tried so hard despite my age."

"Your age. Even you say it. I don't mean to be rude, but how do you think he feels about your age when he cannot accept his own?"

Auntie Bina's face was livid, the veins standing out on her neck. "Can't we find this Mrityushakti mantra in some Vedic text?"

"It is special, granted only to immortals. How many of us are immortals in this world?" Jalebi pursed her lips. "But the mantra's got to be somewhere."

If only Jalebi and Sonya would talk.

"How would we get him to read it even if we found it?"

"The saving grace is, he doesn't know what it is," said Jalebi. "He has never read it, for if he had—"

"He would be dead."

"If we could only display the six words of the mantra in really big letters, he would be forced to look upon them, and his mind would absorb them as word-pictures." Jalebi's eyes glinted wildly. "Isn't that reading?"

Of course.

Something crashed against the door.

There was no smell, no wind, and no scintillating lights.

Dev? A cold shiver ran right through me.

Auntie Bina clutched Jalebi's arm. "Is Dev listening to us?"

"He wouldn't wait outside after hearing everything we said. He would come in and kill us both."

Is it Sonya then? Please, please let it be her.

The windows rattled. Auntie Bina gripped Jalebi like a vise.

"It's only the wind," muttered Jalebi.

On the porch, an invisible cell phone vibrated. Millions of dots surged around it only to fade instantly. A message appeared as if on the invisible screen several feet above the ground, and it was from the fiend:

Why don't you text? Is Jalebi at Bina's?

Yes. The keyboard clicked, and then with a burst of visual static, the device went silent.

Beads of sweat oozing Sonya's scent floated in the air.

I almost squealed with excitement. *She now knows how to use the image of the mantra. Is she using her old phone with the image or the new one?* I could not tell.

Invisible yet scintillating erratically, she raced toward the gate. In her haste, she stumbled against a Chinese lacquer pot by the flowerbeds.

It swayed noisily in the silence, almost tipping over.

The curtains parted. Auntie Bina and Jalebi peered out tremulously.

"A few nights ago, a gust of wind blew its pair over." Auntie Bina sighed. "It was damaged beyond repair. I had to throw it away."

"This pot looks okay," said Jalebi. "Yet that sound. It was like someone bumped into it."

Auntie Bina closed the curtain. "I must install heavy-duty folding security gates at all the entrances. Let's find the security experts in the yellow pages and contact them right now."

Chapter 48

I lost Sonya only to find her a block away from Asha's house where she emerged as if out of thin air, her wet sweaty clothes clinging to her like a second skin.

A black truck pulled up, picked her up, then whooshed away.

"Who's truck?" asked Sonya.

"Neel's," the Romni at the wheel replied. The fiend's voice gave him away.

The truck headed out west, toward Southwest Freeway. "Your Corolla is in his garage and all your belongings in the master suite."

Is that where they are headed? I felt terribly uneasy. *Sonya must live with Neel?*

Sonya gazed out the window at the passing scenery.

"You seem preoccupied, Sonya. What did Jalebi say to Bina?"

"Oh, only about her upbringing."

"I adopted her at the age of thirteen, gave her the best possible education." He took a raspy breath. "Did she say anything adverse?"

"Um, no."

"But your hesitation to discuss what she said tells me she did. If she did, it's only a story. Her story. If she begins to spread rumors, which I do not doubt she can fabricate with her very fertile imagination, she will get herself into trouble. I will be gone and there will be no one to help her out of it."

"Silly girl." Sonya met his gaze.

"Don't worry about her. Let's focus on the Sunny-Nikita episode, which must happen tomorrow. The potion is ready." He eased out a tiny pouch from his pocket and handed it to her. "Here, a few drops on each eyelid before the alarm goes off tomorrow morning—remember, no sloppiness. It's the little things that trip you up."

"There's one hitch. While on my way to Gran Bina's, I spotted Paul and Sunny at Trader Joe's. I was invisible, so I ventured close. They spoke about an early-morning appointment tomorrow with prospective buyers of the Mehta estate—Nikita's home."

Her loyalty!

His eyes darted. "Why all of a sudden?"

"She's been trying to sell it since her parents' accident."

"That can't happen. That won't happen." The fiend drew a sharp breath. "Sunny and Nikita must get engaged tomorrow, and Leda silenced forever." Giving no details as to how he planned to achieve his second objective, he reminded Sonya that he would call Sunny like they had decided.

Sonya's wide grin blossomed across her features. "What if we could get both Sunny and Nikita to sleep through the day and wake up at half past six in the evening instead? I could wet Nikita's eyelids with the potion while you chat up Sunny."

"Good. I have been observing you, Sonya. Love your attention to detail and your work ethic." The fiend took an arm off the wheel and patted her thigh.

Eek!

Sonya betrayed no sign of disgust! Instead, that wide, bright smile continued to grace her face.

How does she manage it?

"When do I get to see Hema, Uncle Dev?"

"The bat!" The exit to Rosenberg approached, and the fiend's hand returned to the wheel. Signaling right, he merged onto the exit ramp. "Whenever you want to really. I almost lost her. Thankfully, Guru, the caretaker of Herenhuis found her."

"The last time I saw her, she threatened to run away."

"She was hiding in the woods at Herenhuis. Guru recognized her. Anyway, I've asked him not to mention any of this to Bina. She doesn't know about Hema or her bat version at all. And I know you haven't told her."

"No, of course not."

"Now, just to keep you updated. The bat demands immediate freedom. It's her mother, my sister, inciting her."

Sonya scrunched her brows.

"Guru is terrified of her sudden towering rages. Yet you are not." He glanced at her.

"Hema is not always in a fury."

"Well, Guru is so traumatized, he's moved out of Herenhuis. And now he is shit scared in case Bina should drop by to check on the property. He's afraid that he will lose his job. She's already mad at him for allowing Jalebi in."

"It's my job to appease the bat. Do you think I should go and check up on her tonight?"

"She's still in the woods. It's better you go during the day with Guru's binoculars." The fiend tightened his hands around the wheel. "All this had to happen now, just as the Master is ecstatic about the souls I gave him." He dug his fingernails into the wheel. "Hema must be crushed."

"You shall have my full cooperation." Sonya beamed.

If only Sonya would ask questions.

"I will text you Guru's number, Sonya. It might be a good idea to get in touch with the man. He might have some information, if not the courage to physically help you, should you need help."

"Of course. I really appreciate your thoughtfulness, Uncle Dev."

The fiend pulled up to the curb of Neel's house and passed Sonya the keys and a basket from the cargo bed. "You will find all sorts of snacks and drinks in here."

"Wow! Thanks!" Sonya accepted it graciously and disappeared into the old, dark house, devoid of any human scent except that of the fiend.

Neel couldn't be living here. Then why keep it?

The fiend drove away preoccupied.

Whatever his thoughts are, he's not going to hurt Sonya, not yet. She's still useful to him, almost indispensable. But where's she heading?

Deep in the downspout of Asha's roof, worry-filled "what-if" thoughts about Sonya's future returned to plague me.

Sunny and Paul drove past.

"Nikita is drifting from me," said Sunny. "It's no point returning to England. I can't focus on my job." I hated the deep despair etched on his face.

My anxiety for my children skyrocketed. I crept out of the downspout to ponder my despair in seclusion.

An owl wheeled across the leaden sky, drawing buoyant hues with its fine quills.

Deepak's scent overpowered me.

"Deepak, my kids—" Gusts of wind drowned my voice.

He tossed some feathers over me. The new disguise of a Lincoln sparrow fitted like a glove.

"You are at the beginning of the last phase of your stay on Earth, and I came all this way to tell you that." Deepak soared into the tangerine skies, tugging me along.

"But what will happen to my children? My daughter is with the rogues—"

A vision of the future No.7 emerged over our ash-covered property.

Mesmerized, I floated toward the beautiful mansion that stood in the middle of lush gardens with water features blending seamlessly with the landscape.

"See that board among the tangle of wisteria with the name 'Shantih' carved on it? That will be its new name."

The thunder predicted that peace, shantih, would be achieved through the three 'Da's. "Looks like the curse will be revoked after all, doesn't it, Deepak?"

He faded with the vision.

Wriggling within my sparrow disguise, I plummeted into the pool of yellow streetlight shrouding No.7.

A drizzle swept gently past in a drifting haze. Not a drop fell over the property.

A hermit-thrush hopped around the ash, looking up at the skies, singing, "Drip drop drip drop drip drop drop."

Leda's voice penetrated my core though I neither saw nor smelled her. She spoke like she was on the phone. "Bina is just avoiding me. She won't take my calls, won't answer my texts. I have a feeling something's up."

Perhaps Jalebi is stopping her. She avoids Leda like the plague.

"I've been to the house several times, but every time she's been away," came Nikita's reply. "And the key I have doesn't seem to work anymore. But I can try again."

"Yes, please—" There was a groan, then a thud before Leda finished her sentence.

Neel's black truck drove past and stopped at the curb in front of our neighbor's house. The fiend, disguised as a Romni, spoke to Neel on his phone. "No, Neel, no luck with the silver,"

The intrigue of magic. The sorcerer can't find it, and Leda can.

"When can you come, Neel?" the fiend asked. "You know we won't have much time once the brat is offed."

Offed? Who?

"Dev, there is one important thing you must tell Sonya. She should not use the truck—"

"Hang on." The fiend placed Neel on hold to answer an incoming call.

It was Guru. "Sonya is mortally injured at Herenhuis. The vultures are gathering . . ."

The fiend returned to Neel at once. "Get the OB at once. I'm coming. Sonya is at Herenhuis, mortally wounded."

No! Even as I rocketed though the hundred and fifty miles that separated the two properties, Leda talked to the emergency services.

That was a quick recovery. Is it Aunt Camelia's magic?

I landed at Herenhuis and stumbled on a pool of blood. It smelled of Sonya.

And she was unfazed about the bat's temper. Is she dead?

Up in the branches I glimpsed the bat and shuddered at her bloody claws. "Hema! Where is Sonya?"

She bared her sharp fangs.

What if Sonya's dead and they drenched her body in their identity-effacing sprays?

Searching for her, I stumbled on Mashi, Hema's mother, struggling to escape the rainbow-color spirit traps dangling from creepers on the walls. "Someone, help," she cried. "These skeins are stifling me. My evil brother, he is relentless."

I threw myself at her, fiercely, once, twice, thrice. My cladding felt tougher than ever before.

Strangulated sobs racked her body. "I understand why you are angry, Priya. I did try to save your daughter from Hema's violence, but Hema was driven insane by her impatience. She tore some flesh off Sonya's arms—"

"Where is Sonya?" I rammed into her until she dropped to the ground. There she lay dazed for a second, then realized she was free.

"Thanks, Priya," she whispered feebly. "How could I think a good soul like you could hurt me? I'm sorry I cannot help you to find Sonya. She was picked up by a rogue, Neel. There was an OB with him. They forced the chunk of flesh out of Hema's mouth, but I have no idea where they went. I am so sorry, Priya. Hema has done great wrong, but you must excuse me. I must race to Heaven and plead for forgiveness from the Heaven Elders on her behalf." She vanished in the sudden rush of sirens and flashing lights.

In the blinding, deafening chaos, the bat lurked in the shadows.

"How could you?" I dared. It required a significant exercise of will not to pounce on her and tear her to shreds.

She lurched at me and sunk her fangs into my disguise. Before I could react, she was sucked into a green, fetid mist which dissipated almost at once.

Was that the Devil? Did he take her?

An eagle swooped down, his wings as broad as they were black. His head was white as a paper cut out. He smelled like Deepak, yet his talons squashed my core hard against his bosom and tossed me across the woods.

"I am sorry I must do this, but you must stay away from the Devil. The wait's nearly over." Deepak's voice faded with his scent.

The world blurred.

Woozy, I tumbled through the air into the pond of irises in the woods. There was a soft plonk and then only the quieter, undulating sound of ripples . . .

Chapter 49

I came around at the bottom of a pond. My memories wiggled their way out of the mud of my core. Hema bit a chunk of flesh off Sonya, then attacked me. Deepak shoved me to the bottom of the pond. He said my wait was nearly over.

Rising through the clump of irises, fluttering in the afternoon breeze, I tried to analyze Deepak's words. *What does he mean by "The wait's nearly over?" I do so desperately need the support and guidance of the Heaven Elders.*

I wondered if Sonya had had some slipshod surgery and lay sedated in some covert little hideaway. My first guess was Rosenburg where I had last seen her.

There was no one in the house except Hema. She spun dizzily in a corner of Neel's study, fastened to whirling rotor blades.

Is this some kind of punishment for her aggressive behavior? Who put her up there? The Devil or the fiend?

Instinctively, I searched for spirit traps. There were none.

I am not expected there. The house will make the perfect lookout point. Sneaking into a roofline gap, I focused my attention on Asha's house.

Is Sonya in the lounge? I saw no trace of her.

A police cruiser with flashing lights pulled into the driveway.

Has the officer any news of my girl?

He rang the bell, and Auntie Bina opened the door.

"Mrs. Singh?"

She nodded.

"May I come in, please?"

"S-sure."

He stepped in, glancing around. "Isn't this the house of Asha Chawla, the woman responsible for the murder of Baal Zebab?"

"Yes. I'm her mother. I'm just visiting." Auntie Bina denied knowing about her daughter's whereabouts.

The officer stopped to scan the framed photos on and around the console table in the foyer. "We are investigating the case of Sonya Gupta," he said, "the girl found unconscious on your property, Herenhuis." He handed her a picture of Sonya.

If I had been granted the perk of talking to humans, I would apologize to Auntie Bina on Sonya's behalf.

Her brows furrowed. She trembled. "I have no idea how she landed at Herenhuis. I've barely used the house since I came into possession of it a little more than a month ago. She was staying with me here since she returned from India after her parents' funeral and then suddenly left without telling me. We were close. I . . . I um, have known the girl since she was little. She is like family. Sonya was best friends with my niece's daughter, Nikita. I used to babysit the pair." She paused for a breather.

The officer's brows scrunched. "Would you have any idea where she could be now? It's been three days since she disappeared from Herenhuis."

It's been three days!

Auntie Bina shook her head. "But you could search my Galveston condo."

"Why? Has anyone seen her there?"

"N-no. It's just my gut feeling that she could be there."

The officer watched her with narrowed eyes. "Hmmm. How long are you here for?"

"Until the end of August. But you might not always find me at this house. I have other properties in Texas." She shared the addresses with him.

He took copious notes. "Well, that is a lot of property," he said.

"I am an Indian princess." Auntie Bina beamed.

"Then you must have a lot of maids." The officer craned his neck to scan the kitchen.

"No, I'm a fusspot."

That's honest of the socialite.

The officer's gaze swept over her wedding photograph on the console table in the foyer. "Where is your husband?"

"No idea. We don't live together. You could go look for him in Victoria. You might find him there."

The officer sighed. "What does he do?"

"Astrology. That's what he told me when we got married, but now I hear that he does black magic too."

The officer squinted at her. "Do you think he has a hand in Sonya's plight?"

Auntie Bina shrugged. "He can do anything."

The officer inhaled sharply. "Does your niece's daughter live here?"

"No." She reached for the sticky notes on the console table and scribbled Nikita's address. "Here," she handed it to him. "You should find Nikita home now. She might have some information."

She seems desperate to get him out of the house.

"Thanks." The officer tucked away the sticky note in his pocket. "Who else lives in this house with you? I saw a young woman as I came in."

"Oh, I have a devoted companion from India. After all, I need help with the housework. I am eighty next year." Auntie Bina slipped into the kitchen and returned with Jalebi.

She appeared a little protective of the girl.

"What is your name?" the officer asked Jalebi.

"Rumki."

"How long have you been in this household?"

"Since I came to work for Mrs. Singh last month." Jalebi looked the officer dead in the eye. "I will return to India with her in August."

"Thanks. That will be all, Mrs. Singh." He left the premises with a deep frown.

Several hours passed. I scanned Asha's house, from my lookout in Rosenberg, for any clues that could help me find my daughter in vain.

The late afternoon sun angled down when Nikita pulled up on the driveway. Again, she wore Estée Lauder's Beyond Paradise, one or two spritzes on her wrist.

The house seemed quiet. She pushed open the door left ajar.

Jalebi, busy polishing the furniture in the living room, dropped the chamois leather in her hand and rushed away.

Nikita's phone chimed with a message from Sunny.

Her face grimacing, Nikita switched the phone to vibration mode. *It distresses her to ignore Sunny, yet . . .*

Auntie Bina stepped in and hugged Nikita. "Hello, dear. It's so lovely to see you." She took a lungful of her fragrance. Her eyebrows scrunched together, but she asked no questions.

Jalebi lingered in the shadows of the kitchen, watching, listening.

"Have you changed the lock, Gran Bina?" asked Nikita. "I dropped by a few times. No one answered the door, and the old key doesn't seem to fit."

"My husband changed it. I'll give you the new key once the security gates have been installed."

They settled on the large satinwood settee.

Auntie Bina sighed. "So how have you been?"

"Okay. Just got done with the police interrogation. He kept asking about your new husband. I said we hadn't met. Where is he?"

"No idea. We're splitting up."

"Really? I'm so sorry."

"You needn't be. He's a nightmare."

Nikita swallowed. "It all happened so quickly."

"He's been very secretive, right from the start. I was going through a difficult phase when I fell in love with him—"

The clock struck five.

"Teatime," beamed Auntie Bina. "Would you like some pakoras with your tea?"

"Of course."

"Great. Give me a minute." She waddled to the kitchen and returned with a smile. "My Jalebi is an expert."

Nikita smiled. "The name sounds familiar."

"Really?" Auntie Bina seemed ill at ease.

"There was a Jalebi who worked for someone I knew back in India—Leda."

"The detective?" Auntie Bina grimaced. "Did she send you here?"

"Well, I would have come anyway to apologize for splitting up with Dillon so suddenly at the last moment. You spent a fortune on my dahej."

"No worries, Nikita. You will get married soon. The gifts will not be wasted."

"But all those custom-made items you got for Dillon?"

"Never mind that. I might start a boutique." Auntie Bina leaned forward with a smile. "Now, you tell me about Sunny and you. How are things going?"

I recalled Sunny's despair as he spoke to Paul about Nikita drifting and waited to hear her version of the story.

"He wants us to get back together."

"Then go ahead."

"As much as he sweeps me off my feet with his charm and good looks, I hate the way he treats Sonya." Nikita inhaled sharply. "The poor girl is so vulnerable."

She must find it strange knowing how close they had been.

Auntie Bina glanced over her shoulder. "Now where is the girl? Jalebi?"

"Coming," Jalebi responded promptly from the kitchen.

"Hmmm." Auntie Bina's eyes narrowed at Nikita. "But Sunny is treating you right."

"That is not my Sunny." Nikita sighed. "His behavior concerns me. He used to be so level-headed, compassionate, and empathetic."

Hmmm.

Nikita's phone vibrated with yet another text from Sunny.

Both Auntie Bina and Nikita glanced at it.

I'm coming over, Sunny had texted.

Not at home, Nikita replied.

Auntie Bina watched Nikita with her brows furrowed. "Find someone else. Try Saadi.com. I don't want you to lose all chances in love merely because you are wrapped up in Sunny's charms."

"He changed because Dev cast a spell on his family."

Auntie Bina sighed. "Then why blame Sunny?"

"He's still Sonya's brother. It's unnatural that he doesn't care two hoots about her."

Jalebi came in with the tea and planted the mugs on the coffee table.

"Thanks," said Nikita.

Jalebi smiled. "The pakoras should be ready shortly." She left quickly.

"Look, Nikita," said Auntie Bina, "Sonya's no babe lost in the woods." She drew a sharp breath. "You think about yourself and your grandparents. They're dying. Get married." She picked up a mug and sipped a mouthful, "Dillon is already married."

An acrid odor hit my core.

Jalebi had disappeared from the kitchen. Yet the oil smoked in the pan, and the pakora mix was all ready for frying. I scanned the premises. There was not a trace of her anywhere.

In the living room, Nikita and Auntie Bina continued to talk.

"I bumped into Dillon and his new wife at Galleria. She's pretty." Nikita smiled.

"It was an arranged marriage."

"Um—" Nikita sniffed. "Do you smell oil burning, Gran Bina?"

Auntie Bina rose. "Jalebi!"

She did not answer.

Auntie Bina and Nikita rushed to the kitchen. Nikita switched off the stove.

"Where is she?" Auntie Bina opened the kitchen door and stepped outside. There was no one there. "Jalebi, are you listening?" she called. "Jalebi?"

There was no response.

Chapter 50

Nikita and Auntie Bina searched the premises for Jalebi in vain. I squirmed restlessly in the roofline gap of Neel's house. *The fiend must have got her. There is no escape for her, is there?*

"Let me call Leda," said Nikita.

Leda responded promptly to the call and arrived at the house post haste. "May I have a few minutes with Bina alone, please?" she said.

"Sure." Nikita departed.

Leda found Auntie Bina weeping in the living room.

"My Jalebi is gone," she sobbed. "One minute she was preparing pakoras in the kitchen, the next, she's gone."

She genuinely feels concerned about Jalebi's wellbeing. Their misfortunes have brought them together.

"May I look around the house, please?" asked Leda.

"Of course. Jalebi uses the room above the garage."

"Thanks." Leda studied the photographs in the foyer and returned to the living room. "What is your husband's name?"

"Rishabh."

Leda squinted at her.

"Rishabhdev, the man you are looking for," said Auntie Bina in a loud and clear voice. "We are no longer together."

"Thanks." Leda produced a little wandlike metal rod and whizzed round the house, thrusting it into corners and sliding it across the walls. At length, with a slight grimace on her face, she raced past Auntie Bina, dozing on the living room settee, and bolted up to Jalebi's room.

She rummaged through the drawers and all of Jalebi's belongings. She scanned Jalebi's mother's wedding photograph gracing the top of her wardrobe, slipped it out of its frame, and traced a finger along the torn edge. Her gaze whizzed around the room and finally settled on the other half of the photograph lying face down at the bottom of the empty wastebasket.

Leda flipped it and studied the groom's picture for a fraction of a second. "Neel?" Her brows scrunched, and she rubbed her chin. Thrusting both halves of the photograph into her carryall tote, she returned to the living room.

"Bina," she called in a near whisper.

The old lady jumped.

"It's only me, Bina. I am done. Thank you."

Auntie Bina pulled herself up on the settee with some effort. "Leda, please be kind to Jalebi when you find her." She sighed. "Poor girl, she has had a horrific life. She was sold to Dev at thirteen by her father and abused."

"You did not give me her correct address."

Auntie Bina swallowed. "I gave you what she gave me. Anyway, Jalebi was staying at Budget Stay on Hillcroft, Room 215, before she came to live with me here a few days ago."

"Thank you." Leda raced back to her car.

Auntie Bina limped behind her. "Please try and understand why the girl committed the crimes she did. Dev exploited her since she was thirteen! He—"

"I'll see you in a bit, and then you must give me the whole story." Leda leaped into her car and drove away.

The fiend and Sonya sipped their coffees at the solitary window of Jalebi's suite at Budget Stay, their gazes fixed on the motel's small parking lot.

I willed myself not to move from Rosenberg. Sonya didn't appear to be in pain, though her upper left arm was wrapped in a bandage. She held a mug in her hand and beamed like she was in seventh Heaven.

Perhaps the fiend used some numbing charm on her wound.

"I'm glad you don't have much of a conscience." The fiend swirled the coffee in his mug.

"I only see, hear, and do evil." Sonya grinned.

"I'm glad you remember the words." He laughed. "You will be happy to learn that we're leaving tomorrow."

Again! Where are they going? Has Sonya picked up her old phone from Asha's house? The image of the mantra is stored in it.

Sonya's face froze for the briefest second, then her wide smile broke through. "When will Gran Bina be joining us?"

"We'll think about her once we've got Sunny and Nikita together. There's very little time, and we have a lot to do."

Is he still thinking about silencing Leda?

"Of course." Sonya grinned. "When do we get started?"

"I will slip out and do the necessary." The fiend spoke in a monotone.

Unable to understand what exactly he meant by "do the necessary," I shifted uncomfortably under the roof of Neel's old house, and the front door opened softer than the whisper of a breath.

A cloud of flickering dots appeared and vanished at the entrance door. Quiet footsteps sounded on the floor. The door to the cupboard-under-the-stairs creaked open and shut.

I smelled nobody.

The invisible person retreated to the front door and saw himself out.

Rapid and shallow breathing emerged from the cupboard-under-the-stairs.

It must be someone who has been knocked out and drenched in the fiend's invisibility spray. That makes two prisoners.

"So, where are we going?" Sonya's question jolted my attention back to her at Budget Stay. There was no panic in her voice, yet my heightened senses caught a slight tremor in her knees.

"Mexico," answered the fiend.

"Are we flying?" she asked.

"No, we'll take a taxi to Victoria from Rosenburg, and Neel will drive us to the border.

Sonya glanced around the room. "Where's Jalebi? When will she pack? Her things are literally everywhere."

"Jalebi will never need any of that." He sipped a large mouthful of his coffee. "Jalebi lies sedated in Neel's house, thanks to Damien."

So it's her. Damien must have picked her up from Asha's house, knocked her unconscious, and dumped her here.

Jalebi continued to be invisible and scent-free.

"You will have to light a kerosene lamp in the cupboard-under-the-stairs where she lies before we leave," said the fiend.

"Of course." Sonya nodded, still smiling. I caught a whiff of sweat pooling in her hair.

"She will go in her sleep. The girl has served me well, and I will ensure her death will be easy and painless. That's as kind as I can get." His eyes glinted ominously.

He only used Jalebi.

Sonya's heart pounded dangerously, yet she smiled. "Yeah, so it'll be just us then, Uncle Dev."

"We will hang around here all day, then drive to Rosenberg at night. I have your favorite sandwiches in the cooler bag—bacon, brie, lettuce and tomato."

"Thank you, Uncle Dev," said Sonya. "I love brie."

"I know." He chuckled. "And there are more surprises."

The perfect doting uncle!

"Thank you. Thank you so much. Honestly, you are the uncle I never had." She drained her mug and planted it on the sill. "If only I could be more successful with Hema."

"No worries. The Master has taken care of her surplus energy. He put a dart through her, an "inciter" that will stir her feelings and build her anger a thousandfold, well, until she's at bursting point."

I felt a surge of pity for her despite everything. *Hema lived and died a good little girl, having done nothing to deserve this fate.*

"How does a spirit burst?" Sonya met his gaze.

"Spirits have a core, and the core has a capacity." He seemed pleased with her interest in the dark arts. "Now this inciter I told you about, has a built-in electronic speed controller and a timer." He squinted at his watch. "If all goes well, in exactly three hours, the bat is expected to reach the anger level required, and then the inciter will release her and switch off. The "extensior," which is an ethereal tube with a sensor will shoot up at once and swallow the bat."

"But all the ash?"

"That will fall away through the extensior—it has perforations—but it will store all the anger, all that energy in the bat."

Sonya's lips twisted into a lopsided smile.

She's too tense to give him the full grin.

"We need the energy to stretch the bat out as thin mesh over the whole of No.7." He beamed.

"Over the blanket of ash?" She managed to keep her voice steady.

"Uh-huh, and shield it for eternity."

"Bet Hema can't protest."

"Not at all."

"So, am I fired?" Sonya chuckled.

Horror grabbed me as I recalled Jalebi's statement of how everyone in his life had a purpose to fulfil. *What will he use her for now?*

"You are a smart woman who will be an asset wherever I go."

Sonya lips twitched. "More coffee?"

"Sure."

She picked up his mug and filled it with trembling hands. Oblivious of a little spill, she returned to the window. "Here." She handed it back to him, her heart beating like a blacksmith's hammer. "Isn't that Leda there?" Sonya pointed to the detective, doubling over in pain in the parking lot.

The fiend's face contorted into a grotesque grimace. He drained his coffee and slammed the mug on the sill. "How did she know we're here?"

"No idea." Sonya cast a furtive glance at him.

Before their eyes, Leda yanked out an aerosol spray can from her tote and squirted a white mist over the scar. At once she straightened herself and approached Neel's truck parked not far from her Audi.

So, Aunt Camelia has been able to solve part of the problem.

The fiend grunted.

Sonya held her breath.

Leda produced the wandlike rod, also from her tote, and flicked it over the truck.

"What on Earth is that thing for?" The fiend croaked. "To pierce my invisibility guise? She thinks I'm in the truck. Frickin' idiot! We must get away quick." He darted to the bathroom. In went lotions, bottles, sprays, the truck key fob into pockets I could never have guessed existed in his trousers. Out they came, to be quickly replaced by others.

The process continued.

If only Leda would come up now and witness his wild, unthinking behavior.

Leda took a picture of the truck's license plate and raced toward the manager's office.

The fiend ran around in the little bathroom, stumbling on the stuff on the floor, shooting them unwittingly in all directions. Shrieking a curse to Leda, he sprayed the bathroom floor at lightning speed. Everything, including the truck keys, faded away like a morning mist.

"Sonya!" The fiend's voice emerged from the bathroom as he disappeared in a haze of static.

Sonya rushed toward him, vanishing in waves of flickering dots. Their scents faded with them.

"To the truck," the fiend's voice squeaked.

What will he do when he realizes he's left the keys behind?

The suite door creaked open and shut. Their footsteps raced down the corridor and the stairs and mingled with those of the other guests.

"We won't take the truck," the fiend whispered. "That will keep that firangi waiting here while we flee."

Where are they going?

Leda was still in the manager's room explaining to him the purpose of her visit when the rear door of the motel opened.

A crowd of people stepped out. They dispersed. Sonya and the fiend's footsteps faded and died in their midst.

Pacing the space under Neel's roof, I strained my core to pick up their voices, but all I heard was the traffic.

I tried to stay calm despite the restless energy coursing through me. *The fiend said they would take a taxi to Victoria from Rosenberg. I shall wait here.*

"Sure—but not interfere." Deepak appeared out of the blue and gripped me like a vise. "Sorry about my harsh treatment of you the other day. I come with great news. You are to join me in Heaven in a day or two."

"W-what?"

"Believe me, they're making grand preparations in Heaven to welcome you." His voice smiled.

"But Sonya?"

He sighed. "Priya, you've got to understand. Honor this prestige Heaven is about to bequeath on you. You have earned it. You were unconditionally kind to a spirit whose child hurt yours."

"I care for nothing more than my children at this point. You have powers. Show me what will happen to Sonya next."

"Not like you can change the inevitable."

A tangerine fog swirled out of him and split like curtains upon a stage.

I saw Sonya gasping in smoke, Sonya in a deluge of ashes . . .

"Bet she'll be stuck at Neel's house with Jalebi and share her fate. I must stop it."

"You know the consequences. By interfering. you would only sponge on Sonya's energy and lose your hue, which is just perfect for Heaven now."

"Can't you do something?"

"Denizens of Heaven are powerless in this one aspect. Or we could've stopped accidents, drownings, plane crashes—sorry, Priya, but I must be off. The Heaven Elders are waiting for me to help them with the preparations for your welcome event. Take care. Please."

"Can I release Hema?" I called after him. "She's a spirit."

Deepak had blended in the fiery light of the setting sun.

"The Devil is dealing with Hema." The fiend's voice drifted into my core.

Is that the answer to my question? I would never mess with the Devil.

No longer invisible, the fiend and Sonya stepped into a taxi three blocks away from the motel.

"Rosenberg, Fiesta Mart," said the fiend.

The taxi pulled out into the street.

Chapter 51

The taxi carrying Sonya and the fiend to Rosenberg pulled off the highway and sped toward Fiesta.

Neither spoke. Sonya sat quite still, though her heart pounded like the thundering hooves of a thousand wild horses.

The fiend looked back over his shoulder at the road behind repeatedly until the taxi slowed, crawled to the Latino-American supermarket, and stopped.

The fiend paid the driver and stepped out with Sonya. Quickly, they blended into the diverse clientele the store served and found their way into the restrooms.

People exited the restrooms. There was no sign of the fiend or Sonya.

Perhaps they have already left in their invisibility gear.

I shifted anxiously under Neel's roof. *There are two prisoners in the house already. Is Sonya to become the third?*

If only I could communicate all this information to Leda so she could come to their rescue!

I glimpsed Leda bolt up the stairs behind the manager at Budget Stay.

"Would you happen to see a tall, elderly Indian man around here with the girl in the picture I showed you?" She frowned at her own question.

"No," said the manager. "Not the man, but the girl, yes."

"When did you last see her?"

"Two days ago, no, three. Perhaps four."

"Anyone with her? A young woman by the name of Sonya Gupta—five-foot-eight, tall and lanky, with long, thick, chocolate-brown hair and eyes."

The manager shook his head.

Sonya uses the spray. The fiend does not consider Jalebi important enough to have access to it.

The manager spoke to a cleaner walking past in the corridor about the occupants of the room.

"The **Do Not Disturb** sign always hangs outside their room, so we cleaners never enter it," she said.

He walked Leda to the room and knocked on the door.

There was no reply.

The manager knocked again. No one responded.

"Open the door." Leda slipped on her gloves.

The manager unlocked it at once and Leda rushed in, swaying her wand.

Nothing happened.

Leda ran up to the window and peered down. "The truck is still here." She turned around to scan the room, and her gaze drifted to the two mugs on the sill. She sniffed the dregs. "Fresh coffee." She photographed the room and took notes.

The manager squinted at the countertop. "Fresh coffee spill."

Leda squinted down at it. "Someone must've been here just minutes ago."

"Her clothes are lying all over."

"Hmmm." Leda glanced around, then checked the contents of the mini fridge under the countertop. She grabbed the paper bag from Shipley's Donuts, squeezed in among bottled water, soda, candy bars, and nuts and peeked in. There were two glazed donuts in it and the receipt.

"It has today's date." She pulled it out. "4519, Reading Rd, Rosenberg," she read aloud.

"That's around half an hour away," said the manager.

That address can take Leda to Rosenberg, but how will she find Neel's house?

Leda lingered at the motel, pointing the wand toward the immaculate bathroom. The stick glowed and beeped.

The manager walked up behind her, frowning.

Taking one step into the bathroom, Leda swept the wand over the floor, and everything that the fiend pulled out of his pockets during his panicked moments materialized.

"Jeez!" The manager gasped. "It looked like there was nothing on that floor. Are you a magician like the man you are looking for?"

Leda shook her head and scooped up Neel's truck key fob from the shadows of the toilet.

Has the fiend realized yet that he has left it behind?

Leda excused herself from the manager and raced down to the truck. On the way, she made a quick phone call for the owner's information.

"The registered owner's name is Mr. Neelabhro Das," came the reply, "and he lives on 1111 N Washington St, Boston, MA, 02114."

The stink of sulfur distracted me from Leda. It flooded the air in Rosenberg and intensified around Neel's house.

The Devil must be painfully close.

I drew consolation from the fact that the cast iron vent pipe in the roof would repel him.

Beneath me within the rooms, the darkness rippled like living ink, shifting with unseen currents.

The bat continued to spin dizzily in the corner of the study, still fastened to the whirling rotor blades. Something glided along the walls with unnatural stealth, the edges of its silhouette pulsing with an insistent rhythm. The air around it shimmered.

The Devil can appear in various forms. It's him.

I found myself shaking uncontrollably. *If only I could sneak out real quick.* No sooner did I conceive the thought than the rhythm disrupted, and the creature of the wall stilled.

I froze. *What now?*

There was a prolonged, muffled hiss. Then the Devil slithered out of the cracks in the walls. Colossal wings spread above the house as broad as they were black.

The air rang with an avian cacophony one minute, the next the sounds faded to a deafening silence.

He was gone.

The two prisoners remained helplessly trapped—the bat spun against the wall in Neel's study, and Jalebi lay in the cupboard-under-the-stairs, still invisible, still scent-free.

I wondered when the magic spray would wear off. *If only Leda would arrive here before it is too late.*

At the parking lot of the motel, the detective typed the address of Fiesta, Rosenberg into the car's GPS and drove out into the traffic that had piled up on the road. She checked and rechecked the time on the dashboard.

How will Leda find Neel's house? All she knows is his full name. How many will be familiar with it even if she asks around?

I shifted uncomfortably in my roofline gap, and the entrance door opened again. Footsteps echoed in the foyer. The door closed with a soft thud.

"Perhaps we should grab our stuff and run." Sonya giggled.

Yet her heart raced. Her eyes darted, and her gaze settled on the door of the cupboard-under-the-stairs. She pursed her mouth.

"Not the right time," said the fiend, "and though we must run eventually, we must ensure we don't leave any evidence behind. That will be a lot of work." He sighed. "Now I repeat. It will be your responsibility to light the kerosene lamp and lock Jalebi's door as we leave. By the time her body decomposes and rots, and the cops come flocking, we will be miles away with not a soul to recognize us."

Did he plan this with Jalebi's father. This is his house.

The darkness of the fiend's eyes was cold and demon like.

The only joy a demon feels is in torturing others. Will he hurt Sonya?

She stumbled mid-stride but grasped the stair railing in time.

I waited on high alert, ready to dive-bomb, peck or scratch the fiend as and when necessary.

The fiend turned on a little bulb hanging from the ceiling. "C'mon in, Sonya."

Sonya stooped down to pick a scrunchie from the ground and followed the fiend in.

The wooden floorboards groaned beneath their weight, and the echo of their footsteps seemed to reverberate through the empty rooms.

"I was really beginning to wonder about the doors." Sonya squinted into the darkness beyond. "Are they soundproof or is Hema resigned to fate?"

The fiend's eyes took on a slight, dangerous glint. "Her screams could awaken the dead, so we have a noise-cancelling device—a 'nuller' in place. It creates anti-noise signals that cancel out her screams."

Sonya scooped up a Gucci earring, also hers, from the floor.

"The bat scattered your stuff all over when the Master dragged her to her trap. The brat! She clung to your stuff like some mysterious power would rise out of it and save her."

She said Sonya was her only hope. Poor Hema!

Sonya flashed her wide smile, though I thought her fingers quivered a little.

"She overheard the Master discuss her predicament with me at the daemo sedere," continued the fiend, "my special meeting with him. I would have blown her to pieces, but I restrained myself only because the Master had plans for her. You should see her now, crushed by the contraption. Ironical, isn't it?"

I fought an irrepressible urge to save Hema. *If only the Devil wasn't involved.*

My sparrow wings fluttered uncontrollably. The fiend shrieked a spell at me.

Instantly I landed in a special chamber in his pocket.

"Thanks Priya," He patted me over the fabric. "The Master will be delighted."

I sank rapidly into cushy yarn that puffed around me, soft as cotton wool. I tried to keep hope. *Deepak always comes to my rescue.*

"Is the Master here?" Sonya's smile was intact.

Oh, Sonya, wipe off that insufferable smile!

"Was. He has a busy schedule, keeping people primitive and lusting for revenge and status. Yet, he drops by every so often to check on Hema and regulate the speed of the inciter." The fiend paused, then said, "It was the Master who alerted me about Priya lurking around. How lucky is it that she should play into our hands just when we couldn't wait to lay hands on that lovely core?"

A compound eye, practically transparent, floated by, utterly free of gravity as if it had air-control guiding it in.

"Hey, Tartarus," the fiend mouthed, "everything okay?"

A voice like 'Siri,' the digital assistant, responded, "Everything just right, Dev."

"Good. Good." The fiend stared after it. "Tartarus is the remote control for the inciter."

"Hats off to tech-savvy Hell." Sonya grinned.

The fiend nodded. "Is it a wonder? Crowds of high-tech souls have ended up in Hell." He fetched two chilled beers from the fridge in the kitchen, and they settled in the living area before the fireplace.

It glowed with a disgusting green flame, the Devil's color, yet there was not a whiff of his scent. The flame crackled, churning wisps of thick, black smoke into the putrid air within.

Infernal.

A skull stared out of the flames, all the little holes bursting with the unsightly fire.

The Devil's eyes cannot look ghastlier.

The fiend chuckled. "How do you like my latest acquisition, Sonya?"

Sonya cracked the beer, all smiles. "Perfect! Is it a real, the skull?"

"Of course—my conduit of communication with the Master." He popped his can, and his phone rang.

Chapter 52

The caller was Neel, calling from Victoria. "Dev, where are you?
"At your place."

"Then why is my truck in Hillcroft?" Neel's words were rushed, disjointed. "The firangi has my truck and the keys."

The fiend jumped to his feet, yanking out the contents of his pockets. Out flew tubes, bottles, aerosol cans. He drove his fingers into the corners, then retracted them, seething.

"Dev, this is serious. I was about to tell you not to use my truck when Guru called you about Sonya the other night. Then you got busy tending to her injuries." Neel swallowed. "A couple of my utility bills were in the truck in a secret compartment. The firangi found them. I must leave this place ASAP. Don't come to Victoria. I'll meet you in El Paso."

"Has she got hold of the address of this house?"

"No chance, Dev. The owner was from the Sundarbans. He died in India, and his death wasn't formally announced."

"Good. With Jalebi lying sedated in the cupboard-under-the-stairs—"

"Should have wrung her neck at birth," Neel shrieked. "Is the invisibility spray wearing off?"

"Not yet."

"Well, good luck."

For shame!

The fiend hung up on Neel, grinning like a madman.

Sonya met his gaze full on, beaming. It felt like a shared understanding flashed between them, yet her heart pounded a frantic rhythm.

How long will she keep up this pretense?

The fiend tossed Sonya a bunch of keys and pointed with his chin toward the locker. "All your stuff is in there, phone an' all."

Whew! He obviously hasn't checked her photos, or he would be dead.

"Thanks." Sonya voice squeaked ever so slightly.

Even as he watched her unlock the cabinet and yank out her bag, I felt the cushy yarn tightening around my core, slowly, and gently. *Is it trying to sever it from my spirit?* I shuddered. *I'm sure Deepak will want to rescue me, but will he dare, now that the Devil is involved?*

"Your phone's charged," the fiend said to Sonya. "Get Leda here. Quick!"

Sonya glanced over her shoulder. "Of course." She slipped out her old phone and switched it on.

The fiend took a few steps toward her, his eyes narrowed. "Ask her where exactly she is."

Where exactly are you? Sonya typed. "Anything more?"

"No." He plucked the device from her hand and peered down at the words. "We'll wait for her to reply and as we do, let us plan how we shall get her here."

He said he would finish her off. I shifted uncomfortably. The yarn cut into me. I twisted and turned in a vain attempt to wiggle out. If only I had controlled myself instead of fluttering around.

Sonya's phone pinged with Leda's reply:

On Interstate 69, approaching exit 106. Where are you?

That's six exits from Rosenberg.

"What should I write?" Sonya was composure itself.

"Wait! We're not done planning how to get her here." The fiend rubbed his chin. "You text her and say that you are at the Brazos River Nature Center, where I will drop you off in a minute. Tell her I locked you up in a strange house, and that you escaped with just your phone—your old phone. Beg her to pick you up."

Sonya nodded.

He handed her a vial from the refrigerator. "Rub a small amount of the liquid on your hands as you wait for her. Rush up to her car in tears when you see her. Tell her about your colossal mistake of coming to me and as you do, wrap your hand around her scar. That will knock her out." He checked his watch. "Drive her straight here. She should come around in a bit, though she will be in unbearable pain. I'll get her to sign a document withdrawing her allegations of mischief and malicious magic against me, then throw her in with the bat."

Sonya beamed. "Great!" She did not glance at the phone, not once.

Her self-restraint!

I was growing impatient. The yarn trap was inescapable. Spasms of pain tore through my core.

The fiend watched her approvingly. "Let me increase the speed of the inciter. There is still an hour before the timer is set to go off. If we can get Leda inside the study before then, the bat will off her in his fury."

"But, Uncle Dev, one question." Sonya sounded dispassionate and involved. "Isn't it all programmed by the Master? I thought the bat would be sucked up by the extensior as soon as she is released."

The fiend shook his head. "Have you forgotten that the Master was here to regulate the speed himself. The inciter deals with different spirits whose anger can vary significantly in terms of intensity. If the anger is more or less than expected, the speed of the inciter must be regulated so that the job is still accomplished in the time estimated. Now, I know exactly how to manipulate the speed so that the bat is released a little early."

"In which case, the extensior will not be ready to grab her."

"It will in a few minutes, though, so wastage of anger is minimal." He drew his mouth back in a vile smirk. "As much as the Master controls the variables, he realizes that we can never be sure of the mood of the spirit on a particular day." His eyes glinted wildly. "The Master just wants results, and I shall ensure he gets them."

Sonya's phone chimed with yet another message from Leda:

Only a couple of miles from Rosenberg now. How far from Shipley's are you?

The fiend read the text aloud. "Bet she found the receipt from Shipley's. Let's not waste any more time." He handed Sonya back her phone. "Here, take this. Draft the text while I adjust the speed on the inciter."

I felt myself rip. *Is it my cladding? If only Sonya would hurry up.*

"Great." Sonya began to type the message.

Why is she typing the message?

"Hey, Tartarus," the fiend stepped away to grab the device, and Sonya opened the camera app on her phone.

At last! Hurry! The yarn was like a blunt knife sawing away at my cladding. It resisted as never before, yet I doubled over with pain.

"There, the bat will reach the required anger level at least five minutes before time." The fiend fixed his hawkish gaze on Sonya even as she clicked on the last picture captured in her phone.

The words of the Mrityushakti mantra appeared on the screen, looking apologetically insignificant.

Sonya's eyes darted.

The fiend sniffed, walking back toward her, tapping his fingers on his trouser pocket. Spurred to action, the yarn squashed me thin as in a canine bite.

Raw pain seared through me. *Did Jalebi hear right?*

"Um, Uncle Dev, I think I've typed up the message." Sonya touched her neck. "You wouldn't phrase it any differently, would you?" With a quick, almost imperceptible twist of her hand, she turned her cell phone around, displaying the screen to him.

"Wh-wh-what is this?" His voice choked. His eyes bulged. He stumbled back a step and crumpled like a puppet with its strings cut.

He lay so still, he could be mistaken for dead.

The magic has taken effect. Still in the throes of excruciating agony, I sighed with relief.

Stealthily, Sonya plucked a metal chip clinging to his magnetic shirt button and rubbed it against the threads that held me. The yarn cracked, heaved, and split.

Sonya did the right thing by living with the fiend. I was foolish not to realize. I wiggled out of my ripped disguise, my cladding intact.

Chapter 53

Even as I tried to get my bearings, a sob tore from Sonya's chest. "Mom, sorry for my indifference, my disrespect, disregard—"

Jalebi's groans emerged from the cupboard-under-the-stairs.

The invisibility spray had worn off, and I saw her slender body bound and gagged.

Wiping the sweat dripping from her brow, Sonya snatched the fiend's bunch of keys off the locker and rushed to the cupboard-under-the-stairs.

Her phone rang and she picked up.

It was Leda. "Sonya, why don't you answer my texts?"

"Sorry! Too much has happened. Please come quick," She balanced her phone on her ear with her shoulder, while trying to match key after key to the lock in vain. "I'm at 20789 Ricefield Road, behind Domino's Pizza."

The call disconnected and Sonya tried yet another key. It worked. She removed the padlock, slid the bolt back, and pushed open the door.

Jalebi wiggled in the darkness, her wrists and feet tied bone-crunchingly tight. A strangled groan escaped around the thick gag in her mouth.

Sonya bolted to the kitchen and grabbed the kitchen knife and the fiend stirred.

No!

Without a backward glance, she raced back to Jalebi and sliced through the bindings.

The fiend shot up, writhing.

This must be the last surge of energy.

A sickening green light glided across the neighborhood. The overpowering stench of festering garbage flooded the air.

The skull rattled in the fireplace.

"Forgive me, Master, that I dared mess with your tools." His eyes voids of darkness as if the sockets had been hollowed, the fiend dragged himself to the hearth and banged his head repeatedly on the cement. His mask dropped off.

The skull in the fireplace sucked it away with a cackle.

The malodor intensified. Flakes of ash scurried through the air, swirling into blinding flurries like locusts.

Oh, for some clean air!

They coalesced into black ominous clouds that swerved clear to let me pass.

How strange.

Moon rays came as whispers of light. I rode the avenues of the warm milky glow and landed on a smile of bold silver beams arced across No.7.

There was not a flake of ash left at the property. *Is all that ash from No.7?*

Thunder rolled in the distance. Three hooded silhouettes floated away. Leda and Patrick talked animatedly. The third turned around and the light lit her face.

Sonya! Her self-restraint has been remarkable.

I lost the shape in the bright runways meandering through the gloom and ash.

The flakes tore around Neel's house.

I recalled Deepak's prediction of Sonya gasping in a deluge of ash. I tried to rush back to her but was hurled back against the roof.

The windows burst open, as if by some chaotic wind, and the black flakes streamed in, smoking hot, moving toward the fiend as if to unseen instructions. They filed into his empty sockets—black holes—where gravity was so strong that none could escape.

The fiend thrashed around on the floor. The ash clogged his body cavities, swamped the organs, and saturated the fluids.

Yet the ash continued to flow in. The flakes swirled into a live wire within him, frying his innards. His flesh split open.

His agonizing groans echoed through the house.

Such a painful death.

In the teeming darkness, each cell in his body swelled and burst. His breathing stopped, then his pulse and heart ceased, mimicking a cardiac arrest.

The ash retracted promptly, as if acting upon a signal, and streamed out of his eye sockets, and into the little holes of the skull. There it disappeared, smothering the fire inside the firebox.

A mournful wail echoed through the quiet streets, and the Devil's bray erupted like some siren call.

I pressed against the cast iron vent pipe despite the appalling stench. *Iron repels the Devil.*

His howl faded out with the stink and the wail. The air felt strangely clean.

Sonya's phone chimed. It was a message from Leda:

Nearly there. Did Sunny call? I messaged him that you had found your old phone.

Sonya did not notice the message. She struggled to remove the gag from Jalebi's mouth.

The fiend is dead; the curse is broken. Sunny and Nikita must have gotten back together.

Ten miles away in the Mehta estate, Sunny and Nikita's conversation confirmed my guess.

"Why doesn't Leda answer my calls and texts?" Sunny inhaled sharply.

"Perhaps there is a problem with the signal. You can't get through to her either." Nikita sighed. "Wonder where they've taken Sonya."

"I hope Sonya is okay." Sunny tried Leda's number one more time. "What if the rogues have done something to her. What if they left her with that that bat that almost killed her three days ago? She could've done anything." He sounded seriously concerned about Sonya.

My core throbbed with a flood of emotions, and the door of Neel's study burst open. Hema charged through the doors.

The flakes of ash unlocked around her and tumbled as confetti and scattered. She flapped her wings in a joyous dance over Sonya's head and vanished like she was sucked away by some almighty force.

The Devil had vanished. *Is it the pull of freedom?*

There was a knock on the door, then Leda's cry. "Sonya!"

Sonya staggered to the door and turned the knob with trembling fingers.

Leda pushed her way in. "Hey." She looked past Sonya. "So, this is him." She walked in and peered down at his face. His mouth and nostrils were still. She shone her cell phone on his eyes. His pupils were fixed, dilated, and unreactive to the light. "Dead," she said in a quiet whisper. "When did it happen?"

"Like an hour, forty-five minutes." Sonya trembled.

Leda glanced at her watch. "So, at around one. I can't believe it's nearly two. I was going round and round the town unable to enter. There was this dark smog that blurred my vision. My phone wasn't working. The signal was weak." She messaged Sunny about the current situation, sighing as she hit send. "How did he die?"

"Slowly. For hours."

"How many? I spoke to you just after nine."

"Since before—" Sonya's voice trailed.

Leda rushed around taking pictures, and her gaze drifted to Jalebi's feet sticking out from the cupboard-under-the-stairs. Her brows furrowed. "So, you were not alone."

Sonya shook her head. "Jalebi was gagged and bound in there. I just managed to untie her. The fiend had planned on killing her by carbon monoxide poisoning."

Together Sonya and Leda helped Jalebi onto the settee. She seemed disoriented and babbled incoherently.

Sunny replied to Leda's text. He and Paul were on their way to Rosenberg.

"Good, we need both the doctor and the lawyer." Leda grinned. "Now a few questions before they arrive. Why were you at Budget Stay?"

"I was recovering there." Sonya touched her arm, and her gaze dropped to Leda's wrist.

"A few minutes before I arrived here, the scar vanished." Leda's eyes glistened. "Thank you, Sonya." She patted her on her shoulder. "There's lots I would like to talk about, but right now, we need to protect ourselves from the police." She glanced at the two popped cans of beer. "Did Dev eat or drink anything?"

"Just a beer. He took a sealed can from the fridge."

"Hmmm. Tell me what happened from start to finish, sparing no details, please."

They sat down on the floor, and Sonya took a deep breath. She related how the fiend and she got to the house, his plans, the bat's predicament, the Mrityushakti mantra, and of course the ash.

"Thank you, Sonya! What an accomplishment, and how ironical that the mere image of a mantra should kill a powerful sorcerer like him." Leda wrote down every word Sonya said. "Was it really all that simple?"

Sonya blinked. "In the end it was, but I have had to live in constant fear, fear of the fiend, fear of the bat. I had to placate her when she became frustrated with her lot. It was always a bloody affair, and the last time at Herenhuis, I passed out."

"How is the wound?"

"Okay, thanks to the fiend's magic and the quick surgery."

"Where did you have the surgery?"

"At Neel's friend's clinic. She is an OB."

"Hmmm." Leda took a deep inhale. "Thanks for filling in the gaps. However, we will have to modify the story slightly for the police. One, you were in Victoria taking a self-guided walking tour of the historic town with your boyfriend, Paul. I'll let Paul know. You strayed into Herenhuis because your mom had started renovating the property before she passed. Two, the ash bat attacked you. The police know about her. They know she gave me the scar and have witnessed me in the throes of agony in her presence. Three, the bat did not bite you. She only attacked. You fell over and hurt yourself. Paul took you home and your wounds were treated by your brother. Four, there was no Mrityushakti mantra, and you never really saw or interacted with Dev—his marriage with Bina was a troubled one right from the start, and Bina was thinking of a divorce."

Sonya swallowed. "No one saw us together except Bina and Jalebi, thanks to the invisibility spray."

"Good." Leda heaved a sigh. "I will share the points with them."

"What if the police ask why I am here today?"

"Well, you will have to say that you came here with Bina. She got wind of her absconding husband's visits to this house, and she came to talk to him about legal separation." Leda peered into Sonya's eyes. "Don't look so upset. The police will understand if you tell them she popped back home and will be back later with Nikita. Bina always needs a companion, which brings us the next point. Jalebi came to this country on tourist visa but moved in with Bina, as she suddenly became unwell. Jalebi will return to India with her."

Sonya nodded, and Leda texted the modified story to Auntie Bina, Sunny, Nikita and Paul. "Sorry, I could not be more helpful, being a detective. The scar got in the way. Aunt Camelia experimented with a variety of spells but could not make it completely unresponsive in his presence."

Neither Leda nor Sonya noticed Jalebi sit up on the settee.

"How did you live with Dev and gain his trust?" Leda asked Sonya.

"Long story," Sonya's voice trembled. "When I first came to him from Digha, he was at the abandoned house, torturing a woman who had dared to be disloyal. He shouted, Uttana. Uttana,' to her fingers and they stretched upward rapidly."

How dreadful! Uttana is the Sanskrit word for stretch.

"She was in a lot of pain and on the verge of passing out when he cried, 'Viparita.' It must have meant 'reverse,' for then the woman's fingers returned to their original size.

"'From now onward, you shall only see, hear, and do evil,' the fiend whispered to me later, 'or else . . . '

"I remembered the incident in all its details, especially the words because of their impact on the woman's hands. It was a lesson learned. I used the words time and again to stretch the corners of my mouth, upward and outward, and then bring them back to normal. How well it deceived him, the scoundrel!"

And me too, even with my heightened senses.

Jalebi looked from Leda to Sonya and back again. "Neel's the greater scoundrel," she muttered.

Leda and Sonya swung around.

"Hey, Jalebi," said Sonya. She hugged her.

"How do you feel?" Leda asked kindly.

Jalebi stood up, swaying. "Like perfect trash. How else does one feel when their father is complete scum?"

Leda produced the ripped half of the picture she had found in the wastebasket at Asha's house. "This?" She planted it on the table before Jalebi.

Jalebi seized the picture at once. "The rogue of a man who brought me into this world. He sold me to Dev at thirteen." Her eyes streamed. "My cursed life."

"It'll get better," whispered Leda. "Now listen carefully." She prepared Jalebi for the upcoming interrogation.

That done, Leda called the police and gave them a briefing about the events of the night.

As she finished, a pair of headlights swept across the house, cutting through the darkness. Sunny and Paul leaped out.

Leda raced to the door.

Sonya followed behind, slower, a little unsteady.

"How are you, Sonya?" Paul looked deadly pale.

She barely nodded when Sunny pulled her into a hug. He did not utter a word, only his eyes glistened.

Silence speaks volumes.

Sonya snuggled into his embrace, and Sunny's arms tightened around her. There was something so incredibly warm about the hug, something that felt right, smelt right.

My mind was at peace. *How could the fiend mess with a love so pure?*

"Where's Dev?" Paul took a step into the house.

Leda led him and Sunny into the living area. "There, on the floor."

They stared at the wrinkles and folds of his skin more pronounced than a deflated balloon.

"Do not touch anything." Leda watched the receding figure of Jalebi disappear into the kitchen. "The police will be here any minute. But before they come, let me tell you about the outstanding feat accomplished by this young lady." Her voice choking with emotion, she enlightened them about how Sonya had triumphed over the monster.

Sonya trembled, smiling through her tears.

A flicker of pride crossed Paul's features. "I knew you could do it," he cried.

Sunny's eyes brimmed. "Wow, Sonya, you accomplished the impossible! I am so proud."

His voice was drowned by Auntie Bina's convulsive sobs. She had arrived with Nikita in a state of shock.

Chapter 54

Paul and Sunny helped the elderly lady into the living area when the emergency vehicles arrived with blaring sirens and flashing lights.

The ambulance parted with the fiend's body.

The police interrogation began. Sonya was the first to be called in. It was a long and intricate affair. She avoided talking about the black magic, maintaining that she had been visiting the place with Auntie Bina, an old friend, when her husband suddenly suffered cardiac arrest.

"What do you think led to it?" asked the officer. "Did he argue with his wife?"

"No. Uncle Dev had peculiar interests. One was playing with ash. Leda's scar—" She paused.

The police officer nodded. "Sergeant Leda has briefed me about Rishabhdev's bizarre personality. I haven't witnessed her agony in his presence, but I've seen her with his queer bat. The scar on her wrist played up when she flew in and calmed like a live thing when she disappeared. I have also been notified that it just faded with Rishabhdev's death."

Sonya heaved a sigh.

Leda is a godsend.

"There has been widespread unrest about an influx of locusts in the greater Houston metropolitan area, specifically in Fort Bend County last night," he said. "Did you see anything?"

Sonya shook her head.

"That will be all."

Dismissed, Sonya shut herself in the guest room and threw herself on the bed.

Her emotions are finally breaking free. All that self-restraint!

Everyone was too busy to notice her.

Leda made tea in the kitchen while listening to Jalebi's woes.

Sunny checked Auntie Bina's vitals. "Everything looks good." He put away his instruments, trying to make light conversation with her.

The officer called her in.

Nikita walked her to the door. "Good luck," she whispered in her ear.

Shaking from head to toe, Auntie Bina entered the study. She forgot to close the door behind her.

Leda carried the steaming hot tea into the living area in paper cups that she found in the drawers. "Where's Sonya?' she glanced around.

In walked Patrick with Dish.

"You?" Leda looked surprised to see her husband.

"I had to come look for you." Patrick helped himself to a cup and sipped a mouthful. "Why don't you pick up your phone?"

"I'm sorry. Did you call?" Leda scrolled through her missed calls.

"If it wasn't for Sunny, I would never have found you."

"Hey!" Sunny walked up, almost stumbling on Dish making his way into the kitchen. "Poor Patrick's car broke down at No.7 last night, and he had to wait like forever for AAA to arrive. He called me several times, but unfortunately, my phone was engaged."

He was trying to call Leda.

"Thanks to you, I experienced this phenomenal occurrence from the curbside, the cleansing of No.7." Patrick grinned. "All that ash is gone. There was a sudden turbulence on the property last night, just on your property."

Hmmm.

Leda stared at him.

Sunny squinted at Patrick.

"The wind howled, the land rocked, and the ash cracked," Patrick continued. "Everything was a blur for a second, then the flakes, millions of them, filed through the air as if after the hypnotic notes of some symphony."

I must have gotten too engrossed with the death of the fiend to notice it.

"Apparently, the ash came here," said Leda. "They streamed in through Dev's hollow eye sockets, ignited, and charred him to death."

Patrick and Leda's 400-Watt smiles lit up the dim room.

"And all thanks to Sonya." Leda sighed. "Where is Sonya?"

Paul hung up on his client, telling him sacred secrets she would have carried to the grave, and glanced around.

"In here," Jalebi's hoarse voice drew everyone's attention to the guestroom. She stood back, allowing Sunny, Paul, Nikita, and Leda to rush in.

Sonya lay curled on the bed. Her eyes streamed.

"Hey, Sonya," said Nikita. "You seem to know your way around this house."

"I have been staying here on and off," she sniffed.

Paul watched her quietly. His bottom lip trembled.

Leda planted Sonya's cup by her side on the bed. "Have some tea, Sonya, and you will feel better."

"Thanks," Sonya did not move.

Dish bounded in as if from nowhere and leaped onto the bed. He drenched Sonya in slobber. Sonya sat up, and he showed her his belly.

Aww.

Sonya smiled through her tears.

Sunny perched down on the edge of the bed and pulled her into a comforting side-hug. "I can't believe how brave you've been."

"I knew Mom and Dad would never come back. Everything else that we had, I wanted them back for you and me much more than I wanted to draw another stupid breath."

If I had eyes, they would have overflowed.

Sunny blinked. "The ash has blown away from No.7 all because of you. Want to come see?"

"Only after the interrogations." Sonya wiped her wet cheek with the back of her hand. "I'm really worried about Jalebi. She is in no state to be questioned at this time."

Sunny nodded with a sigh.

"Jalebi will be okay, won't you, Jalebi?" Leda studied the girl.

Jalebi swayed. "I'm more okay than I've been since my father sold me to that monster. I owe you big time, Sonya. You have no idea what you've done for me."

My heart swelled with pity for Jalebi.

"Paul!" Auntie Bina's screech rent the air like a siren. "I messed up. Where's Paul?" she cried. "I need to talk to him."

"Hope she's okay." Nikita ran out.

"I'll be right back, Sonya." Sunny followed Nikita out.

Auntie Bina perched on the edge of the settee, panting.

"How are you doing, Mrs. Singh?" asked Paul.

"The brat of a dog," Auntie Bina cried. "Goodness knows how he got hold of that picture."

Worry etched on his features, Patrick looked up from his phone.

"What picture?" Paul's gaze swept over her panic-stricken face.

"Jalebi's dad's picture. How am I to know that Neel is her dad? He's a criminal and the police have arrested him. Now she will be incriminated."

"It doesn't quite work like that," said Paul.

The police officer emerged from the study. "Miss Jalebi."

In the guestroom, Jalebi sobbed. "Yes, I'm evil, yes, I lied to Leda and Patrick, yes, I stole strychnine from Dev to kill Bina and Meghna's money that Randy gave her. But I helped Tino escape from the monster by paying a coworker to take him away. They were talking about killing him and selling his body parts.

So what Gladys said was true. Thank you, Jalebi.

All eyes stared at her.

"Miss Jalebi," the officer called again.

"Leda, can you do me a favor, please," Jalebi begged, "in case the police take me away?"

"You will be alright."

"Will you do me a favor?"

"Of course."

"There is a bag of money under the mattress in my room at Bina's. Dev had given it to Randy, and he was furious that Randy had presented it to Meghna. Dev asked me to get it back, so I stole it from her. Could you please return it to her?"

"Done," said Leda.

Jaleb dragged herself away.

"Drink your tea, Sonya, before it gets cold," said Leda.

Sonya fidgeted with the hem of her sleeve. Her eyes streamed.

"What is it, Sonya? You know you can tell me."

Sonya drew a shuddering breath. "I have been so scared, so scared."

Oh, my baby!

Leda wrapped her arm around Sonya's. "I can imagine. How did it all happen? I mean what made you decide to go stay with him?"

"A few nights before I went away, I had a bizarre experience. I was woken up by a strange noise. At first, I thought it was the wind, then I noticed something strange at the window."

Leda frowned.

"A light outside cast an eerie glow in the room. Moonlight doesn't look like that. I tried to get away, but I couldn't budge. Somehow, I pulled my covers over me, but there was no hiding from the unnatural light. It kept peeking through the threads."

"Where was I?" asked Leda.

"Sleeping. It was the night before Patrick arrived. I hoped the nightmare would be over when the sun rose. Hours passed. Dawn did not come. I peeked over the cover. Though the light at the window had disappeared, the pale light still engulfed the room. I lay perfectly still. The day broke finally. Patrick knocked at the door, and it was all gone."

I recalled Sonya appearing at the front door, drenched in sweat that morning.

"Why didn't you tell us?"

"I was scared you would tell Sunny, and he would be wild. Dad was vicious when Mom thought she saw the spirits of her near and dear ones."

I did see them.

"Scared that the light would visit again the following night," Sonya continued, "I called Rao in the evening. He didn't know what the light was. We got talking, and he said he probably had gaps in his knowledge and had not been able to revoke the curse. He suggested someone should try living with the fiend just to find out how to."

"But not you?" Leda squinted at Sonya.

"No, but he told me the story of *Samson and Delilah*—the story of the Philistine who, bribed to entrap Samson, coaxed him into revealing that the secret of his strength was his long hair. She took advantage of his confidence to betray him to his enemies."

Leda nodded. "That was enough to make you go?"

"It felt like the perfect solution. For months, pangs of guilt had kept me awake at night, my mind hovering within this void, full of empty feelings—hollowed-out feelings."

"But you had me and Nikita, if not Sunny."

"I didn't belong with any of you, you included Leda, despite all your compassion. I had no one to compare experiences with. None of you could relate to me. You were all miserable for the suffering I had caused. I was alone in my grief, so I decided to try out what Rao suggested."

"How exactly did it happen?"

"As I hung up on Rao, something grazed past me. I saw no one and groped for the thing as if I was blind.

"I barged into someone. Invisible hands dragged me down. I found myself disappearing in a mist of spray. In minutes, you were all looking for me. I couldn't speak out of shock, not even when the spray wore off and you found me. I thought it was the consequence of my interaction with a ghost. Mom used to talk about otherworldly visitors towards the end . . .

She's right. It had become a vicious cycle—I saw ghosts and interacted with them because they reminded me of "my old Ravi." They lured me to the verge of death. Ravi was mad at me; I craved his love and sought the spirits who seemed to fulfil that need . . .

Sonya drew a long, deep breath. "It was only later while living with the fiend that I found out that it had been his special friend, Damien, in the invisibility disguise."

"He has been arrested together with some Sue and others." Leda sighed. "Why were you at the beach later that night?"

"I woke up in the early hours to the light. There were sounds in the room so quiet as to be practically imperceptible. I did not see anyone. I was numb with horror when I heard my dad call out to me. It was like he knew I needed to hear his voice more than anything else at that moment." Sonya's eyes streamed. "Fear had crippled my thinking. I ran out in response to it and bounded over the sand. Too late, I realized I had been tricked by the fiend, but I was already with him, alone among the desolate rocks."

Leda swallowed.

Sonya pulled herself upright. "He was kind. We sat on the rocks and chatted. He offered to help me with the curse. He invited me to come and stay with him. We discussed the terms and conditions. I agreed to his proposal." Sonya drew a deep breath. "Hours passed. I did not change my mind. The next night, Gran Bina picked me up from the gas station opposite your store apartment."

Leda opened her mouth to say something then shut it.

"I was just determined to find a solution to our problem."

"It must've been hard when the bat hurt you. She could have done anything!"

"That was the deal." Sonya bit into her lips.

Gratitude, pride, and respect for my girl overwhelmed me. *Alas, ghosts cannot cry.*

Leda wiped away a tear from her face.

"I invited you to the yoga session and lied about the instructor. You must forgive me. I never quite forgot the girl who dared betray Dev and his torture. But I didn't know about the cuff. Honest, I didn't."

"It's okay," said Leda.

Nikita rushed back in. "Sorry, Sonya. I got busy with Gran Bina. I'm honestly so relieved to have you back. I did try to find you, but who could have guessed you were hiding in places such as this?"

"You wouldn't find me. The fiend made sure of that." Sonya picked up her cup and sipped a mouthful. Her face contorted.

"It must've gone cold. Let me make you a fresh cup." Nikita extended her hand to scoop it up.

Leda gasped. "You are engaged? Congratulations!"

Nikita touched the petite twisted vine diamond ring scintillating on her ring finger.

We all missed it in this pandemonium. Even I!

"Sunny proposed in the early hours of the morning," she said in a quiet voice, "and I accepted."

Chapter 55

Leda was jubilant at the news of Nikita and Sunny's engagement. "Yeah!!!!" she roared.

I would shout out for joy, too, if I had a human voice.

"Congrats!" said Sonya softly, like she struggled to process the information.

"What is all this commotion about?" Auntie Bina lumbered in. "God have some compassion for my poor nerves."

"Sunny and I are getting married." Nikita gazed at her ring.

Auntie Bina stared so hard at it, she didn't see the bed and stumbled against it.

Sonya moved, making room for her, and she lay back on the mattress.

"The wedding is on me," she mumbled. "I will pay for everything."

"Gran Bina," said Nikita, "we're planning a courthouse wedding."

"But I have the resources to organize a celebration that you will remember forever."

"Sunny is dead against it," Nikita protested. "We decided on a small celebration on the gulf beach later."

Auntie Bina grimaced. "Is it because of the curse?"

"The curse died with the fiend." Sonya stroked Dish who leaned against her.

Dish pawed at Auntie Bina. She glowered at him. "I shall prepare the gifts as always."

"Not another dahej, Gran Bina," Nikita cried. "As I said, Sunny will not hear of it. He said we should help you to sell the stuff you bought earlier."

"Well, I have plans to start a boutique in Kolkata with Jalebi. If she can only handle the police interrogation."

"She will," said Leda. "Jalebi is smart."

Sunny walked in.

"Where are Paul and Patrick?" Auntie Bina yawned.

"Outside, talking."

"You missed Nikita too much." Auntie Bina smiled. "Congratulations!"

Sunny blushed.

"The cat is out of the bag." Leda giggled.

Sunny shot a glance at Nikita who caressed the twisted vine diamond ring on her finger.

"How did it hap—?" Sonya began when Auntie Bina's loud snore cut her off. She almost jumped out of her skin.

Sunny gave her a gentle pat on the shoulder. "It's okay, Sonya."

She sighed. "T-tell me about your engagement."

"Well, I was at Galleria engagement ring shopping when Auntie Diya called. She reminded me how Gran was certain that Nikita and I would get married. On a sudden whim, I bought the ring. I was walking back to my hotel, when Leda texted that you were associating with a master criminal called Neel." Sunny cast a furtive glance at Leda, and she nodded. "I thought you had sought his company by choice, as you had Dev's. Terrified, I called both Paul and Nikita to share what I had heard and my plan to find you. Neither answered. I left them a message."

What time was it?

All eyes turned to Nikita.

"I was suspicious of this sudden change of attitude," she said. "Besides it was nearly nine and I was at dinner. The clock struck the hour, and something strange happened. The new housekeeper mentioned that she had been cleaning my bookshelves and had come across an old album with pictures of me and Sunny. 'There is so much goodness in this man, it comes through in his eyes,' she said. As if her words worked some magic on my mind, I responded to Sunny's text at once."

Hmmm.

"Where was Sunny at the time?" asked Leda.

"On my way to Nikita's house." Sunny's eyes locked with Nikita's.

"He came in a mad rush," said Nikita, "all worried about Sonya. We tried to contact you, Leda, but in vain. I guess the signal was weak."

"Yes." Leda nodded. "Is that what took Sunny so long to propose?"

"Well, it was your long text message that relaxed him and probably reminded him that he had a ring in his pocket."

Everyone laughed.

My core did a little, involuntary dance.

Jalebi rushed in. "I have to go down to the police station. Bina, why on Earth did you have to tell the police that the man in the picture was my fucking father?"

Sonya retched.

Auntie Bina rubbed her eyes, sitting up groggily. "I never said he was your father. I didn't even know he was your father." She met Jalebi's glowering gaze and winced. "Dish ran in with the picture in his mouth—goodness knows where he found it. I shrieked out Neel's name. He ruined my daughter's life, and he was responsible for Jay's death too." She wiped her eyes. "Believe me, I did not want to get you into trouble. I um—why are the police after you? Is it because they can't catch him?"

"He has been arrested." Jalebi stormed off.

"Even so, that cannot be the reason why Jalebi must go down to the police station," said Leda.

Jalebi must've messed up the interrogation.

Leda found Paul, and together they talked to the officer in the study. He explained how Jalebi had divulged information about the disappearance, murder and decapitation of Gladys, and more.

Jalebi must have felt a psychological need to come out with the truth.

Auntie Bina limped to the family room as the officer escorted a wailing Jalebi out of the study. "You couldn't reason with him, Leda?" she cried.

"Jalebi gave away information about Gladys's murder that the police didn't already know, like the victim's body parts were removed by operation and who did it. Anyway, Paul and I are going to follow them. Paul's taking the case. He's a seasoned criminal defense attorney. Jalebi should be fine."

"Nobody can save me," Jalebi screamed.

Auntie Bina's eyes flowed. "The girl has suffered enough."

Somewhere in her heart, Jalebi has made a special place. Perhaps it's because they have been betrayed by the same man.

Jalebi did not look back. The officer opened the door to his car for Jalebi to enter. She stepped in and he drove her away.

Auntie Bina wept disconsolately. "Jalebi is mad at me because of that dog. How did he get hold of the picture, Leda?"

"No idea. I found it in your house, in Jalebi's room in the wastebasket, and showed it to Jalebi. She took it away when I wasn't looking."

"I saw something like a torn picture lying face down in the wastebasket here in the kitchen," said Sunny.

"Guess that's where Dish found it," said Leda. "Jalebi must have chucked it in there."

"Neel sold her to Dev at thirteen. Do you blame her?" Tears rolled down Auntie Bina's cheeks. "Jalebi and I made plans for our future, now I shall be all alone."

"No, you won't." Leda wrapped her arm around her. "You have all of us."

"And right now you must take care of Dish." Patrick scooped up Dish, whining at Auntie Bina's feet, and planted him on her lap.

That's perfect to give her the much-needed oxytocin boost.

Auntie Bina sighed.

Dish rolled over and offered her his belly.

Her eyes softened.

He licked her lovingly, the soft continuous splats punctuated only by the gagging and retching sounds emerging from within the bathroom.

Oh, Sonya!

There was a call from the police officer, and Leda whispered to Paul, "We've got to go."

Paul nodded, struggling to tear himself away from the room. "Take Sonya to No.7," he mouthed to Sunny.

Sunny nodded.

Leda picked up the lock and key from the side table.

"I'll take Gran Bina home," said Nikita. "It's been a long day."

"I'll go get us all some dinner," said Patrick. "Dish, c'mon."

Auntie Bina wrapped her arms round the terrier. He licked her playfully.

Leda eyed them. "Bina, would you please take Dish home with you? Patrick and I will pick him up on our way back to Dallas."

She thinks of everything.

"Of course." Auntie Bina petted Dish gently.

"Thanks, Leda," said Nikita.

"Thank you!" laughed Leda. "You are doing me a favor."

Sonya emerged from the bathroom shaking.

Nikita grabbed Patrick racing out the door. "Patrick, could you please give us a ride back home?"

"Of course." While Patrick supported Auntie Bina to his car, Nikita whispered in Sunny's ear, "Drive Sonya to No.7. Take my car. Give her back her brother."

Thanks Nikita!

Sunny wove a brotherly arm around Sonya. "Let me take you for a drive." He guided her toward Nikita's car.

Sonya melted in his warmth.

It is just like old times.

Leda pulled away from the driveway, waving to them.

Paul followed her, watching Sonya fade in the small frame of the rearview mirror until there was only the empty road behind him.

Sunny drove through the quiet streets of Rosenberg and merged onto the highway.

Sonya stared out the window, lost in her thoughts.

"Everything okay?" asked Sunny.

Sonya attempted a smile.

"I'm sorry I wasn't kinder to you, Sonya."

"It was easy to misunderstand me, the way I was behaving." She sighed. "I had to stay loyal to the fiend."

"Let bygones be bygones. Care to sneak a peek at No.7? You've got to see for yourself what you have accomplished."

Sonya inhaled sharply.

It's like she's struggling to believe that the nightmare is finally over.

The car sped along the highway. Sunny's eyes glistened. "I'm sorry I've been an awful brother to you. I didn't even so much as look for you. I honestly don't know what came over me."

Sonya closed her eyes.

Sunny exited the highway and zipped down the road toward No.7, humming the cheerful, upbeat tune of "Yellow Submarine," Ravi's favorite song.

Sonya did not join in but blinked furiously at the road ahead.

She's been too strong for too long.

No.7 rose into view.

"Holy smokes!" cried Sunny. "This is incredible!" He pulled up to the curb.

Sonya sat upright, wiping the tears from her lower lids with her forefingers.

The freshly cleaned grass, transformed into a sea of amber and gold in the light of the setting sun, swayed gently in the breeze.

"It feels so peaceful," said Sunny. "Look at those daffodils, dancing over the rubble."

Sonya nodded. "And it's like the pansies are laughing," She spoke, her lips barely moving.

"If only Mom and Dad were here," Sunny's voice trailed.

I resisted the temptation of beelining right to the windshield. I alighted, though, not far from them, and chose my direction by the bluebells that seemed to have spread and flowered among the charred ruins.

"I have a feeling Mom's here," said Sonya.

"Me too," Sunny scanned the grass.

Bouquets of butterflies, wildly colorful like oil-slicked patterns, cascaded down as if from the Heavens above, blending and swirling as playful waves upon night sands.

"Look, Sonya," said Sunny. "That was where Mom and Dad's bedroom stood, and mine was over there, and yours to the left . . . "

It was like the rooms materialized bit by bit, resurrecting our home before his eyes.

Is it magical, that iridescence of the wings?

"The day they brought you home and put you on my lap, I couldn't let go." Sunny's eyes glazed over like he was reliving the memory.

She smiled dreamily. "You were just four and already perfect brother material."

"I couldn't help it. You were so adorable. And you had this heightened sense of empathy even as an infant. They say morning shows the day."

A tear snaked down Sonya's cheek. "Only I was feisty, a little too feisty."

"Every blessing is a curse, every curse a blessing, and they come in equal strength. It's the balance of the universe. If you won't accept the curse, you can never be blessed." Sunny wiped her cheek with his thumb, and Sonya's dam broke. Her tears flowed like her stress and pain had at last condensed into a deluge of rain.

"There is so much comfort in being with you." She sniffed. "This you."

"I'm sorry I grew so distant, so angry, but I was terrified of what was happening to us, you, things spiraling out of control." Sunny dabbed his tears with his sleeve. "I did not believe in the curse and look what it did to us. It turned us into real, arguing, fighting siblings." He laughed, and she did too. "I always loved you; the anger was temporary, and this is the way real bonds are."

My core throbbed and swelled. It filled my being. *If happiness has a definition, it is this feeling of fulfillment.*

Two cars honked at the curb. Doors flung open and Leda, Paul, Nikita, and Patrick leaped out.

"Do the pair of you want any dinner or not?" yelled Nikita. "Gran Bina is waiting."

Chapter 56

The cars departed with all the chatter and laughter, and the amber glow faded to a soft black. The world was just shadows and silhouettes dancing playfully in the dark.

I yearned for Heaven's light and soared up in search of the eternal home. Granite-gray clouds moved in shoals, refusing admittance. There was not a crack anywhere, spilling Heaven's light.

Am I to believe that Heaven is still not ready for me?

Alone in the darkness, my attention drifted to Asha's house.

The three happy couples had just arrived, and a yapping Dish led them to the dining room, Dinner awaited them in warming trays. Everyone talked about how brave Sonya had been. She, however, was quiet, her dark eyes pensive.

What's bothering her now?

Diya called Sunny in response to a text he had sent her about his engagement. She congratulated him heartily. "Sorry, beta, I couldn't get back to you earlier. Leena went into labor last night and has just delivered a beautiful eight-pound baby girl. They named her Priya." Her voice choked.

I couldn't be happier for Leena and Ganesh and felt so blessed for their love.

Sunny switched on the speakerphone, and everyone congratulated Leena.

"Thank you," she said. "Why Meghna not coming for her sister's wedding?"

"No idea." Patrick picked up Dish begging around for scraps. "She did not tell me a word about it."

"She tell her parents Randy leave her lot a money, so she help," said Leena. "Then she say she lose all that money and go away to Amrica."

"The money's been found," said Leda.

"Great, or I could have replaced it," said Patrick. "Meghna is one of my best employees. She is reliable, has strong communication skills, a solid work ethic, and the ability to collaborate effectively as part of a team."

There is no way Leena can understand his rich language and accent.

"Tell Meghna a neighbor buy Rao's flashy scooter," she said. "Rao die from rotting finger."

"May his soul rest in peace. When was this?" asked Leda.

"The neighbor buy his scooter three weeks ago."

The call disconnected.

Leda did not call back. "Poor Leena has just given birth. She's tired."

Patrick frowned. "I have a busy day tomorrow. When shall we hit the road?"

"Right now. Where's Sonya?"

"In the restroom." Paul pointed with his chin.

She's been in there for ages.

Leda knocked on the door

Sonya switched off her phone and opened the door.

Leda squinted at the device.

Almost at once, Paul's phone chirped. It was from James, his dad. He excused himself to read the message.

"Everything okay, Sonya?" asked Sunny.

"Of course."

"Why don't you come and stay with us." Sunny wrapped his arm around her.

"Gran Bina returns to India tomorrow night," added Nikita.

Leda, Sunny, and Sonya gasped in surprise. Dish wiggled free from Patrick and yelped at Auntie Bina as if in disapproval.

She picked him up from her heels and kissed him. "Please don't take Sonya away, Sunny. I need her here, even if it's for just one night. Nikita, Sunny, Paul why don't you come over for breakfast tomorrow?"

"Of course." Nikita accepted the invitation graciously.

Paul hung up on his dad, "Thank you so much for the invitation, Bina, but unfortunately, I can't make it. Something very important has come up." He cast a furtive glance at Sonya. "Anyway, goodnight, everyone. Goodnight, Sonya."

Paul's velvety voice startled the girl.

Where is her mind?

"Goodnight," repeated Paul.

"Goodnight." Sonya managed a smile.

Paul rushed away.

Sunny and Nikita followed him out, but one step out the door, Sunny stopped and eased out some chocolate bars from his pocket. "Oh, I got these for you, Sonya. Your favorites."

"Thanks." Sonya's eyes, soft with thanks, found his.

"Try and get some sleep." He kissed her on her forehead. "See you tomorrow."

God bless.

The party broke up.

Patrick tempted Dish away from Auntie Bina with a chewy treat. "Let's go, Leda."

"Give me two seconds." She pinched Sonya aside. "I'm going back to Dallas, but before I do, I need to know you are completely safe."

"I am."

"Look, I care." Leda squinted at her.

Sonya met her gaze. "I only left the table to apologize to James. It took a lot of effort to find the right words."

Is it about the internship? Does she want to do it now?

It was the best feeling in the world watching things finally fall into place.

Alighting on No.7, I bumped into Hema's sketchbook, sweeping across the lawn. It was the book the fiend had used to cast the evil spell on my family, and to that end he had trapped Hema's spirit within its pages.

Where is she now?

"Coming to Heaven?" Deepak's voice pierced my thoughts. He hovered over me in the disguise of a bird with golden feathers.

"Is Heaven even ready for me?"

"You are still chasing the book."

"I'm wondering about Hema."

"Her case is complicated. There have been a lot of pleadings on her behalf. She will be born multiple times on Earth but will not survive her first hour. With every birth, her soul will cleanse itself. She will flee the cycle in less than a decade and come to Heaven."

"Good for her."

The pages of the book fluttered in the breeze. The first seven depicted the story of creation that Hema illustrated under our teacher's supervision, the next seven, the spirits that haunted her during her illness, the seven immediately after, the ghosts that derailed my life.

"How I hate the spirits and what they did," I said.

"Heaven will erase them from your memory forever."

"How much longer must I wait, Deepak? Yesterday the Devil could have seized me."

"He wouldn't. Unlike earthly fiends, the archfiend must abide by some rules. He has lost to Saint Ignatius—the clearance of the ash from the property is his admission of defeat. He can no longer touch you."

"You're right. The Devil assigned the job of capturing me to Dev. Now that he's dead, the Devil seems to have left me alone. Yet, it intrigues me how someone who adheres to some rules can be totally lacking in basic principles. He subjected Dev to the most horrific death. I know he would have died anyway—he read the mantra— but to be burned alive?"

"The Devil punished him for messing with his equipment and for trusting Sonya enough to let her into his life. She found the mantra. Dev's death wrecked the Devil's plans. All the energy was wasted. The Devil cannot use Hema again. The Heaven Elders have decided her fate, and it's not like the Devil has a replacement for her."

A dalliance of wind gusted warmly. It bared Deepak's core. Our glows and our claddings matched perfectly.

Deepak's joy was contagious. "It's time to go."

A whirr resonated through the air—the low, continuous, regular sound as of propellors.

The sky turned honey-peach, the black tree-tops green. It was already dawn.

"Time races with the divine chariot," said Deepak. "It has come to take us."

Tremors of excitement rippled along my core. *At last!* We rushed in.

"Now hold on tight." The cherubs spread their wings upward. "We shall take the scenic route to Heaven. You will see the prettiest sights Earth has to offer all at the same time." They lifted us into a dance.

The early morning sunlight, soft and diffuse, gave way to broad daylight.

My eyes sought out Asha's house, where Sunny, Nikita and Sonya enjoyed a hearty breakfast in the dining room.

"I'm late." Sonya, dressed formally, gobbled her last mouthful and pushed back her chair.

Nikita hugged her. "Good luck."

"All the best." Sunny stuck his thumb in the air.

"Thanks." Sonya grabbed her handbag, and Paul walked in through the door.

"All ready for the interview? C'mon then. I'm your chauffeur this morning. Dad's orders." He held out his hand, and she accepted it.

Is this true or am I dreaming? I cuddled with Deepak.

He chuckled. "Isn't this the perfect route?"

"Couldn't be better."

We whistled over the future-telling mountains, kissed to their summit by Heaven's divine sunset.

Creamy pastel oranges streaked the meadows beyond, with little gold bees swarming among the wildflowers, delicately spinning out an ethereal melody.

The cherubs flapped their wings vigorously and we started our descent.

Heaven loomed large all around. Never was a sky more brilliant. Never was a breeze more refreshing. Never was a dance more mesmerizing than that of the ambers, pearly pinks, and purples merging into happy watercolors.

"Welcome to our forever home," whispered Deepak. "Heaven was never Heaven without you."

Chapter 57

The sunset splendor stretched far and wide. It flowed into the streets, radiated over the flawless architecture of the city, and melted into woods and rivers of gold and crimson.

Wow!

Deepak chuckled. "This is just the beginning of an eternity of awe."

The inmates came to welcome me. "Everyone's route to Heaven is different," said one. "Hope you enjoyed yours."

"She missed out on a lot coming here, preoccupied as she was," the cherubs remarked. They flapped their wings and soared over the sun to perch on the horizon as in a perfect painting.

"There are a few events that you will be expected to attend," the inmate announced, "but your visibility at the gatherings is your choice. They are organized to help you access apps that will answer any questions you might have about cosmic affairs, your future, that of other spirits, and earthlings. Regular attendance at the events will earn you protectors, angels who will plug you in fully to their energy stream. The more you can connect with them, the better will be your chances of becoming one."

"Is it true what they say about the events?" I asked Deepak.

"Yes. It was at one of them that I found out about Hema."

"Where's Ma?"

"In purgatory, where the chill cuts through her core, but she's due back on Earth soon, and guess what? She gets to choose her parents."

"She will no doubt choose to be Sunny and Nikita's little girl."

"That's what I would have expected, but she would rather be a ladybird—its life cycle usually lasts about a year. She is in a real hurry to be united with your dad."

"May I see him, please?"

"Well, he's preparing to become an angel."

"Wow! That's impressive. Where's Asha?"

"There's the spark in both Asha and Ravi that innately discriminates between right and wrong. They are still part of the Divine, still connected. They will be put back on Earth, where they will evolve through trials and tribulations."

As much as I enjoyed the peace and tranquility of Heaven, I missed my loved ones on Earth. The angels encouraged me to indulge in activities other than watching my kids.

"You could not focus on your Heavenward journey at all," said one. "You were so completely consumed by thoughts of your children. This obsession will lead you back there, and then you won't know how to get back."

"But Deepak does."

"Oh, Heaven was never at ease about his Earthly trips—we always had to call him back before he was happy to return. Yet the support and guidance he demonstrated toward you qualifies him for the position of a guardian spirit. He will get busy. Try and settle down. You will know that you have once you hear the music of the spheres. It will lead you back here wherever you go."

Life was nothing short of a dream.

The angels radiated positive vibrations, and the rest of us soaked it up. The gold bees made the world rosier, offering their daily dose of bliss. Their drone was the river of the air, a flowing music that hydrated our souls.

With the passage of time, the drone created its own sonic textures. It deepened. Its magic sweetened, until it was like softly spun sugar, almost tangible.

The music of the spheres? At last! Now I can go see my children.

The Heavens parted like curtains on a stage.

The ocean brought a flash of blue in the amber light. The joyful cries of the gulls drifted in, the soprano to happy sounds as of a wedding.

I glided through the briny air. Upon the white sands of Galveston, Nikita and Sunny posed for a wedding photo.

My dream come true!

Dish, the ring bearer, stole the show in his Harris Tweed wedding day attire.

By Sunny's side stood the groomsmen, those steadfast mates among whom the best man, Paul, was the most striking of all. Sonya, Leda, Meghna, and the other maids of honor mixed and mingled, stunning in their bright red dresses. They talked about Jalebi in low whispers. Apparently, she had got a ten-year sentence, though Paul, who was handling her case, was confident that she would be released on probation before the assigned term was complete.

The wedding guests—mostly residents of Auntie Bina's village in the Punjab—sat in neat rows on snow-white Chiavari chairs bedecked with sky blue organza sashes. The wedding meal was served cocktail-style, which mixed heavy passed hors d'oeuvres with food stations so that guests could eat when they wished.

The photographer, Tino, presented a full-fledged slide show for his audience.

"Beautiful pictures of Meghna." Patrick winked at him. "However, I love this one the most." He pointed to one of himself and Leda. "Tino has caught all three of us together."

"I thought Leda was expecting." Tino squinted at Leda's belly, and she beamed.

"You're pregnant, Leda? Congratulations!" Sonya leaned against Paul; an elegant solitaire engagement ring dazzled on her finger.

Engaged? Oh, bless!

"Not that far along yet, only eighteen weeks," whispered Leda. "He is growing quickly. I can barely fit into anything, though now I look forward to mealtimes instead of dreading them."

"The hospice at No.7 will be complete by the time the little one comes along." Sonya counted the weeks and months on her fingers.

"He will be baptized in our very own chapel, which will be blessed with the special collection of silver from the property," said Leda.

"I love the plan, the bungalow-style building with sparkling ponds weaving through the lush, manicured lawns. The place will be so perfect as a hospice."

"We'll call it Shantih." Leda beamed.

"I'm sure it will the abode of peace as the name suggests." Sonya beamed.

"Thanks to you! Peace could not have been restored at No.7 without your self-control and strength of will. We could only salvage the property from that monster because of you."

Sonya sighed. "It would've been impossible without your compassion and Patrick's generosity. He paid for Jalebi's air ticket to the US—she had the much needed-information about how to use the Mrityushakti mantra, and you did not turn me in after the yoga suit incident as your job prompted. If you had, I would never have accomplished my mission."

Peace has come to No.7 through the three 'Da's. Just like the thunder said.

The music of the spheres tinkled, drowning the chatter. The reception ended. The guests faded. Only the newlyweds remained along with Sonya, Paul, Leda, Partick, their lives on fast-forward. One moment they were raging successes, the next, they were surrounded by babies. The babies grew; life went on.

Shantih grew and flourished under the supervision of the three couples, and later their grown children. They became like family, bonded for life.

What seemed like a curse turned out to be a blessing.

I followed the harmonic tones back to Heaven. I would watch the generations from my eternal home.

Glossary

Aghori: A small Hindu sect known for their use of taboo substances and engagement with death rituals
Alu bhonda: A deep-fried Indian potato snack
Attar: Natural perfume oils
Bahu: Daughter-in-law
Beta: Child
Chapati: Indian flatbread
Dahej: Dowry
Datta: The giver
Dada: A respectful term of address to any familiar older man or a man with higher social status
Dāmyata: self-control
Dayadhvam: Compassion
Didi: A respectful term of address to any familiar older woman or a woman with higher social status
Ektara: One stringed instrument made from a gourd with a hollow body and a bamboo neck
Firangi: The term refers to foreign individuals or things originating from the west
Garam masala: A mixture of cumin, coriander, cardamom, pepper, cinnamon, cloves, and nutmeg
Ghee: A type of clarified butter, originating from India
Gita: A sacred text within Hinduism
Horlicks: A British sweet, malted milk hot drink powder

Ji: A gender-neutral suffix placed after a person's name or title as a mark of respect
Kamishikimi Kumano-imasu shrine: A Shinto shrine
Kangan: Bangle
Lakh: 109,754.50 United States Dollar
Mangalsutra: A necklace worn by married Indian women that represents their marital union and commitment
Malai: A clotted cream from the Indian subcontinent
Meenakari: Enameled
Narabali: In India, human sacrifice is mainly known as Narabali
Pajamas: a pair of loose pants tied by a drawstring around the waist, worn by both men and women in some Asian countries
Pakora: Spiced Indian vegetable fritters
Pallu: The loose end of the saree that is draped over the shoulder
Paratha: A flatbread native to the Indian subcontinent
Pooja: The act of worship
Puri: A type of deep-fried bread
Rajrani: Queen of the kingdom
Romni: The singular term for a Romani woman or wife
Sadhu/ Sannyasin: An ascetic who has given up worldly life to pursue spiritual liberation
Sādhvīne: Female sadhu
Sanskrit: An ancient Indo-European language of India, in which the Hindu scriptures and classical Indian epic poems are written
Salwar-suit: South Asian ethnic combination dress for women comprising of a pair trousers called salwar, a long tunic called Kameez, and a scarf called dupatta
Sabji: Vegetable curry
Shaadi.com: An Indian online wedding service that operates globally
Shantih: Peace
Sindoor: A traditional red powder used in Hinduism as a cosmetic and religious symbol
Tantrik: Sorcerer
Thums Up: A brand of cola sold by Coca-Cola in India
Upanishad: The latest addition to the Vedas—Hindu scriptures
Yajnas: Any ritual done in front of a sacred fire in Hinduism, often with mantras
Zewar: Jewelry

ABOUT THE AUTHOR

Texas resident, Nandita Banerjee, grew up in India. A teacher for years in India, in the US, and in the UK, she discovered her passion for writing when a book concept descended on her completely out of the blue. She began to write and never looked back since.

Her novels include the No. 7 series: They're Calling and The Date, and In B'tween: The Wisp.

Banerjee has also published two collections of poetry, namely, Thoughts Recollected in Tranquility and Alice Through Wonderland.

Visit her at authornandita.com or on Facebook @ Nandita Banerjee, Author.

www.ingramcontent.com/pod-product-compliance
Lightning Source LLC
Chambersburg PA
CBHW020738310726
48969CB00002B/310